A BREAK IN THE WALL

Bruce LACHTER

Published in 2014
by Bruce Lachter

Interior layout and Publishing assistance
by Publicious Pty Ltd
www.publicious.com.au

Cover image by Paul Sellenger

*Catalogue-in-Publication details available
from the National Library of Australia*

ISBN: 978-0-9925533-0-2

Also available in ebook
ebook ISBN: 978-0-9925533-1-9

In loving memory of my father,
Dr Julian Lee, a *mensch*…

"Ever it was thus, boy. Ever it was thus."

"The word 'I' is repellent to me as a vain affirmation of the self which contains a large measure of illusion and another of vanity and unjustified pride. Whenever it is possible, that is to say when I am able not to feel myself isolated, when my experience illuminates in some manner that of the men to whom I feel tied, I prefer to use the word 'we', which is more general and more true."

Victor Serge, *Birth of our Power*

"Psychotherapy is an encounter, a discussion between two psychic wholes, in which knowledge is used only as a tool. The goal is transformation."

Carl Jung

"…it's just the same with the Head of Protocol, who's a hunchback. He has only to be in my house five minutes before my fingers are itching to stroke his hump. I can't help it."

Marcel Proust, *Remembrance of Things Past*

Contents

PART I

PRISON BEGINNINGS

SAM

I began my prison year as a visitor observing another world. I wondered what it would be like to live there, and about the sex of prison. Her walls were smooth, and stood above me like a dominant woman, red and massive against the sky. Her hair was sharp and shiny razor wire. Metal gates bejewelled her, their grip-sized padlocks as clasps, female to the male keys dangling on every officer's hip.

I wondered about sex in prison. Do men forget how long since their last kiss, when they are behind bars? Would I forget? Would I kiss them? Probably a fuck is a fuck, and a screw is a screw, and a fuck can be taken, given, or shared. But a kiss? No, men do not kiss each other in prison. That said, of course they do.

On my first day, an officer told me the crucial difference between wants and needs:

"Needs we'll help them with, like a shit or a piss or food. But wants - well, they're in prison, so wants wait."

This simple logic led to conflict, as simple logic invariably does, because in its simplicity it denies the myriad subtleties and possibilities of every living moment. Listen to the first prisoner I interviewed and you'll see what I mean. It was a question of definitions. He defined his desire to call his solicitor as a "need".

"I need to call my solicitor right now," he said. He was

unshaven, and swarthy. He had told me that his wife could read his mind by voodoo, being a witch, so now he was in trouble, and only his solicitor could get him out of it. I thanked him for his time, and suggested he ask the officer about the phone-call. But the officer defined this request as a "want" which would not be immediately gratified. Then the shouting started. I did not see how it ended, being soon busy with my next interview. That is the doctor's privilege: when things get nasty, he can leave because he is busy - always saving lives - but really ducking around the corner to the tea-room to have a nice cup of tea.

"Prison is a brutal place," I would say to others after work, to titillate them and safely share in some of that brutality myself. After all, if it was brutal, then I must be a hard man to venture so near. But there is a world of difference between observing and experiencing. That is the psychiatrist's plight: to be an eternal voyeur, a nonentity, marginalised. Vicarious pleasures become a habit.

I met Sam in the tea-room of the prison clinic. He was a likeable armed robber. A perfectly spherical belly strained the fabric of his faded blue T-shirt, like a big melon jutting above his stubbies. He wore regulation prison-issue Dunlop Volley sandshoes. Not for his feet the flash Nikes of the young junkies. His feet didn't need much cushioning because he spent most of his day sitting down. And Sam hadn't seen his feet in years.

Sam was the clinic "sweeper", a sentenced prisoner who was given chores such as cleaning, washing up, running errands - not that Sam ever ran. To be the clinic sweeper made for a cushy life, and plenty of food to feed his belly. Sam perched on his plastic chair, one freckled and tattooed forearm resting on the laminated table and the other against the grimy sink, like a dilapidated boxer in his corner waiting for the next round. His brain resembled a boxer's, too, although the frontal lobes had been pickled in alcohol, not withered by constant pummelling. And like legendary heavy-weight champion of the thirties, "Two-ton Tony Gallento", Sam had trained on beer and pizzas. But instead of coming out of the corner with his dukes up, he'd stay there, and open up the little wooden box he'd made to hold his cigarettes, and pluck one out and gently press it into his plastic cigarette holder, and light up. Then he would draw back with such languorous pleasure that a non-smoker would wonder if it wasn't worth the risk of lung cancer, after all. Sam's eyes narrowed, his jowls wobbled and tautened with the first insufflation, and then bulged slightly in silent exhalation, smoke rising as one with its source to some higher plane of rapture. Then he'd return to the known world, and gently enquire in his husky drawl:

"Hope youse don't mind if I has a smoke. It's me first of the day."

I never complained, nor commented on his fruity hack. Sam was useful. Sometimes when the nurses were too busy I would ask Sam to sign the consent forms as witness to an interviewed prisoner's signature. Sam wrote his moniker slowly and with great care. The curve of his "a" was perfect, resembling the convexity above his shorts. Then he'd look up and say: "I expect me payment, doc. Twenty bucks a pop, like youse agreed."

"Cheque's in the mail, Sam," I replied. "Trust me I'm a doctor."

Sam would chuckle as heartily the first time as the hundredth, and sometimes to get the last word in he'd add: "Yeah? Trust me, I'm a crim."

These are the simple pleasures of prison life. An idle

exchange becomes ritualised to reassure the prisoner of his humanity, and the pleasure in every smoke is savoured when smokes are precious, and time is not. That's only sensible.

Sam took me on a tour of the prison yard. At each gate he yelled, "Gate up!" and then we waited. Along the rampart, an officer patrolled with his rifle slung over his shoulder, its burnished butt jutting back and up to where the sky hung blue and clear. The sky is beautiful from enclosed space, and we were given plenty of time to enjoy it. We waited and waited. The sentry strode to his post at the corner of the wall, and then walked back the way he'd come. Nothing very much seemed to be happening on our tour.

"Do we always have to wait this long to be let out, Sam?" I asked.

"Mate, I've been waitin' for years to get out of this place. One thing you need here is patience, and a sense of humour."

"That's two things," I didn't say. I didn't want Sam to think I was a smart-arse.

Then an officer arrived and said "Gedday, Saaam" and Sam said, "Gedday, maaaate. Alright if I show the doc around the yard?"

"Sure, Sam. Just don't leave him behind."

The officer opened the gate and we passed through to the yard of the main prison, where prisoners roamed in little knots, and huddled on seats, and lifted weights and played hand-ball and tennis and generally ignored us as we walked around. But I could not ignore the prisoner serving on the tennis court: long black hair, bright lip-stick, and pert breasts. Sam caught me staring.

"Not bad for a cat, eh?" he said.

"Not bad at all, Sam," I didn't say. I didn't want Sam to think I was perving at a bloke, even if it was a bloke who looked more like a woman.

"Havin' a bit of a perv, doc?" he teased.

Then we came to another gate and Sam yelled "Gate up!" and we got through that one too. But the big gates remained closed even to Sam, or open only to let him in. He couldn't seem to stay out of jail; maybe he didn't want to.

An officer called Barry told me about this. Barry himself had been at the prison for the last twenty years, "apart from two years in a real job", but he still only had two stripes on his epaulettes. After three stripes they got a 'pip'. Three pips became a 'crown', the rank of governor. Out in the yard, among the plain blue T-shirts, the signs of rank were less obvious, but theirs was a hierarchy just as strict.

"There's two turning points for a crim, which maybe should be called his 'straightening points', because they are his chances to go straight," Barry reckoned. "Most seem to wake up to themselves at thirty. A bloke in jail at thirty says to 'isself, 'I'm a bloody mug, wasting me life in here,' and gets out and stays out. But if it's not occurred to him at thirty, he'll likely be around another ten years. Then at forty, the same thing will crop up, that he oughtta get out for good. But a few stay on longer, like Sam. He'd be lost on the outside."

Sam's career in detention began in boy's homes, then jail at 17.

"I was a punchy rascal," he said. "Would have got meself flattened but me dad's mates looked after me on the inside, so I never had no trouble."

"Now you only cause trouble, eh Sam?" the Kiwi nurse, Shauna, said.

She teased Sam, but he liked the attention, and took her comments as flirtatious. Shauna was cute in appearance, rough in her language, and kind in her behaviour - a combination which appealed to Sam and to most of the other prisoners. The clinic staff appreciated Sam, an old-fashioned crim with an old-fashioned integrity and loyalty. He was the first sweeper they trusted not to steal drugs from the medication trolley. After Sam knocked off at three p.m. Shauna told me he was celibate, but her boss, a male nurse called Chia, wasn't so sure.

"It's very hard to know," Chia said. "We only found out the other day how another sweeper - been in 23 years - raped his teenage cell-mate. But they reckon there's been plenty more too afraid to squeal."

"Why not squeal, if you're having fun?" Shauna said, and gave me a wink.

"That's enough, Shauna," Chia said. "Rape is no laughing matter."

"Who said anything about laughing?" Shauna persisted.

Chia ran the prison clinic, but Shauna was not going to let him run her. No-one knew whether 'Chia' was his first name or his surname. He was Chinese, we assumed, but his origins, like his accent, were obscure. Although Chia seemed as anonymous as the night, his clinical acumen and respect for patients were clear as day. The main diagnostic question Chia and his GP, Nick, faced was detecting genuine need among the malingering mass of prisoners. A prisoner had to earn the right to become a patient, to accrue the privileges of the sick role, but Chia had been around long enough to know that even malingerers occasionally became ill.

An officer joined in our chat over afternoon tea. He was a pugnacious "baggy" - a new recruit without stripes or sense.

"Bloody laughable," he said. "The sweeper's a sweeper 'cos he's trusted, and he turns around and rapes a bloke in his cell. So how many others has he been chocking? Are you here to work that out, doc? That'd be bloody useful research, instead of this stuff 'bout scizzyphrebia. They shouldn't have these bloody sweepers. It's a security risk."

"Which means you don't like it because you can't bully Sam," Chia said to the officer. Then Chia bowed his bald pate to take a sip of lemon tea and a mouthful of plain boiled rice, hot from the microwave.

"No Soya sauce, no nothing, eh Chia?" Shauna said, smiling at her boss as he waved his chopsticks in the air. This seemed to signal that the conversation was over, and that the upstart baggy could formulate his hypotheses elsewhere. I never saw Chia consume anything other than this frugal fare of rice and tea, a cultural equivalent of bread and water. He was fastidious and gruff and, everyone agreed, a bloody good nurse.

My structured interviews to diagnose mental illness – including 'scizzyphrebia' - among the prisoners were long and frustrating and tedious for interviewer and interviewee, so we would often break to yarn. During one such lull, a prisoner said: "Nothing is real in here. I think it's a dream, like I'll wake up and it'll be gone."

Freud held that dreams are generated by an unfulfilled wish. Freud also knew that dreams are not easy to decipher.

One morning Sam brought in some raw meat, a big slab of beef which he divvied up with a scalpel on the tea-room table. The meat was from the prison butcher; the scalpel, from Nick, the clinic GP. When we met, Nick said to me: "You look too normal to be a psychiatrist."

"Looks can be deceptive," I said.

Despite the lovely steaks he was carving, Sam seemed morose all day. It was awkward with him sometimes. I thought he was saddened by the death that morning of an obese prison officer who had collapsed while doing step aerobics at the prison gym. After Shauna had tried to resuscitate him, she sat in the tea-room, quiet and close to tears. And Sam just stared at the floor, and dug his scalpel into the linoleum table-top. Sam, heart of gold, I thought. A prisoner cutting up the lino because he's all cut up by the death of one of his guards. A lot of the younger prisoners cut themselves up. In frustration or despair, they would slide a razor blade across a tattooed arm or thigh, drawing blood between the ink, adding scars to the tattoos. Sam disapproved of self-mutilation. He preferred to dissolve his frustrations in alcohol.

We were one happy family in our little clinic, so I thought. Close and caring. Turned out Sam didn't give a stuff about the deceased officer. He was moping because his missus didn't visit that day - Valentine's.

I was moping, too, but attempted to keep that to myself for those first weeks, while I could still lose my pain in the prison clamour. If not close and caring, then at least prison was noisy and distracting.

LOVE AND DATA

Love took many forms in prison. The trannies as erotic mates were chaperoned through their lag by a succession of handsome bucks. When one was transferred or released, another took his place. Charlene was the gorgeous Maori transsexual whose serve I had admired on the tennis court during Sam's tour. Nigel was her buck. He protected her, in exchange for favours, and they had become attached, an "item". Nigel was big and mean and threatened bloody violence when he was to be transferred to a country prison, sent away without his love.

Shauna went to see him before he left, but to no avail: he was heartbroken and enraged, a man who had never been loved or valued or cared for in his life until prison romance. It was tough on Charlene for a while after he went, until another buck took Nigel's place as protector and provider. But Nigel did not forget his first true love. Like D.H. Lawrence, he believed *"On reviens toujour a son premier amour"* – one always returns to one's first love. But unlike D.H., Nigel was illiterate.

He dictated his love letters from the country jail to whoever would listen, and care to write them down. The written version was often somewhat more lewd than Nigel's spoken words. It was hard to keep things secret in prison, and prisoners did not respect a man's tenderest feelings, so Nigel quickly became the butt of ridicule in his new home. He didn't care. Nor did he care that his letters were read by the officers at the receiving end, for security reasons, again to much hilarity, and that Charlene's new buck pinned them to the noticeboard on the landing. Nigel lost his appetite. He no longer worked out in the gym every day. He moped and said little, apart from the daily letters spoken to Charlene. Soon after he stopped sending them, he hung himself.

I heard two officers discuss his death.

"They lost another one up in the bush."

"Who was it?"

"Nigel the spiv."

"Dunno him."

"You've read his letters. The love-lorn poet."

"Ah, the one with the hots for the cat. Will she go to his funeral?"

"Mate, she wouldn't even spit on his grave."

"Suppose that means flowers are out of the question."

What's love? Kevin knew the answer. He told me as I led him from the holding cell to my office in the clinic. He was gaunt, with grog-withered eyes. A tight bun held his black hair hard against his small skull.

"Love is a long-shot, doc, but with my little lady I reckon I've hit the jack-pot. Wouldn't be alive today without her. We were playing poker in the back-bar, and some dickhead reckoned I'd switched cards on him. Me missus saw his mate about to jump me and she whipped out her knife and put it straight through his heart. He died. She did six years. I call that love," Kevin said.

"Well, you could say it's a form of devotion," I said.

"Yeah, it's love, that's what it is. You gotta agree," he insisted.

"It's certainly a demonstration of her commitment to you, Kevin."

"Sure, doc. You said it: devotion and commitment, that's love," he concluded.

What would I know about love? Love is two empty vessels pouring their contents into each other. Its satiation is necessarily ephemeral. I could reduce love to constituent parts: a yearning to possess, and a surrender to possession, neither owning nor being owned. The ultimate gift has no strings attached. My prisoners seemed to understand that, when they gave their consent.

"This interview won't help you directly, and it's completely voluntary. It is an investigation of the mental health of prisoners," I told them, a soothing mantra to be chanted six hundred times. That was the size of my sample, for statistical reasons, and because I liked the sibilance of 'six hundred subjects'. It was glorified market research, pretending to some higher moral stature than mere commerce. "This is in the name of science," I announced to a reluctant prisoner, but such grandiosity made me feel even more like a salesman.

"You married, doc?" Shauna asked me, while signing her name as witness to another pile of consent forms. It seemed this favour had strings attached.

"Nope."

"Girlfriend?"

"Not really."

"Lonely?"

"Look, what is this? I'm here to work, not give my life story."

"No, you get your stories from the prisoners. I just wanted to find out a bit more about you. What makes you tick. You've been here for weeks, and we don't know the first thing about your life outside work. It's like you don't have one."

"My work IS my life. Research is all-consuming, like an artistic pursuit, and I need to get ahead in my career."

"You need to get a life. And when you do, don't be afraid to share it."

"I appreciate your concern, but I don't think my private life is any of your business."

"Listen, we're both in helping professions aren't we? At this rate you won't be able to help anyone. I've seen it in other hot-shot docs, that's all. You give everything to your work, and it sucks you dry. So, be too busy for a life, if you want to fade away. Hey, why should I care?"

"It's a question of priorities. I happen to have a disciplined approach to my work."

"I'm sure you'd enjoy a bit of discipline, too."

"It's satisfying, to complete a task."

"Geez, I hope you're joking, or you're more of a boffin than I thought. Do you know anything about women? About their needs or enjoyments?"

"I've got two sisters. We are quite close."

"Listen, there's some things sisters don't tell you. There might be secrets, things a sister keeps to herself, away from their brother, so busy with his work all day. And night."

Chia had been listening to the nurse's interrogation, and was becoming as exasperated as me by her persistence.

"Shauna, that's enough," Chia said. "Why don't you give the doctor a break - he's got work to do. Work that he believes in, and that has never been an easy path to take. Let's not make it any harder for him than it has to be."

"What is it with you and work, Chia?" Shauna protested. "It'll see you to an early grave, that's for sure."

"Whether you like it or not, sister, our work defines us. Criminals become criminals because they are too lazy for work, which is just as well because it is that same laziness that usually sees them get caught. That's how criminals become prisoners: they are too lazy to dig their victim's grave deep enough, too lazy to keep quiet about their robberies, too lazy to properly hide their tracks in all sorts of ways," Chia replied.

Shauna shrugged, and it was back to work for each of us. I felt relieved. The prisoners - my work - had arrived in the holding cell. But I found Chia's idealisation of me and my work harder to handle than Shauna's criticism. I had always yearned to be placed on pedestals, but once elevated felt unsteady upon them. Shauna was right: I had kept my past secret, but for now I had no intention of letting my guard down.

This wounded bird was seeking somewhere safe. Shauna could sniff out those wounds, but it was not for her to open them up. The more determined she was to remove my mask of aloofness, the more firmly I clung to it. If prison had become my life, then that was just as well. For me, life outside prison had lost all meaning. This is the opposite of the prisoners' experience, of course: for the prisoner, life behind bars is life on hold. They pine for the outside, to have their life back. For a while I could convince myself that I was as absorbed, as besotted, with this place as any man would be in the first blush of a love affair. Perhaps there was a belief in there somewhere – a belief in what I was doing - as Chia suggested.

After about twenty of these structured interviews, they began to enter my dreams. I was somewhere cold. There were wolves, with enormous teeth, but the wolves were friendly, or I sensed they could not harm me. Then I heard myself, a disembodied voice, reciting the questions over and over. My dead-pan delivery soothed the wild dogs. This pleased me, to attain in my dreams the perfect monotone of disinterested investigation, which I strived to reproduce when awake. I had to control for confounding variables. Systematic errors could ruin the data.

"Be a wooden Indian," my supervising professor had advised. "That way you will not introduce bias."

She had said this when I still trusted her, in those first weeks. A wooden Indian: that suited my purposes, to remain aloof, to coldly observe. By clinical detachment I shunned attachment. My task was to entice prisoners into voluntary anonymity as subjects, as data, while avoiding their insistent individuality, expressed as so many pleas for a phone call or a favour, or merely succour. They sought intimacy; I clung to my isolation. What else can a wooden Indian do? He cannot flinch, nor falter in his stern task. Was I a hardwood, or a softwood? When others are encountered in greatest numbers, the singularity of each is most readily ignored. A chorus of prison voices swept over me as an impersonal and vast vibration. It struck no common cord. This tension corrupted me: I used them, and discarded them, and felt I had sullied their trust.

"Come, talk to me, to meet my needs. I will fall for your story. Its details and lies will not be lost on me: I am an open container. Pour out your heart to me, that it may merge with mine."

How could they resist? At first, the refusal rate was less than ten per cent. These were the halcyon days. My past was private. My prison project was humming along. I was feeling stronger bit by bit, more confident among these hapless cases, impregnable in the face of their rants and pleas. It was a pleasure to have no clinical responsibility for them. They were there for me, not vice versa.

Answers to my questions emerged in the welter of irrelevancies which the prisoners considered relevant, such as where they sprang from, and how they came to this, and what made up the waste of their days. I allowed them to squander my time with their hesitant replies and confused babble, because each subject brought me closer to my target. Six hundred. I felt in control, as long as the dialogue continued.

From the beginning, the prisoners meant less to me than I could ever let them know. But as research fodder, I was forced to schmooz up to them, feigning interest in the myriad shoddy tales which washed over me in the accumulation of data.

I thought of buttering some of them up:

"You could be no other than yourself. You encompass and entail your experience of life in perfect honesty. You are as true a reflection as a face in a mirror," I could say, but I preferred to encourage co-operation by gestures, rather than words. It was less overt, and more effective because it worked subliminally. So I mirrored their movements, a crude mimicry in my clinic office. I swayed back to one subject's retreat, and leant forward to another's hunched eagerness. Nodding, posturing, grinning, bracing - these movements coincided like dance.

In this silent choreography, I pushed through the tedium of the questions, and the obstacles and distractions of the prison and the clinic, to seek the details of another man's mind. I gently pried, and prised apart the convoluted petals laid in curves, a bulging calyx, to reveal the stamen. I was a painstaking and attentive biologist, but I despaired that my technique - fifteen ambiguous questions - could not support such rigour. These doubts only spurred me on to examine and explore, to extract all I could from the data, and from each face and each utterance. I was alert to the words, and the spaces between the words, and the grunts and coughs and snorts. I fed on the details of each subject, who gave obliviously, with no strings attached, until my interview was completed, and the data recorded on my hard-disc, and the prisoner was returned to his holding cell. We discarded the fact of our meeting with a shrug, in order to move on. Love is tireless, and voracious.

Then one prisoner was encountered who sought out my weakness and bound to me through it like a virus to fragile protoplasm. He touched the wooden Indian and found that it was flesh. I became ineluctably attached to this man, a political prisoner and personal nemesis named Antonio Gramsci. But this came later, when, of course, I least expected it. Psychiatrists observe through a lens, rendering themselves myopic because the whole is ungraspable in others' lives as in their own. My glasses cracked, and here, in prison, in this morass of social detritus, I was to learn the meaning of human relatedness, and its risk. In closeness we become most vulnerable. From seeing the prisoners as brief dots on a radar screen, or flickers of light on an oscilloscope, to myself reverberating, feeling, and alive. I failed as a wooden Indian. Another failure to add to the list. This much I had in common with the prisoners, none of whom came to this place for their successes.

Before I descend further into the prison encounter, I will first describe the twists and turns in my psychiatric career which led me there.

PART II

PSYCHIATRY FROM WITHIN

INCARCERATION

Most prisoners are sent there; I had chosen my destination, or so I thought. Naïve to feel that one's choices are determined consciously. Prison's difference fascinated me - much as the psychiatric ward had excited me in my first year as a doctor, and led me on the path of psychiatric training. As an intern, I had been thrown into the strangeness - the shambling, raving, despair - of psychosis. I felt I belonged, and took to the books and mentors who could guide me through.

Both prison and asylum existed as another world which I could explore each day, and leave at night. The psychiatrist visits other's psyches, and then departs, with a trace. Now I had departed the clinical role altogether, to assume a new identity as researcher. I had closed the door on my professional consulting room, its green leather armchairs, Oregon timber desk, and yellow walls which had contained the voice of each patient lulling and captivating and soothing and berating like the crash of waves rolling onto the beach beyond my window.

That work had exhausted me, its waves had washed me high and dry, and languishing on the shores of emotional devastation, physical ruin, professional incapacity. Prison loomed as an opportunity to rebuild a shattered self, in embarking on a new phase of my career, no longer as carer.

Prison as refuge and rehabilitation holds little validity for most inmates, but it was my last salvation.

Demons had driven me from the care of my patients. I cannot strike the necessary note of distance now to fictionalise my suffering, not in the voice which says 'I'. And if I were able to assume that distance, and equivocation, between narrator and author which serves for an account in the third person, then no such history would bear telling, for I would be cured of the need to ruminate, and ruminate on the symbolic product of my rumination.

Motivation is a slippery critter. Superstition prevents artists from exploring its wellsprings - the fear that if the lid of the kettle is lifted, the affective drive to create will dissipate like so much bubbles and steam, and the artist will be as bereft as others, or more so for his depth of narcissistic regret. I have no such doubts, and nothing to lose, and shamelessly present this story of descent from observation to experience as another mode of therapy: part indulgence, part necessity, and an unambiguous response to the question "Who is the story for - reader or writer?" Writing is analogous to self-laceration. The pain of torn skin is eased by the release of blood. A display of self in ink may do just as well. Or badly.

Prison is lowered as a grid upon the chaos of thoughts and feelings and episodes which make up a life. Its routine adjusts and fixes each man's reptilian and vegetable functions to the same rhythms: when to eat, when to sleep, when to wander in the yard like so many chooks pecking for morsels of meaning across their daily rationing of concrete space. Prison sets high walls between its inner and outer, between self and other, between awareness and experience. Only psychosis breaks them down.

The facts of daily tedium fail to contain, or block. Prison demands adherence to external routines, external regulations, as though stability will thereby be introjected. But the struggle is already lost where awareness cannot emerge. The inner narrative of self is usurped by the primitive agonies which prison inevitably arouses. Histories shift as we tell them, loose as dust, precarious as the heightened self-consciousness of a man whose very experience of self is constantly threatened: a life at stake. A yacht's keel acts to counter downwind drift. These men are at sea, and blown across its surface, like so many flimsy hulls. Their course is random, but served to guide my own.

This preamble is to orientate myself, and reckon up the balance of griefs - how I lost my work, how I lost my way - before I begin the story of my prison year. A confluence of despairs had swept me towards the prison gates. Overwhelmed by experience, I turned to a mythical scientism - an objectivity of self which defines the mind as an appendage, to be ignored, if not exorcised - and hoped that in the detachment of observation I would find the control and certainty which I had lost. I could look **at** each prisoner's eyes, not **into** them. The torpid man seeks a dulling of vitality in others. This wounded bird, a squawking limping flightless bird, needed refuge, care, sustenance, safety, and a decent wage. Is that too much to ask?

I would prefer to trace here a trajectory of heroic and noble achievement; I would prefer a litany of success, to the ensuing threnody of woe. I would prefer the warm glow of narcissistic gratification to life's insistent restrictions, and the clammy grip of envy enveloping my regard and turning it to scorn. Such is the shroud of mourning across my shoulder, and all the more pathetic as stooping to the fact of loss as self-imposed.

A career in madness had driven me crazy. All careers are ultimately soul-destroying, and I do not exclude creative pursuits from that generalisation. Weariness, and the formation of a callus, are the inevitable effects of any rubbing up against the world. Ageing itself is a drawing out of being over the wrack of time, as time slows to the body's deceleration, involution, and eventual stasis. In prison consciousness, the dawdle of days becomes a stultifying sameness.

The body changes with the mind in time's flux: fluids filter more sluggishly through the kidney's net; marrow decalcifies; immunity dims as the boundary between self and other elides, in preparation for decomposition to dirt. And thoughts, too, no longer arc at lightning speed across the neo-cortex, but hesitate, and double-back, and in senility never make it to awareness, save as the signal of something absent, the negative of knowledge, the gap between the sense of something known and the inner expression of that something. A life can be forgotten, beginning with the end, and working backwards until the self is no longer. We are our memories; without them, the meaning of being disappears. So it is that grief numbs the senses. In its attempts to shut down, to remove what cannot be contained, grief destroys all continuity. When the attachment to one's own past is broken, there can be no hope for a future, only a constant immersion in the morbid present.

Prisoners who dwell on loss - of freedom, of sex, of drugs, of work, of relationships - are driven to despair. It is far healthier to ignore, to suppress, and to carry on as though nothing is missing, or being missed. Rebuild the social world inside, assume a likeable knockabout visage, hide the misery, especially from yourself. Be a bloke. The truth is that no-one cares here, because no-one can afford in the act of caring the unleashing of their own personal suffering. And the truth is that here, talking won't change anything. Nor is there a pill to make the pain go away. No wonder-drug, or shot. Every moment hurts in prison, if you let it. Pain becomes a reflex. His severed past lancinates the inmate consciousness like phantom pain from an amputated leg. The prisoner hobbles, teetering toward collapse, staggers up again, and leaning upon a fence cadges a durry for distraction: "Thanks, mate. Gotta light?" Ignorance is relief.

Imagination breeds fear, and fear impairs performance as writer, as doctor. I am the nameless bracing of wish in the cold wash of experience. Praise, virtue, even love dissolve in the face of an indifferent universe, in the face of the silent and unyielding prison wall. When the metaphor of 'face' returns to its origin in maternal pre-occupation, the man returns to a trust and a yielding. This is the stuff never found in prison. Nothing grows inside, where poison spray coats concrete, where men are dulled to their routine, and coalesce in the tribalism of adolescence. This is the uniform regression of prison officers in grey and prisoners in blue. Two colours of the sky define their social existence, and difference.

Being placed between heaven and earth, neither of one or the other, man feels most keenly the very problem of categorisation: distinction *per se* causes a space to arise which terrifies me. I quake in the rift, a threat of engulfment, or of falling into an abyss. I am always between two worlds, never seeing because there are two ways to see. Only blindness can ignore them. If I shut my eyes, sameness reassures me of my safety.

I am in a room with a murderer or rapist, but I can disregard the token images of his viciousness. I can disregard the bristling crop of hair, dullness of expression, tattoos, slouch and languid voice. I can ignore the brooding menace of a stereotype if I do not see these points of difference, but slant my vision to the need and softness which still float in the man's inner swamp like uninhabited islands. He, too, was once a baby.

A lazy crocodile ambles over warm sand, its heavy tail dragging up the beach. The reptilian brain discharging conscious lust in a man's mind circles the naked woman lying in the sun. This is his island, she is his creation to devour. Then he is 'put away', incarcerated for his violation, and basks with sly croc grin in his prison slouch and amble. The pain which begets more pain is never touched.

The comforting illusion of intersubjectivity is that our differences arise only as distinct expressions of our relationship, and cannot exist in themselves. The psychopath takes comfort in the blurring of difference which he defines himself by exploiting.

Awareness had never merged with experience in any way I could put into words, save the scream of parturition which must be stifled to preserve decorum. Baby and mother co-mingling in sound as in amnion, and the guttural groan "I" of men entering prison, swallowed whole. The serpent devours its own tail, then feels sated, and digested simultaneously, and wonders where its next meal will come from, or go to. Let us coil around the huddled emptiness of prison time, of prisoners' lives which are partitioned into this lag. Let us search there for the bed-rock of certainty - a certainty which clinical toil could never attain. And let us in prison bury ourselves in others' laments and despair, the better to detach from our own, or fictionalise it. So to the cast of prison characters, the detached observation, the relentless pursuit of truth in numbers, in statistics, in data. The prisoner hoped it was all a dream, so it would all go away. I shall now vanish. You wish.

PANACEA

I must introduce you to the broad ways in which psychiatry pretends to some knowledge of the human condition, for these ways had become my ways. My learning and practice had made me, or been the container for the pre-existing content of my habitual neuroses. Medicine is a harsh mistress. She demands stoicism, a resignation to the real. Over the years of my clinical practice, these demands wore me down, until eventually I sought relief, first in psychoanalysis, then in prison research.

I had struggled at the clinical coal-face, not knowing whether to go through, around, or over it, and failing in each attempt. The first question which the doctor must grapple with in becoming a psychiatrist is: who is the patient, who is the doctor? The recognition of self in other is terrifying. The lines of retreat from this terror lead to a biological model. The shoddy shrink can be resurrected as doctor again - a physician of mental illness - donning the white coat for austerity, clutching a stethoscope as symbol of expertise, prescribing anti-depressants, beneath the slogan of 'depression as chemical imbalance'. He cuts clean and cuts deep, like a surgeon, to ward himself off from his patients' suffering, and his own.

I felt safe for a while in this guise, this professional façade, which assigned the distress of each patient to some putative diagnostic category. I was committing what is known even within medicine as the 'Procrustean crime', after Procrustes, a villain from Greek mythology who forced his victims into a bed of the wrong size, by mutilating them. However, as the years passed, I too was to feel that I had been squeezed into a Procrustean bed as psychiatrist. I squirmed, protested, and eventually leapt free, via psychoanalysis to prison, another retreat to scientific detachment, a perfected objectivity. But perfection is just another form of cruelty.

Before that escape, I daily attempted to assuage my patients' protestations of individuality by my soothing insistence: 'This is the diagnostic bed to which you have been allotted. Now lie still and take the medicine.' That medicine again and again was anti-depressants, and not just for depression. No, these wonder drugs were indicated for panic disorder, for obsessive-compulsive disorder, for personality disorder, for generalised anxiety disorder, for post-traumatic stress disorder, for anorexia, for obesity, for gambling and for migraine, irritable bowel, and chronic fatigue. You name the illness, here is the panacea.

This pharmacological mythology gave me a professional identity. Here I was, following clinical practice guidelines, and evidence-based medicine, and not thinking too hard about it. The trouble was, my patients kept pestering me with pesky trivialities, such as:

"Taking a tablet won't solve my problems."

"I am frightened that it will change my personality."

"If I stop the tablets, will I get depressed again?"

"I don't want to become addicted."

"I don't want a medication to prop me up. I can solve my problems myself."

These were the baleful voices which stymied me each day. Each resistance to my ministrations caused a tiny but irrevocable erosion of my professional confidence: disappointment in the response to medication became cracks in the patina of smug assurance which had sustained my career. I would counter superstition and subjectivity with science, the facts of quantitative research by pharmaceutical companies striving for market share. Their studies compare, say, one thousand patients treated with the medication, with another thousand untreated, and…

You, too, will believe that life can unfold as a shining path to paradise, with no messy residue of despair, hopelessness, or nihilistic resignation to an indifferent universe. The world will glow again as though leaden scales have lifted from your eyes. Beauty will abound, and light breezes of optimism will whisk clean the musty alleys and corridors of your cognition."

Cut to

Pearly grimace, as mother saunters over greensward with boisterous, healthy family. Setting sun, lilting music, and a soothing deep male voice-over defining the moment as safe.

The mother had suffered from depression, until her doctor took control. He applied a nudge to the modulating tone of her neurotransmitter soup, bathing her again in the anodyne wash of 5-hydroxytryptamine, and noradrenaline. Husband continued to disparage her, and her child no longer even bothered to attend school, but she was able to maintain a sublime resignation, thanks to the wonders of modern psychopharmacology. Not only was the burden of depression lifted, but so too was she relieved of the ridiculous urgencies of life, such as meaning, change, doubt, struggle. Compare this outcome to the pervasive depression and guilt which may have continued to torment her even through a divorce, custody dispute, and retraining into work.

The judicious identification of patient need, and application of appropriate treatment, have preserved the family. Meanwhile, the child is responding well to the amphetamine prescribed for his attention deficit disorder, and he no longer complains or draws pictures of mummy as a clone from outer space. The husband's affair is going fine, too.

There is no need to reject an easy answer, simply because it is easy. My scepticism - as much as my patients' fears and quibbles - was tarnishing my professional role. It may well be that depression is in fact a disease, whose pathophysiology is simply not yet elucidated. The brain is the final frontier of medical science. Only in recent years has the technology arisen to search its recesses.

The first anti-depressants were discovered in the 1950s when doctors treating patients with tuberculosis noticed that some were becoming strangely ebullient. It turned out that the antibiotic for the tubercle bacillus had a mood-elevating effect. This discovery gave rise to the mono-amine oxidase inhibitors, and later the tricyclic anti-depressants. Then came Prozac, the first of the selective serotonin re-uptake inhibitors. The psychiatrist now has a veritable pharmacopoeia of agents from which to select his anti-depressant. How does he make his choice? With care, and knowledge. The free pens, free dinners, free lunches, free holidays, free coffee plungers, free toothbrushes, free desk diaries, free cameras, and free pads from the pharmaceutical companies are handy, but hardly influence prescribing decisions. More relevant factors to consider are the side-effects...

"Doctor, my head feels like its full of the green foam that florists stuff flowers into."

"I have this thick wall of glass between me and other people on these pills."

"There's this weird feeling that nothing matters any more."
"It's a manufactured happiness, but it's not really me."
"A kind of slowing into quicksand."
"You promised me the world with these pills, and all I got was an atlas…"
"I can't, you know, get it up any more."

I could not win. Even when my patients' suffering was relieved, still they complained. At least the last complaint - erectile impotence - is listed as an adverse effect. The other stuff is too subjective to show up on their studies. At first, the drug companies reckoned impotence would occur in up to five per cent of (male) patients – not much more than with placebo. After a few years, that rate was more like 70%. Funny how the epidemiology got it wrong to start with. Funny indeed that such a finding might have hurt market share. Other "recognised" side-effects (recognised by the drug company, that is, and not merely by pernickety patients) include: nausea, insomnia, drowsiness, diarrhoea, headaches, anorgasmia in women, dry mouth, blurred vision.

So, what did the patients expect - miracles? You don't get something for nothing. This is a tough world, you layabout. The bottom line is, you gotta gee yourself up. I can't do it all for you. At the end of my private practice sessions, I felt worn out, a sponge sodden with others' miseries and inadequacies. If I squeezed myself, a grey muck dribbled to the carpet, and I was left deflated. I needed a greater purpose, some personal saga, a quest to steel my days towards. This routine of prescribing and periodic review was dulling me. The other lives I might have lived loomed in my imagination like so many unstarted journeys. I yearned for the vista of fulfilment which cruel fate and some lousy decisions had denied me. Of course, I could detect in my own musings the narcissistic whims of an overgrown adolescent. I dreamt of crafting from the dross of my daily list of patients some unique monument to myself. The greater my disillusion, the more pressing and immediate was the will to change.

This growing urgency to act, however, was countered by a growing realisation that - for all my moaning about my moaning patients - without them I had nothing. I needed my patients to fill my emptiness, just as they sought me to fill theirs. At least I could tolerate my patients' suffering, but not their indifference, whether expressed in a failure to attend, or a failure to pay. If a patient did not turn up for a session, I would fly into a rage; another space opening up, another emptiness, another proof that I did not matter.

I became pre-occupied with my earnings, tallying them to the last dollar over and over in my head. What else to do with that inner deadness than line it with wads of cash like some subterranean bank vault, or coffin? Locked tight, held deep down, hoarded away – holding in what is of no value, but what one cannot bear to release. Freud recognised the nexus between shit and cash and death, that anal fixation. It is what we do with our deadness that defines character. Cash can take the place of meaning, as though it were of equal value. One's preoccupation with money varies in direct proportion to one's deadness. They say fear and greed rule the stock market. The same could be said of my private practice.

The very bane of my life had become my only means of livelihood. I was ruined for real work. Like some perverse shepherd, a flock of suffering supported me. I was the victim of an intricate deceit beginning with **their** need, and ending with my own. Further symmetries emerged as the very symptoms for which I was treating my patients began to appear in me. Although descending the declivity of despair, I could not ask for help. The vulnerability of patient hood appalled me. Surrendering to another's will, and declaring oneself unable to cope, and accepting the possibility of need, of dependence, of trust. Not to mention the **meaning** of my depression. This was a murky pond of questions and memories which are better left undisturbed. An occasional lumpy fluidity spreads beneath the meniscus' slime. Is it the ridged dorsum of submerged monsters, or the drowning form of my narcissistic alterities? Perhaps they are one and the same.

Pondering this question, I felt the lurking threat of suffocation which introspection entails. If only I had listened to my mother's warning: "Introspection leads to depression…" Or was that the other way around? Over and above these hesitations was the terrifying stain upon my formerly pristine self-image: that I, too, was tainted with a mysterious but palpable neurotransmitter imbalance. An imbalance so subtle, so arcane, that it cannot be seen by positron emission control tomography, or magnetic resonance imaging, or electroencephalogram, or even in the very cerebro-spinal fluid which bathes my brain, my thoughts, my self. Depression. Mood swing. Affective disorder. These labels which I had handed to my patients as a soothing answer to their doubts, and as promise of relief (if there is this beast called depression, we have this panacea called anti-depression), were now beginning to encroach on me. I struggled in the gloom of a shadow which I had seen always cast upon my patients, but never saw behind me.

Help can overwhelm. Help can prise the fragile grip, finger by flexed finger, until help's victim drops into the other's empathic abyss. Can the physician help himself? He is given sample packs of antidepressants. I stored batches and batches in the bottom drawer of my Oregon timber desk: reversible monoamine oxidase inhibitors, selective serotonin reuptake inhibitors, serotonin and noradrenaline reuptake inhibitors, tricyclic antidepressants, and the latest - a serotonin type two receptor blocker. One dull morning, I listlessly opened the packets which I had formerly only thought fit for my patients. I fingered the tablets, the capsules, the pills, and made little piles of them on my desk. I randomly mixed and merged the different coloured discs until a colourful mosaic laced and curved before me. I was enthralled at my design, and the possibilities which grew from its chaos of hundreds of shapes and colours, like a child seeing through wondrous eyes what the grown-up dismisses with a weary glance, a shrug. The drone of patient after patient could not distract me from this kaleidoscope. As they talked, I fiddled and tweaked. Patients are never concerned by the apparent indifference of their psychiatrist. Either they are so self-absorbed that they cannot even accept the possibility that their discourse is anything but engrossing, or they are so self-reproachful that they cannot imagine that anyone would even bother to listen to them, even if paid to do so.

After some hours of random fiddling, I had serendipitously created a concoction of antidepressant chemicals so potent that a single dose could stimulate every known synapse in the human brain. This led to a fantasy of the final breakthrough in brain chemistry

...I had a new purpose: to deliver on an impossible promise to not merely lift the mood, but send it in a sky-rocket to nirvana. The first patients to try my new concoction confirmed the promise. Not only were they cured of depression,

they no longer had bad hair days, or self-doubts, or even fleeting recriminations. Life was aglow. The hang-dog losers slumping in to see me each week became confident, vibrant, and successful. Some took up careers in politics, others went in to sales, or advertising. A refreshing ruthlessness lit up their eyes. Soon, they stopped paying me, and not long after that, they stopped seeing me. After years of intimate contact, these ungrateful wretches who had crawled to me begging for help were treating me with contempt, like a loser - me, their saviour. Was this another symmetry?

Although patient after patient recovered from depression, and deserted me, my own depression never left. The persistence of my own misery became the cruellest irony of all, but I could not bring myself to swallow that pile of pills…

So much for the fantasy. The history of psychiatry is littered with too many maverick cures which turn out to be worse than the disease: insulin coma therapy, deep sleep therapy, barbiturates, and benzodiazepines. And for every maverick cure, there is the maverick shrink whose omnipotence blinded him to the risks. Some are struck off, some commit suicide, some become professors. By sheer fluke, I had created a dose of polypharmacy which would cure depression in a bull elephant. The only side-effects were an inordinate lengthening of the ears, a coarsening and greying of the skin, a gradual protrusion of sclerosed tissue either side of the trunk-like nose, the development of an immense girth around torso and limbs, and a lumbering gait. Many of my former patients went to Africa, where they were shot by poachers.

When asked for answers, for the solution to the problems of living, my response was to retreat. *"Doctor, why am I still thinking about killing myself? Why should I live?"*

How do I know? To live or to die. Such questions jolted me. They swam in my head as a residue of this work, swam as so many lumpy, spiny, creepy eels. Albert Camus* thought this was the ultimate question of philosophy, and he died in a car accident, probably while smoking. Ridiculous: existential, even.

The eel coils back on itself, tail sliding into mouth, and body disappearing like the meaning of a life untold whose first question is the final answer. When I work it out, logically and completely, then I will know that suicide will be the right choice. A dedication to the cruelty of the rational, of the sealed compartment which does not leak, or allow an inkling in of the fluid stuff of feelings. The perfectly impermeable barrier between a self and its content: this is what my patients were seeking.

"There is no reason to go on. I would be better off dead."

Each day, each hour with a different patient, each adding a final straw to the burden of their constantly unmet needs. The answer rang shrill as a gangster's percentage deal, as an equation which proved that awareness plus meaning over understanding equalled zero. Nullity. Nothing to gain by all this talk:

"Just give me something to take away the pain. You can help, can't you? Your are a doctor, aren't you?"

No journey to this patient's centre, no way through, because the sheer emptiness of the core is incommensurable. There can be no signs, no navigable route, along this rutted path of an appeal to my guilt, which itself merely covers my own helplessness. The

---

* from The Myth of Sisyphus, by Albert Camus

ignorant would-be healer of the mind is caught like a compass needle which spins without bearings. I had no workable knowledge then of psychoanalysis, no framework within which to locate myself and my patients. I am appalled to look back now at those faltering steps, staggering towards the possibility of a relationship between doctor and patient, but each veering away just as some inkling of connection and closeness and meaning may have been about to emerge.

I was in the grip of the transference, without awareness of it, and attempting to fob it all off as some symptom begging for relief. How wrong can a man be? Imagine a carpenter who hates wood and you will have some idea of the practice of the biological psychiatrist dealing with people's minds all day, their subjectivities which he crushes against the anvil of his spurious objectivity. After all, to him all that exists is the brain; the mind is an epiphenomenon, a chimera. For every twisted thought, there is a twisted molecule.

Send in the next patient to face a diagnosis, like a prisoner being sentenced. The past is never disclosed – abuse, trauma, deprivation. Of course, that silent evasion is itself disclosing some abusive re-enactment right here, in the transference, if the biological shrink can but open his eyes to that painful fact. No, they remain closed, colluding with the patient who carries her compartment which life does not dare open, and death will seal over ever more completely - air-tight and water-tight. Her sentence lasts forever, because it is invariably passed onto her children, and her children's children.

The doctor reassures himself: "But there must be something I can give you other than a diagnosis. Perhaps a pill. Never mind your past. [Never for a moment considering that it is being played out right now, in this eternally recurring present.] Never mind at all. I am not fobbing you off. Trust me. No sense digging around in that muck. Let bygones be bygones. Cheerio…Next!"

Nor had her mother fobbed her off, in ignoring her complaints about daddy, and her urinary symptoms, and her fretfulness each night, and her failure to learn.

This patient's scream is silent, for she has never found the voice to utter a single syllable of her own. Her mouth widens in horror and confusion, but does not betray the secret: she cannot be moved to reveal to others what she cannot identify to herself. She doesn't know where to begin. Another perfect seal, which the psychiatrist claims as some success, by pressing the edges more tightly shut, like pursed lips, like the clenching of a fist, the squeezing of the bleeding lids imposing blindness on the void. See no… Speak no… Hear no…

"Take this agglomeration of medication, which blocks every pre- and post-synaptic receptor so tight that not a drop of psychic juice will escape. You literally will not feel a thing, because you will not feel yourself. The subjective and objective will merge into a being beyond division."

The universal anti-depressant is prescribed. One hundred per cent cure rate. One hundred per cent improvement in quality of life. The answer you've been waiting for, the answer to your prayers. Another religion, where your pain can be diluted in the greater pain of the universal soul. Hallelujah, and pass the cocktail. Gulp, slurp, gurgle. Feeling better already.

Was this the answer? I believed for a while in this attempt to relieve symptoms, to seal my patients against fears, in an impermeable cage in which to float, free from the influx of questions, doubts, needs, losses, pain, trauma.

Death was merely a side-effect, a price proving one thing: that the only perfectly sealed box is a coffin.

The burden of my patients' expectation of cure had been lifted, and in its place was the boredom of routine. I had seen dullness in my colleague's eyes, the vaguely inattentive look of the burned-out shrink, immaculately attired, and never at risk of a single original thought. The categories of existence neatly stipulated in their diagnostic manual, there was no more to discover. I bought myself two new sports jackets, one a burgundy coloured linen, the other of light wool with a herring-bone design. I was in a state of confusion, like a man exposed to advertising for the first time who has no resistance to the hype. Psychiatry appalled and fascinated me. I tried but failed to emulate its suited practitioners. What made me so special? Nothing, no wit or talent or particular calling. I had fled to the safety of the medical profession, and was in no position to complain. It fed me and clothed me and paid the mortgage on my home and my investment property and the lease on my European sports saloon with leather upholstery and CD-stacker and air-bags. The show must go on: nothing to show for it, but put on a good show. Have a sumptuous meal at a drug company's expense. Relax and watch the show.

Thoughts of suicide are an indication for anti-depressant therapy, for such despair must be the *sine qua non* of any category of melancholy. And never doubt or delve beneath the surface of despair, because to find in the urge for death some sense of soothing escape or respite begs the question - escape from what? And then the journey is directed inward, to descend into the labyrinths of past, unearthing bones of long-buried skeletons. The molesting hand of a deceased grandfather, the persistent rebuke of a parent, the pain of lost enthusiasms. No, enough morbid introspection, which itself is merely another feature of the depressive syndrome. We can treat the mood, and its accompanying ruminations, and etiolate the past.

Order another test. Tease another neuronal synapse. Meaning had disappeared from the possibility of relevance, when doctors of the brain disregarded the mind. The mind grows in the embrace of relatedness. An isolated brain remains just that - a brain. As alienated as a pickled viscera I saw years ago in a jar on the counter in the old anatomy palladium, hazy yellow with the glint of sun through formaldehyde, and the snickering students and the doddery lecturer mumbling to himself and the gardener below who was shocked at being thrown a cadaver's hand by a student later dismissed for his levity.

I had chosen medicine not out of interest, let alone a sense of vocation, or to help people (in case you hadn't gathered *that* already) but for reasons of status: being a medical student meant others could be certain I had scored higher marks at high school. And from their certainty, I could draw smug sustenance - a sugary satisfaction, for its sweetness is also its decay. Chasing status can be a life-long pursuit: it gives a sense of purpose - if not purpose *per se* - and fuels a career. The drive to prove some point to others suppresses the feeling of pointlessness, when things go well.

I had remained in medicine by force of habit, and chosen psychiatry by interest and *mien*. But I had come to know things were not well, because I had come to know too much: that my patients demanded a truth which was beyond me to give. I, a man of a thousand disguises, a hundred dissemblings. I, who had bamboozled even himself in the twists and turns of his deceit. This is the confessional mode, a narrative to set the record straight, in tone if not in substance, as the substance has evaporated. When all a man's energy is devoted to the currying of favour, and the embellishment of image, the inner self is depleted. What remains is the shell, the face in the mirror, the accoutrement, the carapace as identity. There can be no private language for such a man, merely the social palaver of a psychological cadaver; the world refracted in the prism of narcissism, whose self-sufficiency prevents him calling out, "Give me a hand". Like the hapless gardener, I too would be thrown that lumpy- fingered flesh from a corpse.

No point, no purpose, no way through the morass. The habitual expression of disdain was distorting my face, not to mention keeping patients away. I was burning out, a wreck, a smouldering cinder of a man. To retreat from the world with loathing is logical, even laudable, but you need determination and either an independent means, or a marketable talent. I simply could not take the risk. I was too used to my comforts.

Psychiatry straddles imagination and madness, mind and brain. But what I sought as a bridge between the two became a barrier - another wall. If a man is what he is paid to do, I was a bulwark of logic beyond self-doubt. As vessel for others' fears and moods and fantasies, I was sinking, I was in danger of capsize. Most working days sap the energy; mine sapped my soul. There was nothing left within me to burn out: cinders can be relit only so many times, until all is reduced to ash.

I tried to become philosophical, which is to say, detached. It is not necessary to *care*, so much as to be *interested*, and the two are not incompatible. Interest is simply care without sentiment. Interest defines professionalism, care defines the clergy, the benevolent, the preposterous martyrdom of charity. I attempted to cultivate a detached yet interested stance, trying it on much as I tried on my new sports jacket, or any other trappings of professional identity. A sense of emptiness ensued.

I sought colleagues for reassurance, but gathered only scorn. Drowning in a sea of doubt is a grim enough fate, but all the worse if that doubt is irrelevant. Philosophy does not wash well with the crowd at the free dinners put on by drug companies. Another new anti-depressant, another city hotel, international speaker, and courtesy car-parking. The dull-eyed mob of psychiatrists feigns interest while gossiping over the latest divorce, the latest colleague to be struck off for fucking a patient, the latest killing on the stock market, and rifling their goodies: the drug company pen, notebook, T-shirt, cap, toothbrush, coffee mug, coffee plunger, tie clip, and calendar. There are also scientific papers purporting to prove the newest drug's superiority in the Darwinian struggle for the exogenous molecule to relieve sadness. I felt alone, but risked conversation with a crusty and eminent colleague. He wore a bow-tie, and pin-striped suit, and exuded smugness, and tilted his head to mine with a mixture of indulgence and indifference, between sips of cabernet sauvignon and chomps of veal.

"You say the problem of caring for patients is too great a burden? I don't follow you. The only real care is whether they pay. Face up to it, man. We live in a capitalist technocracy. The vastness of urban angst to which we psychiatrists are exposed can only be compensated in the pursuit of financial security. And perfecting your golf swing. The government issues all doctors with a provider number, so you can go forth and provide for yourself. This dilemma of choice - caring or interest - makes no sense at all to me. You should concern yourself with useful dilemmas: shares or real estate? Would you like some more veal? These drug company meals are really very good. Must be doing well, the anti-depressant pushers. And why not? A perfectly reasonable market. Depression really is an illness of the brain, you know. The neurochemistry is almost elucidated."

The rational response is to pull back. Bathe in colloquial shallows: relax, don't try so hard, it's not so serious, take it easy, don't let it bother you. Anodyne gulping, the swallow which follows the herd to oblivion. I, too, could drink the maudlin days away, because there's no point, not a care in the world, not a patient to care for. This despair feeds the deceit of exemplary benevolence: my true need was not to be needed, but to be known. And clinical psychiatry simply was too small a stage. No grateful patient could mimic the sweep of applause, the resounding clamour of acclaim. And the most hateful patients were those who were never grateful.

THE HATEFUL PATIENT

So I too was another nobody with all the trappings of privilege, another shoddy shrink, albeit a well-paid one, and could probably have tolerated the intolerable, which is the defining theme of most self-centred lives, were it not for a concatenation of fateful events, beginning with Harold, the hateful patient. He aroused a desperation which finally drove me from the work of caring for others, and although now free of that clinical burden, he continues to haunt me, like an apparition from a past life, someone else's nightmare.

The fusion of two selves presents an escape from the imprisoning logic of self: where self-reflection cannot exist, regression to psychic union is inevitable. The horror of Harold was in his abject yearning to meld our minds. He caught me at a vulnerable time, just as my doubts about my work and my self were escalating. We met three times a week for two years, a mere drop in the infinite ocean of the unconscious. But in those two years Harold's life seemed to follow mine into a pit, or vice versa. Perhaps he identified with me too closely - by an unconscious process, of course, as he knew nothing about me. I was appropriately reticent.

This professional reserve allows the patient to more completely project their fantasies, as though onto a blank screen, Freud's *tabula rasa*. I was moving towards the analytic method at the time, although still oblivious to its technique and theory. But in Harold's case, the projections swung wildly out of control. My blank screen served only to goad him further.

Over the course of his therapy, Harold's pleas to be known, totally and absolutely, and to know me, became a burden which I loathed. I increased his fees, changed the appointment times, the days, the venues. But still he clung to the contact with me, the reluctant guru, attempting to reincarnate me as smothering mother, and becoming her himself.

This transference phenomenon remained impermeable to my every ploy, because I never was able to penetrate its meaning. His silences became as intolerable as his barrage of questions. The scrutiny with which he examined my every movement, grimace and flinch for reference to himself induced in me a feeling of floundering in thick goo, some psychic soup. In the consulting room with Harold, there was nowhere to run.

Eventually, I simply stopped turning up to see him. Although the patient cannot charge the therapist for missed appointments, Harold's persistence wrecked my practice. I would phone the rooms to check with my receptionist, asking furtively, "Is *he* there?" Invariably, he would be patiently waiting for hours after our scheduled time, ignoring the receptionist's explanation that I had been "held up at the hospital" and would not return that day. This meant I had to abandon other patients, and avoid Harold like some vile contagion. If I saw him walking past my favourite café, I would quickly hide behind a newspaper, or waitress, especially if it happened to be the hour when I was supposed to be subjecting myself to Harold's emotional onslaughts.

He laid siege to my practice. Each morning the flash of the answering machine light bore a terrible malevolence - its signal of Harold's invariable message. The more I tried to avoid Harold, the more needy he became.

I sought supervision from a psychoanalyst.

"Zere is no problem, you see. Zis patient is perfectly regressed, and is now fixated on the anal stage of control. Continue wis your vork. That vill be four hundred dollars, please. Plus GST."

"You said it would be $250."

"I haf had some losses on ze NASDAQ. Do you know anything about hedge funds?"

"But this is intolerable. Harold is destroying my life."

"Ach. Zat's his job - he is a patient."

"Look, you don't seem to understand..."

The analyst gleefully interrupted me. A twinkle lit up his *arcus senilis*, and his perfect dentures glistened with clear central European saliva. "Ach," he said. "Zis is the perfect case of the parallel process: first, ze hateful patient seeks a total mind meld wis ze therapist, and then the therapist seeks it with me."

I was humiliated, and never returned to analytic supervision. But the therapeutic impasse became a rift, deepened into a ravine, and eventually the problem of Harold plunged me into one of Dante's abysmal circles of Hell*, the seventh one where the violent are tormented in a river of blood. How could I extricate myself? I needed a new paradigm, something precise, measurable, reassuring in its certainty: neuropsychiatry.

---

* Dante Alighieri, The Divine Comedy, illustrated by Gustave Dore, published by Omega Books

The prosaic of Prozac would banish these nascent psychoanalytic speculations. And besides, it seemed a shrewd political move. This is the age of accountability, of managed care: how could I justify the hundreds of hours devoted to a single neurosis, when I could be treating patients every fifteen minutes by writing a script? I visited the hot-shot professor in his research institute.

"Impulse control problem, associated with deficiency in 5-hydroxytryptamine in the fronto-striatal synaptic cleft. We can demonstrate the defect on positron emission tomography scanning. Several publications confirm a significant difference in assays of cerebro-spinal fluid metabolites such as 5-indole-acetic acid between cases and controls on lumbar puncture. Send Harold here and we'll be glad to work him up. We're looking for more subjects to volunteer for our research protocol. He'll be given a free sandwich for lunch."

"Yes, a free sandwich. Excellent. I'm sure he'll agree. And you will actually stick a needle in his back? Yes?" I was thrilled, and not just at the possibility of inflicting pain on Harold, my hateful patient.

I had heard of the notion of sadistic counter-transference, and the punitive therapist, but at the time was happy to scorn such pseudo-scientific folk psychology as inadequate alongside the pure science of 5-hydroxytryptamine. My motivation was clearly now one of furthering science. I felt part of a magnificent enterprise, and thus had embarked on the journey which was to re-build my ailing career. I turned my back on the clinical coal-face, a thankless task where talent such as mine was unable to soar above the mundane indulgences of patients.

In parting comment, I would not deny that Harold had demonstrated for me the limits of control which the practising psychiatrist must face. The intrusion of another invariably arouses this question: who is on top, who wins out? Lacan called it the 'fight for pure prestige', which is the only phrase of his I ever understood. Those men least able to function socially will typically prefer the company of women, and cite an aversion to competitiveness for turning away from the fellowship of men. It is not an aversion to competitiveness that irks them, but an aversion to *losing,* or at least to taking a risk. As patients, they do not risk saying a word, for fear that it may be wrong. The infuriating silence is exacerbated if any coercion is employed, for this only confirms the fear. What is the answer?

The professor wrote back to me the following month:

"Dear doctor,

Thankyou for referring your patient, Mr Harold ... Unfortunately, he does not meet the parameters for our clinical threshold protocol, i.e. there is nothing wrong with him. However, we would be happy to include you in our study, based on Harold's lucid account of your psychiatric condition. Please complete the enclosed consent form.

Yours faithfully,
Professor..."

This reply shattered me. No professor was going to stick his bloody great lumbar puncture needles into my back! No way. I knew that Harold's *mind* resembled the tentacles of an octopus - designed not only to grab, but also to exert suction. I had hoped to hand his *brain* over to the neuropsychiatrists to relieve me from such loathsome imagery, from a necessary but dreadful density of metaphor in which I could not think, and barely survive.

THE CURE OF LOVE

When a man feels he needs a reason to go on living, that he has suffered too much, he in fact has not suffered enough. Psychiatrist, heal thyself. I felt like taking a break from my life to have a nice cup of tea and a good lie down. If only I could find a kettle which would take a few years to boil. That kettle turned out to be psychoanalysis, but I got scalded.

I yearned for some authenticity of being. The fact that I had never known such a state only heightened my nostalgia, rendered it all the more poignant, all the more sincere. The places we most want to go back to are those we have never been.

Psychoanalysis paved the way for that prison epiphany. I had begun to fret over the impact on the depressed patient of being told that he or she is suffering from a 'chemical imbalance'. I could no longer ignore the fact that this 'explanation' encouraged a flight from self-reflection for both patient and psychiatrist, and perpetuated the former's suffering and the latter's ignorance. In the clinical setting, in announcing to patient after patient that they were chemically imbalanced, I was parroting a *non-sequitir*. This wearied me.

Although disheartened by my supervisory experience, I persevered with psychoanalysis to find a new language for my distress, and became a patient. This also meant I lost contact with my colleagues from the drug company circuit of cocktail parties and dinner parties and harbour cruises. No great loss, and I am sure that feeling was mutual. However, it meant that I now had to buy my own pens and pads and coffee mugs.

Finally, with the collapse of my clinical practice under Harold's relentless onslaught, and the insulting letter from the neuropsychiatry professor, I had sought the help of Blind Freddy, one of the only analysts thought of as 'kind', although this is not what most people *said* of him. He had a reputation as indulgent, lacking rigour. Such kindness sounded fine to me.

What did he do with my distress? Nothing, but it was a special nothing: he sat and listened and offered comments and allowed my perturbations to follow their course, willy-nilly. I resolved to follow Blind Freddy's lead, which is to say I resolved to go nowhere, and take my time getting there. This is the magic of psychoanalysis, the magic known as 'holding'. Within the peculiar sanctuary of analysis, my thoughts expanded around the question of the mind-body split. I sided with the mind in an unwinnable battle against the brain, and lost. This merely expressed my own inner conflicts, and my transference struggles against Blind Freddy's subtle influence, although I was not aware of that at the time…

That depression is caused by a chemical imbalance has become a tenet of modern psychiatry. Psychoanalysis took a different view of mental life from such biological reductionism. Its perspective was more complex, imaginative, and occasionally almost accessible. But it never quite contained my misery, never quite held my agitations, which were soon exacerbated in the narcissistic regressions of the analyst's couch.

It was a greenhouse effect: my flowers of evil luxuriated within its sweaty garden. Blind Freddy had unwittingly unleashed a Frankenstein of infantile rage within me. I was sooled onto the enemy. Where previously my hostility was sprayed about ineffectively, like buckshot tossed in the air, now it was being honed daily beneath the benign ministrations of my analyst. Those loose pellets were forged into bullets, which I fired at the very foundations of modern psychiatry. Curious how the cure of love can unleash such hate.

Point your index finger, now, while reading, and you will notice that three fingers are pointing back at you. I had not recognised this anatomical fact until after my missiles were launched. My attacks were initially gratifying, like any infantile release, but in the end, I deprived myself of my clinical livelihood, and wound up needing prison as a new career.

BIOPSYCHOSOCIALISM

The revolutionary notions which I began to spruik in the heyday of my analytic fervour soon had me marked as a troublemaker within the psychiatric profession. Of course, I became as guilty of fanaticism as those biological psychiatrists I was attempting to discredit. No-one likes their beliefs being challenged; I was pointing out the cracks in their hallowed 'biopsychosocial model'. This had for decades been psychiatry's lodestar, but its moulding of biology, psychology, and sociology represented at best an uneasy triumvirate, at worst a nonsense.

In defying the chemical imbalance notion, I became a self-proclaimed champion of psychoanalysis. *"Antidepressants exist; they may even be of use,"* I declared, to anyone who would listen, mostly Blind Freddy, who was being paid for the privilege. However, because I lay on the couch and he sat behind me, I was never quite sure that he *was* listening to my propaganda. Sometimes his breathing slowed, and he seemed to come to with a jolt, but I went on and on in my magnificent eloquence. Breathtaking stuff, like: *"In narrowing the range of affective experience, antidepressants may bring welcome relief, or intolerable petrification."*

After these sessions, I would make copious notes, documenting my own significance. Soon, I had assembled enough material for several papers, which I began to present at various conferences, workshops, and seminars, to the traumatologists, the somatic therapists, the Lacanian analysts, the object-relations analysts, the Freudian analysts, the Jungian analysts, the self-psychologists, the attachment theorists, the neo-Reichian bioenergeticists. And no-one doubted my message. On and on I went, barking up that same tree, preaching to the converted.

I also began to assert the primacy of meaning and subjectivity to my own patients. I am not sure that many of them quite knew how to take my comments. The clinical setting became another opportunity for my extended harangue. Patient after patient sat there baffled and silent as I declared: *"While there is no biological marker for so-called biological depression, the psychiatrist's adherence to the notion of depression **as** biological is itself a social marker of his or her professional orthodoxy. And while the notion may serve the brain scientist well in opening up fields of discovery, it has the effect in the clinical setting of shutting down the mind."*

The patient would leave, without a script for their antidepressant, and never return. Soon, my referrals dwindled. When I attempted to present these notions to a general psychiatric or medical audience, I was similarly met with unconscious and conscious resistances, but this did not deter me. On and on I went:

"Psychiatry is a deeply fractured profession, pretending to unity for political and sentimental reasons, but whose factions could not be more polarised, because the polarities in psychiatry define not just a job of work, but a conviction about the human condition. The schisms between biological and psychological - brain and mind - run as deeply as ancient religious beliefs, in a permanent state of conflict.

*Are we our chemicals, or our relationships? Or, as light can behave as wave **and** particle, are we both? These schisms are all too evident in daily psychiatric practice to be ignored. The profession rests on an eclecticism, whose ungainly portmanteau - the 'biopsychosocial' paradigm - evokes nothing more than its divisions. So the eclectic psychiatrist falls between three continents, and the specialist who chooses one or other focus defines himself as irrelevant."*

In all this, I was defining **myself** as increasingly irrelevant. And it was I who was falling between continents; for a while, my own hot air alone allowed me to maintain some altitude. By their nature, psychoanalysts are reserved. While some may have appreciated my message, they detected in its strident delivery the playing out of my own unresolved narcissistic issues. Mainstream psychiatrists were even more dismissive of the messenger, and of the message. The work of psychoanalysis is the process of the emergence of meaning, but how many psychiatrists could tolerate that, and how many patients? It was a pursuit which was beginning to defeat me, as well. It may be that as someone once said, psychoanalysis creates that disease which it purports to cure.

The more I scrutinised the fractures in psychiatry's fondest shibboleth, the more despondent I became. To soothe myself, and find some meaning in it all, I accelerated my campaign, and took it into enemy territory: the psychiatric hospitals, and university departments. I needed to generate more and more hot air to remain aloft. Here, in the bastions of biological psychiatry, I fed on the disputes I aroused…

*"The assertion that **patients with depression suffer from a chemical imbalance** represents the most prevalent paste which smoothes the crevices within the biopsychosocial*

model, obscuring psychiatry's gaze, hindering the work of thinking and finding out.

"*The analytic method required resisting the impulse to repair. It is this impulse which closes down the mind. In place of an exploration of fragmentation and conflict and uncertainty, the psychiatrist enacts a futile attempt at potency, at integration, at certainty. But when it comes to human processes, certainty is oblivion. To reverse the retreat to a dull complicity with putative brain models that are irrelevant to the clinical discourse, the impact of medication - and of the act of prescribing - must be brought into question. For some, such questioning represents nothing more than the jeremiad of a psychopharmacological luddite. For others, an exhortation to scrutinise the cracks in biopsychosocialism is an exhortation to think.*"

By this time in my tirade, there would typically be loud guffaws and cat-calls, but this only spurred me on…

"*To prescribe medications is a doing, but it is not necessarily more or less psychodynamically informed than other aspects of clinical work. Interpretation, too, is a doing. The real distinction to be made is that the explanatory notion of a 'chemical imbalance' - so often a correlate of prescribing - is directed one-way and one-way only. The thrust of a great deal of contemporary work in psychoanalytic theory and practice is that therapy is an interpersonal process, a mutual exchange. The setting up of a frame for treatment, including regularity, and payment, can also be seen as 'one-way' - defining the patient as patient - but it is often here that further exploration occurs over questions of trust, and vulnerability. Medication, too, may be incorporated as part of a frame of care, and its meaning discussed. The chemical imbalance notion, however, moves the exchange from the interpersonal to the impersonal, a mode which may be more comforting for both participants — more comforting, and less intimate or relevant.*"

The occasional irrelevant and erudite quotation seemed only to inflame the audience further, which of course suited my inflammatory purposes. For example...

"Theory need not inform practice, and indeed the latter can be perfectly sound even when ignorant of the former, as Aristotle noted in his Ethics: "...some people who do not possess theoretical knowledge are more effective in action (especially if they are experienced) than others who do possess it. For example, suppose that someone knows that light flesh foods are digestible and wholesome, but does not know what kinds are light; he will be less likely to produce health than one who knows that chicken is wholesome.

"The problem with prescribing anti-depressants is not that it challenges psychodynamic theory, but that it encourages a tendency to a particularly mindless discourse of which 'chemical imbalance' has become a slogan."

This was pure theatre. I relished the opportunity to insult the scholarly professors who typically had nothing better to tell their patients about than this or that chemical imbalance.

"When the depressed patient asks 'Why am I depressed?', it is a clinical non-sequitur to respond with an explanation of neurotransmitters, analogous to a response to the question 'Why are you sitting there?' which describes the effects of gravitational forces. What depressed patient suffer from is not a chemical imbalance, no matter what they may have heard. There may be a chemical imbalance - which itself says nothing about the direction of causality between mind and brain - but the suffering is about loss or fear or hostility or trauma, to name a few. The psychiatrist may well correlate a subjective exhaustion with an 'objective' exhaustion or depletion of brain molecules, to be chemically rectified. What matters clinically is not solely an anti-depressant's brain effects

per se, but also the patient's disposition towards them - which is a feature of mind.

"The biopsychosocial model merges separate pieces of reality into a nonsense, a hegemony of one part over the other, and a loss of that sense of which part of the unwieldy portmanteau belongs where.

"Let us consider how the three entities of the biopsychosocial paradigm are related. Mind (psyche) emerges from brain (biology) through a social interaction - whose template is relatedness with the (m)other, mediated by language.

"Do we take the stern methodologies of brain science for objective truth, for its patriarchal certainty? Brain science works its direct route from cause to effect; the mind, however, experiences the vague drift of lived time. Such concepts as chaos theory, uncertainty and quantum principles, and fuzzy logic are from time to time grafted onto psychology, bearing the promise of a 'scientifically' legitimised integration of subjective and objective fields, but never quite deliver. How can they, when integration is a fond myth?"

This next bit really pissed them off, those that hadn't already walked out.

Guaranteed antagonism. Oedipus shmedipus, as long as you love your mother…

"Speaking of myth, is contemporary psychiatric practice a displacement of the Oedipal drama: a slaughter of the (feminine) mind to marry brain, to be governed by its masculine, active, doing principle? The result is the same as in the original: where the mind's eye shuts, the psychiatrist becomes as blind as Oedipus.

"There can be a reassuring merger for patient and doctor in the chemical imbalance notion. The doctor may hold up a picture of the brain, or point to small coloured spheres entering geometric clefts, just as his and the patient's views can lock

together like jigsaw pieces. Patient and doctor can rest snug and warm, encased in an explanatory concrete.

"If the psychiatrist is not able to see that depressed patients suffer from something other than a chemical imbalance, then how can they?

"Even in the face of a patient's sustained tirade, the task remains to trace in his or her utterance what is closest to their meaning. If a patient insists that a chemical imbalance is the cause of their distress, then this belief, this attitude, becomes itself a symptom of the patient's disposition to himself, and it is in the terrain of one's disposition towards oneself that we grope for meaning, and do our work.

"If the patient cannot begin to register an attitude to himself, a self-reflective capacity, then we must consider why, but also be prepared to accept that ultimately a productive conversation whose emphasis is on meaning may be precluded. The space in which to think about oneself may not be accessible for all sorts of reasons; in suggesting chemical imbalance to our patients, we merely add another obstacle to self-reflection.

"The patient who is adamant that he suffers from a chemical imbalance may have sought refuge in a spurious objectivity, as flight from the subjective. It may be possible to offer a comment which attempts to get at what is going on in the mind, and to allow that going on to be felt and acknowledged. The patient's assertion of a chemical imbalance tells us something, but we must hear what it tells us; in each case, the message may be quite different."

Yes, occasionally even the most hard-boiled biological audience appeared impressed. My *coup de grace* was in the form of various case histories. These vignettes were all I had to offer as 'proof', but at each performance of my one-man show, I felt my charisma and zeal were swaying hearts and minds…

*"A female patient in her fifties had attempted suicide while being treated with Prozac by her GP. He then referred her to me. (A previous psychiatrist was no longer available, having himself committed suicide, but not before he had sedated patients — including this one - and then sexually molested them.) Another antidepressant was tried and brought rapid but short-lived relief - her misery soon returned. This response indicated a placebo effect, and was in keeping with her eagerness to please others. With the failure of the second antidepressant, she was doubly pained to have "let me down": the antidepressant trial contained a clear imperative that she **should** get better - for me, if not for herself. Was her relapse a covert defiance, or an unconscious sabotage? She saw me twice a week, and between our sessions attended a therapy group. After many months without medication, she said: 'I read this book that gave me some understanding about myself - how I tend to have people treat me like a child...and then I blame them for it but it is my responsibility, and I have to grow up...'*

*"She was in tears with the pain of this knowledge, and remained silent, staring at the ground. When the session ended I felt concern that in the crash of this realisation there may ensue a feeling that it is **all** her fault, and that there could be no involvement with any one else, no possibility of help, particularly in light of her experience of having been sexually abused by the former psychiatrist. In what ways did she feel guilt at his death?*

*"In the next session, her personal discovery had become an accusation against me, and perhaps against him: she had been unable to tolerate her insight, and blamed me for it. This retreat from the pain became expressed as a retreat from contact with me, as follows: 'I thought about what **you** said to me last time and it made me angry that **you** told me I was to*

*blame, and it was my fault the way people treated me...how do you know this isn't a **chemical imbalance?**...'*

"In telling me how hurt she felt, and in clinging to the possibility of chemical imbalance as a cause of her distress, she had paradoxically become more lively and more involved in our relationship. Now that the anger had been mobilised and brought into the work with me she could talk, feel, and respond. Again, the fact of her experience with the previous psychiatrist may also have contributed to her anger, her reluctance to trust me, her preference for placing trust in a 'chemical', and her belief that I, too, was not treating her properly.

*"If the patient attempts to impose that tyranny of chemistry on us, demanding that we accept their suffering is the fault of chemical imbalance, then we are being given material to ponder. How does this tussle with the patient affect us, particularly if the decision to prescribe **is** made and the patient sees this as proof of their projections? This is an emotional exchange in which we fail only if we retreat to the medical model. The challenge is to remain open, and acknowledge our uncertainty, and search for meaning even in the patient's adamant assertions about chemical imbalance.*

"Is not an honest dissonance which can be recognised and thought about preferable to a sham harmony? For if we accept the chemical imbalance as valid, and see it as somehow explanatory, then explanation's victory is Pyrrhic - won at the cost of the defeat of understanding. If we parrot the chemical imbalance as explanation, then we are obliterating the patient's mind, or colluding with the patient in a crushing of thought, and of the possibility of growth. These operations within the patient's mind are likely to have brought them before us in the first place. Teasing out the

experience of depression and its origins is hard work. So too is feeling depressed.

"The relief which antidepressants may bring is not to be confused with a cure. The 'explanation' of depression as chemical imbalance is likely to offer relief that the depression is not the patient's 'fault', but it also reinforces a lack in the patient, by taking away a sense of his or her own possibility of initiative, of agency.

"It does not follow that antidepressants are banned from psychoanalytic discourse, but that there is a need to forge a language which acknowledges the fact of antidepressants - a language which can prescribe, but whose metaphors allow the work to continue in a register that is psychologically relevant. Metaphors such as the medication as a 'glue', or as a 'container' - perhaps until the therapy's container is sturdy enough. These metaphors do not deny meaning: they indicate the way in which productive searching can be sustained."

Stunned by my own eloquence, I would leave the podium, shaking, and elated. I felt at last that I was commanding professional respect, because I knew that if you ask nicely, you don't get it.

Without being aware of it at the time, I had merged with my analyst, become his Harold equivalent. I was so proud to announce to the world that I too eschewed the quick-fix, and had struck out into the vast territory of the unconscious, lost and intrepid, like Blind Freddy, groping for some clue, some direction towards an unknown destination. What a noble pursuit! Yes, this was the new language, this was the voyage I had yearned for – into the mind, or so I thought…things did not turn out as I had expected. This Frankenstein monster within me had lurched from the biological to the psychological – from the brain, chemicals and antidepressants, to the mind, transference, and psychoanalysis. But I was as lost on the second continent as I had been on the first.

Now that I was not even giving them a pill, my patients were even more ungrateful to me than before. They did not seem to appreciate the sheer emotional exertion, not to mention cost, of my continuing personal analysis. So much for the vast unconscious: to me it felt that I had tapped into vast reservoirs of rage and despair, no longer papered over with that universal panacea, but arising raw and disturbing before me.

I discovered through bitter experience what old Sigmund* had written long ago: that depression is anger turned on the self. The anti-depressant turned out to be an anti-anger pill, and without it dulling their passions, my patients' anger – a part of their dependency needs - was directed against me. The bloody transference. From being faced with reasonably compliant but slightly disgruntled zombies, my days were now filled with enraged monsters. I was soon longing for the good old days, when they depended on the anti-depressant tablet, rather than on me. It felt safer that way. Their complaints didn't feel quite so personal back then. But it was too late to return to that. That biopsychosocial paradigm which I had railed against so heartily now looked cosy and snug. Why had I been so determined to leave the mainstream? Better to flounder with the mob than feel stranded, lost, and under attack. Having located those cracks between biology, psychology, and sociology, I had fallen right through them. Like the design faults of human anatomy – the knee, the appendix,

---

* Sigmund Freud, in Mourning and Melancholia, first published 1917

the Eustachian tube, to name a few - the mind too was proving to have several mistakes built-in.

More and more anger erupted against me in my daily work, anger at the cancellation fee, anger at the comments I made, anger at the duration of misery, anger at the world. Like any parent in the face of the infant's daily barrage of fury, I was sick and tired! Enough!

I unleashed my own infantile rage at Blind Freddy, in terminating the analysis just when I needed it most. But I could not persevere. It seemed to have become a battle to the death, and I needed to live, or at least survive. I decided one day to simply not turn up. That was that. Cut clean, cut deep. I never saw him again, and I wondered if he had ever really seen me. I relished that power, such complete annihilation of the transference - to stop. But I had not bargained for its persistence in the unconscious, and its later re-emergence in a prisoner's thrall. All very well with the benefit of twenty-twenty hindsight, of course. The fantasy at the time was that Blind Freddy needed me more than I needed him. Nice try.

RAZZLE DAZZLE

My career highlight came when I presented the full and unabridged critique of biopsychosocialism at the prestigious annual world-wide psychiatry congress. This was the psychiatric equivalent of a football grand-final, of a Broadway hit musical. From the top, there is a long way to fall. I was expecting much critical acclaim. At least I got the first bit – criticism.

An icy silence descended over the auditorium after I had finished speaking. I felt dismayed, and alarmed. As it turned out, this was pretty close to what the audience was feeling, too. Finally, a lisping, bearded professor of biological psychiatry from Spain rose to his feet.

"You like big words," he shouted. His comment brought loud laughter from the audience, but I took it as a compliment. His attack seemed to galvanise me. My arduous apprenticeship had taught me how to handle these hecklers. I retorted:

"Seems you biological guys don't mind a few big words yourselves, like 5-hydroxytryptamine. Why don't you spell para-hippocampal gyrus for the audience?"

He was outraged, and stormed from the auditorium.

"Hey, signor, don't dish it out if you can't take it. Hasta la vista, baby," I yelled at his back.

Quite a few of his cronies followed after I said this. "What's the matter - can't take a joke?" I hectored. Those remaining shuffled about with little purpose.

The convenor quickly invited the next speaker to begin. A confident young professor from Nebraska strode to the dais. She gave me a strange look as I made way for her. Her teeth were very shiny. I wondered what anti-depressant she recommended, and whether she took it herself. Her delivery was clipped and precise, like her hair, as she presented a unique perspective - complete with computer-generated illustrations and diagrams - of the neurobiology of alien abduction. She received resounding applause for what I considered dubious science. The smarmy convenor had to extend question time even into the lunch break, such was the interest in her material.

I retreated to the foyer and proceeded to harvest the free lunch and other drug company giveaways – pens, pens, pads, pens and a trinket or two - alone until I was approached by the president of the world-wide college of psychiatrists. I had noticed him asleep during my talk – sleeping despite his loud bow-tie. But now he was all too attentive. He smiled sweetly, and presented me with a snow-job which I instantly succumbed to.

"That was quite a colourful story. You have a great deal of talent and an independent mind. We could use a fine fellow like you in research," the suave and observant president said.

I thought him a fine judge of character. This was what I realised I had yearned for from Blind Freddy, but my analyst had obviously been too consumed with envy to praise me.

The president continued: "You seem to have decided that our precious biopsychosocial paradigm is nothing more than a three-ring circus. That makes me the ring-master. Good for you. You've done the biology, and the psychology, so why not take on the *social* aspect? Get into the society of prison: take one of those prison research positions in your country. It is an area of need. You could make a name for yourself. They could do with your abilities, even if Blind Freddy didn't see them."

The president chuckled as he said this, and winked at a passing drug company floozy in a short skirt.

"I would love to talk with you some more, my boy, but do excuse me - have to run. Here's the number," he said, and lowering his voice to a growl, ended with: "Call now."

I strode to the telephone. The prison professor answered. Hearing her voice for the first time was calming, almost mesmerising.

"Ah, yes, I was expecting your call. We might have a place for you. Come up and see me – and bring a research idea."

By now, I figured that nothing could be more oppressive than the prison of private practice, not even prison. Burnt out, personally devastated by the demise of my practice, financially ruined by my supervisory and analyst fees, and without a place in my profession, the prison study became my way back. I felt a surge of determination before the interview with the professor there. She could not deter me, much less intimidate. I was of her ilk: a psychiatrist who would never again treat a patient. Relieved of the clinical task, I would be free to research, to write and present. As an added bonus, those least involved in care become the tyrants to the carers. That was to be my salvation. The dominant chord in my life had been ambition, competition, victory. How could I look after patients? I was perfectly suited for academe.

The president's hook baited with blandishment had caught in my gullet. But other coercive forces were involved in my decision to take on prison work. When I first met the professor, she was not at all what I expected. Despite her black leather pants, cascade of grey hair, and richly rouged lips, she was nowhere near as formidable, and nowhere near as impenetrable. She led me upstairs to her study, and stood with arms laid back against the writing desk. She jutted her legs out, and backed herself against the table edge, her slender body tracing a concavity.

I had worked out what I would say to her on my long drive down the coast to the prison – my research idea. I knew already that she had recently won the academic appointment there. Her faculty of forensic psychiatry was offering research positions. The professor needed fodder for the mill of publication, and I needed to quit clinical work. I hoped we could come to some arrangement, but there was competition for her largesse. I did not have a plan, but I did have an idea, and this at least had gained me an interview. One idea, that is one more than most psychiatrists.

This was my chance to get the show on the road again. I began with all the enthusiasm I could muster.

"You asked me to bring an idea. Here it is: *'Is evil innate, or acquired?'* As you know, Freud had ventured beyond the pleasure principle*, and found a biological imperative, an extended metaphor on death. The death drive comprised several tendencies: to entropy, to repetition, to inanimate origins. Melanie Klein's later

---

* Sigmund Freud, Beyond the Pleasure Principle, first published 1923

66

findings in the psychoanalysis of children, or rather of infants' at play, supported this supposition of a primary destructiveness. And before long, she had found in the nursery a richness of material around envy, hate, hostility. I refer you to Klein's paper, 'Criminal Tendencies in Normal Children' whose subject is *'to see criminal tendencies at work in every child and to make some suggestions as to what it is which determines whether those tendencies will assert themselves in the personality or not...'**

"Much later, the American analyst Heinz Kohut challenged this theoretical position. He suggested that frustration and trauma gave rise to such negative elements, which were thus not primary, but rather represented fragmentation products of the self. He asserted that these by-products could be dissolved in an adequately soothing relationship.

"The debate rages on. Freud's notion of a passive and ubiquitous death drive may not so readily translate into the willed activity of sheer destructiveness, and it is perhaps another leap to evil. Further puzzles arise. And where else but in prison would an answer be found? Prison gives the opportunity to observe the play of thugs and thieves and murderers...overgrown children, in a nursery of their own."

The professor smiled when I had finished. Creases formed across the thick pancake of make-up, but its patina did not crack. No breaks in her wall, I mused.

"Interesting in theory," she told me. "But perhaps a little grandiose for our humble research facility. Why not

---

* from 'Love, Guilt and Reparation', a collection of Melanie Klein's papers, published by Virago, 1988

begin with a simpler and more immediate question, and move on to your idea later?"

By this time, I had not the least concern about my one idea. It was just for show, a bit of razzle-dazzle. I had always been quite competent getting a foot in the door, but maintaining the contact had been a struggle. This is what had been beyond me in the clinical pursuit: the patient would engage with me readily enough, and I might typically even have something useful to offer at first, but just as things began to deepen, as inevitably they did, I would find some way of avoiding the intimacy. The same pattern of course explained the demise of my analytical marriage with Blind Freddy. There had been compatibility between us, even fondness, but I took myself away whenever closeness loomed. I felt something was catching up to me, despite my determination to keep on running. I was running out of time.

PART III

PRISON DESCENT

THE CURE OF LOVE
ENDS IN TEARS

Psychoanalysis had slowed this flight from my own emotions, although not held me in them altogether. My inner world was shaken and crumbling. In those months after Blind Freddy and I broke up, I felt that the death drive had driven right over the top of me, like a truck. I was ruined for clinical work, where previously I had merely been inadequate. So the patients gradually detected this deadness in me: the flicker of concern which I had managed to sustain was snuffed. I was loveless, emptied, and no use to anyone, let alone those most in need. Within a short while, only a handful of my regular therapy patients persisted. For each of them, the roles had been silently reversed: I was now the patient to be revivified, as my slump evoked for one the malaise of a depressed mother, for another the mother's alcoholic stupefaction. There was always a tale to tie each patient to his or her peculiar mode of repetition in the transference. And I finally withdrew my services even from those who would continue to pay to look after me. It was all too much. My savings dwindled; I could no longer afford the overheads on my rooms, nor my financial planner's exorbitant commissions, even as my analyst's demands had been terminated.

This was the near-ruin that I had reached at the time of my leap into that forensic opening. This was my big break. The wounded bird would learn to fly again – behind bars. And there was to be plenty of opportunity for *schadenfreude** amongst the miseries of the inmates. I knew it would work out. I could latch onto the professor, cling to her, find refuge in her research empire, and restore myself to professional life.

Good riddance to Blind Freddy and his futile analysis. I was striking a new path for myself. I was sure my financial planner would be pleased with the superannuation loadings in the public system which funded prison research. Leave the wreckage of private practice behind. Yes, that was strength of character. That was will. It felt like a pre-oedipal conflict had been resolved at last. Something about autonomy versus shame and doubt. The transference? The interpretation? The to-and-fro of the clinical exchange? I was happy to abandon the lot, and could feel my narcissistic restoration: it was for others to wallow in the care of the mentally ill. I was being called to a higher vocation – research. Yes. The lure of publication, of statistical rigour. I would banish those imaginative flights which attempt to make sense out of the nonsense of neurosis. I was to be reborn, and my intellectual fires rekindled…

"You seem to be veering into another manic episode," my analyst had suggested at our final session. I had forgotten that he was there at all. So much for free

---

* schadenfreude: gloating over another's miseries

association. There was always the spiteful interpretation ready to pounce upon my freedom, to curtail its expansiveness. I was brought back into the room. Supine on his couch, I heard blind Freddy yawn behind me. He let out a quiet burp. I wondered if he would doze off, again.

"At the risk of sounding sesquipedalian, you know you really are rebarbative," I asseverated.

"…"

"'What inner decision, what inner murder or prison break must I commit if I want to speak from my true deep voice…' Who said that?" I probed.

"You did. Just now." He roused himself.

"No. Well, yes, but no. It was Sylvia Plath. She didn't really say it, but. She wrote it." For some reason I seemed to be stammering to find my own words; eloquent only with someone else's. Déjà vu: I had not felt this sort of mind merge since the hateful patient, Harold. And when indeed would I find my own 'true deep voice'?

"I see." Blind Freddy, smug and condescending his default tone.

This was too much. Clearly he was not at all impressed with my literary magnetism: even bored with my flights of genius, particularly when they belonged to someone else. Was Blind Freddy also deaf? Or, like me, waiting for my true deep voice?

I suddenly knew I had to leap for freedom or else fall forever into Blind Freddy's psychic goo. Yes – terminate! So, here you have it, pal. Cop this! Enraged at last, and locating in that rage my authenticity, and my break from his imprisoning wall of humbling metaphor and studied indifference. For a moment that greenhouse-fervid consulting room went silent, silence concealing an act of inner murder, the murder of Blind Freddy! Before utterance, before the word, I murdered him with a thought…

Hostile-dependent: that just about sums up the human condition. That, plus fear and loathing. Like Plath furiously attacking the monolith of self to prise poetic shards, I, the analysand, was locked in solipsistic regression. I refuted the presence of the analyst, as a fanatical atheist refutes the existence of God. So much for attachment theory; I was determined to perfect detachment, but was left merely with shoddy irony.

Humour deserts us when we need it most, as when struggling alone between life and death, because humour presupposes an audience, a sharing. Cancer is not so funny, sometimes. Particularly a cancer of the personality.

But the joke as always was on me, to die alone. If history repeats in the form Karl Marx suggested, then just as Harold the hateful patient had been my tragedy, so in this duplicated mind meld with Blind Freddy I had become his farce.

For the murder **of** Blind Freddy turned upon its cruel ambiguity, as my fury became an inner murder of vulnerable alterity. That fragile needy part of me was murdered not by Blind Freddy's gentle pale podgy blotchy abstemious hand, but by my own. I was not ready to leave him. Could I bear to speak this simple and awful truth: I needed Blind Freddy now more than ever! Plath's puerile quest for 'true deep voice' had triggered my own bleak echo, reverberating in an empty chasm of tortured and abandoned self: my authentic voice as falsetto. Even as I was killing dear Freddy - cuddly warm nice teddy Freddy who helps and soothes and cares - even as he would not die, I knew this leap was unwise, imprudent, to say the least. One great leaping self-sabotaging act of ruinous destruction, such as patients tend to make. I had missed the unconscious message in my chosen literary quotation. Sylvia Plath had murdered herself one month after my birth: her death juxtaposed with my neonatal neediness. And I re-enacted in terminating therapy that same juxtaposition of murder and vulnerability, of hostile and dependent. I could not bear to need him. Who wrote '*Death Anxiety in Clinical Practice?*' Who cares? Blind Freddy would know, he who knows all. Suicide is a pre-emptive attack on death, and a murder of the internalised other. Such hasty terminations abound, mine now enacted thus:

"This will be my last session, Blind Freddy." My voice trembled with suppressed rage. "It is time for *me* to tell *you* that we have come to time, instead of the other way round. So long, and thanks for trying, but I don't think I have changed one bit. Perhaps my narcissism is impenetrable. As Bob Dylan sang: 'I'm just glad it's over. I'm seeing the real you at last.'"

But is it ever possible to encounter - in oneself or other or thing - the 'real'? As doubts multiplied, clouding my mind, a black van arrives in anonymous menace. Stick figure operatives (half-weevil, half-human, paranoid-schizoid part-objects) alight to their assigned perimeter around my crumbling subjectivity. A notice reads, 'Stand clear, please. Reality testing in progress. We apologise for any inconvenient dissembling. Structural faults within the personality. Unforeseen cathexes. Technical difficulties. All agency subsumed. Normal services may never resume...'

Blind Freddy's voice interrupted my autistic state.

"Or am I seeing the real you? Perhaps we are seeing the real in each other. And perhaps your narcissism is as you say, 'impenetrable'," he said. "I wonder if you have taken on analysis more as a career choice than as an act of love. I have tried to stay with you, to learn with you, but you reject my presence. Remember, self is a process, not a position. I hope you keep searching, and I hope your book brings love to you, in ways that I have not been able to. 'Every psychiatrist a writer manqué, exiled from the kingdom because he has to talk.' And no, I didn't say that, either. It was a writer named Patrick McGrath. 'Trauma' is his chronicle of the demise of a brilliant psychiatrist, of vanity and futility. You should read it, doctor. And one day you may have plenty of time to…"

I was stunned by this speech, which was more than he had ever said to me before. The paragon of pith had turned loquacious. And whose career was he talking about – mine or his? He was not just stepping out of role, this was transgression of taboo. He had finally cracked - we had simultaneously cracked - and behind his wall of silence coiled the desire of the analyst, like some serpent, now slithering across the shattered fragments of his analytic persona. I felt used, but what was he using me for? He must be jealous - that's it! Attempting in this vile analytic trench to thwart my ambitions, holding me back because he was stuck in his own rut, and jealous of my looming freedom, and fame! Blind Freddy had never once previously given advice, nor called me 'doctor'. And his mention of my book surprised me even more. Although I had in earlier sessions revealed my literary ambitions, I did not for a moment expect that he had taken me seriously. I thought to him such yearnings for artistic glory were merely another expression of my narcissistic regression. What had he once said about it? 'Writing as reparative act to heal the wounded breast.' Blah, blah, Kleinian blah to all that. And 'one day I may have plenty of time'. What did he mean by that? I was busy. Too busy to join his pathetic reading group. Too busy to lie around under his oracular spell. Too busy by far to recognise in myself an unravelling into manic defence, as herald to another collapse – aka hubris.

In keeping with incipient psychosis, which even Blind Freddy had diagnosed, a trio of tormentors past and present now lined against me in collective arraignment. Foreman of the jury was my analyst of course. In the immediacy of the increasingly psychotic transference the increasingly loathsome omniscience of Blind Freddy had shattered my feeble defences. And I recalled that perspicacious headmaster from long ago who wrote on my final school report card: 'I hope he isn't really feeble.' Further back, too, a long dormant identification with the villain Dr Zachary Smith, from the TV series Lost in Space, erupted into consciousness, particularly that episode when an alien with the capacity to expose the secrets of Dr Smith's criminal mind declared: 'You are the lowest form of life in the universe, Smith. A failed medical student!' I cringed to recall that vicarious humiliation which had evidently embedded itself deeply in my young mind, alongside Dr Smith's effete catch-cry 'Oh the pain, the pain…'

If the unexamined life is not worth living, what of the less-than-half examined one? Had I just failed my self-examination? Never once did I consider the obvious fact that Blind Freddy simply wanted to get rid of me: I had to defend myself to the bitter end against that ultimate humiliation.

But I was surprised at how his words had hurt me. It **must** be time to leave, if he was getting under my skin like that. I rose from the couch, and peered menacingly into his lachrymose and myopic eyes.

"There is the matter of outstanding fees, and I will charge you for all this weeks' sessions, even if you don't return," he bleated as I left.

This final barb pleased me. Money had again taken its familiar place in the scheme of things as a signifier of aggression. Money seemed to restore things to their natural order of conflict, to titrate love and hate in equal measure. I resolved to pay him. There was a perverse satisfaction in expunging any debt to this teddy Freddy blind and deaf freak: I owed him not a cent that way. How dare he speak to me of love, or a search, or some such cliché. He simply lacked imagination, talent, fortitude. That lack is what defined him as a psychoanalyst, and doomed him to the futility of his clinical toil. I was destined for greater things, or so I yearned. So the cure of love ends in tears. His, not mine. My eyes were clear, a steadfast gaze at certain future glory, in prison science if not in clinical art. I left the room, left the building, left that psychoanalysis, and headed for prison.

Another interview with the professor awaited.

"Your mind is contaminated by clinical work. Dealing with patients all day long is tedious and unproductive. It has hindered your career," she told me. "You have had too much time for philosophical and romantic notions of attachment, of transference, of trauma. What you will learn here, in my faculty, is discipline. The quality that gives rise to clarity of mind. Statistical rigour is the foundation of sound research. Are you familiar with the chi-squared test?"

I cannot recall my answer to the question, as my head was spinning with the implication of her words: that I had been granted a research fellowship. Thoughts whirled, like eddies moving upriver, building to the heights of my ambition, to glory as a researcher. But what would I discover, now that she had dismissed my one research idea?

The professor continued: "I have a project I would like you to take up, a simple but important piece of work, with social and political implications."

I was hooked already. The celebrity psychiatrist, interviews on radio and TV. Hell, my own chat-show.

"What is it about?" I asked.

"I want you to find out how many prisoners have severe mental illness – schizophrenia, manic-depression," she said.

"OK," I answered, again seduced by the promise of easy fame, but without any idea of how to set up and run such a study.

"You have every right to be confused. Just because you are a psychiatrist doesn't mean you should be spared the confusion which is the lot of our time. In fact, maybe you will be more confused than most," she said.

I was even more confused now that she had apparently read my thoughts. Or had I unwittingly spoken them? The professor continued:

"I do not want my researchers arriving here with the paint wet on the canvas of their emotions: research requires cool detachment, objectivity. So it is good that you have terminated your interminable analysis."

"How did you know about that?" I demanded. This was too much. Who had betrayed me to her?

She ignored my question, and continued: "The analysts don't want you. Your friends don't want you. Your mother never wanted you. I think you will fit in well here in prison, where those whom no-one wants belong. Let us meet next week to decide on the format for the research questionnaire."

I left her office. So I had a place here with her, in prison. Somehow my elation gave way to a familiar bleakness as I drove away. Its effect began rolling over me, like a coastal fog - that same quality I had known in private practice when patient after patient would fail to attend. I had been let down. The patient had found it necessary to communicate something to me by their absence. Was this what it had felt like to be abandoned as a child? Was the failure to attend retaliation for some inadvertent insult, or for my looming holiday? Despite these attempts to place a psychoanalytic slant between me and the experience of abandonment, its morose quality pierced me through and through. Each patient who failed to attend, each patient who failed to improve, wore away at my enthusiasm for clinical work. Of course, the patients were failing to look after me. How inconsiderate; how selfish...

Most of the attitudes and prejudices about psychiatrists are true. I can attest to the fact that most are as flaky as their patients. That listening to depressives all day is depressing. That most patients are too bound up with their plight to ever loosen their hold on it. That the root cause of mental torment remains unknown. That patients only tell you at the very end what they think of you, and it is usually then a relief for both parties that the end has come. So the end for me in clinical practice came as a relief, and coincided with the end of my personal analysis. No sense in doing things by halves.

Were these endings failures? What was originally felt as failure often comes to be understood as something else. But the learning experience is no less painful than failure itself. I look back over a pattern of wreckage: no-one can teach someone who refuses to learn.

Prison research was my attempt at some sort of personal and professional rejuvenation. We all need our rewards, our recognitions. I now sought mine in prison. An irony that it was only when my prospective data was held captive that I could feel safe and secure in its pursuit.

Entering an asylum is like venturing to the further reaches of the psyche. Entering prison has a similar effect, although more oppressive. Even the pretence of therapy - embodied in such euphemisms as 'corrective services' or 'rehabilitation' - is discarded. But the psychiatrist is as much at home here as he can be anywhere else. As alienist, as shrink, he too - like the psychotic patient, like the prisoner - has been ostracised, and forms defences of varying brittleness. These are the barriers against attack, stopping invasion. Prison walls, however, prevent escape. Nothing is impermeable: prisoners' flesh is violated hourly, often by each other. The blood flow eases tension, and conveys the prisoner along the corridors of dissociation which form lacunae in the mind, the gap in place of the memories of abuse. Heroin has a similar effect. And the circle completes like a snake swallowing its tail when the prisoner overdoses and is brought to a 'trauma department', as the body's trauma mirrors the mind.

The territory in which men of promise strike out for fame has always been uncharted. Therein lies the challenge, and the reward. This stylised hubris implies its tragedy: protagonist marked for doom as his pride is revealed. But the style of *my* fall - a descent from observation to experience - bears telling. I expected to emerge from prison after twelve months with data, and findings derived therefrom, and a research doctorate to add to my lavish lettering. One solid year of work can make a career, and set a man up for life. I did not envisage being set up in any other way.

The study of mental illness among prisoners was initially the study of difference. Their experience was not mine, but was mine to observe: the human wreckage which winds its way through police custody to magistrate's bench to the holding pens of prison to the prison yard. I was perfectly detached, controlling all variables. Many journeys begun in cold detachment lose their way through thickets of attachment and deceit. Like an explorer embarking on a voyage to strange lands, I made plans to ensure that my work would unfold as an orderly process of investigation. To my mentor and new tormentor - a burnt-out and cynical professor - I suggested a pilot study.

"Yes, yes," she drawled, bottom lip wobbling beneath the black cigarette holder. "We must identify the variables, and control them. Have you considered the statistical power? This is crucial, to maximise the possibility of publication. When does your funding expire? Apply for a renewal."

"I've only just been awarded the grant, professor. There's still twelve months to go."

"Righto then. Off you go. We must accumulate facts before we attempt to pursue causes. Attempting to find the ultimate 'why' is like lusting after a barren virgin. Remain on the plain of the definite and the defined, and you will have a successful career in research. Now, how do I switch on this computer?"

"It is on," I said.

"Fine, good. On your way, then."

The professor had been accumulating facts and nicotine stains and characterological despair for decades. She had never once proven a cause, let alone understood one, nor had she lusted after a barren virgin, as far as I could tell.

POLITICAL PRISONER

I can thank one remarkable prisoner for what he taught me, and for challenging my assumptions about motivation, about prison, about myself. The professor had warned me about this man, Antonio Gramsci, the last political prisoner in the state, but in warning me she had also enticed me to engage him as a patient. He was something of a mascot for her, a means for her to toy with her own unrefined notions of psychoanalytic theory and practice. So I was drawn into a peculiar therapy, to take on Gramsci as a patient, to treat his fanaticism, and allow its underlying melancholia through. Having joined the prison research faculty as a refugee from clinical practice - worn out and demoralised by the task of care – the prospect of another clinical engagement was anathema.

Antonio Gramsci, yes, I had heard of him. Poor sod. The last of the raving Marxists, wasn't he? A bitter hunchback, with an axe to grind and nowhere to grind it, now that the class struggle has been suspended, through lack of interest. People are too distracted by their mortgages, by their cable TV, to bother with questions of proletarian revolution. It had been hard enough in private practice to get people to come along to therapy, to pay *my* mortgage. I didn't fancy Gramsci's chances of fomenting revolution.

Even when confined in prison, he apparently persisted in his neurotic scribbling, the great manifesto of his prison notebooks, which were permitted to continue. It seemed the prison governor reckoned Gramsci's ravings kept him occupied, and were so obscure as to lack all meaning for the masses, including the prison masses. But after Gramsci set to work wrecking my research, I could well sympathise with the magistrate who had uttered those wonderful words in Gramsci's trial: "We must stop this brain working for twenty years…"* Marvellous.

The trouble was, in such cases of malignant narcissism, all such reproofs are taken as some justification for further vanity. Well, if his brain could not be stopped by the full force of the law, perhaps more subtle means were called for…

The professor had given me access to the Gramsci file. But as I opened it, in taking the case on, I had forgotten that first maxim of clinical work: why this referral, and why now? There was no mention of a rupture in the therapy with the professor. Why was she handing him over to me, this prize patient?

The file documented her diagnoses of Gramsci: adult attention deficit disorder, paranoia, and narcissistic personality disorder. Fairly run-of-the-mill stuff, from a psychiatric point of view – mere prison fodder.

While I was busy with the pilot project to test out my structured interview, and the logistics of the research, the Gramsci issue remained a sideline. My primary task was to assess the number of prisoners with serious mental illness.

------

* from "Selections from Prison Notebooks", by Antonio Gramsci, published by Lawrence and Wishart, London, 1991

In a massive global social experiment, asylums for the mentally ill – known as 'bins' - had been closed over the past decade. Around the world, community psychiatric facilities were unable to meet the added clinical load of former hospital patients, most of whom were flung onto the streets. Given that the mentally ill urban homeless are likely to be picked up by the police, often for trivial crimes, and that they are likely to be poorly defended in court, the expectation was that prison had become the new repository for the chronically psychotic. An ersatz asylum, as it were. But an asylum which was not equipped to look after its inmates as patients. These were the hypotheses which I was attempting to test.

The prison project thus provided an opportunity for a snap-shot of the social effects of a political and economic decision – closing the bins. What argument could the Marxist agitator have with that? Indeed, it occurred to me that this project should surely be in keeping with Gramsci's revolutionary ideals, if indeed those ideals were aimed at improving the lot of the most underprivileged members of society. But he had set himself up as a rebel within the prison.

His ranting and propaganda threatened to derail our research, just as it was going so well. Gramsci's failure to incite rebellion on the outside seemed to goad him to wreck all progress on the inside. My project became a target for his vandalism. He circulated a disruptive manifesto around the wings, accusing me of working for the police, gathering data . Notices appeared warning the men not to take part, that the study was a plot. More and more of the prisoners were refusing my request to participate. And there was nothing we could do to stop Gramsci's malign influence upon them. The prison mind is mercurial and fickle, for the most part, but once moved to a decision, it tended to stick. My study had become a target, and that was that.

From ninety per cent participation, my strike rate dropped to just one in five. At this rate, the project was doomed.

THE REFUSERS

Angry men milled behind the bars of the holding cell. Gramsci had spread the word among them to tell me to get stuffed, as though it was my fault they were there.

"We're not innerested in yer friggin' study."

"Yer too lousy to pay someone else to do it."

"Wot's in it for me?"

"We only want our pills."

"I don't need no trick cyclist to tell me what I already know: I'm a psychopath."

The last voice in this chorus from the holding cell belonged to a man trembling and sweating in withdrawal. Pus had collected in the corner of his eye, and his nose was dribbling. He clutched a book, 'Cities of the Red Night', but was too crook to read it. The others lounged on the grey benches, smoking and watching the TV which was perched high in one corner so they couldn't reach it to change the channel or volume. Only the officers could do that, by remote.

There was nothing in it for them. I had neither carrot or stick to induce participation. It was frustrating to hang around, rejected by a social underclass.

The professor called the men who refused to be interviewed my "narcissistic injuries."

"Have any injuries today, mmm?" she'd ask. "Too bad. The statistics won't look good now, no matter how we massage the numbers. Too many refusing, aren't there? Gramsci's up to his old tricks."

She stood with her leather-clad legs entwined, leaning back with arms braced against her desk. Her chin jutted, and the afternoon sun caught its bleached hairs through her heavy make-up. The tone of her voice was both niggling and dismissive. I was presenting my preliminary data - being supervised, academically, or toyed with, emotionally. She was bored with my project already, perhaps bored with me, as the stench of failure hung about my work. Like most academics, the professor wanted it easy. Now that things had turned hard, she would have to find her publications elsewhere.

Her intellectual curiosity had vanished when she became a professor of psychiatry years ago. The prison was as good a place as any for her to avoid work, and no-one else in the faculty had wanted the prison job. But she relished the challenges of administration, and its rewards, like controlling others by memos and rosters and appointments - such as advocating my appointment as a researcher under her supervision. She expected I would be useful to her: she would be co-author of the publications which my work promised, despite her scant role. I resented this, but played the game. There were rules and a hierarchy to the academic career, as to any other.

Chia finally came up with an answer to this refusal rate. He was aware of all the knock-backs I had been suffering, and told me over a cup of boiled water about the remandees.

"You need men that are not yet contaminated with the germ of Gramsci's Marxist cant," he said. "You need the remand prisoners. The fresh meat."

Brilliant. I could have kissed his chubby face. He looked concerned at my excitement, waving me away with his chop-sticks.

"Thankyou Chia, I think your fresh meat has saved my bacon," I exclaimed.

Yes, the prisoners arriving straight from arraignment, to be held in custody, awaiting trial. Remand. I could capture these men before they and their belongings were processed and they were assigned to a wing and a cell and let out to the yard. These became my subjects, the new arrivals into the remand prison. They had not yet been found guilty, or innocent, but were to await trial in custody, because bail had been refused, or they were unable to meet its conditions.

Ah, I still recall the satisfaction at discovering this simple ruse to avoid Gramsci's hold on the prison mind - my first and only victory over him. Yes, remand provided just that stream of prisoners I needed, and I dived right in, once more gathering data, accumulating my statistics. More research fodder, men eager to please, and too frightened not to. None were game to refuse my invitation now.

The professor was again interested in the progress of my work: more publications for her, more scientific credentials, more funding from the university, and more researchers. Growing the faculty was like growing any enterprise.

"Our project is again coming along well. I understand the refusal rate has dropped considerably since we began our screening in the remand," she said, taking full credit for the solution. "This isn't like clinical work, you know. It is all in the numbers," she continued.

"Yes, the numbers are going fine," I replied.

"No word from Gramsci?"

"No, seems to have quietened down. His influence obviously doesn't extend to the remandees," I said.

"I wouldn't be so sure about that. The governor has been in touch with me. Wanted to know how Gramsci's therapy was going. Any progress?"

I felt that familiar pang which I had known for most of my school days – that steely moment of truth, when one has been caught out, 'sprung bad like an old bed', as we used to say. Where I could once have feigned a cherubic insouciance, I now lacked any semblance to a cherub. I had not yet seen Gramsci, much less begun therapy. His *eminence grise** role in hindering the pilot project had disconcerted me, and there was also my own aversion to clinical work. Gramsci was well and truly on the back-burner – my back-burner, if not the governor's. Turned out that the senile old turnkey who ran the place had a misguided opinion of the potency of psychoanalysis. He took the magistrate's order seriously, and it was up to us shrinks to carry it out, to stop Gramsci's brain from working. As though we could anything with such a hardened case as Gramsci.

"Look, there's no point attempting to treat the guy. Why not just lock him away and forget that he exists? Any other approach is only going to inflame his ego," I said.

"Please, no unsubstantiated psychoanalytic babble in my faculty. We observe only the most rigorous scientific language," the professor said.

---

* French for the grey eminence, a term originally used to refer to Cardinal Richelieu, whose power ran pre-revolutionary France from behind the monarch's throne

"Sorry. You are quite right: to any self-respecting scientist ego is a dirty word. But how do you suggest that Gramsci be approached? It's certain that he will again refuse all offers of treatment."

"Precisely. The problem with you clinical psychiatrists is that you think your role is to *help* people. That is why you all get so burned out. And cynical. People don't want to be helped. They certainly don't want to be changed. The only way to get someone like Gramsci on board is by appealing to his narcissism. Let him know that you are not there to help. That helping him is the furthest thing from your mind. Let him know that you are looking for *his* help. That you are so impressed with his political and social doctrines, that you would like to learn more. Get hold of some of his writings – he's always craving a reader. Praise his brilliance. Then draw him in. And nullify him."

I wondered what she meant: nullify? No sooner had I switched my research to the remand prison – and successfully 'nullified' Gramsci as far as my work was concerned – than I was being forced into contact with him. Despite these initial reservations, I wondered if it might prove interesting to engage with him, and advantageous to my new career. A tough nut, by the professor's account. Difficult to take on, difficult to keep, and difficult to crack. But perhaps success would win me kudos: this was my chance to shine.

I knew from the inside how to grapple with these narcissistic types. Therapy must topple that edifice of self-sufficiency, of grandiosity, of malevolent solitude. It was to be my task to get Gramsci back to an original state, a regression to the point where his distress was repudiated, and humanity frozen. His trauma had been channelled into a paralysing arrogance. So much for theory. Applying it was not going to be easy. Particularly as he didn't think there was anything the matter with him. Another narcissistic blind-spot, the professor told me at the first of our weekly supervision sessions.

How can a man like Gramsci with such hatred of society deny that there is anything the matter with him? Does he think that society is the problem? I wasn't sure that society wasn't the problem, myself, given my latest run of social failures. But it wouldn't help my social standing with the professor to be so glib. Of course, society is a fine old place to be. Not much choice, is there? It's pretty difficult to avoid society. And here I was, in prison. I gazed over its red tiled roofs, the grimy buildings, the concrete yard spread before me from the professor's office. Gramsci was out there, in one of those barred cells. How could he still be so enraged? What was fuelling him?

The familiar scent of histrionics hung about the professor's description of his clinical history. So what if the fellow's father was wrongly accused of corruption by some regional administration? And that the wrongful accusation led to his arrest. And so what if his father was murdered in prison? And the mother was left to fend for herself and her seven children in poverty. Gramsci should get over his early difficulties, and get on with life, despite his past, and his physical deformity. In launching himself at the state like an ideological incendiary, this hot-headed cripple named A. Gramsci had achieved nothing but a long prison sentence. And how was it that this clinical task had been foist upon me, when my role was supposed to be research? This was becoming stranger and stranger. The battle had begun. The nemesis was about to descend.

PERSONAL NEMESIS

I faced Gramsci in his cell. He sat cross-legged on his thin mattress. On the opposite wall, a steel exercise bar gleamed in the sunlight. He noticed me staring at it, and said: "I hang upside- down a lot, doctor, to relieve my kyphoscoliosis, you see." Despite his hunchback, he was tall. A grimy stain pasted his jowl. "Napoletana. Beautiful with a touch of garlic, some sun-dried tomatoes, marinated olives, pesto. Welcome, doctor, welcome to my palace." Sunlight upon his outstretched arm seemed to cause his deeply tanned skin to glow like some Mediterranean movie-star from the fifties. *La dolce vita* set to *jail-house rock*. His face was smooth and unlined. The good-looks soon banished awareness of his deformity. "Quite a view, no? This is the capitalist's ambition, this expanse of sun-dappled ocean. Look, see how far it goes. Way, way out there. So far, so far into the distance. If we could see that far into the future we would be looking at the workers' paradise. From each according to his ability, to each according to his need. Yes, I can see all that, to the horizon, and beyond, and I have it here, for nothing. For nothing, because I have committed no crime, no crime. But I have it for twenty years."

Although I had not spoken, Gramsci had intuited my every thought from the direction of my glance: the exercise bar, the stain on his chin, the view beyond his cell. His conversation was artfully choreographed to my slightest gesture. I was under intense scrutiny, and vice versa. The constant mutuality of assessment is what makes therapy so exhausting. I wanted to leave, to return to the objectivity of my research, away from this entwining of subjectivities, each bound up in the reflections of the other.

He began to cough a fruity hack. He bent down, which accentuated the knuckle of bone jutting like a second head behind his first, covered in a cashmere gown. I was wondering at the outfit, so unlike prison garb, when his consumptive attack ceased and Gramsci abruptly glanced up, a crooked line creasing his face, spittle at the lower corner. His beady eyes wrinkled still narrower.

"How can I help you, doctor?"

"Ah, yes, well, it is nice to meet you," I said, flustered.

"Yes, it is nice to meet me. It is even nicer *being* me. Just as well, given that I have few other choices. Ha ha. And I plan to spend a lot of time with myself. Might as well be content with that. But I assume that one's self, of course, is merely a shell, to you, doctor? You would have no use for such a shallow notion as a self, no? Ah, to have your equanimity, your psychoanalytic poise. It would be quite grand. Quite the exquisite path to wisdom. I really do admire you Freudians. The link with Marx is quite strong. The superego is the analogue of the capitalist oppressor, and both are mired in unconscious guilt." This was going to prove harder than I expected. Gramsci had stolen my best lines, even before I had thought of them.

Gramsci gestured at the notes piled high upon his writing desk against the corner of his cell. "I would so dearly love to abandon this mass of work, to recognise within its pages merely the silent poison of ambition, that conceit which worms its way into the work of all narcissists like myself. However, there is nothing for it but to persevere. To remain bound up in my vanity is of course to accept myself as yet another case of a failed analysis, as I am sure the professor has told you. She tried so hard to sublimate my political urges, to generate a more creative libidinal flow. Yes, she tried very hard indeed. Erotic counter-transference, perhaps. But I am a very attractive man, and she is a virile woman. Ambitious to a fault. Ha, I digress. You are a new page, a new chapter, perhaps."

He paused, winked at me, and looked away into the distance, before continuing. "But how I would love to fall into her transference maze yet again, where the therapy fuels itself on the morbid conceits and histrionics of desire. But that is the lot of all artists. The fanatical repudiation of society requires a narcissistic wound to remain open, weeping, suppurating. I cannot allow myself to conform to a cure. That is to surrender to commonplace misery. Ah, I am so colourful in my expression. All the more impressive considering that English is my second language. Third, actually, after Italian and Russian. Well, so much for the transference. All that analytic terminology is passé, is it not? The post-modern vogue is all to do with cognitive schemata, and templates for organising affective experience. Well, it is all transference to me. Ha, nice to speak with you in the language of relativities, and phantasy, doctor. Am I right that the phantasy is distinguished from the fantasy in that the former is unconscious? But our time – time that is a metaphor for death, for all absolutes - is coming to a close. It will be most beneficial to my mental life to engage with you, I am sure. You are just as I have been told. The governor is most generous. Give my regards to the professor, and I hope she is recovering."

Gramsci beckoned me to the door. He handed me a typed document. "This is the direction my scholarship is taking," he said. "Let me know what you think."

"Yes, thankyou, very nice to meet you," I stammered. His parting comment baffled me. The governor's generosity? Professor's illness? What on earth was he getting at? I wondered too at the pages he had given me. Perhaps his written words would reveal more than his spoken ones.

Outside his cell, I attempted to retrace our conversation, to allow some diagnostic acumen to be brought to bear. It seemed that in the short time since I had discarded clinical work to enter the prison, my ability to take command of the clinical encounter had deserted me. Perhaps that was it. The familiar counter-transference experience of being tyrannised and trivialised, of myself coming under the patient's command. That was the clue to Gramsci's personality: the most virulent and odious narcissism. And in naming the transference, he was at once showing me the way through to his miasma of self, and shielding himself from my intrusion. Blocking me again, just as he had blocked my pilot project in the prison with his propaganda. He was also launching a pre-emptive attack, in usurping theoretical language – my language - so as to weaken its impact upon him. One tricky customer.

To get my bearings with Gramsci, I was forced to return to the foundation of psychoanalysis: that peculiar and shifting foundation known as the transference. Perhaps a more accurate metaphor is that psychoanalysis orbits around the transference. This astronomical perspective allows for perturbations and black holes, meteor showers and solar flares. Although everyone agrees that it exists, and exerts a massive gravitational force, no-one is quite sure what the transference is. Suffice it to say that psychoanalytic therapy evokes in both patient and therapist archaic modes of relating, and from these patterns, a whole historical narrative can be constructed. We do not live in the past, but nor do we live entirely in the present. The amalgam of the two – the way in which the past is lived as present – is what psychoanalysis considers. As someone once said: there is no such thing as history, only present evidence.

The transference of the patient has its corollary in the doctor – the counter-transference. Given this mingling of inner realities, psychoanalytic therapies rely on an assumption that the doctor is less disturbed than his patient, so that he or she can maintain some objectivity – or at least a perspective - through its stormy course. Therapy is intrinsically disturbing for both participants. The pain of being twisted inside out, of being utterly laid bare, that was the price I paid for taking on the prison nemesis.

I was familiar intellectually with the path that Gramsci's subjectivity must take in the psychoanalytic experience. He must enter what is known as the depressive position. But I had not yet *felt* my own demise. Not yet taken in the full emotional intensity of failure, humiliation, collapse. I was driven to rediscover that the transference never follows a straight path. But nothing could have prepared me for Gramsci's convolutions.

I recalled the benign ministrations of my own psychoanalyst, Blind Freddy, beneath whose kindly and myopic gaze I had rested, prattling on hour after hour, year after year, in delightful and tax-deductible indulgence. The regressive allure of the nursery, a bubble bath of my own vacuity, would be shattered not by Blind Freddy's interpretations – which I was able to hear as adoration and fascination for my unique case – but by the bill which he handed me each month. Despite the tax deduction, right there, at that moment, came the crashing fact that he did not love me, that he was not interested in my innermost magnificence for its own sake, but that he expected to be paid even as I introduced him to the most fascinating psyche that the world had ever known – me. Or more correctly, me at whatever age I had regressed to that session – typically age five or six. 'I want. I want. I want.' And, 'Look at me. Look at me. Look at me.'

Finally, I had to call a halt to Blind Freddy's free ride; he ought to have been paying me. However, the weeks after I had terminated the interminable process of analysis saw me descend to a state of squalor. I did not at the time link my malaise to the ending of my treatment. Only in hindsight could I acknowledge that I had become utterly dependent upon that analytic process, run by a man all the more dangerous for his veil of blandness. I too had denied my dependency needs, but I could not return to Blind Freddy; that would expose me to insufferable humiliation. By day, I was now a researcher, objective, calm, rational. But by night, I dreamt of gigantic men with amputated limbs, of bloody carnage, of mutilation. An ungainly analytic monster with dank hair and thick spectacles and a stooped posture tormented me in my sleep. This unconscious blurring of Gramsci and Blind Freddy held a portent whose significance I was unable to acknowledge.

It is only in hindsight that I can recognise that the precipitate termination with Blind Freddy left me with a yearning for more attention, for more indulgence, and it was this yearning that rendered me so vulnerable to

Gramsci's manipulations. I had lurched from the analyst's couch to the Marxist's cell.

I had come to prison as a cosy sinecure that no-one else wanted, and no-one at all cared about. Although it was a professional backwater, and a retreat from the clinical career in psychoanalysis which I had planned, prison research became the opportunity to live again, to get out from under the scrutiny of Blind Freddy, to shed some light in that shadow he had cast over my psyche.

Psychoanalysis had hurt my brain. I just wanted the pain to stop. Is that too much to ask? In prison, I could hide away, like a wounded bird. Or so I thought. Love is the best anti-depressant, but hate comes a close second. I was attempting flight from both. This seemed to be repeating something.

Excuse me while I clear my authorial throat. You see, I had intended to keep my own past out of all this, just as I was happy to ignore the personal miseries of my prison subjects, but the abscess of my history burst beneath Gramsci's pertinacity. So much for all those years of analysis with Blind Freddy. The way to become an expert is to ignore all experts. It took Gramsci, an amateur, an auto-didact, to crack me wide open, like an egg. Watch the goo run out. I look back over a pattern of wreckage: no-one can teach someone who refuses to learn.

This background may be unnecessary, but it seems to me that that is the same as saying the donut does not need its hole. Is the hole a part of the donut? I suggest that the hole defines the donut, so this is my hole, this is the black hole, into which my world had collapsed. The stuff that I had kept from Shauna's prying grasp in those first weeks in the clinic, the stuff of my unravelling, came spewing out in my subsequent meetings with Gramsci...

SELF-MUTILATION

Self-mutilation - the topic of the paper that Gramsci had handed me - is one of the most fascinating behaviours that the psychiatrist encounters. Years before my prison work, I had cut my teeth, so to speak, on a female patient in her thirties. She had begun cutting herself at age twelve soon after she was molested by her father. A dream arose during her therapy with me, in which her father was suffering from a cancer of the eye. She felt sad in the dream.

In her subsequent associations, she arrived at the revelation that the father's lust was analogous to her own self-mutilation. In both, an experience of tension would build up, to be relieved by a behaviour about which each felt terrific guilt: the father's molestation of his daughter, and the daughter cutting herself, drawing blood. The cancer of the eye was the lustful father's punishment, perhaps a cancer of the eye of the penis. And the sadness referred also to the patient's peculiar sadness that with the passing of her own cutting activity, she had lost a means of obtaining her own relief, for after this dream she never cut herself again.

Before I entered prison, I also knew that incarcerated men cut themselves more than any other social group.

I had dabbled in the area of self-mutilation, reading articles, and attempting to treat the perpetrator/victim as best I could. But my experience scarcely prepared me for the intellectual acrobatics of one Antonio Gramsci. His paper seemed an extraordinary combination of wit, drivel, and scholarship. Here it is, unabridged…

Cut by the Hand doing Time

(**Self-Mutilation and other indulgences among prisoners**)

by Antonio Gramsci

"Perhaps it is only in really vicious lives that the problem of morality can arise in all its disquieting strength."
Marcel Proust, Rememberance of Things Past

*The central questions which I pose in this paper are why and how pain and pleasure become conflated. If we take as the origin of all pleasure the gratification of our infantile dependency needs, then the Oedipus complex may give an answer to the **why** question. The presence of the father, both metaphorically and literally, prevents the infant from endless gratification of his or her pleasure, from endless indulgence in the mother's body. So it follows that the infant's dependency needs - the gratification of which is the original pleasure - become also a source of pain in their frustration.*

*I will consider the self-mutilating prisoner as a particular example to examine **how** pleasure and pain are conflated. If suicide is the most self-indulgent of acts, as Nabokov [1] says, then self-mutilation cannot be far behind.*

The body is the organ of dependency, which the mind repudiates at its peril. But prison attempts to render the most incorrigibly autonomous of psychopaths dependent for food, for warmth, for shelter. The psychopath habitually denies his needs, corporeal or emotional: he denies his needs as needs, by fulfilling them instantaneously, because all is seen as his own. The recognition of needs presupposes recognition of separateness.

Self-mutilation represents an interruption both corporeal and mental: a cutting of integument, and of continuity. A stream blood - and consciousness - is released to form a cicatrix whose granulations I now invite you to observe.

Literature and psychoanalysis enrich experience by observation and representation. Henry Miller wrote of the novelist John Cowper Powys: "Literature was for him like manna from above. He pierced the veil time and again. For nourishment he gave us wounds, and the scars have never healed." [2]

Beyond the metaphor, or before it, lies raw experience, exemplified here as the self-mutilating prisoner. This exemplar can be romanticised as free, celebrated in some anthem to savagery as release, penned in his blood. Or he is scorned and shunned as a diminution of humanity, an obliteration of mind. There are many points from which to view the prisoner's self-inflicted wounds.

Aristotle writes of Justice in the fifth book of his Ethics: "...a man who cuts his throat in a fit of anger is voluntarily doing, contrary to the right principle, what the law does not allow; therefore he is acting unjustly. But towards whom? Surely not himself, but the state; because he suffers voluntarily, and nobody is voluntarily treated unjustly. It is for this reason that the state imposes a penalty, and a kind of dishonour is attached to the man who has taken his own life, on the ground that he is guilty of an offence against the state." [3]. The prisoner-citizen is vulnerable to the prison-state. In prison, ownership of the body is in constant dispute.

In the same book, Aristotle invokes an inner relation between objects as "...there is such a thing as justice not towards oneself but between certain parts of the self..." [3] which he likens to the relation between master and slave.

This brings us to another political point of view. In Hegel's parable adopted by Marx of the master and the slave, it is the slave who attains the deepest, indeed the only, freedom - that of authenticity - by remaining tied to the means of production. [4] The prisoner is free to change his flesh, and more free than his guardians. The master's incarceration is no less real for being psychological: alienation from the means of production becomes an incarceration of spirit. But what of the product? For our purposes, the product is the prisoner's blood released: self-laceration as a mockery of freedom. (Cut again the granulating scabby effluent. Such adjectival caress, another Nabokovian indulgence, is surely acceptable at this, a seminar on inscription.)

The master, then, is never more free than his slave. Although neither can escape the prison of consciousness, the master must maintain a vigil over his slave which is not reciprocated. In seeking to define the slave, the master defines himself as lost, for a meaning imposed is meaning denied. Slavery's truth lies in not pretending to freedom.

From the spiritual point of view, the cut is not invariably a transgression against the body's temple: there are many cultural sanctionings of inscriptions in the flesh. However, the prisoner cutting himself again and again is greedy. In his disfigurement, he mocks our sanctity, and celebrates his profanity. It is a defiant act, which may harbour its own revolutionary evangelism. The histrionics of self-mutilation straddle the boundary between private and public, and the stage is ever-shifting. Its secrecy begs discovery. Like masochism, self-mutilation repudiates the other but begs some response.

What of the biological view of contemporary psychiatry directing causation relentlessly from brain to mind - where it acknowledges a mind at all? It may implicate some deficiency of cerebral serotonin in the act of self-laceration. [5] The act is defined as impulsive, not compulsive, because the cut is inherently gratifying. [6] Our prototypical prisoner cuts his hands more assiduously and more often than he washes them.

We also recognise an aesthetic point of view, of which Genet [7] would be the exemplar: no act is too depraved for his artistic flourish. This returns us to the romantic response.

*Let us, after Genet, envisage our prisoner as apotheosis of life's lyricism. It seems to be the noblest retreat. Retreat from what, you say? From ignorance? Perhaps we can only observe, and satisfy ourselves with vicarious truths, unless something rings truer than we ever knew, and releases a dormant impulse, a coiled spring within our minds now impelling **us** to cut...*

But the empathic impulse to observe need not overcome our own volition: language and image allow the space within which to create, allow observation as refuge from the sensuality of experience. Holding in our eyes the image of another's blood, we can release the haemorrhage of ideas, whose flow leaves no stain.

Psychoanalytic meanings of self-mutilation include the act as displaced castration. [5] This notion contributes to a prison prototype, fabricated also from recent newspaper reports [9] of a man charged with the bilateral enucleation of his mother. He had told a doctor some years before that he wanted to cut off his penis with a razor blade because he believed it was an "impediment to the enjoyment of life." [9]

The penis is itself the guilt, impeding joy. This is the matter of psychosis as concretised life, the literal, beyond the 'as if' or the 'taking to be' or the 'standing for' of neurosis, or normality. This is the bravado to see in the penis what can never be forgiven, never expiated, and so must be cut off.

Perhaps in tearing out the eyes of his mother he ripped again at the monster of guilt whose abjuring vision was the mother of all self-awareness.

Our fabrication begins with the prisoner prototype awaiting trial, cutting himself repeatedly. To be observed in prison is to be persecuted. On our encounter with him, we frantically project some personal analogue of suffering to account for his. But he is blissful, serene, albeit freshly scarred, and stares blankly like a lizard, into our caring, needy eyes. Blood trickles from his wounds like the sugary ooze on mango. Taste it and you will taste sweetness, not at all salty. The prisoner is in a self-sufficient state, a paradise.

To us in court, then, the prison prototype is an ignoble savage. Let us conceive his existence as brute experience, lived in the immediacy of enactment, obliterating any space between thought and deed, on the arid plain of the actual. It is as though the prisoner is deaf and mute, unlike we who speak and hear and cannot bear the echo of our own words in the chasm of consciousness. We are aware, and in constant pain; the prisoner is anaesthetised. He dwells at the reptilian core of mental life, its (m)idbrain.

His self-mutilation is a private act, a tender communion of knife and skin, no less pure for being furtive, and no less a sanctification for being corporeal. The indulgence of martyrs must command respect. If self-awareness entails a cutting off of self, self-cutting is the glorious affirmation of being cut off from such awareness as pain, to see its egress as blood, to sanctify sanguine release from the prison of mind, to seek inscription in the flesh.

See that hyphen between self and its awareness now a gash, now bleeding. We want action, a bold cut, and a rising up of passions. We risk madness to get there, but do not fear: the prisoner is dexterous, and skilled in his incisions. He knows what he is doing, if not why he is doing it. This is pleasure dressed up as pain, but pleasure just the same. A grooming, a caress, and an impulse gratified. Is our language not itself experienced as soothing? The anodyne to prison tedium. Do not accuse a man of a crime of which he is the voluntary victim. Or at least be aware as was Aristotle that the only justification for the act as criminal is in the sense of a transgression against the state [3].

We imagine this imaginary inmate engrossed in the act, head bowed to each deft nick, the steady silent surgeon in solitary theatre beneath the glow of forty watts, arm rested on thin grey prison issue drape. The patient is anaesthetised, but he is in good hands, for the patient is also the surgeon. At his feet lie the blue plastic shards of the disposable razor vandalised for its blade. A neat little shiv, another mark in prison time, whose dilations are now stilled for one mind. But the mind evokes new causes with each stroke - blunting Occam's razor [10] - for this act like any human truth is multiply determined. Our story confounds the scientific method, because the story itself is the casting around for threads of truth in diverse forms.

*The prisoner who cuts himself is not wrong, not committing a crime. He is merely incomplete: just as Socrates claimed that man cannot do evil and know it [11], so I assert that the prisoner cannot cut himself **and** feel the pain.*

Further, the prisoner who begins to feel the pain will no longer inflict it on himself. In this crucial respect, then, we are not observing masochism, unless all masochism presupposes some such mechanism of shutting down, or disavowal.

And what pain must our prisoner face? From what is our savage running scared? The pain of being aware of being cut off, that consciousness of the hand of time which works its hidden decay even as we create. The consciousness that from time there is no escape, not even a good behaviour bond.

The self-mutilating prisoner analyses himself, of course: self-analysis as the continuation of war by other means, but spurning the other. This is the ego, emerging from the body ego, to place itself on the couch, and itself in the chair, and describe itself in blood's rhythm of tension and release, of wound and repair. Our prisoner speaks:

"Why do I cut myself, you ask? My eye takes in what my hand releases on the skin. And so identified with my own projections, this blood frees me from the prison of my integument. Thoughts cannot be imprisoned for a moment. You learn that in solitary, and forget it when you leave.

"With lavish touch I have raised furrows in my flesh, on the corporeal temple, whose sacrilege is a private act, like grooming, or meditation. This cutting is an act of love, by which I feel attached, and saddened by attachment's fragility, and knowing at last that the walls inside me are dissolving, even as those around me remain insurmountable...

"But this beauty is forlorn, for I am alone, and growing old, and the diurnal variation of my mood is recognition at dusk of the waste which each day has brought. Prison imposes a priesthood, being without women, but the only purity attainable to me is the purity of evil. I cannot pluck Eve from this cage of ribs. I groom my skin with razor blades in case she

should show up, maybe on a visit, and take pity on me and lead me from here, or share my suffering."

The prisoner holds his freshly sliced forearm to the court-room and continues in mocking melody:

"Self-mutilation is cheap and convenient, you won't catch VD, it's available at anytime, and it's absolutely free. That's why, I'm a cutter, I'm a cutter, I'm always cutting myself...[12]

"Now leave me alone."

He then flicks blood at the judge, and is led ranting and scuffling from the room.

The first expert is called to give evidence. Dr Israel Rosenfield is a neurologist from New York. His book "The Strange, Familiar and Forgotten" [13] ponders our relation with our bodies by considering a case from the annals of neurology, Madame I, who says: "I am no longer aware of myself as I used to be. I can no longer feel my arms, my legs, my head, and my hair. I have to touch myself constantly in order to know how I am. I have the feeling that my entire body is changed, even at times that it no longer exists. I touch an object, but it is not I who am touching it. I no longer feel as I used to. I cannot find myself. I cannot imagine myself. My insensibility is frightening, as if everything is empty."

Rosenfield attributes this woman's distress to a peculiar loss of the relation between her self and her body as object, that is, her body image is somehow abolished, and with it her ability to feel pain. "In running her hands over her body, she was trying to establish the human being's most basic frame of reference" - the body. Rosenfield supposes a lesion in the limbic system, and in support of an anatomical lesion are her loss of proprioception, and of pain sensation.

Now we can return to the prisoner who is cut off from the social body: this social amputation is analogous to the neurological lesion in removing the reference points of human existence. Without the familiar landmarks of identity, prison entails a quotidian free-fall. The prisoner, then, cuts himself to assuage the severing of a social meaning; the cut reminds the self of its existence, at a time when that self is most acutely alone.

Our next expert is called, an obscure psychiatrist from Vienna named Sigmund Freud. In response to the preceding testimony of Dr Rosenfield, Freud mutters, "The ego is first a body ego."

It seems that the prisoner's tendency to self-mutilation since arrival on remand moves him beyond the pleasure principle, for Freud declares: "The new and remarkable fact, however, that we have now to describe is that the repetition-compulsion also revives experiences of the past that contain no potentiality of pleasure, and which could at no time have been satisfactions, even of impulses since repressed." [14]

Just as his incision mimics a severing from social life, its dried product mimics death. For we must stay with the cut, at least until its drying, and scrutinise the wound's detritus for its truth. In evidence, Freud invites us to follow our prisoner out of his cell to the prison yard, where he is among other prisoners, milling and pacing and yarning and waiting. Now the prisoner is mustered and as he shuffles into place a crimson scab falls from beneath the sleeve of his sloppy joe onto the concrete. When all the numbers have been called, and each responded to, and the prisoners again dispersed, Freud scuttles across the yard and fetches the scab as evidence for the court.

Then he leaps beyond the prison walls as the prisoner had leapt beyond the pleasure principle to weave it with Nirvana, joining death to life as instincts. Our marginalised prisoner, who cuts at his own margins, enacts this fusion in his compulsion to repeat.

Freud's exposition of something so bold as a theory of death has our self-cutting prisoner as its exemplar. Freud begins with an acknowledgement that the traumatic neuroses contradicted his earlier theory of dreams as wish-fulfilment: "…now in the traumatic neuroses the dream life has this peculiarity: it continually takes the patient back to the situation of his disaster, from which he awakens in renewed terror…" [14]

He then observes the play of a little child of eighteen months, throwing a reel into his cot, and withdrawing it again by its string. This game's significance is found in relation to the mother's disappearance, which the toddler had evidently learned to tolerate, as Freud put it: "…he could let his mother go away without any fuss…" Although the child's "effort might be ascribed to the impulse to gain mastery of a situation," Freud does not find in this case any direct contradiction of his pleasure principle. Now, we are perhaps at the same stage with the self-cutter, who may be re-enacting in altered form abuse endured in childhood. The trauma is presented, not represented, evoked, or rendered in any way but as itself. This is the truth in the act, the act as truth. Corporeality: the thing in itself. And we can only attain this state as an ecstasy, which utters no sound, paints no picture, desires no symbol.

"The act is repeated in spite of everything; a powerful compulsion insists on it…" [14], and further "that there really exists in psychic life a repetition-compulsion which goes beyond the pleasure-principle…"

As you can gather, Freud's standing as an expert witness is harmed by his tendency to excessive speculation which took him far from the details of the case before the court. Several times, the judge intervenes to return the doctor to the point, or rules his comments as out of the jury's consideration. It is not even clear whether Freud regarded the accused as in fact mentally ill, neurotic or psychotic, which surprises the rabble in the public gallery.

"Being castrated - or being blinded, which stands for it - often leaves a negative trace of itself in phantasies, in the condition that no injury is to occur precisely to the genitals or the eyes," Freud says [14].

Returning to the psychic interruption of dissociation, Freud states his Economic Problem of Masochism thus: "If pain and pleasure can be not simply warnings but actually aims, the pleasure principle is paralysed - it is as though the watchman over our mental life were put out of action by a drug." [15]

Asked to account for the prisoner's self-cutting since remand, Freud says: "Loss and failure in the sphere of the affections left behind on the ego-feeling marks of injury comparable to a narcissistic scar…" [14]

The skin is then analogous to the ego as being a border, for Freud states "consciousness must lie on the boundary between inner and outer…". [14] The deadness of the inner stimuli, the sense of void within, may itself be so terrifying that a need arises for the production of some stimulus in the form of cutting, to reassure oneself that life continues - if only as the sentience not of pain, but of blood. The simplest expression for this is cutting as an attack on one's own deadness, and an expression of it upon an "outer layer which by its own death has secured all the deeper layers from a like fate…" [14]

Freud continues: "an instinct would be a tendency innate in living organic matter impelling it towards the reinstatement of an earlier condition…" [14]

The judge is unimpressed, and asks: "Please explain."

Freud concludes that "The goal of all life is death, and casting back, the inanimate was there before the animate." [14]

As evidence, he then produces the scab from the prisoner's self-inflicted wound, holding it carefully between thumb and forefinger for the jury's scrutiny. He is labelled a buffoon and laughed out of court.

The next psychoanalytical opinion, given by Hanna Segal, is that the prisoner had demonstrated "an attempt to get rid of all perception, and it is the perceptual apparatus that is primarily attacked, destroyed and obliterated." [16] Segal glances at the jury as she speaks, at an artist's twisting index finger upon an eyelid crust, at the scraping of flakes of skin within a musician's ear, at the plumber's nail prising his nasal mucus free. But they are as contemptuous of her opinion as they had been of Freud's.

Their contempt is shared by the next expert, an eminent forensic psychiatrist, Dr Forsure, who had never heard of Freud and wondered how he could utter such outlandish notions. Dr Forsure is scientific, and pleased to expound his science. Unlike Freud, then, this expert witness exudes expertise as he strides forth to address the court.

The jury appreciates the colourful pictures of the faulty brain of the accused which demonstrate his biochemical abnormalities. Not for them the idle speculations of psychoanalysis: they want facts, and Dr Forsure delivers them, plain and simple.

During Dr Forsure's peroration, the judge shares a wink with the accused, each seeing that this is fine sport.

The verdict is announced: the prisoner who had removed his mother's eyes is declared insane, and not guilty by reason of insanity, which is to say, the law closes its slow and deliberate circumnavigation of madness, ending where it began. The prisoner is to be held at the governor's pleasure, although the governor's pleasure becomes increasingly difficult to define in light of Freud's startling discovery that "repression changes a possibility of pleasure into a source of pain" [14].

In any event, the prisoner himself has the opposite predicament from the governor, inasmuch as for him a source of pain, in the form of self-cutting, had somehow been transformed into an apparently pleasurable one. The increasingly neurotic governor is in psychoanalysis for many years trying to sort out the difference between pleasure and pain.

The prisoner is returned to his cell, and cuts again. Blood stains the sleeve of his blue sloppy joe, its darkening fold spreading now before his eye a memory, an image of another folding blue. The image had leapt into the prisoner's mind, as he would leap to his feet on a wave, as the blood would leap beneath his blade. The quality of this experience which is crucial is its suddenness: this is a visceral and temporal quality. Freud noted that pleasure and unpleasure "cannot be referred to an increase or decrease of a quantity (which we describe as 'tension due to stimulus')," but depend... "on some characteristic of it which we can only describe as a qualitative one. If we were able to say what this qualitative characteristic is, we should be much further advanced in psychology. Perhaps it is the rhythm, the temporal sequence of changes, rises and falls in the quantity of stimulus. We do not know." [15]

The prisoner feels a surge of freedom which is as painful as it is exhilarating. "The taste of salt from blood or ocean tastes alike," he thinks. His eyes are blistered in a gush of spray, but the vision holds of wave and light, a wall spun overhead.

The blade is poised above this memory, poised to slice his skin as a fin slices a wave. He is still. Parts fuse which had for years been kept apart, parts whose fusion had once brought him life, and he remembers how he thought then when meeting twilight upon the beach for an early surf: "If I am not *mad about the ocean, sun, or both, then I am mad myself."* For is not the origin of life as simple as a distant paternal sun, joining a close embracing oceanic mother? Finger-tips cleave the moving wall of blue into white lines of foam. He had loved surfing, and wept with guilt at the damage to his sacred gift. There were reasons now not to cut: feeling that guilt, feeling that pain, he no longer needed to enact his punishment.

Dissociation has been invoked as some mental mechanism which lays the ground for our prisoner's self-mutilation: necessary, but not sufficient. The desire to be familiar to oneself adds sufficiency: he cuts his flesh as proof of existence. I and my body live, cleaving observation and experience. Inasmuch as pleasure may be a coming together, and pain a tearing apart, the conflation of pleasure and pain may lie in the ambiguity of that verb, to cleave, which means both to separate, and to join.

In the instant of unfastening flesh, self becomes detritus: which is to say, a product of one's body is met as object. I suggest that the man entering prison may know this feeling as a severance from the social body. He has been cut off, and will often cut himself.

References
1. Nabokov, Vladimir. Despair. Panther, 1969
2. Miller, Henry. The Books in my Life. Icon Books, 1963
3. Aristotle. Ethics. Penguin Classics, 1976
4. Singer, Peter. Marx. Past Masters Series Oxford University Press, 1980
5. Favazza, Armando. Why Patients Mutilate Themselves. Hospital and Community Psychiatry. Vol. 40, No. 2., February 1989

6. *Diagnostic and Statistical Manual of Mental Disorders, Fourth Edition, American Psychiatric Association, 1994*

7. *Genet, Jean. Our Lady of the Flowers. Panther. 1966*

8. *The Manly Daily, articles of August 5, 7, 8, and 11, 1998.*

9. *Occam's razor defined as "the principle that in explaining a thing no more assumptions should be made than are necessary" [The New Shorter Oxford Dictionary, Clarendon Press, Oxford, 1993]*

10. *Dialogues of Plato, 'Meno', in Great Books of the Western World, vol. 7, Encyclopaedia Brittanica, 1952*

11. *Rugby ditty, "I'm a Wanker", partially mutilated to "I'm a Cutter"*

12. *Rosenfield, Israel. The Strange, Familiar, and Forgotten. Picador. 1992*

13. *Freud, Sigmund. Beyond the Pleasure Principle, in On Metapsychology, vol. 11 of The Penguin Freud Library 1984*

14. *Freud, Sigmund. The Economic Problem of Masochism, in On Metapsychology, vol. 11 of The Penguin Freud Library 1984*

15. *Segal, Hannah. An Introduction to the Works of Melanie Klein. Basic Books. 1973*

So much for the magistrate's order to stop Gramsci's brain from working. If anything, this extraordinary paper indicated that it was working at fever pitch, if somewhat crazily. In contrast to his metapsychological virtuosity, my own brain was winding down - again immersed in the routine of the prison task. This deceleration was what I needed: Gramsci's paper was more than I could digest. It raised too many questions. Although these were not the questions I was in prison to investigate as a research psychiatrist, in those first sessions with Gramsci I succumbed to the idle prison pause, where thoughts meander, a free-floating stream of consciousness, before being brought abruptly to order in the task of accumulating data - important data about the prevalence of mental illness among prisoners.

By entering prison, I was hoping for relief from such rarefied theoretical and clinical speculations as Gramsci's. They had only gotten me into trouble with the college. My patients had exhausted me. Following the president's advice, I had assumed that in prison I could leave biology and psychology behind and set up a project in social psychiatry, pure and simple.

SELF-DISCLOSURE

It is not a good idea for the psychiatrist to tell patients about his or her personal life. It gets in the way, offering too many distractions from the unfolding of the patient's pain. I was somehow unable to resist a personal unburdening to Gramsci, however. My guard was down, in the face of his wily and bamboozling presence. I was beginning to wonder if this was the same experience which had led the professor to hand him over to me. I realised that he must have gotten under her skin, but I did not yet know how far under… In any event, I sensed a strange nexus between the political prisoner and the professor, wondering again at her insistence on my treatment of the incurable wretch.

My second meeting with Gramsci was even more unnerving than the first. I found him sitting cross-legged on the concrete floor of his cell. He seemed to have been expecting me.

"Make yourself comfortable," he said. There were no chairs. An old football injury, and an innate rigidity of my musculo-skeletal system and its various articulations, limited my postural options. I sat stiffly against the wall opposite him, with my legs straight in front of me.

In my anxiety, I broke the rule of allowing the patient to begin, and asked him:

"Gramsci, how did you come up with that article on self-mutilation?"

"Ah, you liked it, then? So much for that famous magisterial decree to stop my brain from working for twenty years. You see, mind is the verb of brain. And the mind is universal. I have access to books through the governor. I have time to read them. And time to write. Luxury for an intellectual. But who will read me? Only my psychoanalysts. To answer your question, I just reached out and found the ideas in the ether. Ideas are quite free. Psychoanalysts do not own the ideas of psychoanalysis," he said. "Do you believe me?"

I nodded dumbly.

"In fact, the professor contributed quite a bit to my paper, too," he continued. "Such influence is only natural in the intimacy of the analytic relationship. Cross-pollination, you could say. And she showed me your article. Fine stuff. Revolutionary, in a way. So when I write '*What of the biological view of contemporary psychiatry directing causation relentlessly from brain to mind - where it acknowledges a mind at all?*' you should feel flattered."

"What? But you were her patient. She's not supposed to…"

"Violate a boundary?" he interrupted me. "Come, come. Don't be so strident. No wonder your own private practice fell to pieces. You are altogether too uptight. Bad for business to be so strict. The professor told me all about that, too. Allow this poor miscreant Marxist some comforting identification with his former analyst. I assure you, the comforting was mutual between the professor and I. You see, I do not believe she had ever properly mourned her loss."

"What loss are you referring to?" I asked.

I knew nothing of the professor's personal life, other than that she was divorced, and childless. I suspected she had a drinking problem, and probably owned a cat. Big deal.

"I will tell you her story, if you like. It really is a most remarkable clinical tale. It was what flung her into prison. I don't believe her cliché about furthering a research career, any more than I believe yours. As you know, doctor, the essence of psychoanalytic technique is to provide the conditions for a mode of utterance which does not dissemble, or at least whose dissembling is revealed. So it is revealed that we are all here for punishment, whether we know it or not. For some of us, the punishment is self-imposed. Would you like to hear the professor's story?"

This was too weird. What on earth had the professor been thinking, to allow herself to be drawn into such a mess?

Again, a silent assent was all I could muster, and so Gramsci began the betrayal of the professor's most intimate confidence to him.

"The professor had once been idealistic, thinking that psychiatry was necessarily personal work, dealing with people's feelings. But it got way too personal for her," Gramsci began. "This is what the professor told me, or close to it, early in our therapy together, when she was explaining it all to me. Shall I tell it in the first person? OK, here is the professor's tale…

Some years ago, before I quit my private practice to pursue research, a patient in her fifties was referred to me by her GP with a depression. She had been sexually abused in an appalling way for several years in her childhood. It was not until several months into the treatment that she told me of her auditory hallucinations. She had never told her husband or children that she was beset by derogatory voices, suicidal impulses, and occasionally cut herself. These symptoms had been present for three decades.

She attended twice a week at the same time each week, and for fifty minutes each time. This form of treatment (known as a 'psychoanalytic therapy') becomes itself an intimate relationship, and brings into that relationship a patient's past anxieties and struggles with relating. This emergence of past relationship patterns in the present therapy is known as the transference. It is a powerful tool for exploration, for support, and for treatment, allowing a resolution over time of underlying emotional conflicts.

Such meetings must occur in an explicit atmosphere of confidentiality, and the structure and routine are paramount. A major criticism of the psychoanalytic approach is that it fosters dependency, and indeed it does, but dependency issues are precisely what the therapy addresses.

Now, it is important that the work proceeds as far as possible without interruption. She had been in therapy with me for about three years, when during a session, the phone rang, with a call being put through from the receptionist. This was the first time in my private practice that I had been interrupted during a session. I answered the phone, and standing in the door-way of my room, must have looked appalled as I heard the news.

I will not tell you right away what I learnt that day, but hold you in suspense, just as the patient was. I said to her that I had to end the session, and apologised, and told her that I would see her next week.

She began the following session without a question about that interruption - she continued as though nothing had happened. A bit later in the session she mentioned the following anxiety to me: that her parents were about to drive down from the country, in the rain, and that she had to prevent herself from thinking about the possibility of them having a crash, for fear of just such a thought in fact causing the crash. Her mind was a tangled web of omnipotence and fear.

It seemed that she was telling me indirectly how much she depended on me, and that the possibility that I might crash was unthinkable for her.

She must have known that the interruption and my response to it meant that there was something wrong, something bad had happened. She was expressing an anxiety as to her own responsibility for whatever disaster had befallen me. I believe that she was not ready for the news, that it would be taken up in her magical thinking and release a terrific guilt directly into the transference — that she had caused my pain.

There were numerous previous expressions of a similar nature. They are in fact typical of the abused child: why is this happening to me, the child asks, and their answer is that it is happening to me because I am bad. This sense of one's badness lodges within the personality, and gives rise to symptoms.

The therapy continued, and I will now leap forward in time to her description of a dream one year later. In the dream a woman was holding a baby, standing in a doorway. The patient could not recognise the woman's face, only that she was in a doorway. The following session, she told me that that woman was in fact me, and that the baby was not a baby, more like a teenager. She told me that the feeling in the dream was one of evil, that the evil was coming from the woman, and the teenager was in danger.

So, an evil was lodged within me, and the fact that this was at the first anniversary of the interruption is significant, as is the fact that the woman in the dream was framed by a *door-way, just as I had been one year before when I had taken that phone-call.*

I suggested to the patient that she may be referring in the dream to that interruption during a session one year ago. She said this was likely, too. And when I asked if she would like to know what had happened that day, she told me that she would. So I told her: that phone-call had been from my husband to tell me that our only child had been run over and killed, at the age of fourteen...

Gramsci finished speaking.

I was stunned. This was something that I had never known about the professor. Her aloofness now took on a new meaning. Her loss must have paralysed her; she was in a state of frozen grief, a suspended animation.

Gramsci continued speaking, seemingly blind to the impact of his words.

"So, you see that there really was nothing more I could do for her. It is written in the Babylonian Talmud that in our time the power of prophesy is vested only in the very young, and the insane, such as her patient's dream. In our dreams, are we not all insane? After I told her that, she seemed to need to retreat from the intensity of her relationship with me. So we made a mutual decision to terminate the therapy. You see, we had both ridden this particular wave as far as we could. Time to paddle out, catch another, and make the drop."

"Gramsci, will you cut this surfie lingo," I snapped at him. "A surfing Marxist intellectual can't expect to be taken seriously."

"Doctor, I have never set foot on a beach, let alone a surfboard. But you can see from my cell that fantastic point break. Look."

I peered down at the heaving ocean, and sure enough, as the cliff wrapped around below the prison perimeter, from his cell I could see a line-up of black figures each straddling a little craft. Now and then, one would paddle in a flurry of arms and spray, and take off on a monstrous wall of water.

"I surf vicariously. Much safer that way," he smiled. "But I have also dabbled in the Babylonian Talmud. And the mystical Zohar."

"What about the Kabala?" I asked.

"No way. A man's gotta know his limitations."

"Clint Eastwood. Dirty Harry."

"Touché."

Everything about him was becoming frustrating or bizarre, and often both. It is difficult to say how we moved from this second interview to a process of psychoanalytic psychotherapy with an emphasis on object-relations theory - but that is what happened.

An intellectual and emotional itch had begun, which was to become a torment. I felt drawn to find out more about this man. What was his crime that he should become a political prisoner? Gramsci continued this session in praise of his own paper, and enlarged upon what was turning out to be his pet topic - narcissism.

"All roads lead to Rome," Gramsci, said. "Narcissism is at the core of capitalism, and insanity. The crime of Narcissus was not to love himself excessively, but to love himself in the wrong way: lacking substance, he could only love his image. You see, doctor, it is a fact that we two, you and I, are united in our apprehension of this. Unconscious guilt, that is what we are running from, and what drives us. But where does unconscious guilt end and conscience begin? We persevere, bravely, in the great work. That is the ultimate futility of the Marxist and the analyst: to be irrelevant. That is even more painful than the lousy pay. A fictionalised lament does not make the pain disappear, doctor. Think of your reputation, the damage caused by the demise of your first two attempts at establishing a professional life. Will it be third time lucky, or strike three and you're out?"

What I was thinking about was how he knew so much about me. I hadn't mentioned this stuff to anyone in the prison. Had I already told Gramsci? Nothing felt clear in his presence. Least of all my own mind. I had never understood what the Kleinian analysts were getting at in their theory of projective identification. I wished now that I had listened more carefully in their lectures, read more assiduously. I was in the grip of a force, emanating from Gramsci, and I was powerless.

The more obscure Gramsci became, the more I felt he had peered into my soul, had grasped its grimy fabric. This was a deeper hold than Blind Freddy had ever exerted over me, and I was to learn a far more malevolent motivation lay behind Gramsci's prying. I wasn't even paying Gramsci. What was he on about, what was he playing at? I fell into the interstices of his utterance as though in a trance. Bit by bit, I began confiding in him. I knew too well the simple relief to unburden oneself, and I was heedless of the vulnerable position this placed me in. Knowledge is power, and I was giving Gramsci both.

Within weeks, however, the therapy had reached an impasse. I was uncertain in which direction to proceed. Gramsci, as usual, empathised - much as the serpent in the back-yard of some suburban Eden Avenue empathised with Eve, probably while she was hanging out the washing, or maybe sunbathing. Empathy itself is neither good nor bad; it's how you use it that counts.

I hankered for a finished product, a cure, a resolution, to release me from this torment. Ah, to hell with product. The process defined us, Gramsci and I: the constant, unworked freedom of means without ends, without accounting or resolution. But the acceptance of the permanence of doubt is a vast challenge, an irreconcilable artistic vision.

My research had collapsed. I had not seen the professor for weeks. She seemed to have vanished. But my sessions with Gramsci had increased in frequency and intensity. I was seeing him daily, and the more I saw him, the more I wanted to terminate the therapy. I knew it was a battle as much for control as for salvation. Gramsci seemed so perfectly equipped for total war: he had nothing to lose.

Vulnerability excited me. I risked pain, and allowed the possibility of being hurt to reach deeper and deeper levels of my soul. Gramsci intuited greater risk from myself with every session, as though the emotional waves we rode must grow and grow to meet a need for thrills. I pressed this bruise.

Pain is from the Latin 'poena', meaning to punish. I did not know who was punishing me, or why, unless it was self-mutilation. This is every doctor's fear: that the patient is in fact healthy, that in every sickness there is growth, and that growth is autonomous.

"How, then, do you deal with uncertainty, doctor?" Gramsci asked one day.

"Why do you ask? Perhaps you are feeling uncertain?" I parried, trying to gain the upper hand.

"I did not say that, doctor, but if you must personalise my every utterance - twist it to your own interpretative purposes - let us allow the possibility, stated baldly, thus:

'Doctor, I am wracked with questions. I do not know who I am or what it is to be me. I am suffering in a welter of uncertainties. Help me. Give me answers.'"

I knew Gramsci was toying with me, but I had heard this same plea from patients whose suffering had seemed genuine. It is in keeping with the extremity of narcissism that when a glimmer of doubt emerges it is often catastrophic. Perhaps the therapy was beginning to take effect. Men with no self-doubt - who never ask questions of themselves - perceive any such questioning as an attack. The political mind exemplifies this most clearly: it brooks no criticism. And Gramsci's was, above all, a political mind. To criticise or question is to betray. Was Gramsci now betraying himself? This could be the crack in his shell that I was looking for, working for. I chose to answer impersonally.

"Well, if there is doubt, and this doubt is ego-dystonic, then it is the doctor's duty to offer some relief," I said.

"How?" he implored.

"By answers. By certainty. Through training and experience we become the experts in the biopsychosocial approach to the human condition. We have the facts."

"Facts, doctor?"

Even as I spoke, I felt I was being drawn into some trap, but could not stop myself. The more uncertainty I felt, the more avidly I grasped for answers, like the aimless pushing of pawns when the chess player lacks a plan. It was a reflex response to doubt. I had resorted to that tired biopsychosocial paradigm. Old habits die hard.

"Yes, facts," I replied. "The medical model for, say, depression postulates a neurotransmitter dysfunction as the pathophysiological substrate expressed in the behaviour and thought processes of its victims."

"And their doctors," Gramsci purred. "But what of this uncertainty which plagues me. Is that, too, a disease?"

"Well, it may be a manifestation of a biological depression – a chemical imbalance. Here's some anti-depressant tablets. Take one each morning. I'm glad to see that at last you're allowing me to help you, Gramsci. I'll see you next week."

"As you wish, doctor, but I fear that you – like so many of your psychiatric colleagues - have corrupted the revolutionary intent of George Engel's* original biopsychosocial paradigm. In the process, you have also unwittingly demonstrated a parallel between psychoanalysis and Marxism. Psychological resistances are identical in form to the reactionary political forces which are unleashed in any revolutionary struggle. Victor Serge, a remarkable Marxist poet, described the need for *'a merciless struggle against confused, reactionary, or romantic ideologies that have become pernicious.'* ~ Can you not see how confused, reactionary **and** romantic you have become? And can you not see that your mind-body split is merely another indulgent bourgeois dialectic. There will be no ultimate victory for either side; there can be no mind without its brain. So for all your hot air, all your agitations upon the biopsychosocial model, you have arrived precisely nowhere. You cannot ignore politics: the logic of the Marxist dialectic defeats you."

---

* George Engels is the late American psychiatrist and psychoanalyst who coined the term 'biopsychosocial' in 1977 in order to alert his medical colleagues to the deficiencies of the prevailing biomedical model.

~ from Birth of Our Power, by Victor Serge, published by Writers and Readers Publishing Cooperative, 1977. page 206

He looked smug, somehow defiant, as I handed him the medication, but I was filled with doubt, bamboozled with his Marxist mumbo-jumbo. Which Engels was he referring to? I was happy to leave the politics up to Gramsci, but I hadn't even got the psychiatry right. It was only after leaving his cell that I realised I hadn't even asked about appetite, or sleep, or even his mood. But I couldn't go back and enquire now. That would be too exposing. Patients have doubts. Doctors do not. We have answers. Yes. Yes, of course.

The officer at the gate caught me muttering to myself.

"Hard day, doc?" he asked.

"Yes. Ah, no, not really. No. Well, kind of," I said, and passed through.

I had heard myself utter that familiar clinical non-sequitir - 'chemical imbalance'. Those words were intended as comfort, as much for myself as for this fiendish patient, but as always the relief was short-lived. They heralded my own descent from a position of scientific objectivity into a paranoid psychosis: my observation of mental illness in prison began to give way to an experience of it. This was what I had been defending against, what I was most terrified of: losing my mind.

An opsimath is one who learns late in life. Was I learning too late the core of my own resistances? These processes of resistance are in us all; they act to deaden the mind, to close it down, or strangle its workings. Avoidance and denial – these are the oldest tricks in the psychoanalytic book of resistances. I knew them well: just as I now fled from Gramsci, so too I had taken flight from my patients, and from my personal analysis with Blind Freddy.

I felt empty, drained of all substance. Where had my work gone? I had allowed this process with Gramsci to devour me, this forlorn recording of psychological observations. I was striving for something which could not be grasped directly, whose purpose awaited elucidation. This is psychoanalysis. We cannot attain happiness - or profundity - by direct pursuit. Imprisonment can be taken as succour, or relief, or an intolerable captivity. It all depends on circumstance and attitude, which themselves depend on each other.

We are given one birth, and one death. These are ours, but we have no control over either process. How many loves are we given, and how much control do we have over them?

Psychiatric medications are an attempt to control the ultimate loss of control: the loss of one's mind. That was only my opinion: I would not seek to control another's choice. But in succumbing at last to the antidepressant, I felt that Gramsci and I were entering the end game. I resolved to leave him be, to let his neurotransmitters find some new equilibrium. I was over it. I told him that I would be taking a break from the therapy to return to my sadly neglected research project on the prevalence of mental illness among remand prisoners. Gramsci said he would miss our little chats, and handed me another paper to read. I never bothered, until it was too late. I couldn't wait to get back to the clinic, to clock up more of my simple and straightforward and structured interviews. Brief contact with an anonymous horde, no clinical role, no free association in which to lose one's mind. What a relief. The prisoners were waiting.

SEX AND DOGS AND ROCK-SPIDERS

The idea of control by rule of law - of forcing others into custody and holding them there - is exciting, just as the crime itself - the rape or robbery - gave some disenfranchised lout a brief expression of power to break the rule. Men on both sides create their victims. Men on both sides relish impersonal, inexorable processes. War is best to satisfy this desire, but is not always available. In peacetime, arrest and trial and sentencing will suffice. Men seek victory, to be on the glamorous side, the side that decides, not the side that is decided on, who are crushed. I saw the beaten ones come out the other side of the walls, entering prison, becoming prisoners, victims of a system. But I did not see THEIR victims; that was not my job. The more aware a prisoner was - the greater his sensitivity to loss - the greater was his pain. For most, loss of freedom was too high a price to pay for the benefits of containment and structure.

"...for what are we,
The beast that walks upright, with speaking lips
And little hair, to think we should always be fed,

Sheltered, intact, and self-controlled?..."*

Take Peter, who winced as he waddled to the chair in my office. I explained why I wanted to interview him, and he said:

"Gee, doc, this survey should've been done twenny years ago. See, my brudder's got schizzofernia, and he just keeps endin' up in jail cos there's no-one ter look after 'im on the outside and he's crackers."

It turned out Peter's brother was being crackers in the prison hospital. Peter was on strict protection, because he had informed on drug dealers. They bashed him, hence the limp, the broken nose, smashed teeth, and reddish puffiness to his face. "They took it easy on me," he said.

When I asked Peter the first question in my interview - "Have you ever believed you were being watched or spied on?"- he could only laugh and say: "You mean paranoid? Bloody oath, doc, after wot they done to me. I'd be mad if I wasn't paranoid."

Prisoners in strict protection were scared. Their confinement was closest, most stifling, but without it they were meat for pounding. It was easy to spot them: usually smaller, furtive, kind of clever. Apart from the "dogs" or "give-ups" who've dobbed in to the cops - given someone up - it was a prisoner's sexual bent which put him at risk. Andrew was a typical rock-spider. He could only be seen when there were no other prisoners in the clinic for fear that they would attack him like greyhounds mauling a rabbit, attack him for the softness of his voice

---

* from 'Apology for Bad Dreams' by Robinson Jeffers, published in 'The Collected Poetry of Robinson Jeffers', edited by Tim Hunt, Stanford University Press.

and features, the neat purse of his lips, his gentle manners and flabby paunch. The appearance which gained the trust of children incited the vengeance of other prisoners. In stomping on the rock-spider they trampled their fathers/step-fathers/uncles.

The sexual question I asked in my brief interview popped up out of the blue, like Andrew's erection behind park toilets. I asked it after the questions about appetite and sleep. The young blokes didn't really understand the question or couldn't stop to listen once I'd mentioned the word "sex":

"Oh, yeah, doc, like I just love the female body. It just spins me out. So yes to that question, I reckon. Like, when I get outta here this Japanese sheila's coming here for two weeks for me, just to fuck. And my wife's around and if she finds out I'll be in big shit. The female body, geez..."

Beyond the office where I interviewed my subjects, visitors passed on their way to the visiting yard. Through one-way glass we watched them without them knowing. We mostly watched the girls go by. Some were all right but most were bony and that was probably drugs, or fashion. This spying was exciting, just as it must have been exciting for these girls, to see their man in prison.

"He's locked up, behind bars, because he's bad and dangerous and the system's scared of him but I'm his girlfriend and I'm not scared and I love him and I'm gonna have his baby." They didn't know we watched.

We find arousal where we can, in sex and power. The other way to sex and power is knowledge, strength of mind. Look at the questions asked of forensic psychiatry: "Is this man responsible for his actions? What of rational choice versus determinism in a delusional state?"

Where does the psychiatrist pitch his court report, where between understanding (empathy, meaning, how this came to be), and explanation (external causes and effects)? It gets difficult and confusing so I don't trust it. The profession cannot afford to be "soft on law and order" because it's already accused of softness in its science. We must produce something more than a social-work report, something harder-edged, but are we more than social-workers? When we try to swagger, we look foolish, not tough.

A pompous prison psychiatrist named Dr King arrived at a meeting with a dressing on his neck where a mole had been removed. But he said he "got stabbed." This man was supposed to be a colleague of mine, but I took an instant dislike to him. Other than unconscious residues of my own sibling rivalries, it was his conceit and self-righteousness that affected me.

"You shouldn't be so popular," I said.

"All part of life's rich tapestry," he said.

But what would nice boys like Dr King know about that? He attended an exclusive private school, not the school of hard knocks. At university, he was shielded from the university of life. Although I met this supercilious psychiatrist on prison grounds, within its barbed perimeter, we were not trapped within its walls. At the end of each day we could leave. Prison braggadocio is most pathetic when adopted by voyeurs like him. A doctor in prison belongs in strict protection, I hope. There is nothing less sincere than a man who apologises for his advantages.

WHO CARES?

Scientific psychiatry is the most inhuman of sciences, which was precisely why I belonged there. Gramsci could go to hell for all I cared. Being paid to care is a terrible way to earn a living. It had felt deceitful. I had too many needs of my own – how could I respond to anyone else's? I had wanted to believe that these anti-depressants would cure my patients - make them stop with all the whingeing, make them play nice, and give them a decent night's sleep after weeks of insomnia. I felt that if the tablets worked, then I was able to give them something after all, even where - as with Gramsci - I had failed in giving of myself. The weight of clinical responsibility was too great a burden for me to carry. I resolved that Gramsci was to be my last clinical case. He had all but exhausted me.

During a lull in my routine interviews, the image of Gramsci would appear before me. What if his distress was genuine? What if the man's morbid histrionics were no less morbid for being histrionic? I felt wound up, knots tightened in my stomach, desire and interest and pleasure dried up like a parched inland sea, and a salty residue remained where no life could exist. A barren expanse stretched before me: a featureless terrain of days until… The grim visage, the stooped posture, the haggard eyes in the mirror. Poor Narcissus, growing old. I was on a familiar slope to despair.

I had the pages that Gramsci had handed me as a parting gift, at our last meeting. After his paper on self-mutilation, I did not feel like reading another of his written excrescences. I glanced at the title page, and read the word "Desire" typed there. The only desire I felt was a destructive one. I tore up those notes, that gift from my nemesis, page after page, like a man freed from a tortured love discarding the letters which flowed between hearts once in unison, now cold. I did not consider that curious fact – that the pages had been typed. I never read them, until it was too late.

My anger waned, and gave way to emptiness. I heard a reverberation in my head of the advice I had given to my patients over the years: 'What are you doing, lying around all day? Take the pills. They are effective in 70 per cent of cases.'

Those words were intended to reassure the patient that his or her brain was the cause of their suffering, and demonstrate the findings from research that an antidepressant would help: that they, like millions of others, suffered from a disorder of brain chemicals. This chemical imbalance notion, for which no credible evidence exists, was the lever to cajole them into compliance with medications, with a self-imposed stupor. Not a bad idea. Medicine's wisdom lies in its pragmatism.

I had returned to my prison work to save myself. But I realised it was not enough. I realised it was now my turn to trust my soul to a pill. Physician, heal thyself. The tablets were the colour of rust, and tasted as bad.

If I think of lifting my arm, the relevant motor plan is enacted and can be demonstrated on a radioisotope scan of the brain - whether the arm is lifted, or not. It is the thought that counts, so Descartes is grinning, or so he thinks; whether he is grinning or not is immaterial. All that matters is that he thinks he is grinning. Or that I do. Think it, that is. Thinking and doing present identical traces, we are as much our thoughts as our deeds, electrophysiologically speaking. But what other way is there to speak? *Honi soit qui mal y pense**. Show me the proof of subjectivity, of a distinctive quality of experience. Yes, that tablet is beginning to help already. A fine cloud settling over my mind, a reassuring haziness.

What trace had I left on my patients? Trivial memories, a few intense longings, the occasional incorporation into an elaborate delusional system. Neurotransmitter systems are self-regulating. Loss is merely a psychological withdrawal response, an adjustment of internal objects. I was a piece of furniture into which my patients had sunk their suffering, but the springs had given out, and my fabric was stained with the spillage of their memories of abuse and abandonment. Sorry to re-enact the latter, but I had needed re-upholstering, a new career.

Another prison to explore - why not prison itself? It had promised two crucial qualities which had eluded me - control and certainty. A slice through the society of prison promised to yield original findings, the researcher's vein of gold. All I needed were the rights to a mine, the tools to dig, and the funding to survive until I struck it rich.

I considered again my current research question: to find out how many men with severe mental illness, such as schizophrenia, were entering this prison. This

---

* Evil be to he whom evil thinks

was a valid and even laudable purpose, and served other ends, personal and professional. Schizophrenia, however, dissolves purpose, or renders it unacceptable, producing in its place a peculiar and diverse set of aberrant behaviours, thoughts, and affects. The social functioning of many patients with chronic schizophrenia declines, as the illness impairs judgement, social awareness, and communication abilities. Such decline is exemplified in the urban vagrant, whose inner city drift between bus shelter, soup kitchen, park, and footpath, reflects an inner chaos. The random passage of such a man can disrupt the urgent scurrying of other men across city streets. Psychosis blurs purpose, or warps it to obscure ends, whereas the adaptive collective neurosis heightens purpose and binds it to the purposes of others, equally neurotic: solicitors, executives, secretaries, politicians, bankers, forensic psychiatrists. I needed a new career, one built on competition, and power - a career whose very essence was the exertion of control. I needed to take the care out of career.

Larger forces are at work than the mere misfiring of neurones across the synaptic cleft. Big asylums were expensive. Medications allowed a measure of control of symptoms, enough to blunt the more disruptive behaviours, and turn the in-patients out - out to 'community care', a euphemism for 'nobody cares'. With the closing of psychiatric back-wards - the old and infamous 'bins' which were erected on the outskirts of most cities like vast repositories for the deluded - madness was let free, and money was saved.

The prisoner with schizophrenia is twice aberrant. I had pursued schizophrenia as a doctor for more than a decade. Could I finally capture it in these men's minds contained in prison walls, distil its meaning and essence?

Probably not. But the attempt was an important career move, my first steps along the path to academic glory, which is to say, a sinecure.

Publications are the bricks which build academic ivory towers. These prison walls enclosed an unexplored terrain. I was digging for facts, searching for that bed-rock of science, of objectivity, of mature discourse; facts encircling our notion of the relevant like a prison wall.

So much for the gold ore. The tools to extract it were necessarily crude. There is no chemical marker for madness, any more than for depression. Investigation of schizophrenia, then, required the painstaking and mind-numbing methodology of hundreds of research interviews.

These would also serve to distract me from my personal problems, about which nothing further need be said here, for this, as I have made clear, is a scientific document, apart from the bits which veer into melodrama, betraying my ambitendency between lurid romance and the harsh duty of scholarship. Although science had brought me to prison, crime kept me there. A crime which began as a glimmer of some personal peccadillo, the grimy creep of shame averting my eyes from the companionship of men, and from the suffering of my patients.

Enough! Such banal tragedy. If I was a novelist, at least I could have created some work of the imagination, instead of this tawdry confessional. The subjective obscures the factual, haunting a pristine objectivity like a shadow over a lens, like that mental woolliness of anti-depressant tranquillisation, like a man immersed in a personal invocation of the metaphor of prison, which could never be completed, or bound. My past had embedded itself as a stain on my psyche. This writing is already helping me to expunge, to expiate. And it's cheaper and less demeaning than therapy. Fancy succumbing in complete trust to another man's ministrations! He would only be gathering information to use against you, or at least giggle about over a bottle of Chardonnay in a trendy restaurant with his psychoanalyst friends, their goatees trembling with mirth, spectacles fogged with their pipe-smoke. ***I am not a patient!***

Yes, that feels better, and it feels better to see it written, like a slogan on a prison wall. I am a man of science, albeit the soft science of mental illness. And at least I acknowledge that it is for my own good that I lance the boils of my past, tracing in pus on the page - a post-traumatic expression disorder. I do not believe any writer who reckons otherwise about his scribbling habit - who, for example, claims to be selflessly furthering human understanding or knowledge. That is the job of scientists. Artists are necessarily self-indulgent, and incapable of the sort of disinterest which we scientists assiduously cultivate. Gaze into the morass of theatre, or literature, or painting, and you see a puddle reflecting the artist's own neuroses. Hear the splash and gurgle of some avant-garde composer, and it is the disjointed plea for attention of a larrikin boy. Read any novel (apart from this one, if in fact it is a novel) and immerse yourself in the vented neediness of the pathetic dolt photographed on the back cover who could not stick at any real work, and so had to survive by some schizoid pursuit such as scribbling his or her muddled musings. That's your business. Frankly, I am intent on greater things than personal narcissism. My narcissus aspires to a universality, a generalisability which only science can claim. The bedrock of our reality. Yes. The truth is so near I can feel her breath on my nape as I work.

Having fled Gramsci's clutching hands, or at least filled them with pills, I took on again the task of amassing data, immersed myself in my work, and dispelled my unease as best I could. But I knew my mind could be suspended only temporarily. The prison had become bleaker still, and the research all the more difficult to sustain. After the Gramsci experience, my interview data took on such a desultory appearance. Who cared for what I was attempting to discover? It seemed to me that the professor had lost all interest. I assumed she was still mourning the death of her teenage son, but it turned out that she had passions to pursue: passions more highly charged than the banal and painstaking process of research.

To keep going now took all my determination. I returned to the prison clinic, to the tough parade, where I belonged, or at least had a place. Research was proving tougher than I thought.

THE TOUGH PARADE

"Are you guys related?" I asked the older of the two men from the bush with the same surname. They were waiting in the holding cell for their belongings to be processed, having just come down from the country courtesy of her Majesty's prison transfer truck.

"That's me son. We wouldn't be in this mess if it wasn't for him, the stupid git. He went troppo when he was dropped from the footie team, so I thought I outta help. But kidnapping the coach only got us put away. Now we're both up shit creek. The coach still won't talk to him - actually doesn't talk to anyone 'cos we broke his jaw. And me missus is ropeable. 'How could youse do it?' she says, but I had ter do somethin' 'cos he's me son, the stupid git. And the missus breaks out in eczema with all the worry and stress. She doesn't even know we was sent down from the bush. Twelve hours in a fuckin' vibratin' tin can yer wouldn't put a dog in, unless yer wanted to kill it and even then why not just shoot the mongrel bastard? That's how they treat us. Me missus is forty, and pregnant. Had all them tests to make sure it's not a Mongolian and all. Twenty-three years since I was in jail. Gave up me criminal activities - well, gave up gettin' caught - when I got married. And now I'm back. Fuck me."

Being from the country, and still respectful of the medical profession, father and son readily consented to my interview. Both were baffled by its content, answered "no" to every question, and were returned to the holding cell in less than ten minutes. But their colourful bush yarn had relieved my nerves. I felt I was 'back in the saddle', even though I have never ridden a horse in my life. Yes, the work could continue; it must continue.

My next subject was at the start of his prison career, a milestone along his tough parade. Wisps of hair straggled down his neck; the rest of his head was shaved.

"Hey, nurse, yer got any moisturiser cream?" he asked as he entered the clinic.

"Waddaya want that for?"

"For me tattoo."

He slumped on my desk and leered.

"Hey, doc, whydya choose a desk job? Wouldn't you prefer somethin' more active, where you can work your own hours and be your own boss and get out and about?"

"What did you have in mind?" I asked, strangely charmed by his slick palaver.

"Selling foils. You'd make three times what you make now. Fair dinkum."

"You mean, selling marijuana?"

"Course. People 'll try anything, but. I smoked some of them bushy purple flowers from me mum's garden last week. Bloody awful. Couldn't sell that stuff. They might smoke it once, but they'd hafter be desperate to come back for more."

"Agapanthus?"

"Don't understand them scientific words, doc. Last time I talked to a shrink, the bastard called me a psychopath. What would he know? I'd like to kick his teeth in. I'm a pacifist, see. Wouldn't hurt a fly if it landed on me. Never flogged no-one what didn't deserve it. Mate, nice talking at you. Haven't got time for your study, but. Got any durries? No? See ya."

These earnest protestations soon became routine in the tough parade. Every prisoner was innocent, been framed, set up, conned and taken the fall, because the system or the cops were corrupt, or both. Sometimes it was the doctor's fault; this was when I was most on my guard. Paranoia and sex are the base metals of motivation.

Allan was a panel-beater with a gripe. He was built like a bowling ball, and just as black from the dense tattoos all over him.

"Bloody doctor got me in 'ere," he said. "This bitch reckoned I raped her, but there was no forensic evidence. Just this bloody quack from Cashoolty sayin' about bruised breasts and lacerations, but they didn't have no photos, and no forensic evidence. How can yer run a rape trial without forensic evidence? That bloody doctor outta be struck off for wot he put me through. Me missus knows I wouldn't do it. She sticks by me, eh."

Allan's blue eyes were wide and innocent, like a child's, pleading to be trusted. He seemed in his eyes to need to know I didn't think he did it. His sincerity was touching. He leaned forward, neck craned, eyes unwavering, looking up at me from a lowish angle, honest. I was certain he felt vindicated.

And it became clearer now to me in his beseeching gaze that I had begun to need my prisoners, to need their neediness, as some sort of glue to hold me together. The failures with clinical work, with my own personal analysis, with the Gramsci case, with my relationship to the professor – all that could be shut out while I was attending to the prison throng. In their misery was my temporary salvation. I was searching for distraction, and answers. But answers could wait; for now, distraction was good enough.

DEATH, THE ULTIMATE RESISTANCE

The routine of my research was tied to the inexorable routine of prison. The repetitions of my interview became more reassuring than stultifying. There is much to be grateful for, in the rise and fall of the sun each day. One day will be your last...

A prisoner was murdered one autumn morning, in his cell. This death in custody was just like any other, but happened to be my first. Nine slits pierced the victim's chest that day. The corpse lay supine for hours before it was found. One eye was split and spilt like egg to dribble and dry across his face. When the officers turned him over, they found beneath his cooling shoulder the biro which had enucleated that eye, after he was dead. There was so little blood; it was a clean, incisive murder, apart from the messy eye. Even his blue T-shirt had been pulled down again over his still chest.

The other prisoners on his landing knew death had struck. Smirks and knowing looks greeted the grim trio of Shauna, Chia and Nick who shuffled from the death pronounced at 3.23 pm in cell 56, wing H.

It is trite to assume fear lay beneath the prisoners' smirks. A murderer was loose among them, with sharpened metal shiv. Some knew who, and some knew why, but truly most men were amused or indifferent. After all, there were already several murderers among them - among the rapists and armed robbers and thugs. One more made little difference.

"Howya goin', doc?" a prisoner asked Nick as he left the wing.

"Fine, and you?"

"Great, doc. It's a joy to be alive. Wouldn't wanna cark it for quids."

We take life too seriously. We should be free like dolphins, free of care, full of joy, and naked. But we are all in custody, veiled in black robes of mourning, mourning for our sins, pining for lost innocence, marching to our graves. Layer on layer like delicate mists no eyes can pierce enfold each of us in solitary confinement. Avoiding light of day, we are in a void, our own. Sharing petty dishonesties allows a sociable well-being. Who can complain? Who can shout "Enough!"? Whose mist evaporated, now seen as naked, would not cringe, fearful, and succumb?

A man had died, bearing neat incisions like gills. He too had sat before me in the prison clinic, answering my questions, entering my research project, when his thorax was intact. Now that he had lost his life, I may have lost my data, for this prisoner was no longer eligible for my follow-up interview. I would need to check with the professor. She would have the necessary methodological and statistical manipulation to account for those who failed to complete the study.

"Do not be concerned," the professor reassured me. "We researchers must adapt to all sorts of insults to the integrity of our data. This is what makes research so challenging."

I had come to prison as a leap to freedom, like that dolphin leaping from the sea, but crashed back to these questions: had the dead man struggled? Had he leapt against or from his assailants? There is nowhere to run in a concrete cell, and I, too, had nowhere to run, other than my prison research. I was losing my nerve. Who could I trust?

I needed to have something to fall back on. But what? My sole clinical task remained Gramsci's therapy, but that had been thwarted. Not only had we reached an impasse, but he had denounced me to the governor, from whom I had received the following memorandum:

"The prisoner Antonio Gramsci is no longer to be subjected to the bourgeois indulgences of the discredited pseudo-science of psychoanalysis. He has confirmed that he will only subject himself to further therapy as long as it is carried out along the lines of neo-Reichian bioenergetics. Only in that paradigm does he feel that his revolutionary sensibilities are respected, and that the mind-body split is satisfactorily resolved."

Gramsci was attempting to gain the upper hand, to let me know that he was finishing with me, rather than vice versa. This was a typical example of the patient's resistance to analysis, a futile repudiation of his vulnerability. For all the grand analogies Gramsci drew between psychological resistance and reactionary political forces, he remained firmly in the grip of his own resistances. This is for the simple reason that resistance operates unconsciously. Gramsci's insights amounted to a row of beans; insight alone is never enough to bring about transformation. It requires also an act of will. Then there is the Lacanian school of thought that the psychoanalyst must overcome his own resistances in a new way with each patient. I gave up on that one, and not just with Gramsci.

In any event, resistance is par for the psychoanalytic course: as the analysis deepens, the patient begins to feel more and more anxious, and mobilises various obstacles against the direction of the work. These unconscious manoeuvres represent attempts to avoid thinking, feeling, and change. They build a wall, but for the analyst to break it down by direct assault is often catastrophic. It is always better to get around the edges, or tunnel underneath. The resistances must be interpreted, brought to the patient's awareness, and understood as a response to this or that dependency experience. And yes, analysis does arouse dependency. This has long been a criticism of analytic work, but it is in fact its great strength and advantage over less thorough-going approaches. Personality itself is formed in us all as a compromise structure out of dependency conflicts – if you can trust theory.

The preference for bioenergetics in particular held an important clue to Gramsci's resistance. Bioenergetics entailed physical contact between patient and analyst, and in that contact lay the seeds of a potential boundary transgression. The penny finally dropped: this is what had happened to the professor. Gramsci had sabotaged the therapy with her by enacting a reversal of roles, such that she began to confide in him – a subtle form of boundary transgression. In telling him of her son's death, via that patient's dream, the professor was seeking her own comfort.

When she terminated the analysis, Gramsci had again been deprived of intimacy, and she needed to have him looked after by someone new. But the intensity and rigour of the analytic experience with **me** was overwhelming him. I was sticking to the rules, presenting myself as a blank screen before him. My stern Freudian orthodoxy was wearing him down, just as it should. He was terrified of revealing himself further to me, and retreated behind a spurious need for medication as a way of keeping me distant from him. And then he tried to further sabotage the clinical work through this clumsy and infantile memorandum from the governor, whom he had also manipulated.

The analysis was in fact threatening to unravel the edifice of his narcissism, weakening that revolutionary fervour. The fanatic, the hero, would be revealed as having feet of clay, with human needs, and anxieties, and a longing for love. But how to gain access to the poor deprived child within the predatory monster that Gramsci had become? How to pierce that shell? Despite the wreckage of the therapeutic process, I took some satisfaction in knowing that I had ventured further than the professor into Gramsci's mental terrain. I did not know then how its swamp was closing around me.

In considering the professor's self-disclosure as a transgression, a new angle arose: *her* vulnerability. Why is resilience such a rare quality, among therapists and their patients? The university ethics committee would certainly frown upon the professor's counter-therapeutic self-disclosure to Gramsci, a patient. Perhaps she would be dismissed, and I would vault into her chair. But it would feed into Gramsci's narcissism were he to play a part in toppling the professor. The greedy infant is not helped by his greed being surrendered to. I kept the professor's little secret for now, figuring that it may come in handy some day. Meanwhile, I could feel quite snug in my research post. I resolved to read up on bioenergetics, and perhaps get a little soothing somatic therapy myself, purely for research purposes. The personal columns of the paper were probably a good place to start.

SAM'S END

I felt most at ease with the prisoners, in my cosy office in the prison clinic, not in the professor's, and certainly not in Gramsci's cell. The professor would never deign to visit the remand prison, and she was seldom seen on the psychiatric ward these days, being too busy with committee meetings and decision-making. I avoided her, just as some prisoners still avoided me, refusing my interview. A few were apologetic, as though ashamed not to take part, not to display a social conscience. Others were eager to participate. They identified with my task in child-like ways. One told me, "I did science, too, so I know what this is about." Once involved in the interview, they accepted my assurance of confidentiality, but many hankered for notoriety.

The life-story of a criminal was in the news. In a few hundred words, a journalist had sifted through the mess a junkie left behind, spinning the tired yarn of victims' lives ruined to feed the remorseless habit of a man without control or heed. The officers knew him well, too well.

"That'll make him happy, being in the paper. He must like it here, he keeps coming back so many times. A satisfied customer."

Two men who had taken overdoses lay in the clinic, one on the only bed and the other on a stretcher. After a while in prison, 'off the gear', their tolerance had dropped. A batch of heroin had been smuggled in, and these boys had 'scored a hit', but the dose which had previously satisfied their craving now almost stopped their breathing. Nick moved between them, checking pulse and blood pressure and respiration and a pupil or two.

"Some hit, that," he muttered.

Both patients were too drowsy to interview. Racking up completed interviews had become all I cared about. But we never realise how much we care about someone until we lose them, and we were about to lose Sam.

The word was out that day that it would be Sam's last as our sweeper. He was to be transferred to another prison. Information about change seeped out as though from between the bricks of the prison walls. Rumours grew and grew and then vanished, typically forgotten shortly before the rumoured change in fact occurred. Prison logic was cruel like that, cruel and fickle, like some impenetrable riddle. There had been rumours about Sam's departure for weeks: that he'd be sent to some prison in the bush, or one in another town. But they had just been rumours. There had even been a story that the clinic doctor had requested Sam be moved "because he knew too much..." This was completely false. If there was one thing Sam knew, it was his place. He was unobtrusive, discrete. If there was another thing he knew, it was how to make Nick a perfect steak sandwich for lunch each day, so why would the GP ever complain?

After Sam was gone, the clinic was in mourning. Sam was irreplaceable. According to Chia, we wouldn't find another sweeper with Sam's integrity. No way.

"He was one of the old school," Chia explained. "You could tell Sam anything and trust it to go no further."

We reminisced, and tried by wishing to force his return through the vast and impersonal corrective services ether. But the object of our wishes is held in the heart and the mind, seldom reaching the hands, and in trying to summon up his presence, we got nothing, not even his essence. Perhaps it was because Sam wasn't actually dead (although as good as dead) so his spirit was not yet detached from his earthly form and free to drop in on old friends like us. When a loved husband dies, the widow still hears his voice at night, and sees his image, and smells the wafting smoke from his cigarette. These hallucinations spring from some deep pining, an amalgam of perception and imagination and memory. But even if Sam had died, his ghost would probably rather haunt a pub, or rob a bank, than hang around prison. We had to accept that he had not exactly chosen to join the prison clinic in the first place. It was simply the best way to do his time easy. So the nurses never knew just what they had meant to him in his three years as sweeper. Nostalgia, like sentiment, smacks of something hollow or false, so we keep these things private, especially in prison, among those we cannot trust. And how close were we to Sam? I had only known him a couple of months, the nurses and Nick a few years, and only in one dimension - as clinic sweeper. We never saw him at night, in his cell, although he did show me his concrete and brick space on our tour. In the far corner, a plastic kettle sat on the toilet seat, a frayed shaving brush alongside. There was a calendar with Chinese writing and a view of Hong Kong Bay on the wall over his bed. I wondered if this had been a gift from Chia. A TV set faced the toilet, at the foot of the bed. So I visited his cell, his home, but I would never have Sam into mine. He remained as far from my life as the clinic tea-room.

Although he was an armed robber, and rough, I felt privileged to have known him: how he would sit with his smoke and nod, and smile now and then, while he yarned about growing up in the inner city, or life in the far north, or blokes he'd known who were "bloody good fighters" and "hard as nails".

"It's changin', prison," he'd say. "They're all plastic gangsters, these blokes. The drugs are stuffin' things up."

Sam's drug was drink. He was drunk on jail brew every day for two months once, he said. He was drunk during his last armed robbery, his son's first. The boy was pulling the heist to fund his habit, and Sam had gone along to look after him. But Sam was dead drunk during the job. Sam hated drugs for putting his son in jail. He reckoned the boy wouldn't get hurt in jail if he minded his own business and didn't let the stand-over merchants intimidate him.

"Depends what sort of man youse are," he said. This was not so reassuring as he had intended.

I remembered how Sam cut the filters off his cigarettes before fitting them into his holder. "You get a stronger smoke," he had explained. He made his cuppa with three tea-bags, squeezing all he could with a teaspoon against the rim, bent slightly to the task with that abdominal hemisphere resting on the sink. Now and then he'd wash all the cups with a Milton's tablet, "So you know they're clean."

He was cranky at me one morning when I walked on his fresh-mopped linoleum floor and muddied it. Cranky too when I marked that lino by dragging a table across it. But Sam didn't hold a grudge. I don't know if that was his nature, or the result of alcohol-related short-term memory deficits. Either way, it meant that he would never refuse to witness the consent of each prisoner I interviewed. And in his signature in careful copperplate on all those consent forms, Sam was eternally enshrined in science. Although I still owe him the money, at "twenty bucks a pop", I figure that immortality was payment enough.

One Monday, I had told Sam how I'd gone fishing with some mates in an old boat, and how we drank whiskey while bobbing on the swell. But then I had felt awkward, and apologised for telling Sam about the outside while he was stuck in here.

"Don't mention it. It's only a matter of time before I'm outta here," he said.

"And when you're out, it's only a matter of time before you're in again," Nick said, chomping on his steak sandwich. Nick reckoned Sam was unemployable "in the real world".

Sam called himself "one dud unit."

"I'm fucked up," he said. "I got no tickets on meself, not like some of these young blokes these days."

At the end of his last day, I said: "Sorry to see you go, Sam."

"Not half as sorry as I am," he replied.

"Wouldn't be surprised if he necks himself tonight," Shauna said, after Sam had left the clinic for the last time. "Others have done it. It's the only way to get out of a prison transfer. Of course, most don't mean to do themselves in, but accidents can happen, and what would Sam have to live for out at woop-woop? His missus couldn't visit him in the bush."

"She never visited him here," Chia said.

"Yeah, but at least she could."

The nurses visited the governor of the prison the next morning to forestall Sam's transfer.

"The governor couldn't have been less interested," Shauna said. "Looked at us like we were a nuisance. Tapped the table, waitin' for us to leave. This place is so petty. The governor wanted to get Sam for being popular with us, but he couldn't touch him so he says that because he's a popular sweeper he must be a security risk."

I thought of writing a letter to the governor requesting Sam be retained as clinic sweeper because he was assisting my research. But the professor told me to keep out of it.

"A letter like that would only annoy them," she said. "You've got to accept that you don't have a voice, which means you don't have any power."

She knew the politics of this place, which is to say she knew her limitations, and mine. Like the prisoners, I was mute. We could not be heard within the walls, and the prisoners could not be heard beyond them. Many were being punished for their anti-social forms of communication - their deeds had done the talking - but prison did not seem to develop their expressive skills. It merely added a few new words, and techniques of delinquent survival.

Shauna feared that Sam wouldn't survive in the newly built jail he was going to. "It's too modern for an old-timer like him - it's all shiny and metal."

A few weeks later we heard he was thriving in a new role as counsellor for first-timers and young offenders. "Do as I say, not as I do" might have been his best advice.

WANTING TO BE LIKED

I was waiting to be let into the wing when the self-confessed psychopath approached. I wondered if he had finished 'Cities of the Red Night'. William S. Burrough's apocalyptic vision seemed a suitable read for this place. The psychopath looked better, now that methadone had soaked up his withdrawal symptoms, but looking better meant he was stronger. I checked beyond the gate. Despite my shouts of "Gate up!" which Sam had taught me, there was still no sign of an officer to let me in. This was when I felt most vulnerable, out there on the fringe of the yard, clutching my little black satchel, prisoners sauntering around. Again I yelled, "Gate up!" as casually as I could, but to me it sounded like "Help!".

"What's in the bag, doc?" the psychopath asked. An innocent-sounding question, which seemed redolent with menace, like the gentle nudge of the snout of a white-pointer circling its prey, sizing up the morsel, before ripping in. Did he expect I was carrying a doctor's bag stuffed with drugs around the yard? And if I told him the truth - that it contained a notebook computer - wouldn't he regard that as an easy trophy? I decided on the truth.

"It's my computer," I said, and glanced inside for an officer.

"What sort?"

"NEC."

"Ha. Piece of shit. IBM's the best," he said. "Now if yer wanna interview me, yer can. Sorry about the other day. I was feelin' pretty crook."

Even psychopaths want to be liked, I thought. Before I could reply, the gate was opened, and another, which led into strict protection, into the hidden fastness, where men are contained most closely and tightly. Six cells for twelve men at risk - at risk for their crimes or their frailty. Being strictly protected meant being deprived of a yard, and usually being "two-out" - sharing a cell. This made for unhappy couplings.

I interviewed old Vincent first, a gummy and obsequious septuagenarian who was stricken with indecision at every question, striving to get them right.

"There's no right or wrong answers, Vincent," I told him.

"That's easy for you to say," he said.

I wasn't sure what he meant. Perhaps no-one was sure what Vincent meant. When he told his cell-mate to smile, Brian snarled. Brian's interview was equally tedious, not because of perfectionism or misplaced fear, but because of a crippling stammer.

"Cheer up, Brian," Vincent said as his cell-mate returned.

"Go p-p-p-p-pull yerself," Brian replied.

"I'd like to, but I haven't had an erection for fourteen years," Vincent said, and cracked up laughing.

It felt good to be back among these honest, earthy fools. Sam was gone, and I felt sad at that departure, but I spared no such sentiment for Gramsci. Good riddance to him.

POWER

Power runs prisons, and prisoners. They lose choice. They must ask, not take, which is hard to get used to for most of them. I like the idea that a prisoner should be returned to society no more damaged (or angry) than when he left.

My power was limited to an ability to say "No" to a whole lot of crappy, stupid requests:

- from a scared young offender who wanted me to ask the deputy governor to have him moved to another wing "to be with my mates."

- from a canny speed-dealer: "Looks like a lot of paper-work here, doc. You outta get a helper - just tell the deputy. Only cost ten bucks a week and you'd have a bloke organise all these forms, keep things tidy. It'd get him out of the yard and he'd be able to stay back late. Just one thing, doc. When you're talking to the dep about this tomorrow, mention Terrence Brian Crosby. I'd be ideal."

Terrence didn't have a guilty conscience. He had never sold to a first-time user, never hurt anyone. He saw himself as a businessman. There's a market for speed, a demand which he met.

- from every second prisoner: "Can I make a phone-call?"

But I said yes to requests for tea, coffee, water, or to see the nurse.

There cannot be power without fear. I recalled Sam's words, "...depends what sort of a man you are." If I saw the prisoners as losers, as no-hopers, it rendered them harmless, and lessened my fear. A herd of men in blue T-shirts and shorts, milling and pacing, yarning and smoking. I watched them pass the dep's office, how peaceful they looked, and peripatetic, perpetually circling like so many sated sharks in an aquarium, idly washing sea-water over their gills. Nonchalant on top of the food chain. With full bellies, there was no need to attack, other than for entertainment. Hours could go by without incident, without a bashing. There were a few familiar faces among them now.

"How's yer book goin'?" Jeff asked me. He was a fat Vietnam veteran, who didn't appreciate the Vietnamese drug-dealers in prison. "Costs money to feed them," he said. I didn't tell him he would eat ten times their intake.

"I'm not really writing a book, Jeff," I said. "It'll be a few articles in a scientific journal, if I'm lucky."

"Just as long as I get a mention, doc," he said. "Tell 'em what I told you about how to check if yer phone is tapped."

"Nah, Jeff, I think I'll keep that to myself. I don't want everybody to find out, or they'll change the system."

"Fair enough, doc."

The guards were scarcely busier than the prisoners. There was a story that if you wanted to get back at the government, become a prison officer and get paid to do nothing. Chia called every officer "officer", even if he knew their name. "They're all the same to me," he said. "Glorified janitors."

Prisoners sometimes clamoured outside the clinic gate, bashing on the door through the metal bars, demanding to see the doctor. Nick was efficient, courteous, and unrushed. A lot of them demanded sleeping tablets, "benzos, moggies, rohies". They complained of fits and insomnia and the "horrors" and cramps. Some succeeded, but for those who didn't, their real punishment was coming off cocaine, speed, smack, or grog.

What did I expect or want from this prison year? Was I there for excitement - seeking these rebels as distraction from the mundane obedience of my own existence? Most bore a stoic manliness. Beneath the machismo was a vestigial honour which too easily became violence. Some officers feared the inmates with a passion which would be laughable were it not for the brutality it engendered.

"The only way to restrain some of these blokes is through extreme pain." The officer said this while his boot pressed on a psychotic prisoner's neck and the prisoner lay bound and helpless but continued to froth and scream. Ten officers had chased him when he tried to flee while being sent to the psychiatric ward. To "restrain" him they had thrown him onto the concrete, and pushed his face in the dirt of a garden bed, crushing flowers which had been carefully tended by a sentenced murderer with blood on his hands and a green thumb. Their prey was a terrified, skinny prisoner, and their hunting ground was a small walled yard. He would not have gone far.

When this case was presented by my colleague Dr King at our weekly case conference, the professor was appalled, but not for reasons of humanity. It had to do with the power struggle between psychiatric and prison hierarchies. Was she as powerless as this patient? The officers would argue that the transfer to the psychiatric ward had required force. 'You want us to bring a patient to you? Well here he is, slightly bruised,' they'd say.

As he lay on the corrugated metal floor of the van which took him to the ward, the prisoner had been kicked in the head for being such a nuisance. He arrived there with bruises around both eyes, 'multiple lacerations and abrasions', and a story which he was too mad to tell.

Dr King, ever the man to make much of his honour, had to tell it for him.

"*Noblesse d'oblige*," he said. "Privilege entails responsibility."

Dr King busied himself with the task. He hoped to impress the professor with his philanthropic enthusiasms. Evidence was needed. Photographs were to be taken that day before the bruises faded. The governor was not to be told the purpose of these photographs, and the negatives were to be kept by the doctor. The physical examination was documented in detail, and anything swollen or sore was X-rayed. Each level of the corrective service hierarchy was to be contacted, with a written report to follow. Dr King's noble plan was underway. The prison hierarchy was expected to make out that the doctors were "soft on law and order", and did not understand the subtle principles and procedures of restraint. Besides, the prisoner had been delivered to the ward as requested, despite his enraged and delusional protests that the "blood doctors would get him." He was far less frightened of the prison officers than of the psychiatrists. He had chosen the wrong time to flee: right on the officers' change of shift. Unrostered overtime made them cranky.

The officers, too, had sniffed out Dr King's affectedness from fifty paces. He had what they referred to as "bad attitude." His enthusiasm for the investigation waned, as the officers began to make it harder for him to get access to his own research subjects. The officers had perfected the passive-aggressive tactic: losing the lists of prisoners Dr King was seeking, leaving him waiting in locked wings, putting him on a wild goose chase for some prisoner long released. In the face of their opaque defiance, Dr King eventually came to understand one simple rule: pull your head in.

Sometimes men I had interviewed one day returned to the clinic as victims the next.

"Intimidation - this place runs on it. Prisons are all about stand-over men and stand-over tactics and how to get out from under being stood over." The prisoner winced as he opened his jaw to speak these words. "This bloody great wog went too far with what he said. No-one else would take him on, so I had to. He'll leave me alone now, he knows I'm not scared of him."

"He might have broken your jaw," Nick said. "You'll need an X-ray, at least."

"Doesn't worry me. I showed him I wasn't scared."

"Did you hit him back?" Nick asked, glancing at the man's knuckles.

"Listen, I might be dumb but I ain't crazy. He'd have killed me. Nah, I just copped it sweet, but he'll leave me alone now."

Bashings happened in spates, but you could sometimes tell who was likely to cop it. Jason looked like a victim, not because he was frail. He was too big for his boots, a loudmouth, full of noise so no-one would think that behind his bulk was a scared little boy. There were stretch marks around his biceps - a sure sign of steroid use. And it doesn't matter how your biceps bulge when you are hit over the head with an iron bar. They hit him several times but the bones did not break, nor did the bar. When the nurse arrived, he was covered in blood.

"They've given me brain damage," he cried.

"No, you had that already," she soothed him.

Some bashings came as a surprise. Terrence Brian Crosby was held from behind, an arm across his neck, while punched by two others. He would have been safer as my personal sweeper, away from the yard.

Terrence was removed to protection, Jason to hospital. Both had been on valium, which put them between a rock and a hard place. The heavies wanted their valium to crush up and inject; the nurses made sure they swallowed their tablets in front of them in the clinic. But I was surprised Terrence was bashed. He'd been out for six months after an eight year lag. Life is rarely lived along a single trajectory of achievement. We flounder and zigzag, but usually manage to stay out of jail, while we wait for some authentic expression of our personal gifts. Terrence had always been "a whiz at numbers". He financed his drug habit by fraud. With computer and modem, he had devised a perfect system. It could have made him famous, he reckoned.

"I got a lot to offer society," he said. "I got greedy, that's all. It was that one extra nought that ruined me. I shoulda been happy with one hundred thou', instead of going for one mill."

He rued the wasted talent in prison, not only his own.

"You meet some of the most creative blokes in here."

He tried to go straight, but no-one would employ a bloke with a criminal record. Maybe his story, like his modem, didn't ring true.

When the officers were clearing out Jason's cell they found a pile of valium tablets - more than his dose over the last day since he'd arrived. He may have smuggled some in, and tried to muscle in on prison distribution.

We tossed around these hunches and assorted facts over coffee each day in the clinic. Our gossip was harsh: who was bashed, why, and whether they had it coming. We fed off scraps of information, learnt of whispered vendettas, and scores to be settled. As nurses and doctors and officers, we were on the outside, wondering what was going on in there, in that strange world. We wondered because we knew we would never know, and were grateful for that. The sweeper was our best access to what was going on out there. Our new sweeper was eager to be accepted. He knew Sam had been the nurses' favourite. He entertained us with a tale from the top landing, a tale of misdirected violence.

"This crim had stored up all his piss for a week in a bucket, and tossed it onto a group of officers below. They raced up, flung open the door of the cell above them, and kicked the crap out of the terrified occupant. Trouble is, they got the wrong bloke. It had come from the next landing up."

By the time of the next death in the remand prison, no culprit had been found for the last. This time, one of the heaviest heavies of them all was found dead in his cell, lying neatly on the ground, head on a pillow, with a fresh track mark in his forearm. This could not have been a simple overdose. If his death had been accidental and self-inflicted, how could he have come to lie so comfortably, in silent symmetry, the gentle demise of a man in his cell? And where was the lethal fix? No needle or syringe was found there. As a heavy, what he wanted, he got. But not this. There were no signs of a struggle, only bruises on his upper arm from finger pressure. This was a common technique in the prison: a mate clamps his hands around the user's biceps to act as a tourniquet before the shot. They call it a sleeper hold, but this was the Big Sleep. Perhaps this mate helped him inject, then panicked and scrammed when he saw the results. Some mate, that.

ANGER AND PARANOIA

My request for co-operation was pitched between each prisoner's anger and paranoia, which was often a narrow space. Suspicion showed in their eyes, and the unspoken question: "How is this bloke trying to trick me?" If a prisoner, by some idiosyncratic and personal logic, worked out an answer, it meant the interview would not proceed. He would interrupt my prefatory speech, which I had already given a hundred times, and stand and say, "Nah, I refuse." Pleading or further explanation made them only more suspicious, so I would stand and reply, "Fine."

Then, thinking maybe there was no trick after all, or else I'd be trying harder to get them to sign, the prisoner would say, "No hard feelings, doc."

"Sure," I'd say, and smile so they wouldn't feel bad.

Some were so keen for the interview that it made me suspicious, but it was always best to appear gullible, to listen patiently no matter what drivel the prisoner spoke. Once he had agreed to the interview, he became a case, a subject, more data, so was not to be dismissed until he had answered the last question. This was how I found myself listening to inane stories, and hollow bragging, and appeals for sympathy. Who did they think they were - patients or something? I was not being paid to care, I was there to do research, important work for the government. Most of us think we are of interest to others; Tim thought he was exceptionally so.

"I have this way of letting people think they're putting one over me, but really they're not so it's turned on themselves and they get destroyed by their own negative energies," he said. "The full cosmic forces are beaming out fluxes which I can tap into, so when I go to court tomorrow they'll do it my way or there'll be bloody trouble for the other bloke when I do it my way or not at all and the drugs are nothing and nobody's right to tell me how to stop using. It's my system in the one universe whole scheme of things from art form to life form a terrestrial goldfish flew over the nest."

He told me this earnestly, as though proselytising some new creed, his crystal gaze holding my furtive eyes as my mind scurried and I picked at the keyboard of my computer and fidgeted through my pages. I was restless. I was so keen to get my questions over with that I had ignored the bizarre flight of his ideas, the acceleration of his speech to nonsense. The man was mad, but I was in too much of a hurry to notice. My eyes and ears had been sealed over by the pressure to collect data. I no longer looked, and only listened to replies which could be fixed in place by my screening interview. Where there is no art, there can be no diagnosis. The doctor as wooden Indian, at one with his computer, fixes response to a pre-ordained stimulus, discarding rogue data, which is where humanity exists, and madness.

Tim was handsome and obviously proud of his thick, curly hair which he stroked frequently. He knew his place - on top of the heap. I assumed he was just another young offender too far up himself to see the light of day. There was so much self-importance among these embittered, jailed men. It must sustain them in some way, offset their torment. I hustled Tim through the questions and thanked him for his time and got rid of him back to the holding cell before he took up any more of mine. He was recorded as negative for major mental illness on my brief appraisal.

CRIMES OF LOVE

Mostly I did not know their crime, and mostly it was nothing they couldn't deny. But the ones from strict protection were marked with the stigma of an awful deed or a fear or an infirmity. For some, like Arnold, it was all three. He waited for the doctor or nurse with the other boys from strict in a small segregated holding cell near the clinic. Other prisoners yelled and hissed at them as they passed. "Bloody rottens!" they sneered. Arnold smiled wearily at the abuse. He looked rotten. His spirit was shrivelled by weeks in 'stricts', pacing an enclosure, roofed one half with iron bars, the other with cement, facing a high brick wall across a concrete landing. When he entered my office his first words were: "I wish I'd never been born." He bowed his head, to sip the sweet tea I had made for him, and a slab of coarse hair dropped across his forehead like hay. He told me he had scarring on his brain, which seemed likely as there was scarring on the outside of his head as well. His face was round and full and lumpy, like a toad seen from above. He was a thoughtful man, a man of theories, which he expounded for me, a fellow scientist.

"If I make love in the morning, see, the day will turn out OK, and if I make love in the afternoon the night will turn out OK and if I make love at night then I'll sleep OK," he said. "I'm always horny, doc."

"Horny like a toad," I didn't say.

Half a lifetime ago was his first time in jail. "They bashed the shit out of me and then raped the shit out of me. At least my dad had prepared me for the first bit, but nothing prepares you for the second. It is pure humiliation, especially when you crack a fat yerself while they're chockin' you."

The nurses found out his crime, which ended any chance of pity from them. He had murdered his wife, chopped her up and put the pieces in a suitcase. "She always wanted to travel," he explained to the police.

Prison cannot be as simple as "us and them". Perhaps I felt more of a man, or safer, by identifying with the threat embodied in these prisoners. I was not shocked, or titillated, not directly, at least. There was more excitement in watching the nurses reading a report of a man who raped young girls.

"How disgusting," they said.

It was, at the time of the act, but later, when the prisoner named in the report sits in front of me as another case on my way to six hundred, I did not feel excitement or disgust. It was as if there was no reality to what happened in another time, another place. Was it done by another man, not this prisoner? This is the nature of past crimes. The deed is not a living thing. It can be impersonally and impassively recounted, and becomes not real enough to have happened, still less to be punished. The guilty man has split off his past. He becomes an innocent, wrongfully accused.

The credo of the ideal prison: "The criminal is sent to prison AS punishment, not FOR punishment." The prisoners themselves see to it that this theory does not become practice. Each prisoner is given a six-digit number on his first lag which he'll keep for life: on his return, the same number applies. Permanent, like some abstract tattoo, the number marks the duration of his prison career.

The next prisoner slumped in silence on the vinyl seat still warm from Arnold's body, but seemed to exude no body heat at all. He was indolent and leering like a reptile whose mandible is fixed in an upward sweep. He looked oddly amused, but did not let me in on the joke, and gave nothing away but answers - which was all I needed - but nor did he appear resentful. I later read his psychiatric report for court.

"I was surprised how soft the man's skull was when I smashed it with a brick after we had sex," he had told the doctor. In coolly describing the immediacy of sensation conveyed by the impact of brick on bone, the murderer attained a perfect detachment, observing like a demi-god the demise of another, and in observing me was perhaps amused to know how softly my skull, too, would fracture. Hence the wry private chuckle spread over his face, which was soft and pudgy and boyish. He had close-cropped hair and a pert nose and flabby arms. Another murderer, who was comfortable with himself, with my questions, with me.

My next subject was tall and well-muscled. Behind him, an old crim smiled broadly - all gums and grizzle - and shouted from the mob milling around outside the clinic: "He's mad, that Jamie - you got a right spinner there, doc!" Jamie shared the banter, which was neither meant nor taken as disrespectful. He grinned and shrugged and sidled into the clinic. Adhering to the standard ritual of his tribe, he paused to scowl at Arnold and his mates through the bars of their strict segregation. And Jamie bore the marks of his tribe. His hair was crew-cut on top and long behind and a tight bush of beard clung to his chin. The tattooed skulls, witches and dragons lacing each arm were uncluttered, almost tasteful, if you go for Gothic. He had an easy manner, good looks, personality, youth. He would go far in his chosen career - crime.

Jamie, being Jamie, had no trouble getting girls. And he had no trouble when they broke up, until the girl found another guy. Then Jamie got vicious, which was only natural. He checked out the girls through our one-way mirror and told me: "I could have any one of them."

My final customer for the day was Robert. He checked out the girls, too, but in a different way to Jamie. Robert giggled as each one walked past, not knowing that she was being stared at. To Robert, this was great fun, and he laughed with the glee of a child who has discovered mirrors. I thought how amusing it would be to travel around with Robert in a bus with one-way mirrors - watching others, ourselves unseen. Robert took up the black biro and pulled its cap off with his teeth and twirled the plastic till it snapped. He kept the plastic twig in his mouth, joggling it between his teeth. Then he wrote in rounded print on the blotting pad: "Hi!" which I thought was nice and friendly. But his next words were less so: "Fuck off doc". I looked away and wondered if this was a threat, and looked again at the message. The final "c" had become a "g", and I felt relieved. He handed me back my pen. "I hate dogs," he said, matter-of-fact. A raised crimson scar weaved down his forearm, crossing the ink of a lavish tattoo. Satan sometimes told Robert to do things, but Robert didn't tell me what.

We looked up the charge sheets each morning. Court results were a kind of sports page.

Jamie got six months for aggravated assault occasioning actual grievous bodily harm. "He beat the shit out of his last girlfriend's new boyfriend," Shauna said.

Robert got acquitted. "What a joke. Guilty as sin," she said, like a blood-thirsty fan complaining, "We was robbed."

One morning I was waiting for three men on the list to enter remand from the reception prison next door, but only two arrived. The third had hung himself overnight. I saw his mother arrive through my one-way glass, to see the governor. She was distraught, sobbing among the other visitors. Gaunt, tattooed, scowling women passed her by. Often they stared at themselves in the window, not realising they were staring at me. They looked, but they did not see. They screeched at their children, who scampered off the path, as the mother wept for hers, adding drops to the ocean of tears for these men.

Another recidivist was on my list of receptions for the day. This was Stephen, returning only a few weeks after his last lagging. Larry, the officer in charge of the remand holding yard, knew Stephen well.

"Drunk and bashed his wife again, I'll bet. Every time he breaks the restraining order, he breaks her bones and ends up back here," Larry sighed.

"Some restraint, that order," I said.

But Stephen, surly like a child, told me his litany of woe:

"How would you feel, doc, if you'd done nothin' and they chucked you in here? The committal went through but the judge at the district court couldn't believe I'd been charged. 'There's nothin' on you,' he reckoned. So what am I doin' here? That same judge refused bail, and the matter's adjourned for four weeks. Fuck me. It's all that bitch's fault. She left me 'cos this place gave me hep C last time I was in so she's shit-scared of catching it. Won't even let me touch her."

Women caused these men a lot of hassles. Another prisoner fretted, pacing the clinic and shaking his head.

"What's gonna happen to me kids? The fuckin' bitch," he moaned. She'd seen him on a visit, accused him of having it easy inside while she had all the worries back home, and told him she'd take an overdose. An officer found her staggering in the car-park, unable to find her car. She had abused "the fuckin' screw" before she collapsed. The officer rang the clinic to find out what to do.

"She can't drive in this state," he said. "She'd be all over the road like a mad woman's breakfast." Chia told him to call an ambulance.

An officer was counselling a nervous first-timer. The prisoner looked close to tears, in the corner of the clinic, and was wondering if it was safe to cry there, whether he would be seen. What could the officer do? What even could he say? He spoke about what he knew, but no-one knows until they've been through it.

"This is the big time, mate - you're in prison now. There's a welcoming committee in each wing - they'll fill you in. Sort of a few older blokes you can trust, if you can trust anyone. You're on your own in here, see. Never been in before, have you? Just turned 19, eh? Dunno why they sent you here and not the young offenders' centre. Well, there's a few rules - not written down anywhere, but still rules. Don't pinch anyone else's stuff. Don't bend over in the showers or pick up the soap, that sort of thing. And don't roll onto your back expecting to get your belly tickled for being such a pretty boy, cos someone 'll come along and stomp on your windpipe."

The kid looked more and more scared as the officer spoke.

"I had a few mates around at the boys' home, but I got no-one here," he said. His hands were down the front of his blue tracksuit pants, below his waist, and jiggled as he spoke. He had thrust them there for reassurance when the officer mentioned the soap.

The next bloke was even younger, and scrawny like a street urchin.

"Did they raid the kindergarten to get hold of you, sonny?" an officer asked, and everyone in the holding cell laughed, including the boy-criminal himself. What else could he do? His big gloomy eyes seemed to beg "more" - plaintive and forlorn like Oliver Twist. His looks would draw tears from a stone, and laughter from a prison officer, but not an acquittal from a judge.

He followed me to my office like an obedient puppy. I soon wished his story would end the same way as his nose and chin - in a sharp point. But his was no fairy tale to conclude "happily ever after." Nor did things begin once upon a time. He was unsure when he first felt depressed.

"It's hard to say. I saw my brother rape my sister when I was eight, and my mother left home when I was seven. My dad molested me when I was nine. But I didn't really notice being depressed till puberty. Now that really fucks people up, don't it? So probably when I was fourteen, yeah. Being fourteen is nowheresville."

His nick-name was tattooed onto his wrist: 'Chook'.

"It's on account of my muscularity," he said. "And because I'm always clucking on about something. I love talking, doc, so you won't be able to shut me up. They reckoned I'd keep talking if they filled me mouth up with marbles and put me head underwater."

Despite his loquacity, we reached the last question: "Have you ever had a period of a few weeks or more when you felt useless, sinful, or guilty?"

Like many prisoners, he was surprised by its tone, surprised to be thrown back onto his emotions after a series of superficial enquiries about sleep and appetite and energy. And, like many others, he said, after a pause, "Doc, I've felt useless for years." I could see in his eyes how long those few useless years of his life had been.

The other typical reply - usually from the younger toughs - was: "Nah, none of that - don't care what I done."

BOUNDARIES

I was given glimpses, brief contact with these men, their stories and style: glimpses of another world.

"The faces in jail - you never see them on the outside. It's like they're particular, unique. There's something stamped into them," Shauna said.

"We look more closely into them - out of wariness. And a man's face becomes more noticeable when he wears the same blue T-shirt as the next. There's nothing else to set them apart," Chia said. He had an explanation for most prison phenomena.

I thought it was because we didn't visit their streets on the outside, and only saw their prison face. Nor were they privvy to our world, except when breaking and entering into it.

"They all go for the same hair-cut. The same tatts, ear-rings and beards," Shauna said. "It's a bloody fashion parade - they've gotta know what's 'in'."

"I think any man that wears an ear-ring is a bit suss. It means he's got problems with his sexuality," Chia said.

"Never heard of pirates, Chia, me hearty?" Shauna asked.

"Or nipple rings?" the officer added.

"My argument holds," Chia said demurely, and sipped his lemon tea.

There were so many crimes, and ways of being caught, that it was unlikely these men who happened to be imprisoned together would have much in common. There was no "type", with set qualities and experiences, but when they wore blue, and were kept behind bars and walls, it was natural to see uniformity, and give them a label of necessary malignity. From this, the numbers, the cells, the steady infliction of impersonal deprivations flowed naturally.

They clamoured for recognition, to be heard apart from the herd. A mob gathered outside the clinic each morning for medication, or to see the doctor. The door opened to a barred gate beyond which swayed a blue bulb with grinning or indifferent or intimidating heads atop multiple stalks. The men did not often push each other or bash on the door or rant. Only one was allowed into the clinic at a time. When each name was called, the others would stand aside so he could enter.

There is no clear boundary between right and wrong, only different points of view: prison is the perfect laboratory for the existential negation of ethic, the amoral society. Arnold could see no reason why I shouldn't contact his solicitor to stop his transfer to the bush. He pleaded with me from behind bars. I told him there was nothing I could do to help, and walked away. I didn't call their solicitors for them or run messages for them or write reports for their courts. This is called being good with boundaries. It kept things simple, but some couldn't take no for an answer. I was threatened by one man behind bars who demanded I phone his GP.

"You're supposed to be a doctor but you don't give a shit. I'll give you a friggin' shiner, yer mongrel," he yelled. An officer smiled at me and winked. Being abused by crims meant I was on the officers' side.

I was walking to my car when a prisoner whom I did not recognise greeted me by my first name. This was unnerving. I wondered if the guard in the tower was looking to see what I had put in the boot after I spoke to a crim, as though I had unwittingly broken the rules of the game. The prisoners were not allowed to use the clinic toilet. Or to have real sugar, the stuff from cane, in case they brewed fermented liquor with it. Or to use the oval beyond certain hours. Rules were the external bulwark against internal chaos.

"There's just one word to sum up this place, doc: 'fucked'. The place is fucked, us crims are fucked, the screws are fucked, and we all fuck each other's day up."

This crim ought to know. This was not his first lag, from his ID number, and from the lines etched deeply like cracks in wood down each side of his face, and from his nose bent and squashed and from his habitual sneer. Yes, he'd know. "So I'll answer your questions, doc, but you've already got the answer in one word: fucked."

I tried to engage him. "Sure, it's fucked," I said. "But there's plenty of different ways of putting it, even if in the end the only word that makes sense is 'fucked'. I mean, 'fucked' isn't enough to paint the full scene."

"What are you - an artist or a doctor," he sneered. "I told you, the place is fucked. End of story."

I was pleading for something from him. Some recognition, or appreciation. He looked up, looked right through me, which I took as a signal to get on with the interview. When I asked him what sort of drugs affected his sleep, he said, "illegal ones". I did not pry further. End of story.

"What's all this for, anyway, doc?" he asked at the end of our interview.

"I'm trying to find out how many prisoners have major mental illness, like schizophrenia."

"Fuckin' good idea. Good luck, doc."

I felt good. The tough guys were on my side, or I was on theirs. This was a good day. My office had been cleaned by the new sweeper. He had replaced the blotting paper and wiped the grime from my window. Robert would have loved it there now: a fresh white sheet to write messages on, and a better view of visitors who still could not see in.

BELONGING

The next time I saw Robert, he was grinning at the GP, asking for a "sick in cell" - doctor's permission to lounge around in bed all day.

"Why should I give you that, Robert?" the doctor asked.

"My shit's black."

"How black?"

"Black as black. And I've had one of them gastrologies - for an ulcer."

"Ah you mean a gastroscopy. Where did you have that, Robert?"

"Down here." Robert's mouth gaped as he pointed deep into his gullet.

"No, I meant which hospital?"

Nick managed to keep a sense of humour. He was avuncular and attentive and occasionally playful, to break the tedium of the daily sick parade.

A prisoner demanded I get the nurse to see him. He was absurdly enraged and desperate. I half-nodded as I walked past. Shauna had him brought in.

"Christ - is that all you were carrying on about, yer big sook?" she said as she changed a dressing on which he had seen blood. But the big sook looked smug with the attention. Chia later said he was amazed how "narcissistic" these men are.

"Entitled," I said.

"Precisely," Chia said.

We saw eye to eye.

The remand prison was a brutal place. But the brutality was mostly between prisoners - in the form of bashings - rather than between officer and prisoner. I was impressed with the reasonable attitude of most officers. One or two bullies among them stood out as exceptions. They were universally loathed: not only did they make life harder for the inmates, but they also caused trouble for their colleagues. The overriding concern of prisoners and officers alike was survival, "doing time easy" - whether it be an eight hour shift, or two months on remand. My equivalent "time" was measured out in numbers of interviews.

"One hundred and eighty down, three hundred and twenty to go," I told the next prisoner. That was my reason for being there: a numerical accretion, signifying research. We all have a sentence to serve, a "lagging". I missed a few prisoners here and there, being slack, which is to say, "Science isn't everything."

After the first interview, I would tell each prisoner he may be asked to do a second, longer one. This was random, part of the routine, I said. And if he should be called back he would receive a cup of tea or coffee, with real sugar, "as bribery," I joked.

"But what's in it for me, doc?" they would often ask.

"Nothing," I said.

A senior officer was interviewing Chia about the last death in remand.

"He was long gone by the time we got there. No sign of respiration, cyanosed and cold. Not much we could do," Chia explained. The officer was taking notes.

"Did you see a syringe?" he asked.

"No, but there was a fresh track-mark in the ante-cubital fossa."

"The what?"

"Just here." Chia pointed to the fleshy confluence of veins at the skin crease on the inside of his left elbow.

"Was this bloke left-handed?" the officer droned.

"I can't say," Chia said.

"You mean you don't know?"

"I mean I can't say because I don't keep that sort of data."

The officer winced, sensing the sarcasm in Chia's reply and unsure how to proceed. He crossed out a line on his page, and returned to an earlier enquiry:

"How do you spell that - anti-cube fossil?"

Chia wrote it carefully on a scrap of paper, and the interview ended. It had been no more futile than many exchanges in prison.

That morning, I felt at last that I belonged in this crazy zoo, this salt mine where nothing went right, except when you didn't want it to. Belonging here gave no cause for celebration. It was more like a loss of innocence, as though I had succumbed to some inevitable numbing, but the sense of defeat was mingled with a strange abandon. Now I was somehow free, godforsaken. My feeling of being accepted had arisen out of the mindlessness and frustration of these prison days - hour after hour of loitering alone with my odd musings in that clinic, observing the sights and words flowing past, observing myself, and trying to make some sense of it all.

THE SEARCH

To belong in prison is to be broken in. This had happened to me on a morning when the paging system was again broken, so no prisoners could be summoned for interviews. My office was being used for Chia to give some buffoon an anatomy lesson – how to spell 'ante-cubital fossa'. I felt bogged down, and my numbers were falling behind. I headed off to strict protection to see if I could gather more data to feed my hungry computer tucked into its little black bag. A prisoner approached as I waited outside the wing for the gate.

"Are you the shrink?" he asked.

A recklessness had replaced my earlier caution. I said: "Yes, but I'm not here to help anyone except myself."

This reply was not received warmly. The prisoner muttered: "Fuckin' smart-arse."

The officer arrived.

"Can you let me down to strict protection, mate?" I asked.

"The stricts are still in their cells. No let-go till ten a.m.," he said.

"But they're usually out by nine," I protested.

"Shit happens," the officer said.

"Can't help bad luck," the prisoner chuckled as I headed back the way I had come, still hungry for data. Just when you think you are broken in, there is more of yourself to be broken.

My search continued. A few prisoners were being sent directly to the psychiatric ward, bypassing my post at the clinic. I decided to chase them up. I found Albert, sitting in a corner of the hospital garden, talking to the flowers and the butterflies and the dirt and anything else that wouldn't listen. He followed me to the doctor's office. He stared at the consent form, stroking his eyebrows like some self-absorbed super-model. He answered "no" to every question, between talking quietly to himself. He was as mad as they come, the sort the officers called a "spinner", but his stock negation of every symptom meant he was not recorded on my interview as a case. My routine was as futile as the rest. I belonged.

Deaths in custody made the governor's job harder, and didn't help anyone else's. To cap off a lousy day, they closed down the prison for the third death that month. All inmates were locked in their cells, and every cell was searched. What were they looking for? They'd know when they found it. The officers brought rumours to us as we sat in the clinic, waiting for let-go. This one had died with the needle still in his vein. He was a sweeper in visits, so he had plenty of access to drugs, but the officer reckoned he wasn't a druggie, so why the OD? The men stayed in the Wings until after lunch. This meant our morning was wasted. I sat around. The deputy refused my request to let a few out from the top landing for my research. No doubt it seemed as strange and irrelevant a science to him as it did to the prisoners. And the deputy was pissed off with this death because the governor was pissed off with him.

At eight every morning, the officers lined up for their roll-call. Each name was answered "Sir", and a post was assigned for the day. Then the three-striper would tell the pip "All present and correct, sir", and the pip would nod and the three-striper dismissed the officers, saying, "All to your posts. Usual routine." I enjoyed watching this ritual, but the officers seemed sheepish when I arrived during it, as though they felt they were carrying on like school-children when they should be adults. But a prison needs order and obedience. The morning roll-call effectively reinforced these qualities which had been instilled by headmasters and teachers and uniforms and school allegiances. We do not grow up in order to discard what we have learnt, but to mould it for present purposes. Sometimes a senior officer - a three-striper - would visit the clinic and a cheeky junior would stand to attention and say, "All present and corrupt, sir."

I enjoyed the routine and its parody. Perhaps my allegiances were starting to show. Four out of the batch of five prisoners refused my interview that day. Eighty per cent refusal rate. Bad for my averages. One had told me: "You look like a cop." Why shouldn't I, after interviewing two hundred crims?

Two officers came to see the clinic nurse that day. One, a strapping, goofy-looking young fellow, complained of chest pain. He looked worried. But medically-speaking the pain was not sinister. The nurse fobbed him off with aspirin, saying: "This is not a fob-off."

"Aren't you gonna give me one of them electro-tests?" he asked. "That's what me GP does every fortnight."

The other officer had a scab on his head where he bumped it last week. Shauna found it even harder to fake concern for him. Otherwise, it was a quiet morning in jail. Voices drifted in from the yard, bantering and carousing; a child whined, being dragged by mum on their way to a visit; birds chirped, and every few minutes there was the familiar clang of an iron gate being opened and closed with a clack of a key in a lock.

WARD ROUND

Most of these men's crimes were tinged more with pride than with regret; their confessions were boasted, sometimes too loudly for their own good. First confessions invariably hint at some deeper secret.

Tim was not so handsome the second time I saw him. The left side of his face was bruised and swollen, which will happen if a face is hit with a right fist. But his grandiosity was undiminished.

"I could destroy everyone here," he raved. "But I choose not to."

"Thankyou, Tim. Now what's been going on out in the yard. Your head looks like rotting fruit," Shauna said.

It was finally clear to us that his was not ordinary obnoxious narcissism. His bragging was too inane to be a typical tough-guy veneer. He was mad, and his madness had rendered him a target. We had seen only a loud-mouth, and not listened to what came out of it. The empty posturing of a vain hoodlum was what we expected. And Tim himself was too proud and too psychotic to acknowledge any need for protection. He was not scared of his assailants, who, in singling him out for close attention, had turned out to be better diagnosticians than us. But there were no beds on the ward, and he could not remain in the remand wings, in a yard where he had antagonised everyone that mattered, so he was placed in a dry cell. This segregated unit contained a toilet bowel and a sink and a brick plinth on which to sleep, not that Tim in his manic state needed to do that. The walls were painted black. He had set fire to two cells on his landing, both of which had been occupied at the time, and the occupants swore to get him. His good looks would soon be gone, along with his sanity.

Down on the ward, prisoners loitered outdoors. The morning was crisp; a brilliant autumn sun hinted at warmth, like a memory of summer, of a lost lover's caress. It was not yet nine o'clock. My subject was easy to spot. He was the one who had been restrained, kicked, bound, and bundled into a steel box for transfer to psychiatric care. He no longer feared the "blood doctors", and the dispute on his behalf between doctors and officers had fizzled out. The full story was less clear-cut than we had assumed. Rumours had sprung up that the doctor had panicked and called in the officers when he could have talked the man down with the nurses. Blame is a fickle beast, as likely to turn on its source as hit its target, and it was too easy to label the officers as brutal. Their task was security. Ambiguity confused them. Captor and captive shared a tendency to action, not contemplation. The logistics of moving a psychotic prisoner were difficult. Fuelling this apologia for violence was our relationship to the doctor involved - our colleague. To the rest of us, he was a pompous upstart. When hints of his incompetence emerged from the nurses, we relished them. Innuendo fed on itself. We assumed he had been brash, giving orders to officers who did not recognise his authority. The doctor was not in their chain of command, and the prisoner - whether or not he was also a patient - remained their property. The prisoner, a powerless token at the bottom of the pile, became the brunt of this demarcation dispute. Like the victimised child of warring parents, he bore the scars of a distant antagonism. His bruising would fade, as the reports gathered dust, and nothing would happen to change life in the prison. I explained my interview to him.

"Will this be filmed?" he asked, earnestly paranoid.

"No."

"Will it be recorded?"

"No."

The interview began and, as usual, I typed his replies into my computer.

"You said this wouldn't be recorded," he challenged.

"It's not."

"Well what's that you're typing, then?"

He was scared. I had shown him the questions on my screen. I had cajoled him to sign the consent form. I had tried to get him a glass of water for his mouth dried from the medications but the officer had told him to wait for morning tea. But my ingratiating, unctuous and practised tactics would come to nought all because the kid was paranoid beyond reason, and could not care less that I was desperate for data.

"I'm sorry," I said. "I thought you meant if it was recorded by microphone."

This hardly placated him. He glanced furtively around the small office. He knew the surveillance cameras were trained on him, from the ceiling or from behind that filing cabinet. He knew because he could sense it, as clear as the light of the day and the pale warmth of the sun outside where he wanted to be. Senses are the most real experiences we have; they do not lie. They are the intimate and constant flux from which we construct our surroundings. They fill us up and we sift through their myriad impressions and become complete every moment, a shifting and fragile completion of the task of being a rational self in a world of irrational other. Who was I to challenge his personal edifice of belief, to realign its precarious tilt? It was not my job - that was for his psychiatrist to do. Nor did I want to be standing under the edifice when it toppled, so I gathered my pens and unplugged my computer, preparing to end our chat.

"Look, I know this is some sort of set-up, but I don't give a shit. I only trust my parents, so you can go ahead and ask your questions," he said abruptly.

We completed the interview, and when I left the ward he thanked me.

PRISON ROMANCE

Charlene, the gorgeous Maori transsexual, had not spent long pining over Nigel the spiv. She had found a new buck in David, and the two were soon inseparable in the main yard. Their amorous ways aggravated other prisoners, particularly Rona, another trannie who resented Charlene's standing as chief cat in remand. Like many prison feuds, theirs was a continuation of resentments from the outside: they had both worked Lover's Lane near the docks. This was the choice beat for trannies, and hotly contested. Now Rona was being forced to cater for the lusts which the example of Charlene and David aroused in other inmates. And once branded as common property, it was difficult to find a buck, so Rona had been denied the security of being a one-man woman-man. The irony was she was even more attractive than Charlene: Rona was all pouting lip and batted lids and almost petite, whereas Charlene displayed vestiges of masculinity, with a more prominent jaw, excess height, and coarser hair. The nurses preferred Charlene, perhaps because she offered less competition for them. Although they preferred her, they did not necessarily like her.

"I think it's disgusting," Shauna said. "I mean, they've still got their dangly bits, so it's just being gay, but they're not man enough to admit it."

Rivalries were as common among the trannies as within any other tribe in the prison, but they could unite for the common good, when it suited them. And, this being prison, their unity could be expressed in strange ways, as happened one morning when Charlene visited the clinic, in some distress.

The day had begun as usual. While waiting for their work to begin - for prisoners to be let out of the wings, and for the needy and malingering among them to arrive - Shauna and a female officer, Muir, chattered in their easy idiom of invective.

"Wosamatter - can't find a tool for yer box, officer Muir?"

"Wouldn't be one big enough for yours after all the kids you've had, nurse."

"At least I had something to feed them with. You'd make a good ironing board."

"Anything more than a mouthful is a waste. Those flabby floppers make you stoop."

In mocking each other's breasts, they showed their manliness. But these were perfunctory barbs, hurled more for the sake of hurling than for hurting, and as practice for the prisoners. Female staff in a male prison did not take a stand against sexism. They created their own. Abuse and denigration were bandied about, as they would not want to be thought soft on crime, or on each other. But they dealt softly with male staff: the sisterhood was not yet equal to the prison task. The nurse phoned each wing for the names on that day's sick parade.

"Hello, Smithie, sweetheart darling. It's Shauna here, the married one. Do you still want my body? Are you listening to me? Have you got our list?"

Smithie was cute, and easily flattered. He read the names too quickly for her to write them, but she didn't ask him to slow down. She did not want to impose, or sound ungrateful for his time. Men always seemed to win.

These prison lists were capricious. Like peek-a-boo, you never knew who was behind the obscuring hand, or the name on a prison list. And in prison, lists were everywhere. There were lists for court, lists for classification, and for the prison clinic. That day's sick parade comprised: a Filipino drug dealer (a "Mr Big Enough"); a conman from Queensland; a recidivist bikie with a long red beard, and various urban junkies, the clinic bread and butter. They all seemed pathetic to Smithie as he recited their names to the nurse. "Another gronk; another fucked unit; another spinner," he said. The longer ethnic names were difficult for Smithie to read, impossible for him to pronounce. He mumbled their syllables over the phone, but never deigned to spell them out, nor did Shauna ever ask. She would not want to impose.

She obediently collated the list for the doctor, who was yet to arrive. This was unusual, as Nick was always punctual. So she was poised between two absent male masters - Smithie on the phone and the doctor on his way - with only the female officer to disdain, until the prisoners turned up. She groaned at the names on her sick parade. Each conjured up a whining face, endless resentments and unmeetable demands.

"National service would give these bloody lay-about crims something to really whinge about, keep them out of trouble and make men out of them, the bunch of sooks," she said, to no-one in particular. "And flogging wouldn't be a bad idea, too."

Shauna was nothing if not tough on law and order. She liked to run a tight clinic - spick and span, spit and polish - and she was a stickler for a neat, if misspelt, list of names taped to the top right corner of the doctor's desk each morning. "If they're not already on the list, too bad, they'll miss out. I don't care if they're dying." She stuck the list into place.

These lists were all the more frustrating because they could so easily alter. It might have been the same prisoner, but with a different name, because names often changed there, for all sorts of reasons. The alias was fairly common. It helped confuse the system, to have a different name for each warrant, and each lag. And if someone in the system was out to get you, it was that much harder with a different name, but they'd get you in the end.

You could also change your name to suit your sex, but the trans-sexual, condemned to life in a man's body, did her time in a man's prison. Even if he became she in name and spirit and identity, he remained he in the eyes of the corrective service, unless her sentence was surgically commuted to life trans-body - life in a twilight of biology. And in the eyes of the nurse, the trans-sexual was seen as caricature or self-parody. Shauna loathed these trannies, the "cats". It was against nature.

So the nurse knew - but did not accept - that nothing was irrevocable in that vast system of corrections. There were always late scratchings and additions to the sick parade, but none more frantic than today's...

The female officer was fretting over the first prisoner to arrive. It was Charlene. Muir would have to adjust the sick list, but such list was beyond her authority to adjust. It belonged to Shauna, who'd kill her if she touched it. "Doctor and his list are that bloody nurse's turf," Muir complained to me. She was uncertain just where I fitted in, and thought I may have been sympathetic. "It isn't fair because she also tries to crack onto any spunky male officers if she gets a chance. Just listen to her on the phone with that creep, Smithie. She can have HIM - he's sleazy, up himself, and he's got bad breath. At least you can't smell it over the phone."

Shauna interrupted the officer's whinge: "Wotsup, Muir? Some prisoner just told you about the birds and the bees?"

"Not exactly," the anxious officer replied. "But you know that trannie came in yesterday? She says she's having a period, so she's gotta be added to the doctor's list."

"Don't you tell me who to add to the list, you idle little strumpet. It's impossible for her to have a period. Anyway, the list's already full."

"She showed me the blood," Muir said lamely, but she sensed defeat. She had ignored the golden rule: never trust a prisoner.

The doctor arrived in the middle of this dispute. It was not Nick, but George, a GP who filled in when Nick took a day off to work in a hospital casualty. George was a jovial reformed alcoholic. He liked nothing better than to see two women stoush. Best of all if it was mud wrestling, but this lively start to his clinic was entertainment enough, even though the nurse and officer were fully clad. He was in good spirits, as befitted a man who was just visiting this place, not there day to day. And his cheer was apt to sour anyone less transient than himself, which was all the rest of us in the clinic that morning. Shauna preferred Nick's quiet efficiency to Geoge's loud jocularity.

"Listening to all this carry-on about blood reminds me of a joke," George announced. "There's this group of kids, see, and they're down the back of the garden behind the shed. No-one else is about, so one of the boys says to the girls, 'We'll show you ours if you show us yours,' and..."

"George, I think we've heard that one. Now you don't want to see this trannie, do you?" Shauna asked.

"Oh, of course I do, sister. Where's your intrepid scientific spirit? A man with woman's problems. Add him - or her - to the top of the list. I'll see her first up - it's not every day you get a chance to make medical history."

George paused. A frown creased his ruddy face. This could be tricky. The price of fame is hard work, and deep thought, neither of which George has particularly excelled at, which is why he had spent two decades as a Navy doctor. He left the ships when the ravages of alcohol and sexually transmitted disease made him as sick as most of his patients, and sicker than some. And where else for an old sea-doc to end his career but in a prison? It was another ship of fools, whose uniforms gave him a sense of belonging. He continued his medical epiphany, to everyone's dismay:

"Mmmm. I did come here hoping to avoid obstetrics and gynaecology. And there are anatomical differences, you know. Even when a man has his penis amputated, and that other operation, what's it called...?"

"Orchidectomy, doctor," Shauna said. George winced.

"Ooh, yes, that one. Well, there are anatomical differences. Even after surgery to become a woman, he isn't really a she. As the Navy chaplain used to say when he was inebriated, which was most of the time, 'We're all here for a reason, as soon as we can work out what it is,' but the sexual reason is perfectly clear to me. The male organ deposits sperm in the female organ, the womb. So this prisoner cannot have a period, period. Absolutely not."

George was adamant in his logic, but the officer remained confused as she went to fetch the prisoner, and Shauna was unimpressed with George's oratory, which she recognised as merely deliberate delay until he worked out what to do. "Tincture of time" was his favourite saying, which meant he'd immediately do nothing. Perhaps George remembered too well the edict of Hippocrates - "primum non nocere" - because so determined was he to "first do no harm" that he seldom did anything. But harm could come from inaction as much as from action.

"I reckon it's that bloody officer's problem," Shauna whispered conspiratorially to George. "Muir's the one always comes to see Nick for scripts for her own period pain, George. Her PMT lasts all bloody month."

He chewed over this intelligence like a big old cow.

"Mmm, I take your point, sister. You invoke hysteros, of the womb, woman," he said sagely. This was George the wise, the omniscient patriarch. "All this talk about periods and woman's problems reminds me of a joke. How do you make a whore moan?"

"George, it's simple," Shauna said, again denying him a punch-line. She was getting more and more exasperated by George's dilatory ways, and hoped Nick wouldn't be away for more than one shift. "If this trannie's a cock in a frock, she stays. If she's had the nip and tuck, she goes to the woman's prison. That's all you need to worry about."

"Right you are then, nurse," George said. This stock phrase was his reassurance of control, with its echo of the fleet, all men to attention, and "right you are, sir."

"Send her in," George said with some authority. "Now who wanted the script for period pain?"

The officer returned with George's first patient, Charlene. She looked like a million dollars that morning:

hips sashaying as she entered the clinic, her brunette hair in luscious waves, and not a trace of stubble to scratch your penis.

Muir hastily drew the curtain across to give George and Charlene and Shauna some privacy, but the officer hovered nearby, for security reasons, and to hear Charlene's complaint of periods confirmed. She knew the nurse was mocking her, but felt old George would sort things out. I hovered nearby, you could say as part of my research.

"Why can't this trannie have periods? She talks like a woman and walks like a woman and men check her out like a woman - so why shouldn't she have woman's problems like a woman? God knows I'd gladly give anyone my own periods. Pain and blood every four weeks. What is it with a woman's body and the moon and the calendar?" Muir whispered to me. The best Muir ever felt was when she went on a crash diet and did every aerobics class at the gym, sometimes twice a day, and her periods stopped. "What a relief!" she said. She had had heaps of energy then - wide-awake like she was on speed, and at the time she thought that was how it felt to be a man. But after she began work as a prison officer with the long hours and rotating shifts, her gym regime stopped and she put on weight and her periods started again.

"So what if I can't stand the monthly pain and take something for it? That nurse is a bloody sadist," Muir muttered as we stood on the other side of the curtain, while listening to the interview between doctor and patient. Few things in prison were secret.

"How can we help you, ah..." George looked down at the file, before continuing. "Ah, Charles."

"That's Charlene," his patient rasped.

"Oh, of course. Right you are. An 'n' can look like an 's' in these blasted files. Norry. I mean sorry." George's joke fell flat. I could barely stifle a guffaw, seeing his red face reddening even more. Shauna thrummed her fingers on the desk behind him, resting her chin in her other hand. The patient feigned indignation, but really was amused, and lapped up the attention. She could tell that this doctor found her attractive. Most did, the male ones at least. I could still remember seeing her long reach for the ball as she served, back arched and breasts squeezed against her T-shirt. Sam's tour seemed so long ago.

Old George had pulled into a few ports in his time, hey what?! Knew a thing or two about working a passage, I bet. The sailors had a name for these girls who were boys; called them "beanies", but that didn't stop a bit of slap and tickle. Some of the beanies even charged a bit more, probably for the novelty value. Not that George himself was ever tempted. Perish the thought. But he liked the old Navy saying: "If life ashore is wine, women and song, life at sea is rum, bum, and gramophone records." What then to make of life in prison?

His lips twitched into an involuntary smile, which he fought manfully to make a grimace. From my angle behind the curtain I could see his tumescence as he leant away from his desk. He swung his arms back, elbows bent, and clasped his hands behind his head, clearly enjoying the slow rise in his Y-fronts, which I reckoned would happen rarely these days, what with alcohol and old age and a history of the clap. George was oblivious to the fact that I was observing his harmless indulgence, this bone in his trousers

The doctor spoke again to his patient.

"Mmm, yes, where was I? Right, so what's the problem?"

"I want to go two out, doctor. I can't stand being alone in my cell."

"Well, that's for the corrective service to decide. I can't do anything about it, I'm sure."

"Not even a letter?" Charlene asked wistfully. "There's another girl here, Rona, wants to share with me."

Charlene tilted her head slightly, pressing her lips to a full crimson pout. This was too much for George, the thought of two beanies in a cage. He hastily scribbled out a letter.

"Now what was all that fuss about periods?" he asked.

"Oh, I just said that to get in to see you, doctor. But I have been having some pain 'down there'. Aren't you going to examine me? Don't you want to see if my service has been corrected?" she teased.

"Well, I don't see any need," George said.

I recalled a surgical adage from my student days: "If you don't put your finger in, you put your foot in." That was the only surgery I could remember, and I was sure George's knowledge was no better. I could see him squirm. He turned to ask Shauna what she had said before - "Something about a nip and tuck?" Now it was his turn to fret over this woman's problems, and he couldn't stand up to examine her because the bulge in his trousers would show. He willed detumescence, demanded it, muttering: "Bugger of a thing. Mind of its own. Never there when you need it, and when you don't..." He gripped his pen tightly, trying to distract himself, perhaps with thoughts of golf, or a cup of tea with strudel, or had he put in his time-sheet?

Charlene seemed to sense his consternation. She relished it. For all their attempt at feminine allure, the trannies retained an aggressive sexuality: like David, her current buck, and Nigel before him, this hapless doctor was a toy she could control, bend to her will, and discard. She taunted him, crossing and uncrossing her legs. She was sure of herself - cocksure, you could say. And she was sure this doctor wouldn't examine her, which was just as well. She would hate to be transferred. For a girl like Charlene, the men's prison was close to paradise: the most intense ogling she'd ever had. So much pent-up male energy, a fearful great yearning in all those young virile men permanently on heat.

Charlene looked proud of her trans-sex, her true distaff nature. She probably felt more of a woman than either nurse or officer. In that environment, they hid their sex and she flaunted hers. Why should she hide her femininity like them? Shauna, for all her loud come-ons, had forgotten what it was like to be a woman, and Muir, like the other female officers, was terrified of being one. Her drab grey uniform - it did nothing for her complexion. But Charlene looked sexy in her blue prison garb. It caught the tone of her hair and eyes.

The doctor enquired delicately: "Is everything in order - been checked and all that? You are all there, aren't you? I mean, lock, stock and barrel?" His voice quivered. Charlene smiled blandly, offering neither a yes or a no, and patient and doctor shared an awkward silence, each with a secret between the legs. This was pure theatre, and I had front row seats.

Shauna by now had also sensed the doctor's consternation, but, unlike Charlene and myself who gloated over it, the nurse felt a need to help George out - even with a dose of his own medicine, a corny joke.

"That reminds me of a story," Shauna said. "There's a little boy and a little girl in the bath. The boy points to his willie and says: 'You don't have one of these.' But the girl points to her naughty bits and says: 'Sure, but I can have as many of those as I want with one of these.'"

Giggles erupted around the clinic. Officer Muir nearly fell through the curtain, before leading the patient - now prisoner again - back to the prison yard, back to the wolf whistles and cat calls and smirks, and back to David. But Charlene had a smirk of her own - at these doctors who never called her bluff.

Shauna fetched George a strong cup of sweet tea - just how he liked it, but without the brandy. His hands trembled as he took a sip.

"Must be getting old," he confided. "None of that in my time. It's disgusting. We're all here for a reason. Preposterous, that I should have to examine her." But doubt shaded his expression, as he muttered that surgical adage.

"What was that, George?" the nurse asked. "Something about putting your foot in?"

"Oh. Nothing." George busied himself with some notes, and I bent again over my computer, analysing data, collating and recording - one busy researcher.

"Ready for your next patient, then?" Shauna asked him.

"Just a tick. No rest for the wicked, hey what?!" George mused. "It's always been all or nothing with me. Trouble is, mostly these days it's nothing."

Shauna looked puzzled by this remark, but I knew what he meant. We did not see old George in the clinic for months after that day's sick parade. That night, Charlene and Rona forgot old rivalries and had a wild time two-out in their cell, but David became jealous. The delicate equilibrium between them had been disturbed. It was as though rutting season had begun. Fights broke out in the yard between prospective bucks. A few days later, the governor transferred Charlene and David to adjoining cells in stricts. Their relationship could not survive being so near yet so far.

On their first morning there David offered his girl a loaf of white bread for breakfast. The bread, prison-issue in clear plastic wrapper, was held out by his hairy hand poking through the bars from his cell in strict protection.

"Here's somethin' for ya, honey," he said to Charlene. His usual gruffness was softened in sentimental entreaty. Her hand - smooth and slight, with long, manicured nails - was extended from the adjoining cell, poised to receive the gift, but languidly withdrawn behind the bars, in a teasing gesture. The bread dangled, an unrequited offering from David to his transsexual lover. He did not like to be teased, being inarticulate and literal and untrained in the subtle arts of seduction. His was a rougher intimacy, without playful dissembling. Before symbol, before the word, sex was sex, and lust was untrammelled by nuance or wit.

The events of David's unexamined life happened de novo, without antecedent or consequence, unembellished. There can be no fiction where desires are immediately gratified. Being true to every impulse denied him the capacity, and the need, for detachment. Irony and metaphor withered in his harsh authenticity, or never took root. Such an existence seemed so clear, so simple, so genuine and heedless to me, the man of a thousand disguises and distractions and philosophies of life. A man with a philosophy of life does not know how to live. But my atavistic hankering for some truer nature, some primitive nobility - whose vestigial reptilian brain is roused from its torpor beneath the convolutions of homo sapien's cerebral cortex, which itself is shed as so much evolutionary waste -

was a thin disguise for disdain and fear of the conscienceless brute. The obverse of that freedom and spontaneity I admired in him was his callousness I condemned.

Most of us have a shared stake in the thwarting of natural urges. It is called society. Society rests on a common agreement to cast our minds back, and throw our hopes and fears forward, fracturing against the fact of birth and the prescience of death that eternal present in which the organism is immersed. Time is never more than now in the body's timeless functions, even as the brave prow of reason's barque carves a passage through time's ocean, leaving a wake of memories. Sleep is the barque becalmed, its circadian hiatus. Men like David had never woken up. Although he was without *mens rea* – or guilty mind - his permanent innocence would not suffice as legalistic defence, because society must protect itself from the rage of sleep-walkers. Innocence is necessarily to be distinguished from mindlessness.

At first, Charlene had found David's animal arousal exciting, but it became less so as he fell more and more under her sway. She found she could control David, like she had controlled other men before him, her "rough trade" as she called them. Culture springs from relatedness, but David was incapable of the decadence necessary to relate. If there is no shared past, there can be no attachment. This was the cost of his solitude, his honest, inflexible and pain-free mode of existence in the here and now. "People who need people are the luckiest people..." This was not David's favourite song.

Charlene was toying with him out of habit. It was an idle diversion. His rages bored her, they were so predictable, like a robot's emotions. Such were the cruel facts of their prison romance.

"Look, just take the bread, ya bitch," he ordered. "Go on, fuck ya. Me hand's gettin' tired."

Then he dropped that loaf which landed with a thud on the concrete. Charlene did not respond. She was hunched over her black and white TV, watching Humphrey Bear in a gloomy corner of her bear-pit, under its concrete roof, sulking in silence.

PULLING POWER

Every second prisoner was again refusing my interview. At this rate, I'd never get the numbers, and without numbers, without data, there could be no research. What was going wrong? Was Gramsci up to his old tricks, or was this merely a phase to get through? I felt like a punch-drunk boxer, an overweight model, an ageing rock star - that old pulling power had gone. Charisma gets bums on seats, fills auditoriums, sells records, and ensures 600 prisoners consent to my interview. Had I lost it? Refusal, knock-back, rejection.

"Bet you haven't had too many of them," Shauna said cheekily.

"She could bring a smile to your face or tears to your eyes, that woman," Chia told me, nodding playfully at his underling.

"Simultaneously," I said.

"Indeed," Chia replied.

I tried to recover from the previous day's narcissistic injuries, awaiting the next batch of remand receptions. Chia had become a source of support, a quiet strength in these difficult days. I wondered if there is a Chinese word for *mensch**.

------

* mensch is yiddish for 'man', but it means a *'good* man'

"Maybe you should bring in a pack of smokes and a lighter," an officer suggested. "You'd get 'em on side, calm 'em down a bit."

"There's no smoking in the clinic. And besides, that would be trafficking. You could go to jail for that," Chia said.

"It's not bloody trafficking, offering a smoke," the officer protested.

Chia pulled out a copy of the Prisons Act, 1952, and pointed to the pertinent paragraph, Section 37. We read in silence: *"Any person who without lawful authority brings or attempts by any means to introduce into any prison or prison complex any spiritous or fermented liquor or any drug shall be liable to imprisonment for a term not exceeding six months or to a penalty not exceeding one thousand dollars or to both such imprisonment and penalty."*

"I believe section 38, paragraph 'c' may also be relevant," he intoned, and directed our eyes to its solemn message:

"Any person who without lawful authority conveys or delivers, or causes to be conveyed or delivered or in any manner whatsoever attempts to convey or deliver or to cause to be conveyed or delivered to any prisoner, or introduces or attempts to introduce into any prison or prison complex any money, letter or other document, clothing, or other article or thing shall be liable to imprisonment for a term not exceeding six months or to a penalty not exceeding one thousand dollars or to both such imprisonment and penalty."

"That sums it up, then," I said. "No bribery with cigarettes or any other article or thing."

But things started to go right. Both prisoners that day consented to my interview; both were psychiatric patients, one straight from a ward, the other awaiting bail to go to a ward. Of all the revolving doors for social detritus such as them, the one to prison was the one they least liked to enter. The first subject looked distracted. His eyes were furtive. He moved in fits and starts, fidgeted, clung to my voice as a respite from his own internal babble. His answers were digressive.

The second man was sluggish. Lengthy pauses preceded his slow, laconic replies. He stared out the window with a vacant and indifferent air. Neither man knew when he was next due in court. As they were being led to remand from the holding cell, the slow man told me he was feeling restless.

"It's the modecate*, doc," he said, shuffling from sandshoe to sandshoe.

The officer told him he'd be in the wings soon and could return to the clinic for medication. He took the two new boys down the corridor and outside, where rain pelted onto an empty yard. Their prison issue blue sloppy joes soon darkened, sagging with the weight of water. Their hair was drenched, their cardboard shoe-boxes of belongings fell apart, and they clutched tooth-brushes and tapes and stuffed precious notes in their water-logged pockets. They looked like forlorn stray dogs newly arrived at the pound, or boarding Noah's ark. The officer who was taking them to their wing wore a great-coat, and carried an umbrella. His charges followed obediently, their flimsy sandshoes splashing in the puddles behind the crunch of his leather boots - these patients, lost in prison, had nowhere else to go, nothing else to do. Chia and I watched

---

* modecate is an injectable anti-psychotic medication with lots of movement side-effects. It can also help.

them cross the concrete, and disappear behind the high brick wall of wing H.

"I worked in a therapeutic community in the sixties with patients like that. They'd stay with us for years," Chia said. "Things have changed, since Ronnie Laing's* day. Now prisons have become ersatz psychiatric hospitals."

"They sure have, Chia," I said.

---

* controversial British psychiatrist from the sixties who challenged the dominant psychiatric paradigms

THE SYSTEM

A junior nurse had been given the job of waiting for Robert to vomit or pass stool. He had complained again of black faeces, but his claims were unsubstantiated - he had flushed away the evidence - so he was locked in a cell with a specimen jar, for diagnostic reasons. It would also teach him a lesson. After several hours of trying, he had brought up bright blood, which he had shown proudly to the nurse.

"No, it has to be brown, like coffee-grounds, otherwise it's likely to be a Mallory-Weiss tear," the nurse informed him, matter-of-fact, straight from the text-book so it must be right.

This did not seem fair to Robert. Here was evidence, clear as day, blood in the jar.

"Perhaps you will produce melena," she continued.

"Don't even know her," Robert said.

"No, I mean faeces in the jar," she said.

"I'd have to have a pretty tight ass to shit into that," he said.

"Don't be disgusting," she said, and walked away.

"Aren't you taking me jar?" he shouted after her.

These malingered claims of illness were the bane of the clinic.

"We need a system," I said. "Like the prison system, we need a clinic system."

"Prison system - what system?!" an officer exclaimed. "When you work it out, doc, make sure you let the rest of us know how this place works."

I should have told them then, told them how it shifts, this prison, this correctional facility, in kaleidoscopic images from bleak to churning chaos. We worked in the empty guts of a hollow machine, without purpose, method, or control, but as part of a system. Our oblivion was surrounded by fragments of prison life barely sustained: the laughter and tears of men crouched in corners, defeated; rows of prisoners mustered each morning and each afternoon, their voices and their foot-fall resonating against concrete as they spilled from the wings at let-go and headed back again at lock-up; the idle and vaguely vicious eyeing up and down of crim to crim, crim to officer, officer to crim; lives of a thousand intoxications staving off the drag of drug-free days, each hour too real.

These prisoners kept returning to the system, following its cruel logic in their roles as junkies, thugs, alcoholics, swindlers, lunatics. They came back, parading an easy familiarity with the system, apparently indifferent to its demands and strictures. The men who were most ashamed of recidivism laughed hardest of all at each lag. But on their first, all were terrified, and showed it. These were the workings and the effects of a simple system.

"I saw these guys in a corner, looking around. Then one of them pulled out a bloody great knife - curved and shiny. Looked vicious as hell. A soup ladle they'd sharpened to a point, and all down one side like a machete. Shit, I reckon I'll keep my eye out for those blokes," said a prisoner from the methadone queue.

These methadonians were dosed daily in a careful ritual. They were the meanest-looking crims of all, whose favourite tattoo was of tears near the corner of the eye. Little salt ever touched that ink. They slouched each morning in quiet menace beyond the bars of the clinic gate, waiting for their name to be called for the brown syrup to be dispensed. They were let in one at a time. Each prisoner was hastily searched, padded along limbs and torso by an officer wearing rubber gloves. Then the prisoner approached two nurses at their desk, his eyes fixed on the flagon of methadone perched between them. One nurse set a plunger and pushed it down the neck of the big brown bottle, measuring out the methadone in a plastic cup. This was taken, gulped and chased with water from an old kettle. The prisoner would then open his mouth wide to the officer's scrutiny, tongue out and wagging like a snake, teasing and venomous, to end the ritual.

OTHER SCIENTISTS

Doctor King, self-righteous as ever, was seeking the most paranoid prisoners, and their stories, for his research. He lectured me on the value of his work, and indeed I was impressed by the detail he obtained from his subjects. Our studies operated from the most divergent perspectives of psychiatry. I took the quantitative, or nomothetic, approach, amassing a breadth of information from hundreds of subjects, whereas Dr King burrowed deeply into the quality of existence of a small sample. This is known as the idiographic method. He described a litany of woe as prisoner after prisoner recounted memories of childhood abuse so concerted and cruel as to equal torture. Dr King presented his cases to our weekly seminar. To listen to the horrors became mind-numbing, until Dr King presented the case of one prisoner whose childhood experiences sounded familiar. The crimes of the father had been visited on the son…

"One prisoner as a boy would be put in a corner for hours and told to stare at a spot on the wall and if he moved he was hit over the back of the head. And another had the string of a kite tied around his neck and was stood in the backyard; when there was a gust of wind he'd nearly pass out. These are typical examples from my research. But one case stands out for its savagery, with subsequent deformity evident in the prisoner's personality, and body. Both are severely warped, you could say. This prisoner gave a history of having been encased in plaster as a little boy from his waist to his neck, and hung upside down evidently for orthopaedic reasons. He had endured this treatment for hours at a time, day after day. However, the treatment failed to rectify his congenital kyphoscoliosis. If anything, the spinal deformity was exacerbated by this innovative approach, but his spine was also stretched so he grew to a considerable height. Later methods had no therapeutic pretensions, as this same boy was subsequently disciplined for any misdemeanour by being again hung upside down - and beaten. This case exemplifies the interplay between nature and nurture in the forming of the personality and its disorders. The spinal deformity was innate, but its meaning as trauma could be considered an acquired characteristic…"

The professor interrupted his musings.

"We need data," she said. "No academic journal is publishing narrative stuff these days. Hard data, Dr King, some numbers for our hungry computers to crunch. You are verging on the mawkish, Dr King. Furthermore, you should be quite careful to maintain the anonymity of your cases."

The professor's facial expression gave little away, but I understood from her words that our special patient had been interviewed by Dr King. To hear my pompous rival thus berated allowed me some pleasure. But Dr King's account also shed light on Gramsci's transference struggles. His relentless antagonism in therapy was merely an echo of that trauma he had suffered as a child. His hatred of his parents became his hatred of society, and his hatred of his therapist. There was nothing I could do about that: his defences were impregnable.

Sometimes the officers did research, too. There was a kindness to the experiments of Bill. He was proud of the letter a prisoner had written to the governor, praising his counselling.

"I just had a few words with him. Treated him like a human being - an equal, ya know. I thought I could help, so I kinda gave it a go, kind of an experiment, like. And he seemed keen to go straight. Got hisself educated, and found a job. Stayed off the drugs. He wrote me some thanks, and sent a copy to the governor. Made me feel bloody good."

This was Bill's case study, a simple but effective research design. Bill looked like a man of science, too. He was wiry and wore glasses. His hair was permanently greased back to a brown sheen. He was always quick to respond to requests from clinic staff and from prisoners.

"They tend to lay off us older blokes," Bill observed of his charges. ""We don't cop the same shit as the officers who are around the same age as the crims. And they get a feel for who they can hassle. I don't mind a bit of lip, or horse-play, but if one of them lays a hand on me, I just snap. Can't help meself. One crim gave me a bit of a nudge and he ended up smack against the wall so fast he didn't know what hit him. This bloody great hook went into his back, too. Didn't get a boo out of him after that."

Bill liked to make himself useful when he was on duty in the clinic. Just to help out, he'd sometimes tell me the charge of each prisoner before I interviewed them.

"Didja hear about that woman killed down at riverside park the other night. This next one's the bloke that got charged. Bashed her senseless, then left her to bleed to death in a storm-water drain. Who knows why - maybe she wouldn't go down on him."

My next customer, then, arrived with an introduction. But Bill, being fair, presumed innocence. He warned the teenage murderer "not to trust anyone in prison," before opening the gate of the holding cell and telling him to "go with the doc."

Bill interrupted our interview briefly to suggest that the boy go to protection. The boy shook his head, but Bill tried to convince him, finally almost begging him to see the officer in the Wing if he changed his mind.

"Don't wait for something to happen, boyo," Bill said. "If yer wanna go to programmes, you let the 'pip' know straight away."

Bill had a bad feeling about this kid. He was a first-timer, a young offender, and he had bashed and killed a woman who may have been only fourteen or fifteen. These were markers for trouble. He looked young and neat, without much muscle, not yet filled out. He answered my questions politely. I thought he must have been drunk or stoned - 'off his head' - to have killed her, but I did not ask. Despite his looks and manner, it was very difficult to presume innocence. It was a question of trust - I didn't.

One of the 'programmers' took a fit while waiting to see the doctor. Frothy blood bubbled from his lips onto the concrete floor. The other prisoners stood against the wall of the small cell, watching his arms and legs thrash spastically. The convulsions petered out, then burst again through his body like electricity.

"Can't yer switch 'em orf, doc?" a prisoner asked. Some laughed, but most were silently observant. One murmured angrily at the nurse and doctor by the man's side:

"It's your bloody fault - youse stopped his pills, that's why he's fitting. Dontcha know anything about the half-life?"

"Is that the sentence you got?" an officer said.

"His pills were stopped 'cos he wouldn't bloody swallow them - he hid them under his tongue. So it's his own bloody fault," Shauna snapped at the know-all scientist-prisoner. He shut up. She was angry, crouched on the hard concrete with a writhing prisoner. Blood and saliva glistened in tiny pools around her knee. She hated her job for the rest of the day. She lashed out at every whining clinic visitor, cursed every knock on the clinic door, yelling, "They can bloody wait." She was determined to finish every cigarette she lit, and that day she lit a lot.

"How dare that crim talk to me about the bloody half-life. Next thing he'll be telling you how to do yer friggin' research," she said.

"I wish he would," I said. "I could do with some advice."

"Everyone's a researcher, in their own way," Chia said sagely.

"Jesus," Shauna said, exasperated.

"Him too," Chia teased.

Chia was counselling a prisoner who was sent up the previous day from the psychiatric ward.

"Well you can't stay there forever," Chia told him. "The doctors thought you were right to leave the ward, so they sent you up here as a trial discharge, to see how you go."

"But I'm frightened."

I'd seen him yesterday, the slow one. His feet still shuffled gently under him as he spoke. Chia sent him on his way.

"I'll kill myself," the prisoner said, more out of habit than as a threat.

"Oh no you won't. You're on the right medication now," Chia said. Somehow the prisoner did not seem reassured. He had told me that he heard the voice of Satan, and had "visions from the Bible, like the book of Revelations - I see the end of the world. But my doctor told me I shouldn't talk about that sort of stuff. Sometime's I think I'm part of God's experiment, like this is all a test."

SARISHA, DIMITROV, AND THE PTERYGIUM

The yard was empty. No-one paced its uneven concrete, or leant against the red-brick walls. No shouts broke the morning stillness. Beyond a metal fence, a few workers were standing outside the butcher shop, their white overalls not yet red with blood from the carcasses hanging on hooks behind them.

The wings were eerily quiet, too. No sign of their inhabitants emerged from the three floors of barred windows. I felt alone with the day.

Down the palm-lined road beyond the wall, the officers were holding a stop-work meeting to protest at the recent closure of their canteen, where they were fed their daily fat: greasy hamburgers, pies and chips and cans of soft-drink. They used to gather there each lunch-break to read the sports pages and yarn about their bloody wives and girlfriends and their you-beaut Commodores and Falcons and the bloody governor and the bloody crims. From the plastic chairs, sweeping east, was a magnificent view of the ocean, shimmering and clear or hazy blue depending on the sun. No-one used to notice.

In the clinic, Chia was irritated by the delay in morning sick parade: the prisoners were not to be let go until the stop-work meeting was over. There was no officer to man the clinic so the prisoners on medications could not be called over for their dose.

"Bloody-minded - that's what it is," Chia said. He was against the unions. "Whatever happened to an honest day's work for an honest day's pay?"

When Chia had gone over to the deputy's office to request an officer for the clinic, he was told there was no-one available, despite the three or four blokes he saw "just sitting around over there, doing nothing. They wouldn't work in an iron lung, those fellows." Chia was usually unflappable, but this delay was all the more trying as it meant the clinic staff had to put up with the idle prattling of another replacement doctor, a woman named Sarisha, who was even less popular than old George. Sarisha was a small, bony GP with an enormous head which bobbed about in time with her sing-song speech.

"When's Nick coming back?" Shauna moaned, as Sarisha told us about her recent appearance in court as an "expert witness" in a rape case. Sarisha was so impressed with that legal designation she was wondering if she could append the letters "E.W." after her medical degree.

"They asked me the extent of damage this hussy may have suffered," Sarisha said. "I told them, as a doctor and as a mother, that this would depend on the size of the organ - it being well-known that the criminal penis is substantially larger than the membrum virile of a law-abiding citizen. But also relevant would be the duration and depth of penetration, the method of thrusting, and the capacity of the receptive vessel. As a woman of science, I find it salutary to reduce a biological process to its component parts in order to understand and predict its effects."

At last, the officers' meeting finished and they returned to their posts. They resolved that the canteen should be re-opened with inmate labour. The prisoners were soon let go, and the day's sick parade was under way.

Sarisha's pedantry, smugness, bobbing head and shrill sing-song antagonised every prisoner she saw. But this was not many: because of her need to repeat every question and the answer to every question before writing everything in the notes with her silver pen, only three prisoners of the ten on her list managed to be seen. Chia, who hovered at his desk in the corner behind the doctor's, was exasperated with Dr Sarisha, and barked questions at the patients over her shoulder. Chia would never do such a thing with Nick, whom he respected.

I snickered at this comical process of question and answer dutifully recorded to no purpose. Sarisha began with a diagnosis, or a prejudice, that every prisoner was malingering, which it was up to each to disprove. Of course, most succumbed through sheer weariness to her withering harangue, so her assumption was confirmed.

Everyone needs a hobby. Sarisha's hobby was fighting battles she could not lose. On her professional pedestal little Sarisha grew to gigantic size, like the criminal penis, and was unassailable. But her third patient, a middle-aged, stocky Slav named Dimitrov, who had seen doctors as bureaucratic as Sarisha in his native dictatorship, fought back. Dimitrov was too canny and persistent to fit this doctor's stereotype. Their voices were soon raised in frustration - a strange chorus of contrasting accents in soprano and baritone, a clash of habitus and history and aims.

Sarisha was unable to locate Dimitrov's doctor in the country by directory assistance.

"So you want tablets you don't know the name of which you say were prescribed by a doctor who doesn't exist," she smugly chanted. She felt she had won, and wrote the details down with satisfaction. But the Slav was dogged.

"Why write down his name if he doesn't exist?" Dimitrov retorted.

"I have to record the details in case you try to take me to court. Not that it would do you any good - I am an expert witness," Sarisha said proudly.

"Well my eyes are sore as well," Dimitrov said. The doctor did not look up from her primary task as scribe. "I need some drops for my eyes," Dimitrov said. Still there was no response. He implored: "You see my eyes?!"

The doctor slowly raised her quivering head, and removed her spectacles.

"You see MY eyes?" Sarisha mimicked. "They're worse than yours. You have a pterygium, and drops won't help."

She felt she had delivered a *coup de grace* - a spot diagnosis which the prisoner could not pronounce, let alone refute. And it was an axiom of Sarisha's prison practice that all prescription requests were vetoed.

"How old are you doctor?" Dimitrov asked quietly, after a pause. Sarisha was relaxed now, thinking this patient had surrendered and was seeking appeasement.

"How old do you think?"

"About sixty."

"Spot on."

But Sarisha had walked into a trap. This was a gambit in Dimitrov's middle game, sacrificing time for space. Now the Slav attacked: "You, doctor, are twenty years older than me, so you cannot compare your eyes to mine."

This disrespect was too much for the doctor.

"I'm referring you to a psychiatrist," Sarisha pronounced, with some sadistic relish.

"I am not an uneducated man, doctor," Dimitrov protested. "Just because I am behind these prison walls does not mean I have forgotten life beyond them - where a doctor tries to help."

Sarisha was already writing the referral request. Her head shook furiously as she dismissed her patient with a wave to the door. Dimitrov refused to leave. The doctor had not heard him out about his bleeding gums and the "cold and sharp" feeling in his side and his headaches. An officer approached and stood grimly behind Dimitrov. This was not a friendly officer. His muscles bulged, round and immense beneath his uniform, and I recalled the glistening slabs of meat hanging in the butcher shop. The officer's head moved slowly on his bull-neck. The tattoos on his forearms rippled as he pulled Dimitrov back in his chair. Dimitrov stood up and thanked the doctor and walked away.

"I'm sending that one to the psychiatric doctor," Sarisha said to the officer, by way of explanation.

The officer grinned and said: "No worries, doc. They're all spinners."

Dimitrov did not attend for his next appointment.

I had come to loathe this bull-necked officer. He was young and arrogant and a bully. He would hover around the clinic, cracking jokes about the crims or singing crude ditties. His favourite that week was sung to the tune of a Glen Campbell song. "Like a well-hung cowboy," it began, and did not get any better. This officer resented any assumption that the prisoners were meaner or tougher than him. He was frustrated by the fact that the prisoner was necessarily more free than his keeper, who must temper his aggression in the job of containing theirs. This officer never succumbed to his task as a role model of decency. He was angry that the crims were free - free to be wanton, hateful, rebellious. He told Shauna that the prisoners were "All fucked units. Why do you bother with them?"

"Why do you?" Shauna replied.

"Well, I'm here to keep them in their place, not to help them like you," he sneered.

I was disappointed when she agreed to go out with him "for a drink" after work that day.

MILESTONE AND WATERSHED

I reached a milestone, the two hundredth interview, with a thoughtful Arab prisoner, softly-spoken and gentle. When I asked him if he had ever heard voices when there was no-one around, he nodded and told me, "That is a very interesting question" at least five times before replying, "Maybe that happens when I am on the telephone, doctor."

At least this counted as data, which was more than I could say for my next attempt, a neat and anxious man who looked like he had changed from his city suit straight into the blue T-shirt and shorts. He checked twice whether the interview was compulsory before apologising: "I'm sorry, doctor. I can't consent. You see I'm waiting for the welfare officer. I don't know what to do. They haven't let me use the telephone since I was arrested. This place... I don't know what I'm doing here..."

My smile when he mentioned the telephone made him even more nervous. I gave up, and interrupted his babble to usher him back to the holding cell. That was as long a hearing as they got from me - unless they consented to the interview. "Don't do the crime if you can't do the time," I thought. He counted as refusal number 21 - still just ten per cent overall.

Most prisoners - even other first-timers - were more stoic about what they faced inside. Some, like Paul, knew exactly what to expect. He was poised for a fight.

"The bloke who set me up is still on remand," he said. "One of us'll end up on that stretcher, and it won't be me."

Dennis, too, thought there was something in store for him out there, in the remand yard. He awaited a brutal reprisal for dogging on his mates after prison riots more than a decade ago. An unruly beard all but covered his face. He pointed to a ragged scar which sliced his nose into two fleshy promontories. "They mightn't reckon this was enough to teach me a lesson," he said. He was shifted to protection, but figured there were enough crims there with long memories. "They'll always get you, in the end. The worst thing is me missus - she's shit-scared."

Dennis told me he was picked up for driving while disqualified.

"They got me around the corner from me house, driving back from weekend detention. But I had no way of gettin' there without a car. The missus don't drive. And if yer don't turn up for weekend detention, yer land in here anyway. This'll make it a bloody long weekend, that's for sure."

The nurses had a few regulars whom they loathed, like Enrico, an ageing South American Communist homosexual murderer with an indwelling catheter. This plastic tube was the nurse's bane.

"He never looks after it. Always complains that it's blocked just so we strip him and touch his penis. He's disgusting," Shauna said.

"*Viva la revolutione!*" Enrico would bellow theatrically. He had learnt that at Communist worker's demonstrations in Peru. Hair grew in thick tufts from his ears and nose.

"You bloody fascists!" he yelled as the nurses demanded he leave the clinic.

Their greatest loathing was for the men from protection and strict protection. It was as though the nurses identified with the other prisoners in their contempt for these "dogs and rock-spiders." Shauna despised the obsequious pederasts most of all. There was one, a diabetic known only as Mr Cardigan, who knew every hour's blood sugar reading for the last week. He always seemed on the verge of tears, and simpered like a spoilt school-girl. He had been on anti-depressants for years, but none of them worked.

"Doctor, do you believe in this Chronic Fatigue Syndrome?" he asked.

"I keep an open mind," I said. "Never know when CFS might come in handy for me."

The only chemical change that would have helped him was a macromolecular paradigm shift: a new brain. His fondest adult memories were of the psychiatric wards.

"They looked after me there. It was a home away from home. I wish I could be back there now. Can you contact them for me?"

I didn't bother to reply. He was a born victim who expected to arouse disdain in everyone, including himself. Why should I be any different?

We notice change in others, but seldom see the changes in ourselves. How had these prison days, these two hundred prisoners, affected me? I was adrift in a psychological picaresque, amassing interviews. The prisoners' fecklessness was contagious, a constant beckoning to entropy which the prison walls were erected to contain. Its bulwark seemed to hold firm - from the outside. Like some medieval castle, this walled city squatted on a rise near the ocean. It was unassailable, with a commanding height on cliffs jutting sheer from the sea, and exuding a solidity and menace to blunt any assault. Its barbed wire and high walls broke the surrounding sweep of open land, an imperious blot on local geography. The citizens of nearby suburbs saw only the slow parade of sentries along their posts between the watch-towers at each corner of the wall. There were no other signs of human activity. From a distance, these guardians of the social order looked grim and determined; close-up, they looked bored. Just as on the outside, all seemed as it should be in the corrective service scheme of things. No prisoners clambered from the walls, no smoke of prison riots billowed above the ramparts, no shots rang out over the prison, which appeared calm and resolute, like a known machine. But the prisoners' lives were chaotic. The numbering, sorting, classification, mustering and marshalling gave only a semblance of control. Behind high walls they could not see the sun setting on the horizon or rising from it, the opening and closing of each day, another closer to release. Once a prisoner was outside, each day of freedom brought him closer to return, to his next lag.

"Done five years - got out three months ago. But I can't stay off the heroin on the streets. No hope. They just kick us out of here and we fall in a heap. No fuckin' rehab. They should've sent me to hospital, not some fuckin' half-way house full of crims. I can't cop another laggin'. It'll be the end of me."

I only heard one side of his story, but this odyssey, told by him, echoed so many more. "I'm a fuckin' junkie. Just social junk," he said.

The shaven head, the tear-drop tattoo, the body quivering in withdrawal - this cannot be seen from the suburbs beyond the walls.

INTERVIEW

Your time begins. You are in jail. You have put yourself behind bars, again or for the first time, and you loll in the cage. I walk to its metal bars. I wonder what you are staring at, up there in the near corner, beyond my gaze. Your mouth gapes and your neck is arched. Then I hear the voices - it is television, and you are under its influence. This is not yet an offence, as long as you did not steal the set. I interrupt your viewing for a chat. Your many heads reply with the same refusal, an identical contempt.

"What's this all about?"

"Look, the cops just verballed me, so I ain't signin' nothin'."

"Wot's in it for me?"

In the face of this chorus of resentment, I wonder why I bother, but I drone out my plea. And all eleven sign today, because my sales pitch is perfect. I accept all objections, and nod in grave empathy, although not too solemn in case I appear mocking. Each man is heard out. I glance at the list of names unobtrusively, so I can call each prisoner separately, and speak to him as an individual. Sometimes, I apologise for talking like a robot, but that is just the way I feel, and I apologise for the more inane questions which nevertheless it is my duty to ask in the name of science. When the more querulous or intelligent subjects find fault with my technique, I thank them for their views.

"Please shit on me - I relish your contempt," I say. And: "There is no perfect questionnaire, no unqualified question has ever been asked. It all depends."

Despite the scorn, if I maintain a dialogue, consent eventually follows, and answers after that, and I am one step closer to my target: six hundred interviews completed. Into the Valley of Death they ride, the brave six hundred, and I am at their head, but I shall fear no evil, for I am the meanest bastard in the Valley. I am biding my time. My revenge for all the scorn comes with the very last question on my screen, my favourite.

"Have you ever felt, for two weeks or more, like you were useless, sinful, or guilty?" It ends on that note, that inflexion, "guilty?"

You can quickly say no. The interview is complete. Or you may pause, then nod, admitting defeat. I will accept your resignation. Cowed, you are led back to your cell, back to where you came from.

PRISON GOTHIC

Remand prison was as impersonal as death, but its prisoners were not yet dead. These unsentenced ghouls inhabited a legal twilight, a living purgatory, poised at the edge of a gaping judicial chasm. Before this Fall, they were neither innocent nor guilty. Below, in the belly of the pit, crouched an abysmal, grinding mechanism to which they were inexorably summoned.

So the remand prisoner awaited his trial, his battle with the Angel of Justice. And on each morning of the trial, regardless of its duration, the prisoner must depart his cell as though never to return, his belongings placed in storage to comply with prison protocol.

That Angel of Justice was too wise for absolutes. Her rulings signified a social decree. The truth will out, but not all the way - just beyond reasonable doubt. That was far enough to fling a prisoner over the walls of remand to his allotted penitentiary, to repent, pent up and penitent. Nothing lasts for long these days, except a prison sentence.

The next list of new receptions to remand filled a whole page. At this rate, I would soon reach the three hundred mark. I looked down the column of names. Bail had been refused for men from a smorgasbord of nations. They were to await her Majesty's judgement in her Majesty's corrective complex, whose lintel bore a sandstone coat of arms inscribed "Honi soit qui mal y pense" between rampant lion and unicorn. Republican prisoners needed protection from the Loyalist majority. They would have lynched Prince Charles's would-be assassin armed with his puny pop-gun, if he had been incarcerated here. Allegiances to Monarchy were proudly displayed.

The crimson stripe of active duty in Vietnam above an officer's left breast signified his imperial service. He cupped his cigarette as he inhaled, eyes narrowed to a slit, as though shielding its flame from the enemy's sight. Death still lurked unseen in the jungle of his nocturnal horrors, and his prison days resembled a war. Each tour of duty unfolded as long hours of tedium, broken by a flash, a surge of violent action. But the tedium took a greater toll. This was where the nerves were frayed, where the mind played twisted tricks, drenching the soldier in a lather of his sweat.

The officer did not mind opening the gate a dozen times for me to lure my subjects.

"That's what we're here for, doc," he said. He offered to call the next name for me, but I preferred to do that myself, to stay in control and avoid giving prisoners the impression that I was part of the corrective service. I told them that I was not part of any system, neither medical nor custodial nor judicial. In fact, I was free and independent, just like them.

Although free, I was not free of doubt. The tension in my practice of psychiatric research was between the idiographic and the nomothetic, the subjective and the objective, the qualitative and the quantitative. I was not there to make friends or write a book. The simple purpose of completing my allotted interviews, of finishing this study, dictated that impersonal numerology triumphed over the individual, private suffering of every man I saw. How could it be otherwise?

"I wouldn't interest you, doc. I'm not crazy," one prisoner asserted.

"Ah, but you are important statistically. It's like a census. Everybody must be counted, because everybody counts," I reassured him.

Of course, the prisoner was right. He did not interest me, any more than a production line robot is interested in its production. I was weary of their tales of woe. But he could help me, by adding his autograph to my collection. I thanked him for his time; he had plenty of it. This work was no rort. It was research - serious stuff.

A few prisoners refused to be relegated to the common denominator of my equation, to be dehumanised for the sake of science. They did not acknowledge my importance, recognising only their own. The boot was on the other foot, kicking down my castle, denting my cockiness. What did that make me? We all must struggle with issues of self-love and self-hate. Boundless in his narcissism, or bound up in it, one such man told me:

"You don't need to ask no bloody questions. I'll tell you all you need to know about prison. Been here on and off for ten years. It's all up here."

He tapped his shaven head, and directed his opaque gaze through the back of mine, like a dismissal of my very presence. His monologue was deadpan. This tough guy was an utter prison product, an animal returning to its pen. The sabre-tooth tiger was depicted on cave walls - captured in symbol by the pre-historic artist - to render the beast harmless. In metaphor, then, I sought to tame the tough guy, to counter his malice by naming. I saw him as ridiculously venomous, pathetic, a caricature of malignity, an empty self-parody, a surly act. Sam would have called him a plastic gangster. These notions soothed me, by distancing him, and his threat. He became less real. The tough guy said little, answering slowly as some mark of his control. Timing is everything when you're playing a part.

His bottom lip was blistered. Where its scabs were broken, a shiny discharge glistened. A plaster cast protruded beneath the sleeve of his blue sloppy joe.

"What happened to you arm?" I asked.

"It broke," he said, impersonal even to himself. There may have been pain, an object struck, a snapping sound of bone. Who cares? Things break.

"Prison is a disgrace," he said. I did not disagree. "You might wanna discuss my case with that female psychologist I saw at the country prison. She was very interested in my personality. And I know you doctors always need a second opinion." This was not so much spoken as sneered. Then he left, a slow, measured gait, arms held away from his torso, swinging from the shoulders, another man in blue with an animal charm.

Like the female psychologist before me, I could not dismiss him. He had made an impact. We were engrossed in his B-grade existence, fascinated despite our better judgement by his hubris. I clutched a fragment of his life, before the detail faded. I held the jagged piece between fore-finger and thumb, gingerly so as not to pierce my skin. Blood would fog the lens. I twisted the shard this way and that, rotating and tilting to see the shafts of light enter and emerge, mesmerised. There were no colours in this prison of a thousand prisms whose adamantine facets cleaved wholly into good or evil all reflected rays. No spectrum filled the space from black to white. That fragment - its living stuff of experience, memory, feeling -

was polarised. The macrocosm is in the microcosm: no part of that man's self was touched by rainbow hues. At the heart of his crude menace lay an intensity of suffering too primitive for words, which fact may be difficult to appreciate as he rapes and bashes you. Let us paint it on a cave, before he is extinct.

His broken bone was reduced according to orthopaedic principles, by which its cortex would knit, only for another bone to break or be broken by the intact arm as weapon.

A needle punctured his skin that night. Its temporary impression became another scab between the images in ink. But they too would fade in time. Even the letters tattooed over each knuckle - LOVE and HATE - would not last forever. Nothing does. When tattooed tears evaporate, the skin will return to innocence. This man too was born an unnamed baby, wailing. Whatever struck the fragment will ricochet, light retraced to ultimate solar origins.

Ten years of prison had brought him a conviction of knowledge. He harboured the very truth of this place, and railed against that "truth in sentencing" which gave him nothing to lose. But he would never lose the way which led him again, via temptation, into prison, as surely as love touched hate when his fists collided. Worlds apart will meet in the end.

ADDICTION

The days weighed down, one upon the one before, a press of time unbroken. Do the tone-deaf abhor a monotone? Do the colour-blind thrill to plastic flowers? Prison unleashed longings, desires never gratified. The men became sick with yearning, aching for a woman's body, or Lady Love in powdered form, crushed, dissolved, injected, and rushing to oblivion. Few addicts counted themselves as "cured". That old yearning welled up, like waters before a dam. Only its outward manifestations were suppressed - for a while. Fulfilment may be thwarted, but the urge to be fulfilled remained. If you look at it as a pathological appetite, those victims "present year after year the unchanging spectacle of their odd and unaccountable habits, which they constantly imagine themselves to be on the point of shaking off but which they always retain to the end; caught in the treadmill of their own maladies and eccentricities, their futile endeavours to escape serve only to actuate its mechanism, to keep in motion the clockwork of their strange, ineluctable and baneful dietetics."*

----

* from page 184 of 'Remembrance of Things Past: Volume One' by Marcel Proust, translated by C.K. Scott Moncrieff and Terence Kilmartin, published by Penguin Books, 1983.

But this is the wrong way to look at it. It is not the appetite that is pathological, but the demand for its gratification. After all, who is not bathed in a soup of urge and temptation and desire? Even as you read this soothing tome, a thousand shrill hearkenings disrupt your consciousness from within a body in apparent repose, for like the prisoner's your body too is ceaseless in its coiling, reacting, sensing, wanting. It is a miracle that anything productive happens, in between such urgent intrusions. The universal Eros, the driven nature of being, extracts a price. (Lacan understood this better than anyone. It is just a pity that Lacan himself is so difficult to understand.)

What counts is the capacity for restraint, a tolerance of frustration. This is one of the core values of psychoanalysis, and it comes hard up against the prisoner's inarticulate world, consumed by and immersed in the madness of the Lacanian real. This is also known as a 'one person world', or a state of 'psychic equivalence', where mental life is itself still-born. Metaphor and symbol have not been achieved, and the psychopath exudes pure menace. Why challenge that? He is not capable of compromise, nor can his original trauma be identified and dissected, for the trauma has the same function as steel bars through a slab of concrete: it has been absorbed into the psychic structure as a reinforcing mesh.

So you find that the addict cannot recover, because the term addiction mistakes the intensity of drive for the necessity of its gratification. Separate the two, and you discover your view of the addict shifts from seeing the suffering of a victim, to the tantrums of an overgrown infant, which itself is a repetition of deprivation. Or, to complicate matters, the re-enactment of a depriving object relation. The addict lacks something. He tells you he lacks the object of his addictive desire. But in truth, he lacks the internal structure to resist that desire, and thus to feel. He is the only person in his world, which defines it as loveless.

When a prisoner demanded "rehab", he was begging for release. His was a voice from the abyss, the bottomless pit they called "rock-bottom", arising as forlorn plea: "I cannot stop myself from falling." Too bad this is not a dream. It is as real as those prison walls, behind which a needle could be sought, or shunned. But once outside, that needle must be sought, without delay, without alternative. Resistance dissolved in chemical craving, involuted men succumbed to an inexorable formulation. They had turned away from life and from themselves. They had chosen to specialise: all drives reduced to one. Their virility was surrendered to narcosis. Junkies could form a clinic for early male menopause, if they cared.

"I'd rather have a fix than a woman."

"When I'm on smack, sex means nothing to me."

"It kills your sex drive, doc. Just overpowers everything."

Life was simpler that way, with other appetites dimmed, until only the intravenous thrill remained. Weight fell away. The girlfriend could join in and be hooked, or leave. Nothing else mattered in this surrender to one shrill priority.

When the supply dried up, a thousand nerve endings would transmit their synaptic rage: "Feed me! Feed me!" A starving chorus, another chemical imperative. This enervated, and chastened, the victim. With continued abstinence, his guts are wracked with spasm, their borborygmi* an intestinal echo of the cry for relief. Sweat

---

* a medical term for the rumbling of bowels

is secreted from shivering flesh, and mucous from his nose. This happened soon after arrival in prison. They begged for methadone, valium, rivotril, relief or satisfaction, but most were given an unappetising cocktail of anti-spasmodics and anti-epileptics and anti-depressants. This pissed them off. They did not believe in medical lore that "Withdrawal only lasts a few days. It's no worse than the flu," or that their writhing and moaning was melodrama. They should read the text-book. An autonomic nervous rebound was to be expected once the dampening effects of opiates were removed - to be expected and endured. If there was no longer honour among thieves, at least could there be some manly stoicism?

THE RETURN OF THE REPRESSED

At first I did not recognise my next subject as he approached me from the holding cell. This was a different-looking man from the proud prisoner I had met all those months ago. His skin appeared almost grey, his face lean and deeply riven, and his body haggard, but he exuded an ironic decadence as though he had never been more at ease. I was appalled at the appearance of his Adam's apple, which jutted and bobbed obscenely like a pig's knuckle pressed against the tense cage of his sinewy throat. He inhaled through the stem of a wooden pipe. He exhaled. He blinked. He spoke.

"This is about mental health, mmm?"

"Yes, Mr, ah." I glanced at my list. He said his name quietly:

"Gramsci. Antonio Gramsci."

We hung in silence for a while, as the smoke from his pipe hung in the air above us. The officer at the gate of the holding cell became impatient.

"He's a C.O.C., doc - change of classification. So he's not a fresh one. Been in prison for years already. Do yer still wanna see him?"

"Ah, sure." I needed data. The officer nodded Gramsci through. Gramsci brushed past us and led the way down the corridor to the clinic.

"'Not a fresh one' indeed. What does he take me for - a fruit?" he said in a tone of indignation, but again he sounded amused.

I beckoned him to my office and tried to present my little speech, to take refuge in my routine. He cut me short with a wave of his pipe. I felt my will dissolve, my self becoming as amorphous as the smoke he exhaled. All attempts at intimacy with Gramsci must overcome an initial abhorrence. But I was drawn towards him, inhaled, a vertiginous drift, succumbing. I was in an instant stripped of professional trappings. He spoke again:

"Well, I'm no different to any other revolutionary poet or political prisoner. We're all insane. Language addles us, and our lyric is a toxin to society. It poisons the technological zeitgeist. All we can hope is that some of the poison remains in the soil after we die. Even Mayakovsky shot himself, after twenty years of work."

Gramsci handed me a consent form which bore his moniker.

"Where did you get that?" I asked.

"Same place you got yours," Gramsci replied.

"But I got mine from the professor."

Gramsci smiled. Prison had taught me to ask few questions outside the structured script of my research. If you ask questions, all you get are answers.

Now sitting opposite me was the oddest prisoner I had ever seen. His body had crumpled in on itself, his head was perched almost horizontal to his frame, as if that hunchback had simply engulfed his form, and his legs were entwined. He resembled a living question mark, rocking gently at the end of a line on a page without words. And although wearing regulation prison blue, he looked almost elegant in the precise cut of his trousers and the fit of his sloppy joe. He wore a slim, black, leather arm-band.

He caught me staring at it. "Yes, it is a *memento mori* for a dog about to die," he said.

This made no sense to me at all, so I tried to begin my interview.

"Some questions…is that all right? Not too much to ask?" I stammered.

"Carry on, doctor, with number two hundred and thirty-seven in your study. After all we have been through together, we two, I am reduced to this - just another data set for you to collect and collate, on your way to six hundred. More dead facts. Factory fodder for the production line of the capitalist's will to power. You seek to murder me with sameness, that repetition expressing death, technology, trauma. Like a malignant proliferation, we are all the same to you, from our undifferentiated prison cells. Consult Oswald Spengler's 'Decline of the West'* if you have doubts of your own: we live in an age of technic, not lyric; an age when the West is in glorious free-fall, an oblivious descent. That should be clear enough. All else follows, including the argument of Herbert Marcuse˜ that technology itself is an expression of the death drive, of *thanatos*^: results are all that matters, and the repetition of a process. Please don't accord me any favours. I am a

---

* The Decline of the West, by Oswald Spengler, published by Alfred A. Knopf, 1926

˜ Eros and Civilisation, by Herbert Marcuse, Abacus, 1972

^ the death drive, described by Freud in his paper 'Beyond the Pleasure Principle' as contrasted with Eros

prisoner, hence a man without culture or grace, lacking subtlety, *sans* aesthetic sensibility. An ignorant and self-ignorant felon."

After this strange speech, Gramsci spoke only to give careful and concise answers to each item of my structured interview. His acquiescence must have disarmed me, as though all knowledge of his duplicitous ways dissolved from my mind. As I shut down my computer at the end of the interview, so too was my wariness shut down, my disbelief suspended. My survival instinct gave way to the need for attachment - I just wanted to be able to trust this dear fellow. Trust is too much to ask for, but I gave it up. I wanted to feel that whatever damage we had inflicted each upon the other, there was some means of repair. I was in the thrall of my own need for love, a dangerous fantasy to sustain in prison. Gramsci was again able to exert that familiar spell over me, as a cruel mother might exert over her helpless infant.

"You ask me all these questions. You ask them again and again, of all the prisoners here," Gramsci said and tapped the grey plastic lid of my lap-top computer "You think that there, right there, you have the answers. But you must look within – here." And he laid his hand upon my forehead. I felt a wonderful relief, right then, as though some cosmic bioenergy had transferred itself.

He continued, with his palm resting against my skin: "And yet you do not see what is most crucial to see: the answers lie within. It is you who must succumb."

What I was unable to see was again how I was being drawn into the Gramsci histrionic. His gesture of the hand upon my forehead I recalled as Freud's initial hypnotherapeutic technique, which later gave way to free association. Gramsci continued:

"The need for some salvation, some escape; for some freedom, some release. This is such a human need. It aches. It pleads…"

His rhetoric washed over me, bathing me in its anodyne intonations. And his commands were so deftly insinuated into my subconscious that I was later to carry them out like an automaton. He had reversed our roles: I was hypnotised. A part of Gramsci's mental apparatus was lodged within mine, where it was to lie dormant until a time predetermined for its release. I would follow his subliminal instructions, whose mission overwhelmed my own faltering and becalmed agency.

I recall clearly his last words to me: "You need a break, doctor. You are becoming insensitive. Do not worry. I am not trying to help you."

I thanked Gramsci for his time, and ushered in my next prisoner. All the while, I was consumed by that one thought: a break, what a fine idea. This work was getting to me. Yes, I was becoming insensitive, burnt out. Gramsci's words echoed in my head as a confusing plea for freedom. Mine or his?

I would walk the prison wall's perimeter, pace out the measures of containment in my own parade, a march of freedom in the shadow of the sentry. No, I would not have the walls come tumbling down - unleashing mayhem at the clarion of trumpets - because I marched under a peculiar banner in silent celebration of one man's temporary release. This path I trod led nowhere. A quirky, solitary trek was my choice in this prison year, the strangest of my life, and I never felt so free as then. I never was so free. It was a year free of patients. There was no-one to look after but myself. Unlike the doctor for his patients, the researcher is not responsible for his subjects.

I felt irresponsible. And it was a year free to observe the self and other and to leave my personal mark upon the walls, tracing out in hand-prints something unique, idiosyncratic, human.

When on my walk I recognised a prisoner and greeted him by name, he said with some surprise: "Geez, doc, you've got a good memory." Every man who signed my duplicate consent form left his own immortal impression on the wall I was erecting. This signature on a document was an ethical requirement, to be witnessed by prisoner, researcher, and nurse or sweeper.

When any prisoner left the jail - other than by escape - he required a warrant in triplicate to be signed at each post through which he must pass, to court or transfer or for an X-ray or even freedom. The movement of human cargo was closely monitored, because each body was valuable, in a bodiless, legalistic and custodial sense. This body, this sentenced unit, must serve more time behind these walls. It will be fed and sheltered. When its time is done, it must leave.

The professor handed me a leave form even before I needed to ask. I was too addled to notice that the dates had been completed already, and she waited patiently for my signature. My hand shook as I handed her back the document.

"Enjoy your little holiday," she said, smiling.

Dr King offered to continue my research while I was away. Everyone was being so helpful to me today. Of course I refused, as he was no doubt seeking to worm his name onto my publications.

"Too bad," he said. "Could be a chance to interview a few more of those attempted escapees returning through remand. Interesting chaps. Derring-do, eh what?"

"What are you talking about, Dr King?"

"Haven't you heard? The break-out attempt. Old Gramsci was apparently the ring-leader, the five-eighth, you know, calling the shots - trying to tunnel out of the place. Bloody good attempt, by all accounts. Almost made it. Seems they had some inside assistance – maps and diagrams of the sewage system, all those pipes to tunnel into. The governor is furious," Dr King said. "He may even demand your clinical notes on Gramsci's therapy. Seems to think you must have known about the whole plot, and should have notified the authorities. Preposterous, isn't it? We try to help, and all we get is blamed when something goes wrong. Cheer up, enjoy your break. It'll do you good. Pip-pip."

Dr King was a pompous and condescending fool. His toffee elocution irritated me beyond measure, and it took all my patience to remain within earshot of him. But this news was stunning. Gramsci's re-classification through remand made sense now, as did his haggard appearance; digging that tunnel had worn him out. What did I care if he fell in a heap? Enough, my mind was made up. I was out of there. This was my escape, not his.

THE BREAK,
A BARK, BAROQUE

Leaving prison, I felt lost, as though a protector had been forsaken. What did I want with this sudden freedom? Prison took all comers. It fed and clothed and sheltered and numbered them, a haven from urban anonymity. Prison gave a place. You were accounted for and someone cared if you were not present, because an escape meant more paperwork.

And my paperwork was progressing so well, the research proceeding as planned. With this week away from my laboratory would I lose my way? I reckoned that I would miss thirty prisoners as they entered prison's maw, beneath the red brick gums, and the grinning teeth of coiled razor wire. My work would be interrupted. This being science, I could not extrapolate to fill the gap. There was no place for speculation at the shapes and stories of those prisoners I'd miss, each one slightly different. Perhaps I should have engaged Dr King to carry it on.

Would my prisoners miss me? The professor had reassured me: "This place will be unchanged on your return. You need a holiday. Relax. The flow of prisoners continues, even as we sleep."

She had an oracular way with words. I took a break, and felt the nakedness of being on the outside. I was at a loss.

Perhaps this was the despair that Blind Freddy had so doggedly attempted to evoke in me: that despair that he insisted must be my deepest response to the abandonment experience of his holiday breaks during our analytic relationship.

"You must remember how your mother locked you in the laundry when you were a toddler," he said before one such holiday, with baleful emphasis.

"Listen, I don't know if that ever happened. Leave off on my mother, all right?" I replied, getting cranky.

"You are avoiding your feelings," he concluded.

I fell silent, waiting for the end of the session. But all I could ever feel was relief while he was away. His absence meant a temporary reprieve from the struggle to get across town to his rooms, the struggle through each tedious session, and the struggle to pay.

But where Blind Freddy had failed, it was Antonio Gramsci, curse him, who had forced me to acknowledge the collapse of my own narcissistic alter egos. An array of heroes were shown to have feet of clay: those intellectual warriors, those mighty conquerors of the mental sphere, each turning out to be nuts, crackers, crazy…crazy with narcissistic rage. In an awareness of his own craziness, of his own burden of fanaticism, each of my heroes toppled from his pedestal. The fall of a father could never have brought with it such a resounding crash, nor the fall of a god, or devil. And yet, once freed of the ideals, I found I was no longer burdened with others' expectations, with the intrusive dictates of reputation. I was free, and necessarily unhinged. But I could not tolerate this state, and almost as soon as it was brought about, I sought out some source of certainty, some solace, another prison. Curious turn, that, for this desperation returned me to my own source. I merged with Gramsci, as what I thought I had despised now revealed itself as a solace to me. So the hero was constructed out of a need for some escape, but he was left with only escape, and no substance…escape, but with nowhere to run, and no return to an old way of being which was no longer available. We are always under a gaze of our own fearful projections.

I took slow steps to nowhere, on the other side, now free or so I thought. I was beyond the pale, walking anti-clockwise, until a sudden stop. Some clock had struck its moment within me. Gramsci's hypnotic grip held me paralysed. I leant against the wall for steadying, and for a moment wondered at this limbo: excluded, yet not game to venture further out. I was circumnavigating the prison wall. This made no sense.

My perceptions were playing tricks. Some strange figure loomed. Was this the ghost of prisoners released, an eternally recurring recidivist? Was this an effigy of my self-sameness of being? A ghost can merge, but cannot wonder, lacking the cortical substrate of cognition, and the limbic substrate of emotion. Unless, of course, a ghost - being wholly of the mind - is pure thought and feeling and no matter. Let him be a prisoner haunted and haunting, loitering and dawdling, to dog my first day of freedom. There is no need to hurry when a sentence is infinite, an endless string of hours, days, words and silences.

I stooped to pick up shards of rock, litter and junk along the way, and flung them out to sea to sink or float like some encapsulated thing, whose drifted circumnavigation ends where it begins, as if forever present. *'What is going on, what is happening to me?'* some vestigial sentience enquired, that last fragment of my fragmenting ego.

From that place decreed by time, a trajectory is captured in ceaseless orbit, following circles full circle to the next ripple on the pond of space expanding Ad Infinitum and beyond measure until the man and his walled circumference at the centre of a universe have disappeared. No great loss. It is the thought that counts the days and asks: Is there black within this hole, or merely the meander of a prisoner in blue?

A dog wandered up at random and sniffed the strangeness of my ghostly presence, because a dog could tell these things, and cocked a leg to piss.

"A man's best friend is his enemy," I said. In a haze of paranoid panic, I saw again Gramsci's black arm-band; he had told me a dog was to die. He told me, but now I felt he commanded me…Something snapped.

I grabbed the playful dog and swung it by the tail, barking and yelping in accelerating orbit, and dashed its snout and skull against the prison wall. There was no sound now. My thoughts quietened. I looked in horror at the carcass of that dog. 'What have I done?' I murmured, as though returning from a coma to the known world. I sensed that I had been subject to some experiment, whose final results were not yet concluded. What next would be released from that hypnotic capsule which Gramsci had planted within my mind? I was not myself.

I saw myself in court, and imagined a futile plea: "That mongrel dog pissed on me."

"Guilty," pronounced his Honour, and passed sentence to be served behind those walls.

"Please do not send me back inside. Leave me here, in imagined freedom. Do not forsake me for a dog. I'll do anything to make it up to you, to atone. I promise. I'll conjure up horrific sounds, unspeakable visions, harsh sentience for your nightly infotainment, but please don't imprison me. I will fascinate you with the metaphor of prison. Its richness will sink into your mind, dominate your fantasy, and you will experience its ruse and muse while I toil at description, a virtual tedium and brutality. Do not condemn me to the actual. Accept this promise, I implore you. Have mercy."

The judge suspended disbelief and sentence. "This is a good-behaviour bond," he said. "But I warn you, if you fail to titillate my colleagues and I each and every evening, you will receive a custodial sentence."

His honour was not disappointed, and from then on his repasts resounded with mirth, with the wobbling of generous jowls, and the stentorian guffaw of fellow magistrates stuffing the collective gob and quaffing at the Bar. I was relieved to be free, but my victim the dog was dead.

This break was becoming too Baroque. It would break me, and be the end of me as I know him. Was this a psychotic break? My will had been flung about like some manic pinball, between the first person and the third, subject and object, between me and a crazed introject. This was worse than being duped, because I wasn't even sure that it was me that this was happening to. But if not me, then to whom?

The notion of a horizontal split in the mind was Freud's original topographical model. Repression defined what lay below the split as unconscious and above it, as conscious. A vertical split is trickier still, with separate aspects of the self dissociating, breaking apart. I felt like I had both vertical and horizontal splits within me, like a cross-word whose clues I could not decipher because the very letters were in some arcane alphabet. Perhaps Gramsci could translate me to myself. I had become dependent upon him, puppet to the puppet-master.

I longed for something known: a fact. I was not guilty of the murder of that dog, but in denying that guilt I was attempting to deny not just a fact but also a feeling, for I had never felt more guilty in my life. I longed for the security of prison.

ANOTHER CASUALTY

I ran and ran from the scene of my own bizarre crime, leaving the prison grounds far behind, and arrived at last in town. I recognised a prisoner on the street, one of the subjects of my study, now a free citizen, albeit one with a record and a bond and probably on parole. Seeing him came as some relief: it reminded me of my work and my place. He was hunched and walking quickly, with an intensity of purpose as though about to break into a run, or a house. He belonged in these hard streets, as he had belonged in prison. I had recognised his face despite an urban anonymity which helped cover his tracks, blur his features, negate his presence. This was a valuable quality - a criminal does not want to stand out in the crowd, unless he is a Mr Big. And he was wearing a blue T-shirt, out of allegiance or habit. Either way, it was an unimaginative sartorial selection.

I had interviewed him in my research, but all details were forgotten. At the time, recognition brought no name, or feature, only the simple fact of deja vu. But writing this I now recall a slowness of reply, an immaturity, almost naive. He had looked young and pathetic, barely man enough for the six digits foisted onto him by the corrective services computer. The sentence may be short, but the ID number would be his for life and he would surely need it again. Only his death would prevent another lag.

He scurried past a poster about condoms and needles for prisoners, but he did not pause to consider it. Nor did he notice me trailing him; he was too pre-occupied, perhaps with meeting a dealer for a fix. That was a likely motivation for his haste along a dirty street. This might have been his first score since release. I followed him to an alleyway of rubble, scattered cats, and garbage between crooked galvanised tin and paling fences, and watched him enter the back gate of a grotty terrace, and hand over cash for a small lump of foil. This was the journey, then, that I had been drawn into, this forlorn repetition, out of habit.

I heard later from Nick, the prison GP, how this prisoner/citizen was quickly caught in another swing of the revolving door: as patient.

"Stop! I wanna get off," he yelled.

He alighted in Casualty, on an ambulance trolley, kind of asleep, early one morning. Nick worked there, doing some real medicine on his days off from the prison clinic to keep his skills up, as skills atrophy behind prison walls

There is no more perfect solitude than that of sleep, and no sleep more perfect than that of the dead. The Casualty doctor working the graveyard shift became more dead than alive, but sleep was denied. This then was the meeting of two ghouls. Chipping away at the coal-face of humanity, sunk down a pit where all is in gloom, voices were subdued, and the drip of seeping water rang shrill. Water and blood: both were spilled freely, the only difference here was that blood left a stain.

Weary as hell, meeting the twilight with exhaustion and relief, Nick slumped over coffee. Twilight - dusk and dawn as twins. At this hour, all differences blurred - sleeping and waking, living and dying, water and blood, night and day.

Lively sounds roused him. Voices - real voices, not the late, late, late movie. And the sound of our prisoner's body - a deadweight, without tone or resistance - hitting a metal trolley, then the slam of plastic curtains parting as he was wheeled in to the resuscitation cubicle. Nick stood up, and saw another blue junkie. He too recognised the kid from the prison clinic. Nick picked up his stethoscope. From forked ear-pieces, a black tube tapered to a gleaming stainless steel case for its listening apparatus, where the doctor's initials were inscribed. This was a graduation present from proud parents, but Nick used it now more as a reassurance of power and control than for diagnosis.

"He's pretty far gone, doc," the para-medic said, briskly pumping the scrawny chest. Sometimes ribs were broken - a small price to pay for saving a life. Blue was discolouring the prisoner's flesh, deepening to aubergine around the lips. Blue. Blue tainted the border between life and death. For Nick, this was an exercise in colours: bring the patient back, and he'll be pink again, let him go - ashen or grey. Nick looked out the window, above the blue junkie, where golden twilight had given way to perfect blue sky, and he sighed with weariness and the anticipated pleasure of a day at the beach, before turning efficiently to his task.

When the vein was cannulated, and shot full of naloxone, the junkie sat bolt upright. They were always testy when revived: it was an instant cold turkey. Nick might have saved a life, but he'd ruined a fantastic hit, and replaced it with opiate craving and rage. This prisoner junkie was typical. He ripped the plastic tubes from his arms, and the oxygen mask from his face, and bolted out the door, leaving a crimson trail. Then he headed back onto the streets, clutching the cannula into his vein because that would give him great access for the next few days until blood clots and infection clogged it up.

A few days later, near the end of my break, his life ended when he took one overdose too many. He was slumped in a single room with bed and sink not unlike his prison cell had been, but costing fifteen dollars a night - cheapest rates in town, he was told, but didn't believe it, believed nothing, this kid - but it'll do and that flashing neon outside the window he liked, adding a touch of grim urban verisimilitude, as if he needed it, like the cheap movies so he could pretend he was a fallen star here with his head bowed onto his chest and his arm crooked so the needle reached his vein for his last rush to shoot him high, as high as this fall.

A siren wailed brief requiem under his window, as he lay dying, before it trailed off into the night, towards someone else's resuscitation. He got off there, his last stop, the end of the line. The door revolved through an underbelly of city streets, that big revolving door like a threshing machine, the same signs at every stop, of squandered lives spent between street and bed-sit and ambulance and hospital and arrest and prison and court.

Another prisoner was released like a stone tossed over the walls into the social pool, sinking to its level, sending waves of shock. Circles of violence spreading out, the beating of a wife like the beating of a butterfly's wings over the Andes: of no consequence in itself, but with immense ramifications, affecting generations. Secret candles of suffering were re-kindled as many flames to flicker in the breeze and drip hot wax onto skin. One woman stood in the doorway of a tenement, with baby on hip, cigarette and curse on lip, radio cacophony, and flagon of grog, waiting for her recidivist's release. That butterfly breeze brushed her cheek as the slam of a fist. She asked for it, had it coming, defining herself as victim as surely as a recidivist re-offends. Not that she dobbed him in; she copped it sweet. Why couldn't she leave? Why couldn't she become someone else, someone like us? The tenement bricks may as easily become a palace. We cannot change by magic, or wish.

RETURN

I anticipated my return to prison with sadness and resignation. I saw myself entering its perimeter, presenting my ID card as an official visitor, and the boom gate rising to let me in. I will climb the grassy rise to the remand prison and another gate where I will press a green button to announce my arrival. At its shrill ring, an officer will eventually arrive.

"Gedday, doc," he'll say, and if he is a regular, probably add, "Been away?"

Then I will sign in - date and time and name and designation - and await a second officer with an enormous key to open the "back gate" and imprison me again. The concrete, razor wire and brick between the back gate and the reception corridor leading to the holding cell and the clinic will look the same. While waiting for the gate into reception, I will gaze at the main yard over to my left where motley inmates will be dispersed. I will recognise some, as it has only been a week away. I will pass through the corridor and poke my head into the reception office.

"How've yer been," I'll say to Larry or Ron or Stewie or Bill, like old work-mates.

"How've yer been, doc," they'll say.

The final gate, the one to the clinic, is sometimes left open to the reception corridor. But not if there are prisoners around. As I am likely to arrive during the methadone dose-up, this gate will be locked and I will have to wait for the clinic officer who is busy letting the methadonians in and checking their ID and frisking them and watching them gulp the murky brown syrup and chase it down with water and inspecting the gape and letting them out again. Then I will be in the clinic, at last, eager for work to begin.

So I could predict the details of my return. So what? Things never quite turn out as planned. Although prison may have been secure, nothing there was certain. And on my first day back, I felt a sudden and inexplicable curiosity about Gramsci's fate. I could barely wait to find out.

"How was your holiday?" Shauna asked.

"Fine - bumped into Nick down in casualty, hung around town, nothing special," I said.

Why was I giving Shauna so much detail? I knew this would only encourage her nosiness, and I felt phoney in my nonchalance, like I was trying to make excuses for some crime. But the more excuses I made, the more I felt I was exposing myself.

"Listen, Shauna, can you tell me anything about that political prisoner? I think his name is Gramsci. I seem to have missed him in my survey."

"Oh, he's been here for years. Part of the furniture. Enemy of the State. Tried to escape recently, so they reclassified him through remand. Wouldn't bother with him."

"Oh. I'm not bothered. Do I seem bothered to you? Just curious, that's all."

"Terrible how his dog was killed," Chia said. "They still haven't caught the culprit."

"It was such a faithful mutt, waiting for Gramsci all those years. Must have been an animal, whoever killed that dog," Shauna said.

"Or a vivisectionist," I said. They looked at me oddly, as though I had said the wrong thing. "Perhaps it was a hungry Korean," I added hastily, to ease the tension, then felt even more nervous. I gulped. I felt Chia and Shauna's suspicious eyes upon me.

"You look nervous," Shauna said.

"You gulped," Chia said.

"This is absurd. You don't think I had anything to do with the death of some mongrel dog, do you?" I asked.

"Your words, not ours," Shauna said.

"Your nameless dread, or worse," Chia said.

"You do not believe I could be capable of cruelty to a dog, do you?" I stammered. "Such a vicious act. Nothing to do with me. I denied everything in court already."

Shauna tilted her head, her eyes widening.

"Are you quite all right? No-one is suggesting you did it. Calm down," she said.

Yes, stay calm. Gramsci's dog was dead. I carried on as if nothing had happened. It seemed his recently deceased dog had patrolled those prison walls awaiting its master's release. Such faith, but release was unlikely. Gramsci could not harm me from his prison cell. An unfortunate accident with a dog, which may or may not have happened, had nothing to do with me. Perhaps it was a simple case of losing one's temper, and it's not as though anyone was hurt or anything, only an animal, a dog, and virtually a stray. Perhaps I had snapped under the strain of a sudden break, but I resolved not to give Gramsci a second thought. Why should I let a paranoid, dog-owning political prisoner ruin my holiday?

Things were never the same again between us in the prison clinic. How could they be after my psychotic break? But I knew Gramsci held the key to my nascent paranoia.

I resolved to keep quiet, and tried to immerse myself once more in gathering data, which required prisoners to interview. None were received into the remand prison that day of my return. Just my luck.

"Yer missed heaps last week, doc," Bill, the ever-helpful officer, told me. "You'd think we had a sale on the way they flooded in like nobody's business. But none due today. Nix. Zilch. Zero."

"Thanks, Bill," I said, musing how excessive solicitude so often masks aggression.

Without any prisoners, my own musings and devices were all I had that first day back. I was flummoxed, rueful for lost subjects. I could chase the boys I missed, but that would be fruitless. It was difficult to interrupt the routine of a jail-bird once he was well inside the nest, unless there was something in it for him. They were always busy with welfare or legals or visits or buy-ups or work-outs or doing nothing. I had neither carrot nor stick to encourage participation.

Groups of three or four prisoners gathered in the yard, dressed in a shabby uniform of singlets, T-shirts and shorts or long tights, like sailor boys, or Robin Hood's merry men, robbing from the rich and giving to themselves. To enter their band, I would need the right costume, and attitude. I wanted to join their set, to mingle and be accepted.

"Please let me in, boys. Please talk with me," I beseeched.

"Admission by personal invitation only, so piss off."

The more I begged the more they were empowered and the more disdainful of my plea and the more I begged. There was no way into their clique. I hovered on its periphery, outside the in-crowd, annotating files of the lucky invited few whose names were listed in four columns on my computer screen. I had collected about 250 so far. Each name gave access to that man's answers to my confidential interview, his responses to the stimuli. I could print them out at any time, and post them all over town. This felt deliciously close to revenge on the club which refused to have me as a member. But then my life would not be worth living. To betray 250 prisoners' trust for mere titillation would be unethical, and foolhardy, and ensure posthumous publication of my research paper, in which no names would be printed, just as I had promised. But being safe and idle, I flirted with danger, and took liberty with the trust of men whose liberty had been removed. I toyed with notions of deceit. Was it deceitful to promise confidentiality, but type their names upon my screen? They would not be identified in any report or published document, trust me, I'm a doctor. I could still hear Sam's wheezy laugh at that old cliché. The simplest recorded fact could trigger a cascade of recollections and images.

One word - "wife" - and I remembered Harry, fat and jovial. "You could say I'm a victim of marital discord - me wife's shot me three times. But we're inseparable, except when I'm in here."

One word - "gym" - and I recalled Howard, the body-builder with a pock-marked face. I asked him if he had ever felt like he was being watched or spied on.

"Your questions miss the whole bloody point. Prison will send you loony even if you weren't loony to start with. I'm innocent - done nothin' wrong - and I end up in here. How would you feel? Of course I've been bloody spied on and watched."

Howard had unwittingly invoked a stress-diathesis model of lunacy, and this was just his first answer to my first question. He qualified everything he said, and justified that, and qualified even more, until I had no idea what he was talking about. The interview was a gigantic struggle. He inhaled loudly with each question, then exhaled a torrential reply as though bench-pressing an inordinate weight. For fifteen repetitions he struggled, straining pectorals and lats, muscle fibres and sinews, until the final question. No, he had never felt useless, sinful, or guilty. Not for Howard the long dark night of the soul. No mental toil to complement the physical. The body-builder lifted weights, not weighty moral questions of guilt or sin, of right and wrong. He was right. He knew that and it was final, and no correspondence would be entered into, just like the judges said at the Mr Universe competition. His muscles were hypertrophied, but less tangible aspects of his being - like his conscience - had atrophied.

"I've had six kids to six different women, and they all love me," he said proudly.

"The women or the kids?"

"Both."

Again it was clear that to have no conscience was to be unattached: this was the price of freedom for Howard as it was for David. Thanks to the disproportionate development of the lateral amygdala (responsible for kindness and trust, and altruism) relative to the medial (which subsumes rage and hatred) we have inherited a society based on love. Has testosterone usurped this utopia?

A prisoner could plead that his life had been his Art, and claim poetic licence for the brutal carving, the violent brush-stroke in blood upon the human canvas, and be pardoned, or at least given clemency.

"I stand before you, bruised and scarred, tattooed with painful experience, a symbol in God's image, a living sacrifice to free expression of the creative imperative."

Prison was full of these noble self-portraits. Some hung themselves, or sculpted themselves into a granite block like Howard, on whose face were etched the effects of weathering.

TOMORROW IS ANOTHER D.O.A.

Prison is an opaque bubble. Although no-one could see in or out, suspicion and hostility and fear flowed both ways. The men were taken inside the bubble in stages: from reception centre to remand reception to the holding cell and only then to the wings or to protection or strict protection. This last was the most impenetrable, an inner sanctum, a bubble within a bubble, whose inhabitants were embalmed by night in cells containing two bunks and a toilet and a sink, and cocooned in outdoor pens by day.

In the quarantine of strict protection, suspicion hardened into paranoia, hostility and fear became terror and helplessness. And even there, the inmate was not solitary. Frank, tall and gaunt and feeble, protested that his incarceration arose from a "misunderstanding between a happily married couple which the cops took too far." Sure, Frank, like the constables had nothing better to do than come to your home and arrest you? Why is your wife in hospital - with broken ribs and bruised face? Now Frank found he could not co-habitate with his stocky cell-mate, Ron. Frank begged me to do something about it. He was quietly dramatic, whining softly. Even Laurel and Hardy had their tiffs; Abbott and Costello fell out with each other once or twice, so I felt tall thin Frank should hack it with squat Ron. Besides, there was nothing that I could do about it, which fact he did not want to hear. I could not grab his bony shoulders, shake him and demand he understand: "THERE IS NOTHING I CAN DO!" Nor could I demand a confession for his crimes, rend the patina of his denial. I did not need to hear that. It was not my job. I was not judge or prosecutor.

Frank was led away by an officer, returned to strict protection through the steel grill and the locked door behind the doctor's desk. Frank felt hurt. Treachery hung close around him, like a slimy film against the pitted concavity of a tunnel wall, like the lurking demons of madness. Even his step-daughter, a gawky pre-pubescent school-girl with anorexia, had betrayed him to the police for what he had called their "little sessions". There seemed no way out from the tunnel, until he saw an exit.

Although it was difficult to hang yourself in stricts, especially for a man of Frank's height, it could be done. Frank had hoped to shock his cell-mate, but Ron had seen far worse than a suspended, bug-eyed corpse. That night, Frank strapped both ankles back to each thigh, which allowed sufficient drop from the metal frame of his upper bunk. Ron was annoyed to be woken by the trembling of the bunk above, but what he assumed to be a more vigorous wank than usual was Frank's death throes. The more gentle sway of the dangling corpse soon soothed Ron back to sleep. When he told the officer the next morning that he had slept right through the night, he was, as far as he knew, telling God's truth.

Shauna and the doctor pronounced the corpse a corpse.

"His eyes were ghastly, like glass bubbles - all glazed over," Shauna said. She had found Frank even more repugnant in death than when alive.

"That's why it's known as vitreous humour," Chia said, which sounded funny but wasn't meant to be. No-one laughed. We sat in the tea-room, silent in death's thrall. Perhaps we could have recommended Frank's cell- mate be changed. Who knows? It seemed he had been terrified of Ron, but no-one knew why. Shauna sucked hard on her cigarette. The clinic was quiet. A death in custody always delayed the sick parade.

This reflective mood summoned memories. Nick, the doctor, shared his, of one Sunday in Casualty, many years ago, when a typical parade of prostitutes and junkies, corpses and crims had roused him to an unprofessional anger.

"Tomorrow is another D.O.A.," he intoned, sparking our interest, if not our understanding, and then told this tale...

Nick's first case that Sunday was straight-forward: a drowning, brought in from the beach, a young girl. He felt the sand on her lids as he drew them back to reveal fixed and dilated pupils. Green froth caked her nostrils, and seaweed clung in tendrils to her hair, as though the ocean, having claimed her, would not relinquish its hold. Her hair was still wet. She looked about fourteen. 'Dead on Arrival', he wrote on her card, and as rapidly completed, the D.O.A. was forgotten in the quotidian spume of his double shift. She wasn't the sort of case that requires follow-up. Nor was his last, sixteen hours later.

"There's a guy in the Lacerations Room who just won't leave," Angela, an intern, pleaded to her weary colleagues near the end of their shift in Casualty. She had been working in 'lass', to which minor cases were triaged such as junkies, alcoholics and schizophrenics.

"What's the problem?" Nick asked.

"Another junkie," she replied. Angela was recognised as a more than competent intern, and she stood unabashed before them, but there was a brittleness in her voice. This battle with a lacerations patient had been fought at closer quarters than she would like. It seemed this junkie in his ruthless ways had come close to scaling her doctor-patient wall. Angela looked around the common-room, at her fellow doctors slumped in front of TV, each silently praying for no more patients: a Sunday night listlessness to end exhausting double shifts.

"Forty-eight hours on call," an intern moaned, his face pallid and looking sicker than most of his patients. Another buried his face in his hands, weariness stark as the blood on his white coat. The click-clack of a stethoscope in idle hands aroused someone's ire, though no-one could hear the movie on TV above the sound of the ice-machine and the coffee-machine and the air-conditioning and the traffic. Nick gave her his seat, saying,

"Well, I'll go and have a talk to him. Shouldn't let these types into the place."

Angela sat over cigarette and coffee, exhausted and grateful.

"Just tell the guy to piss off. Let some other mob feed him," Nick was advised as he left the room.

Attempts to prevent such incidents had made the Casualty entrance a fortress with metal grills, locked doors and a security guard on call, but the determined junkie with feigned symptoms was difficult to thwart. And, as Chia knew at the prison clinic, and these young doctors had learnt in Casualty, even junkies got sick, sometimes.

A swagger in his stride as he approached the Lacerations Room showed Nick was preparing for a contest. Perhaps a chivalrous sense of avenging Angela added to his mettle, although this was not on his mind. Doctors in their clinical indifference keep as much from themselves as from their patients. Nick felt the numbness with which interns are imbued in their sixteen hour shifts, almost as a part of their medical training. To be inured is a necessary response to the pressure, and those who are not thus anaesthetised do not go very far in the hospital system. Patients might have thought Nick callous; he thought himself efficient. He got the job done.

The junkie heard Nick's heavy tread and slid the door back from the inside. But easing the doctor's entrance was neither meant nor taken as a gesture of appeasement. His eyes met the doctor's: nothing was given away in the latter's gaze, but Nick recognised the pin-point pupils of narcosis and eyelids drooping "on the nod" which gave the appearance of a malicious reptile to his patient. They faced each other in silence for a while, until the junkie looked away, slouching lower in his seat. It seemed he would melt into the linoleum floor. This silence unnerved him: most doctors started talking straight away, and you could tell soon enough whether you would score.

"What's he doing just standing there?" the junkie thought. "He's supposed to ask me what's wrong."

Still the silence - a technique Nick had used before. But the junkie's resolve is hard as diamond when feeding his addiction, albeit a diamond buried in a swamp of languid speech and movement.

"It's not for nothing old ladies get bashed. No-one likes to do that, not even a junkie hanging out," Nick mused as he continued watching, feeling his own resolve building through his exhaustion to match that of the gaunt patient. Now he was ready.

"What's the problem?" he asked evenly.

The other did not look up. Slowly he rocked back and forth, tapping the dressing trolley with his fingers, each tattooed with a letter to spell "LOVE". "HATE" was tattooed on the other hand, which hung limply by his side. His long hair was dyed black, a silver skull hung as ear-ring on the left. Between tattoos of dragons, snakes and naked women on each arm, several needle-marks could be seen. There was about him all the lean malignity of his type.

It was the junkie's turn now not to speak. Nick walked to the doctor's desk, keeping out of the other's reach. Both men were about the same age, mid-twenties - beyond rash conflict but before the brooding fires are dulled inside. This would happen later, in the doctor by social and career pressure, in the junkie by meeting a violence greater than his own. Such meeting was inevitable: one day there would be another bastard in his Valley of Death, and only room for one. The doctor picked up his patient's card.

"Now, what seems to be the problem?" Nick spoke as though about to make an arrest. His patient had heard this tone before. He looked up, scowling.

"You're supposed to be a doctor aren't you? I'm hanging out."

"Well, we're not going to be able to help you if you don't let us," Nick said. "Now what happened with the other doctor?"

"She was fucked. She wouldn't listen."

"I find that hard to believe. But if you want to talk, I'll listen." The coldness never left Nick's voice.

The junkie's story unfolded as a threnody of urban woe..."Me dad's an alcoholic and me mum's crook in hospital. I was framed by the cops, see, but I'm out on bail and I can't afford to score and if I get nicked rounding up the cash I'll be put away for sure." His girlfriend was pregnant as well, but Nick wasn't listening by then.

"And all I want is some methadone. I'm on a programme, honest." The junkie's voice seemed to trail off to somewhere far away.

Nick looked around the Lacerations Room, checking the cupboard locks before replying.

"Well, it seems you're in a bit of trouble," he said. "But we don't dispense narcotics in Casualty. The triage nurse should have told you that. I can give you the address and phone number of a clinic..."

The junkie slammed the dressing trolley. Scissors and dressing packs fell onto the lino with a clatter. Nick looked down at them, then to his patient in mock admonishment. He was goading the junkie openly now, but could not restrain himself: things were getting out of hand between the two men. The doctor's numbness was gone. He felt raw, as though his flesh had been rubbed and rubbed and his nerves were exposed and the pain was becoming unbearable. Later a callus would form.

The junkie was taken aback by this doctor. Most of them did seem to care a little, or at least pretend, but this one was different - almost no better than a junkie himself.

"You don't give a fuck, do you?" the junkie shouted.

Nick rose slowly to his feet and walked to the door, now standing over the junkie as before.

"I can refer you to a clinic overnight, but we can't help you here," he said.

The junkie stared at the floor again. Whatever slim chance of a dose he had had, he knew he had blown it now. "Not even some noctec or moggies to help me sleep?" he asked wistfully.

Nick shook his head. A smile escaped and he said to the junkie as parting comment: "On your bike, and don't come back."

The other was rising as he heard these words. He felt a momentary jolt. His strain was as great as the doctor's, and his self-control less. He lunged in fury, his right fist swung to the doctor's half-turned face. But Nick pulled back in that instant, the other's movement sensed as a blur, and reflexively his own fist curved around. Neither man connected, and so they hung, their urge for violence unrequited, the hatred between them smouldering eye to eye.

The other doctors had heard the junkie's shout, and were gathered near the Lacerations Room. Max, another intern, was first to react. He drew Nick away, as though breaking two dogs from a fight. Two security guards held the junkie, but he wasn't struggling with them. He knew his foe. Doctor and patient glared at each other.

Max did not yet know his sister had drowned that morning at the beach. His family had not called their son, the doctor, whose work they thought could not be interrupted. And Max would welcome work the next day and the next, as there he could escape his sorrow, or lose it in someone else's. That is a doctor's privilege. But he knew that to give your passions to this toil was to be yourself devoured.

"You made the mistake, Nick," he said gently. "You should never look them in the eye."

"Just another junkie. Just another D.O.A." had been Nick's response at the end of the shift. How could it be otherwise? He never remembered their names, and no follow-up was required.

Nick finished his story with a sigh, and slumped over his cup of tea. He seemed to recede before our eyes, his shoulders hunched and his back stooped, as though with that concluding exhalation he was transformed from angry young doctor to flabby GP, whose mask of solicitude we knew so well. What distinguished us from the criminal? In demeaning them we demean only ourselves. Nick had revealed himself as human, but Shauna, for all her brusqueness with the prisoners, preferred the mask. She was appalled to hear of such callousness from her favourite GP. In telling that story, he had let his guard down with us, as he had done years ago with that junkie. All our working days we strive to keep our professional facade unblemished. The grimy details of our private lives are split off, until we ourselves forget that the many faces shown to the world are in fact aspects of the one. The upkeep of a reputation is the price we pay for social standing and respect: we lie in order to appear pure. Kudos costs.

"And I end up here, seeing two-bit junkies and hustlers - the same riff-raff as that bloke who could have had me struck off all those years ago, if I had known how to land a punch. I still try to give them good medical care. For what? It's as futile as trying to teach them a lesson. There's nothing this service corrects," Nick sighed again.

Just then, the familiar sound of prisoners clamouring for attention rose up from the clinic yard. They had arrived for morning sick parade, and the GP was soon busy again, his reasons for that work unknown, his anger dormant for another day.

VOICES

Prison contained a thousand voices never heard beyond its walls. And behind its walls tongues were wagged in vain or out of habit, producing a background noise, a white drone, a groundswell which rose and fell on deaf ears. Jail-birds twittered as they paced the yard, lock-step to each other's rhythm and each other's tune. Their ceaseless sound washed against the walls, and rebounded as a surface froth without nuance or sub-text, like the grind of metal in a faulty engine.

They made demands or threats or sought attention, with words mouthed thoughtlessly and in a monotone of indignation and resentment. It was as though that life of the mind or feelings which marks each voice as individual was absent. In a purely communal existence, without the possibility of solitude, the self is subordinated to the group. For all the blabbering of prisoners, or perhaps because of it, the inner voice of each was stilled.

Above the raucous shouts of the mob outside the clinic, Chia said: "They've got no restraint - they're totally selfish and totally unable to see it. You'd never know if there was a real emergency, the way they carry on."

For cases of real emergency, an alarm button was located above the steel sink behind the door of every cell, but no-one bothered to press them because most were out of order. No prisoner had ever bothered to complain that they were out of order because the alarms had never been known to work, and to complain might be seen as a sign of fear, or weakness. Besides, sounding an alarm was close to dobbing. But one indignant prisoner with a ginger Zapata hanging like tusks either side of his chin insisted that his alarm be fixed. He complained to the clinic nurse, although there was nothing she could do about it.

"I'm not responsible," Shauna said.

"Well it's a matter of health and safety so you have to be responsible as part of the medical service here. And if I am bashed in my cell then at least my stand will be vindicated."

She felt like tugging his moustache like an alarm cord as he whined on and on:

"I will be informing my solicitor of the attitude of the medical service and that no response was forthcoming to my reasonable requests which I have made in good faith. If anything happens to me I'll sue the lot of you."

Shauna had learnt it was better not to listen to the prison chorus of a thousand voices, better to dispense the pills and get through the day as deaf.

THE PRINCE OF PRISONERS

Between these musings on Gramsci, my work continued. He was not the only star in this galaxy of rogues, and again I allowed his glare to fade. I had no let-up from the mundane task of amassing data. There were still hundreds of prisoners to interview. I had other titillations and vicarious pleasures. The conventional excitement for a forensic psychiatrist is the brush with notoriety. Mine came in the form of a man who had aroused a police and media and public frenzy by his alleged deeds and by his capture. I saw him close-up, soon after his arrest, when the hunter had become the prey. I barely noticed the other prisoners I interviewed before him that day, such was the excitement of his arrival. There was one whose girlfriend had hitched up with a prison officer. A junkie lay on the ground of the holding cell moaning, "I'm cold," and "I need my dose," while other prisoners walked around him and cursed him to shut-up. And then there was Bogdan, the alleged serial killer. The others were paupers alongside this prince of prisoners.

I could barely wait to interview him, but stuck to the order of names on my list, as a child leaves the favourite sweet till last the more to savour it. Mechanically

I proceeded through the routine of introduction, explanation, consent, interview, and thanks. Sometimes I would forget that, although I'd been through this rigmarole hundreds of times, it was each subject's first. I had to slow down, and explain the interview's purpose and nature with due deliberation, allowing some a hearing, time to yarn - if I thought they would consent.

But Bogdan was not saying a lot. He watched me warily as I spoke. The corner of his mouth flickered into a lopsided grin which may have been a mannerism but which made me feel mocked. Perhaps I was trying too hard, in awe of his notoriety, seeking his autograph as a souvenir rather than as consent for a serious scientific investigation. Whenever a professional man has to justify himself, suspect him of dissembling. Bogdan remained aloof, oddly passive for a man whose alleged actions had... I should not have known what he was accused of, but it was unavoidable. His name had been on the front page of that morning's newspaper, and on every radio bulletin. I wondered if I would have picked him from the day's list as the one, and would my response, unsullied by prescience, have been different? My secret - that I knew his charges - was straining scientific objectivity. I talked more than usual, to fill the space of the silence which unnerved me. Another odd grin creased his smooth face, and his narrow, crystal blue eyes seemed to dance with amusement.

"No worries, doctor. I've got nothing to hide," he said slowly, before signing the consent.

Each word was measured in the way of one for whom English was not a mother tongue. His thickened vowels made him sound like the caricature of a Communist villain portrayed in Cold War propaganda, or American cartoons, which amounts to the same thing. His physique was unremarkable, but I noticed the fingers of the hand which gripped my pen were delicate, and his forearm hairless. It was his eyes which struck me with their appearance, but isn't this always the case when you observe another closely? He exuded a sense of composure, almost of dignity, as though this arrest was a minor setback, beneath his station to be troubled about. If this was chess, his middle game had been slightly ruffled, but he knew he would prevail in the end. Bogdan was a man of strategy, who could afford to be indifferent to tactics. And games were the perfect analogy for one who had seemingly played with other's lives. My paltry game of science was of little interest to him. Although our initial brief interview went smoothly, he refused to undertake the longer one. There was nothing in it for him.

The next day the officer at the back gate wanted to know if I'd seen that prince of prisoners and what he was like. Of course, confidentiality precluded comment.

JUST WHEN THINGS WERE GOING WELL

On a day when things were going well, the ease of my task could show on my grinning face, and I felt I must feign some hardship, or at least concern. It was not prudent to call the prisoners from their concrete cell in a gleeful tone. So I carefully monitored their anger and resentment, and never assumed that what I found amusing would be shared by others. These men were tense, strained to breaking point, and when they broke, it was seldom into fits of laughter.

I watched one prisoner's anger darken and crease his face like wind across a bay, as a nurse and an officer offered complacent replies in answer to his simple question: "What time should I turn up for my morning dose of valium?" A combination of mental docility, physical agility, and instinctive paranoia made him alert to threats and mockery, but alert to little else.

"Well, Collin, that depends on when you get here," the nurse said. The officer sensed the hapless prisoner's confusion. This was an opportunity to put Collin down, and impress the nurse.

"Oh, the valium. You know everyone wants valium. You'll just have to get here before the valium runs out," the officer teased. Collin glowered. Sinews bulged in his neck, and he swayed back slightly, not saying a word. He had had enough. But the impulse to rage was stifled, and after a long pause, he muttered:

"Whatever yer reckon."

There was nothing more he could say. Perhaps the tattoo on his thigh said it all: above a buxom woman squatting astride a man's face was the inscription, "Love Is". The nurse wrote a dosage schedule on his treatment sheet.

There was always more to learn about the species "prisoner". I learnt above all to assume nothing, neither guilt nor innocence, wits or inanity, anger or ease. The face of a prisoner could be impassive, or, as in Collin's case, anger could register upon it like an earthquake on a seismograph. But the prisoner's voice invariably gave him away. No matter how he looked, it was when he started talking that you knew where you stood with him. Some admitted right away they could not read the consent form which I offered as I spoke. There were many who expected some pay-back for their co-operation, such as a letter for the court, more methadone, a favour here or there. Others admitted nothing, but said brusquely, "Yeah, I'll sign it," or "Whatever yer reckon, doc," or "Just get on with yer questions, but I ain't signin' nothin'". For these, I would cut short my preamble, to give them a sense of controlling the process. I would tell them they could have a copy of the consent form if they wanted.

"It's up to you," I'd say. "This interview is totally voluntary. Your choice is respected. No hassles. No questions asked, without your consent."

Sometimes I felt there should be a sign on the wall of my little office like the ones in department stores: "Walk through, feel free to browse. No-one asked to buy." Or, "Obligation-free measure and quote." And, "Do not ask for credit, as refusal often offends." I was one slick salesman, when things were going well. As long as the prisoner felt in control, and felt respected, my day was easier. Best of all was if he realised I was an outsider myself, and hence could not increase the methadone or valium. So the cannier ones would say: "You can't really help me, can you?" Relieved to be free of responsibility, I would reply: "No, I can't." When things were going really well, I might add the lie: "I'm sorry."

When things were going well, prison seemed to abound in idle gestures of kindness, as though, in among the random brutality, a denser fabric of respect held its community together. If he obeyed the codes of respect, a prisoner could get by. The courtesy was understated: to stand aside with a flourish when allowing a prisoner to return through the gate may appear mocking, so the prisoner would stand aside indifferently, in perfunctory acknowledgement of another bloke's presence, of his space and passage. The ritual was simple, sensible, and a matter of course, which is the essence of etiquette. This tameness may have been for show, with the officers and doctor present, but it seemed genuine enough. Most prisoners would share their tobacco with a stranger in the prison if asked.

The paranoid prisoners were my biggest hassle. Not those merely hesitant or suspicious. They needed a little reassurance, that's all. Like Matthew, who kept stopping my interview to check that it wouldn't crop up in court.

"I ain't going to no rat house, doc, if that's wot yer thinkin'. This better be fair dinkum. I been verballed before and I ain't gonna cop it from no shrink," he said angrily."

"Sure. Relax. I signed here to the effect that it's confidential, purely for research. I'm a scientist. Trust me."

"Sounds bodgy to me. And yer signatures look diff'rent on them two forms."

"I'll sign them again."

"Fresh ones."

"No problem. Look."

Matthew was unconvinced. Was I being too glib?

"Nah, doesn't sound right, to me," he said, and I thought I'd lost him. But then he said: "Aw, get on with it."

No, it wasn't the blokes like Matthew who were a problem, but the full-blown, raving paranoiacs. There weren't that many of them, not as many as you might fear, but just one could ruin my day. Their angry threats would arise from the most outrageous suppositions, but the more I tried to refute their infuriating logic, the more they had me pinned as a scumbag liar.

"That first question you ask about being followed - the cops wanna know so they can tighten up their surveillance. That's wot yer on about. It's a bloody scam." Stephen was livid at the end of our interview. He knew he'd sussed me out, he was onto my case, and I wouldn't get away with it. He would tell them all in the yard: "That quack - he's a jack." He would yell it to the prison world, and the 280 prisoners I had already interviewed would be after me, baying for my blood like hounds. That was a lot of anger to deal with.

A scientist's most prized possession - his reputation for integrity - can so quickly come crashing down around him, leaving him psychologically bereft. I felt naked, found out, and vulnerable. When you start to see yourself for what you are, you are looking too closely. "How phoney am I?" I wondered. "What is this research all about, and what if Stephen's claims are true?" Paranoia breeds paranoia, a replicating virus whose toxin of fear corrodes the soul, which after all is merely an expression of our neuronal soup.

What if I had been set up by the research committee, and my "study" was being funded by some dirty tricks slush fund? I was a pawn in their sordid game. Stephen was right. My work was a sham, this study a front. Call me an opsimath*, but at last I had seen the truth: it was all clear to me now, in a revelation of perfidy and deceit. And I felt certain that the professor was in on it too. The professor as patron had buttered me up merely to suck me in. How false she appeared, another traitor. Her odd disappearances, her moods, her shadowy demeanour - everything about her which had once been inexplicable could now be explained by one simple fact, as though an image had suddenly leapt into view from a densely patterned background, and once seen, dominated the senses. She was a woman with a secret. She had deceived me, sold me out to the police who each night were tapping into my hard disc, an incubus extracting data in a ruthless double-cross. Police and professor had betrayed me and the prisoners, and left us to turn on each other. It was a perfect ploy.

"Be careful where you deposit your sperm, and never trust a woman who wears leather trousers." If only I had listened to my father's advice. At least I got the first bit right. I longed for those days of innocence, when I was a good boy and the world was good, before puberty, before knowledge. Like self-praise, self-love alone could not revive my career. It was in a shambles, my dream of scientific glory was a joke. What would my mother have

---

* opsimath – one who learns late in life

to boast about to her friends? Who would publish my research? I felt like a cuckold, whose horns all the world could see and mock. You learn who your friends are when the chips are down, and mine would queue up to stab me in the back. You turn to your parents, in desperation, and they say: "Son, you have shamed us worse than if you had been a faygeleh*, which you probably are anyway. Why aren't you married already? Get lost, and when you get there, wear a black dress and a wig and lots of make-up and change your name so no-one will recognise you or heaven forbid associate you with us. And, what's more, we know you masturbated despite our explicit instructions, despite the lesson of Onan˜. How could you be so cruel? So thoughtless? Where did we go wrong? Oi vey!"

So I would be alone, an outcast to wander the planet all the days of my sorry life. I resolved to trust no-one. That was clear enough, but now I was doubting even myself. It occurred to me that if I were to administer my questions to myself now, I would score full marks on the schizophrenia scale. I needed to get a grip on reality. Maybe I needed a hobby. Everyone needs a hobby. I was slipping into another psychotic break, out on a limb, my little ice floe adrift on a blue sea tossing and roaring in angry tempest all around. At least Stephen was a threat that I could see. It was the other prisoners who would get me, the ones I did not suspect, when I least suspected it. I could hear my lame entreaties:

"Please, fellas, I didn't know they were tapping my files. They used me. I didn't mean it. Honest."

---

* faygeleh – yiddish for homosexual
˜ Onan – figure from the old testament chastised for spilling his seed

"Yeah?! We trusted you once, doc, but we never give a dog a second chance. You're history."

They would probably then end my Trial with an execution, in the manner Kafka ended K.'s, leaving me to die "...Like a dog." Gramsci's dog, that poor hound, pulped. These thoughts sent my mind into such a spin that I could barely focus on Stephen as he left the clinic, talking loudly of my "scam" to the other prisoners nearby, and saying: "Don't trust him - he's a jack!"

"Stephen, listen, I'm sorry, I..."

My confession was interrupted by a red-haired bloke with a mangled prune where his nose used to be.

"Doc, you paged me for your interview," he said. Stephen was still cursing me from behind the gate as the officer let the new prisoner in.

"Ah, don't worry about Stephen," the prisoner said. "He's a raving ratbag."

"Yes, of course," I said, falteringly. "I'm not bodgy. This is serious research."

"Sure, doc." He looked at me oddly, and I looked at his nose, which looked even odder from close-up.

No-one likes to be reminded of his nose, so I didn't comment on this prisoner's proboscis, but its shape was ghastly. There was so much redundant flesh wrinkled and smeared between his eyes, that, before it had been flattened by some horrific trauma, it must have been of prodigious length. This was the John Wayne Bobbitt of noses. Its nostrils were now vestigial - tiny slits beneath a twisted pulp. Still, what's in a nose that can't be left there? And this contemplation of his olfactory organ soothed me, after Stephen had ruined my day, just when things were going well.

I was grateful for this prisoner and his nose, so grateful I could have kissed its hideous morphology. I clung to the fact of the nose like a survivor of ship-wreck clings to flotsam, until washed ashore on the Terra Firma of reality. These bouts of psychosis were becoming more frequent and more florid. Would I recover from the next, or be stranded on Terra Nullus? They were increasingly difficult to pave over with equanimity, as though with each upsurge of paranoia the equilibrium of my self, and my world, was harder to maintain - like the lurching of some wayward planet which began as tiny perturbations but which now threatened to send it careering from the solar system to the oblivion of space. Where once a lodestar - a sense of the continuum of self - had guided me, I now had no direction. If true north was six degrees from magnetic north, where was my true self? I turned to my work for security and relief from these interminable introspections, but saw there only a sorry parade of humanity, more lost than me, and held in orbit by centripetal despair.

SCRIBBLINGS

I was again immersed in my research, interviewing prisoners. Thoughts of Gramsci arose from time to time, and of his dog. "I have nothing to hide," I told myself, but a guilty conscience would darken my false and breezy visage, like bubbles rising to a still surface, pricking its glassy meniscus with their minute explosions. They were light as wisps, these thoughts, fleeting as the memory of a dream, almost imperceptible like the hint of shade beside a tree on an overcast day.

Just when I felt free of the incredible events of that recent break, felt them recede beyond the reach of recollection, I would be overcome by a sense of foreboding, as though of storm clouds gathering on a distant horizon - so distant that what I had at first perceived to be receding was in fact inexorably drawing closer. How desire blurs our perceptions!

The next storm broke when I least expected it: while browsing in the professor's library. I was leafing through a political treatise, daydreaming until I flipped open its title page. It was called "Prison Notebook" and was written by one Antonio Gramsci. I gulped; my hands trembled as I opened the pamphlet, like a guilty schoolboy whose pornographic magazine - hidden between the pages of his Shakespeare text - is discovered by a school-master who had stealthily crept up behind. The few paragraphs I read echoed in my mind:

"The selection or 'education' of men adapted to the new forms of civilisation and to the new forms of production and work has taken place by means of incredible acts of brutality which have cast the weak and the non-conforming into the limbo of the lumpen-classes or have eliminated them entirely…" *, and:

"Womanising demands too much leisure. The new type of worker will be a repetition, in a different form, of peasants in the villages. The relative stability of sexual unions among peasants is closely linked with the system of work in the country. The peasant who returns home in the evening after a long and hard day's work wants the 'venerum facilem parabilemque' [Latin for 'easy and accessible love'] of Horace. Womanising is not his style. He loves his own woman, sure and unfailing, who is free from affectation and doesn't play little games about being seduced or raped in order to be possessed. It might seem that in this way the sexual relation has been mechanised, but in reality we are dealing with the growth of a new form of sexual union shorn of the bright and dazzling colour of the romantic tinsel typical of the petit bourgeois and the Bohemian layabout. It seems clear that the new industrialism wants monogamy: it wants the man as worker not to squander his nervous energies in the disorderly and stimulating pursuit of occasional sexual satisfaction. The employee who goes to work after a night of excess is no good for his work. The exaltation of passion cannot be reconciled

---

* Selections from Prison Notebooks, by Antonio Gramsci, Lawrence and Wishart, London, 1991, page 298

with the timed movements of productive motions connected with the most perfected automatism." *

Finally, I read Gramsci's judgement of psychoanalysis as *"the expression of the increased moral coercion exercised by the apparatus of the State and society on single individuals,"* and his concern at *"the pathological crisis determined by this coercion…"* ~

I had not heard Gramsci speak since that interview before my break, but now I could not free myself from his voice on the page. Here was his odious manifesto, in the professor's study, of all places. He had clearly taken me on as some practical expression of his determination to defeat psychoanalysis. Well, Gramsci, I am beaten, cowed, and surrender unconditionally. No contest. Game over…I vowed to myself to have no further contact with him.

But his phrase *'perfected automatism'* hung about me like a stench. What had happened to me, during my psychotic break, and what part had Gramsci's voice played in my demise? I felt there was a clock ticking towards some catastrophe, and the mechanism was within me.

Despite this dire personal portent, Gramsci's writing style was so typical of the man: aloof and insular. I recalled how I had taken him on as my special patient, and over the ensuing weeks as our therapy got underway, how the initial impressions of his narcissism were to be confirmed. He lived as though in this world he was not just the first, but the only person. Page after page of prison notebooks he had filled, raving on about class struggle, and dialectical materialism, just as he was to rave on and on to me about

---

* ibid, page 304
~ ibid, page 280

his bizarre and twisted inner world, poisoning mine with his intimate nonsense as he had sought to poison society with his ridiculous but dangerous political nonsense. He had been locked up for years by the time he began seeing me. Ah, Gramsci, our Marxist martyr, our unwitting self-parody. A buffoon, but too conceited and committed to see it. Why did I ever take the man so seriously?

He began for me as my special patient, and ended as my bane during the prison year. Gramsci was the strangest case in the strangest year of my life. But this is my journal, not his. I will have the last word. I resent his intrusions, how he inveigled himself into the fabric of my existence, sullying my dreams. Perhaps I write to reclaim them from his grasp. Gramsci had such bony fingers, and, like every Marxist I've ever known, grimy finger-nails.

That year I took prisoners as research fodder, and learnt to take no risks. Prison taught me to be careful. He, Gramsci, was just one of the hundreds of prisoners I interviewed, as part of a study of mental illness in the most restrictive environment, where men are caged, degraded, and abused, but queue up to return - clogging the courts - again and again. This was a simple topic. As psychiatrist and scientist, I was in total control, totally detached, totally defended. My psychic walls were as high as the prison walls. Maybe it was because I felt trapped that I, too, let my guard down, as Nick had done with his junkie patient in casualty all those years ago. I allowed myself to become over-involved in Gramsci's psychopathology. Or maybe it was because I was as smug as my nemesis.

True, I had found our early sessions fascinating. Science. Politics. Economics. Art. Between us, Gramsci and I had dabbled in every promised way out of this universal illness we call the "human condition". Neither of us at that time had yet given up on utopia, I suppose, but I learnt too late how each path leads us only deeper towards the mess we try to escape. Complications set in, unforeseen contingencies. Utopia, like any perfection, is just another form of cruelty.

What was so special about Gramsci that he became my special patient? From a scientific point of view, nothing. Later, when he returned through remand after his failed escape attempt, he represented more data, that's all. Another case to record, classify and collate. I should have left it at that, but could not, because, from a personal point of view, he represented far more: an amalgam of demons, a personal nemesis. Sure, he got under my skin. And the worst thing about it is that I felt I invited him to. Isn't that always the way? I had tried to ignore the man's strange allure, but this only caused somatic symptoms. The usual stuff: irritable bowel, headaches, rashes, lethargy. The antidepressants didn't work for me, any more than my analysis with Blind Freddy.

So I too began writing, as therapy. Notebooks and pens were cheaper than seeing another shrink, and besides, who would I have seen after all those years on the couch? You know how psychiatrists gossip, which is not the worst of their sins. But once I had started scribbling, I couldn't stop. I suffered what the Romans had called *"scribaldi cacoethes"*, the scribbling habit. I am ashamed of it really. To think of Gramsci's vile scribbling and then turn to the same behaviour myself...

At least the physical symptoms have subsided. But the thought of patient and doctor scribbling together still makes my flesh crawl. That horripilation - another somatic response - is a vestige of my neurosis. "Be easy on yourself," I used to tell my patients, the ones I liked.

"A little neurosis is healthy, and we are allowed a relapse now and then."

You bastard, Gramsci. I can still picture his sneer when I tried those homilies on him. So high and mighty, so smug, so altogether bereft of humanity, he was. It showed in his journals - self-indulgent, vain, abstract. It showed in his face. It is hard now to say why I ever took him on for therapy; I could have said no to the professor. Call it morbid fascination dressed up as scientific interest, or a yearning to discover the truth behind my own psychotic core. And what use did I now have for this residue of guilt about some murdered dog. Call it self-destruction. I don't know. We live in a fog.

I need reminding that a doctor should not speak ill of his patient. But why should I be a slave to my honour, a quaint mannequin, weak and pedestalled, in homage to a dignity no-one trusts? That is what has become of our profession. If Hippocrates was around today his only oath would be a single word of four letters. My voice will not be stilled. What do you suggest I do with my anger and resentment - what do you do with yours? A suffering borne in silence is a suffering doubled. And I have had enough. That man tormented me. Yes, I learnt from him, and learnt again that that which we most resent we should be most grateful for, which our parents teach us all if we stop to think about it.

"Every father wants to kill his son," Gramsci used to say. "And every doctor wants to kill his patient. And every God wants to kill his chosen people. This gives survival its only purpose - to scorn the almighty. Of course, we fail nobly." What would a Marxist know about God?

The struggles of our barren and futile psychotherapy now seem heroic to me, all these months later. Like Nick recounting the tale of past heroism in a hospital Casualty, like any man in middle age surveying his variously squandered decades (surveying the seconds and minutes of his tiny history which he can scarcely believe is his, or was, now past, gone, lost, that life he lived), I can only wonder how I persevered, or why. I must have been mad.

I recalled how Gramsci would sit, week after week, then day after day, cross-legged on the concrete floor of his cell. No missed sessions with this patient, but nor did he pay. I can't believe how much time I wasted on him, if only from the capitalist point of view. It was idealism, I suppose: that 'ism' we allow ourselves when we've got only enough money to buy food and pay rent but haven't worked out what else money is good for, or when we've got too much money than we know how to spend, which amounts to the same thing, really. Idealism seeks to reconcile irreconcilable differences, and have everybody play nice together. As if.

What did Gramsci do for the rest of his time, between our little sessions? Not merely wait till tomorrow like a prisoner is supposed to. No, Gramsci would write like a maniac, or a Balzac. I pleaded with the prison governor to confiscate his writing implements. They confiscated drug implements readily enough. Even unauthorised food was seized, and the prisoner banned from visits or telephone use for a week or two as punishment.

I said Gramsci's writing was counter-therapeutic, which was a mistake: the governor frowned at me. He didn't like big words. And Gramsci was left to his scribbling. "After all," the governor said. "He is a special prisoner, doctor. Political, you know. Very sensitive. Very hush hush. Well over my head. Policy, doctor, policy and protocol runs prisons. Cogs in a machine, lubricate regularly."

This was all I needed. Politics and protocol - bulwarks against change. It's the same in any bureaucracy. Prison was no different. But if you want to see lunatics running an asylum, go to prison. If that's a bit drastic, let me take you there, show you what it was like, before Gramsci arrived, before doubt, before torment. And after.

Returning Gramsci's pamphlet to the professor's library shelf, I asked myself one simple question: how did it get there? That question was no sooner asked, than forgotten.

OUR DAILY DOSE

Another junkie was bent with the cramps of withdrawal. His answers came slowly, and he had difficulty understanding my questions. I doubted whether he really believed that the interview was voluntary. Several times he told me how crook he was. But at the end, his symptoms disappeared. He got up abruptly, went straight to the medication trolley and asked the nurse when he would get his dose.

"I'm overdue for my valium," he said. "I haven't had my afternoon tablet."

Shauna checked his treatment sheet.

"You were only ordered three doses," she said.

"Well I haven't had three. Only had it yesterday morning and last night."

Shauna looked worn out by the demands, the arguments, the rudeness of grown men in constant tantrum. She rang the reception prison clinic to check what doses he had had, then turned back to him, a liar.

"They said you had your dose this morning."

"Well, that's not fair," he said lamely. "What if I kill myself?"

Shauna suggested he see the psychiatric nurses. The threat of self-harm was a commonplace manipulation. According to Chia, giving the dose now would only reward him.

Later, over tea, we discussed the week's big news, the prince of prisoners. Bogdan was to have a psychiatric report, about which Chia was sceptical.

"How can you psychiatrists explain what he did - that is if he did it?" he asked. "What can you say? That the id overpowered the superego? There is no sense, no understanding how a man could do that."

Although Bogdan did not return for a longer interview, his cell-mate described him to us. "Bogdan seems like an all right sort of bloke, but he's got an odd way of smiling all the time. Anyway, I'm not here to judge him."

Dr King's psychiatric report said nothing more than this shrewd appraisal, but took longer to say it, and was not given for free. Dr King seemed to have cornered this lucrative market of report-writing. Forensic psychiatrists came in and out of fashion with the criminal lawyers, and the fad for Dr King was at its height. Chia was right, as always, but being always right did not make him smug or cynical. He enjoyed my next subject as much as I did.

There is little ground nowadays between miracles and madness. Tony was born again after he found his girlfriend rolling in the sand in the arms of a new lover. He sat on a nearby pier, watching the swell roll in, and rolling a roll-yer-own, and drinking a six-pack, and thinking, "Shit eh." He was drowning his sorrows, he told me. Then another bloke, a complete stranger, came up to him and invited him to pray right there on the beach, so he knelt on the warm sand, and closed his eyes, and prayed.

"A light went right through me. Jesus told me to walk into the water. I had my arms tensed like this." As he spoke, he threw his hands up in a parody of biblical supplication. "And I went straight into the surf up to my neck and I had my eyes closed. If a decent wave had of come in, I would've drowned, for sure."

Shauna and Chia resisted the temptation to piously ejaculate "Amen". As Tony spoke, he rose stiffly from his chair, backed away, and curled his fingers as though gripping an invisible sphere. I wanted to tell Tony to finish the interview, but he was on stage, in the throes of great drama. Then the miracle happened:

"I started talking in tongues, like this," he said. And young Tony arched his neck, threw his head back and began babbling to the ceiling. Chia, perched at his desk in the corner behind us, looked up and grinned and shook his head.

"That's fascinating, Tony," I said, once his ululations had subsided.

"Shall I tell you about the other miracle, doc?" he asked.

Before I could reply, he began: "This one's about the gold ring which I found in the back of a paddy wagon when I was praying for my brother after he got killed in a high-speed pursuit. I was the passenger. The ring was inscribed with his initials, H.I., which stands for 'Holiness Is'. Isn't that amazing?"

PRISON MUSIC

The prisoner moved in unsynchronised rhythms, as though his body was conducting some experimental chamber piece, fracturing time with jerks and contortions, coughing up notes on obscure scales. His speech was similarly unfamiliar, its awkward syncopations demanding concentration as the words emerged through pauses, hesitations and repetitions. A sparrow tattooed on his neck swooped towards his collar bone. His right eye swayed outwards and slowly returned, and his eyelids drooped and rose again. Although he never quite seemed awake, nor did he doze, and his foggy consciousness was punctuated by a frantic and constant scratching and fidgeting. Fingers darted all over his body, their nails digging in and clawing at random. He could not leave his body alone, as though he was compelled to touch, perhaps to reassure himself that its parts were intact. He had been in jail most of the last five years, and on heroin most of his 35.

"I forget things, doc. Like me brain's sort of fucked. They said I've got cerebral atroffy or somethin'. The drugs 've fucked me up but I still take 'em cos I'm worse off widdout 'em."

Extracting relevant information from him was like pulling teeth, only I was the one feeling the pain. To read his mind was to stare into a vacuum; it hurt my eyes. The last question was especially difficult for him. He grappled not with his conscience, but with the very possibility of conscience: he was unsure if he felt guilt, and asked me what it was like.

"I know I shouldn't have done it, like. I even knew I'd probably get caught, but it was such a cinch, once I'd parked someone's car for them, to nick the change. All those coins added up after a while. But the other attendants got suspicious when I was so eager to park all the customers' cars and they could hang around and do nothing. The harder I worked, the better it funded me habit, so I wasn't gonna stop meself. I'd turn up to work at the car-park straight after a shot, and no-one could tell the difference. Then I'd skim off a few bucks here and a few bucks there. But they were onto me - security. Got me with me hand in the cookie jar, they did. But I can't say I ever felt guilty, even when I was younger and a bit of a thug and rolled alkies for me habit. So that's a 'no' to yer question... This lag's a pity. I worked hard in that car-park, but I don't reckon they'd have me back. Could you write me a reference, but?"

Whatever scientific riches there may have been in a longer interview with him, it would not be worth the effort of immersing myself again in the gluey workings of his cognition. I thanked him for his time.

Enrico was writhing on the bed outside my office. This South American Communist murderer was still the nurses' least favourite patient. His face scrunched up like a rubber ball as he moaned. It was his catheter, again.

"Somebody help me. It's blocked. My urine is blocked. It won't come through the penis."

The nurse worked steadily, unstrapping the catheter bag from the inside of Enrico's thigh, and draining the urine into a plastic measuring tray to show him his last hour's collection.

"There's a hundred mills, Enrico," she said, presenting the tray and its contents to him, cradled between her rubber gloves. "It's flowing."

"No. NO! The blockage - I feel it. No good."

This was a locum nurse. Her fat kind face tightened to a grimace as she crouched by his groin, but she slowly repeated her reassurance. She wondered if it was a language problem with this patient. Enrico squealed louder, bringing Chia from his desk. Chia stood over them, arms akimbo like an angry father, and said: "Now that's enough!" Enrico simpered, then squealed some more in case it was thought that his suffering had subsided. The officers were told to escort him outside.

"You Gestapo! You Nazis! The penis is blocked!"

Prisoners smirked. The officers looked sheepish, standing there in front of a naked man. When Enrico had left, Chia called the hospital where Enrico had had his operation, to confirm what he already knew. Chia spoke to a doctor who knew Enrico well. According to the doctor, this patient had frequented Casualty for years, complaining loudly of "The blocked penis," and generally being difficult and not leaving until security were called. The doctor wished Chia well.

Sometimes after a long day in prison, I felt blocked up, too, like Enrico's penis, and I'd shake my pen but nothing would dribble out. I could always transcribe from the day's interviews a few lines verbatim, such as these from a friendly, pot-bellied prisoner who had greeted the officer with a grin like a regular fronting up to the bar at his local pub. I expected a bit of ribbing, a lend, a larrikin welcome, but when this prisoner opened his mouth, the words flowed and flowed like a lunatic tap:

"You see something getting built right like Creation. I've been around since Creation, since Time started like I'm a traveller from time and space - this is what I gathered from them knowing me and I'm not knowing them. It's just something like I'm created you see and to make things happen like I go back to that building that I'm building something for my people - for the people I love and I need that power it's like putting twenty cents up there and try to stand it up in a hurry. I'm God and I think I've been found out and I start to worry about that."

PRISON AS WOMB

You would think that prisoners would stop their scurrying once they had been halted on the streets, arrested and were holed up behind these walls. They could rest in this red-brick womb, each wing a big placenta to quench the restless appetite, to find comfort in and nestle up to. In prison, life's daily tumult could be relieved, and the prisoners stilled in contemplation. In captivity, given up and surrendered, you would think they could find bliss. Held tight each night in concrete cells, curled on thin mattresses between ragged grey blankets, you would think they could rest and be easy. What more could they want?

By day, the knots of men drew together in muffled voice, their heads bobbing like boys furtively excited over a find or a covert stash. Others were yet more exuberant, bounding up and down the yard with a zany gusto, a spilling out of energy, their knees, ankles, hips and arms flexed and straightened, pumping. The curve, arc, and fall of a leaping man broke the surface of this Breughel of massed bodies captured for one moment while the radiant sky overflowed with their possibilities and yet closed them in.

Their six-digit numbers were jumbled up, random as their comings and goings in this irrepressible present. I could find no formula to clarify their states of mind, but arrogantly assumed some research access was granted.

There was no way to predict this or that permutation. I summoned words to complete their sentence. The herd bustled, brought briefly to muster twice each day, thrown back to their shared cells, then let go again as a spring held tight in the palm uncoils on sudden release, as water flows smoothly inches before its precipitate cascade. This venting of vigour continued in all times and places. It was an erratic energy, a dissonant music whose notes be-bopped, strange and pure, such as a deaf man might never hear as he watched the scuttling of crabs on black rock before the suck, rise and crash of a soundless wave.

If I were a jail-bird, caged in a wing, my false self, the professional facade, would be shattered on the concrete all around and I would feel free to be, not do. I would give my right eye for that freedom, for the release of being in prison. I would no longer need my sight to see the featureless plain of yard as it soaked up blood with a crazed thirst, leaving no stain to show for this brief rain on its dry concrete. Pain quickens and gingers the feet. Now I too am dancing, deaf and one-eyed, and I fall to my knees there, against the concrete, lacing up a pair of prison-issue sandshoes, and I leap...

Back to work. After such frivolous distractions, I resumed hastily raking the top-soil of prisoners' lives, prefaced by my glib speech: "No depth is involved, I assure you, in these fifteen questions of mental health, which touch on paranoia and other modes of thinking, and on appetites for food and sex. They are easy, these questions without right or wrong. A best guess will do; near enough is good enough for me. And it's all voluntary, and totally confidential, so ask any questions you might have, and if it's OK with you just sign this consent form here, where it says 'Prisoner', and here's a copy for you to keep, if you want. The nurse will sign here as witness at the end of the interview. Now let us begin. It'll take about ten minutes. I ask the questions from my computer."

Prison promised to meet my desire for flight from the world, for some obscure refuge, but its sanctuary was illusory. Although always under scrutiny, with nowhere to hide or be alone, I could at least pretend to be an incorporeal, watchful spirit, the unseen eye seeing all but itself. I gave myself this conceit of freedom, this freedom of conceit, as an attempt to disappear. We only leave memories; all else turns to dust.

If you have outgrown these adolescent tensions between intimacy and solitude, good for you. But do you not yearn for some place warm and safe, like the solitude from which we are born? Remand prison was that womb shared by hundreds of non-identical twins, blue zygotes in amnion, numbered and held and mostly kept alive. Some died in utero; some were still-born from their state of banishment; the rest were born, slightly scathed. I saw prison as an opportunity for deepening consciousness by reducing stimulus, but I may have been wrong. Navel-gazing can teach a man a lot - about his navel. And prisoners, like the sick, were obsessed with themselves. These prison themes re-emerged like fraying threads of umbilical cord. If they cannot be entwined, let them fray.

POLITICS

Enrico's accusations were flung across the clinic from the left side of his brain, where a limited capacity for language struggled to express his helpless, hypochondriacal rage, and resorted to the habitual epithets of a burnt-out leftist revolutionary. It is said that a man who was not a socialist in his youth has no heart, and who does not become a capitalist in middle age has no brain. But Enrico had taken a different path: the political sympathies of his youth had become somatised with age, and withered to self-pity. And yet a faint echo of the Marxist creed, of the rousing strains of the Internationale, could still be heard in his harangue against the clinic "Nazis".

He needed a man of Gramsci's determination and discipline to articulate these leftist yearnings, but Enrico would not now understand them as political, if indeed he ever had. Enrico had joined the Marxists as a teenager because he liked to belong, and he liked parties, and their Party had the prettiest boys. He was disappointed that the Party's parties were so dull, full of long-winded speeches, although the bit about rising up to the iron will of Bolshevism sounded raunchy. His sole function at each Party meeting had been to call the roll, which was later altered for Party political purposes, anyway.

Although Enrico, out of nostalgia, may have attended a revolutionary rendezvous in prison had Gramsci organised it, his name would have been the only one on that roll call. No other prisoner would bother to turn up. Gramsci, as far as I could tell, was wasting his breath. Few prisoners even bothered to vote, let alone attend political meetings, voice political views, or set them down in writing. But page after page after page Gramsci filled, as the last political prisoner, the sole survivor among a mob of apolitical prisoners, who were ignorant of his strident dialectic, and indifferent to his incarceration. Gramsci's martyrdom passed unnoticed, and hence was merely a misguided and narcissistic exercise, as most heart-felt causes are. It accomplished nothing but his own demise through exhaustion. I knew he could not hold out. What could sustain him in this apolitical environment, among these apolitical prisoners for whom his notions may as well have been in another language, for all their relevance? Had he plastered the prison walls with political posters, they would only have attracted streams of urine, and not a squirt of notice. These men had committed personal crimes, as far as they and society were concerned: crimes against possession, crimes against the individual. Only Gramsci, the last radical agitator in prison, acknowledged a political context - that the individual and his material possessions were the twin pillars of capitalism.

The prisoners were, if anything, conservative. They were, for example, smitten with the Royal family, and most would have read Woman's Day, if it had more stuff about cars. Even the prisoners' hankering after king and queen and prince and princess was pure sentiment, a longing for the perfect family they never had, and hardly a political notion. If a prisoner ventured beyond the personal to consider some wider system or scheme of things, it was only to rail against the legalistic web in which he was trapped. That struggle was all-engrossing; it sapped his energy for any campaign on a broader front, such as politics. Gramsci's was a voice in the wilderness.

The one issue he may sensibly have campaigned on - if he had advocated democratic elections and not some anachronistic proletarian tyranny - was reform of drug laws. This was wide open for Gramsci to exploit, as it was not a big vote-winner for more conventional politicians. Too risky. Better to lock up the victims of a bad piece of law than risk your political neck changing it. But prisoners who had been around long enough to know how things worked - and not too long to forget or be beyond care - challenged the fairness and justice of the current view of addict as criminal. Gramsci, given any political savvy, would surely have taken up this cause if only as kindling for the fires of revolution he hoped some day to ignite. But he was silent on the whole question. Perhaps he was too engrossed in his deeper exegesis of means of production and class struggle and historicism. I don't know. And who am I to tell him how to run his revolution? To Gramsci, I was a mere bourgeois shop-keeper, cynically exploiting the honest proletariat of prisoners who toiled over my questions day after day, my computer as substitute for the cash register with which my class had always exploited the impecunious. Pressing on my keyboard was no different from ringing up a shop's takings, each day's profit measured out in another man's suffering and debt. Gramsci had told me as much, during that blighted therapy together.

"Ah, I can hear the data in your hard disk clanging as clearly as the coins in your pocket," he had said, accusingly. Was my unease merely the paranoia of possession, the haves versus the have-nots? Gramsci thought so:

"What does the good doctor do before moving into his big new mansion but erect metal bars to keep out the hoi-polloi? Now you can safely be barbecued, grilled on the protective grills, which prevent your escape. It is a cage you have made for yourself, doctor. You are trapped in your own fears, immured in the prison of your childhood."

This was typical of the attacks he had inflicted on me in our sessions. It was only later that I wondered how he knew these details about my personal life. And there was invariably a sidelong threat, veiled in his verbosity:

"Do not invite Molotov in for a cocktail, comrade," Gramsci concluded.

These sessions had invariably left me shaken. I knew they were going nowhere, but felt powerless to stop them. I needed supervision, and should reasonably have turned to my professor for advice about the counter-transference complexities, but a residual mistrust prevented me from confiding in her. No, Gramsci was a personal demon with whom I had to struggle alone.

He had challenged every aspect of my smug routine, applying notions of class struggle to the transference in an idiosyncratic dialectic, a collision between the world views of Freud and Marx.

"This will do you good," he would say. "You analysts need a jolt to keep you honest. Now, doctor, I could not help noticing how you introduce yourself as 'doctor' to the prisoners you use as research fodder, and yet address them by their first name. This smacks to me of some power differential, a setting of the hierarchy from the outset, perhaps even condescension, no? And you invariably take the higher seat, the one closer to the door. I submit, doctor, that the march of your science could learn a lot from the laws which govern the march of history."

I was at a loss. Gramsci's insights penetrated to the heart of the matter, and yet were uttered with an infuriating insouciance. I had tried to meet his sarcasm with bland acceptance, and thereby blunt its edge, but truly I did not know what to take seriously, as he always hinted at some subtle joke by his mischievous and ironic tone. Trying to pin him down was like trying to nail jelly to a wall.

"Yes, Gramsci, I am a shop-keeper. I smile and play nice to make my customers and myself happy. Nobody gets hurt. Then I maybe bring them back for a longer interview, for which they receive a cup of tea or coffee with real sugar, which they cannot get in the wings. Plenty of white powder there to shoot up their veins, but none to sprinkle on their Weet-Bix in case it is mixed with vegemite to ferment an intoxicating substance. But some will not be bribed. That's OK. I don't take it to heart. No skin off my nose."

Gramsci was staring at me throughout my apologia, unnerving me. But I had pressed on:

"I defy all 'isms'. I'm just a regular guy whose ambitions have been dashed on the hard rocks of the real world. I just want to get by, accumulate 600 interviews, write my study, and then retire, live off an academic pension. So, you see, this is my swan-song. Like Moses, you never saw your promised land of worker's paradise, save one Pisgah glance. Will you then begrudge my modest wishes, and mess them up?"

I had almost moved myself to tears with this heart-felt plea. Gramsci was impassive. If any emotion played across his face it may have been amusement. I had tried to go one down to go one up, but felt trampled. Then his face contorted with a sudden rage.

"You must find an 'ism' and be prepared to die for it!" he bellowed. "Subvert the dominant paradigm!"

This was too much. There are rules for therapy, and one is no angry shouting. It was so discourteous, not to mention even more unsettling than his impassivity. I had terminated the session then and there.

"Paradigm is an 'igm', not an 'ism'," I said as parting comment, but Gramsci's voice, and his ideas, continued to haunt my waking hours. I had needed help, but back then was too proud or nervous to ask.

TRUST AND GENIUS

Chia was the one person I could have trusted. He had been a steady and reasonable influence throughout the prison year, this god-forsaken project, but I only confided in him when these struggles with Gramsci had long ceased.

"Science is not an 'ism'," he reassured me when I told him of that long ago conversation with Gramsci . "But wasn't Gramsci that political prisoner. Why did you have anything to do with him?"

"Gramsci was my special patient, Chia. Yes, he's the one with the dead dog, the political prisoner, as you say. You never knew it, but I used to see him for therapy sessions once a week, then once a day. Funny how things can escalate."

I felt calm now, discussing what had once been a terrible torment, like the recovered alcoholic addressing his AA* meeting. Having vowed to abstain from contact with Gramsci, I was several weeks 'dry'.

"But he was involved in that attempted break-out. They never found who gave him the sewage maps," Chia said.

---

* AA initials of alcoholics anonymous, a self-help group with spiritual overtones, begun in the USA in the 1930s

A look of concern ruffled his almost inscrutable visage.

"Did anyone else know about those sessions? And whose therapy was it - yours or his?" he pressed on.

"His, of course. I shouldn't discuss it, really. The sessions with Gramsci are private and confidential, like any therapy. "

"Nothing is confidential in this place, you know. By the sound of it, you were getting a little out of your depth. Just as well those sessions are over. You look flustered, like you haven't had any sleep," he said.

"Chia, everything's fine."

"Maybe you should take the day off. You can catch up on any missed prisoners tomorrow."

"The work must not be interrupted," I said peremptorily.

I did not like Chia's tone, and regretted assuming that I could trust him. I could see that he had been told not to give anything away. Chia was obviously being cautious, hedging. I didn't hold that against him, but felt sorry that our friendship had been unable to withstand this political intrigue which surrounded us all. Still, I had to admit I didn't know what pressure they had put him under. Perhaps his family had been threatened. Wouldn't put it past them. I was up against something big, and it was getting bigger. Once again I kept my counsel and pressed on with my work.

But I could not help thinking that Gramsci had been right, at least as far as his attitude to 'The Cause', whatever cause it might be. Fanaticism is attractive by its all-engrossing nature, which is also its failing, a lack of balance. This was no time for balance: I had been backed into a corner. There was no-one to turn to, so the all-or-nothing promise of devotion to some 'ism' was becoming harder to resist. Besides, the doctor's credo of moderation in all things is merely an apologia for mediocrity. I needed to find some bid for greatness to get me out of this mess. I was still convinced that science was the surest path to man's redemption, so I needed a new experiment, another project.

I had read of a bizarre eighteenth century experiment to map out the pathology of the criminal brain. It was a crude attempt to inoculate the healthy subject with an extract of the brain of a prisoner, to determine how much of criminality was biological and how much environmental. Genius, and such a sacrifice for Science. Those were the days of heroism, before ethics committees ruined all the fun and turned us intrepid scientific pioneers into so many bean counting plodders.

Gramsci had said a man should be prepared to die for his ism. But the next subject summoned for my project was a softly-spoken, effete cocaine addict who was HIV positive. Somehow, I did not feel that the inoculation experiment was warranted just yet. His demand for a gay cell-mate had been refused.

"It's not for sex or anything," he said. "It's just so I can be myself."

I did not care to share his viral contagion. What if I died of AIDS before the innate criminality of his brain could be expressed in my behaviour? Things were more complicated than I had foreseen.

THE ROYAL GAME

Bogdan was daily paraded before the court and hungry media circus, but I, too, was after him. I wanted another piece of the action. His crimes became my vicarious notoriety at social gatherings. The "inside" stories I could garner from prison fed the relish for evil of those whose lives conformed. Do not carp about the ethics of such titillations. The soul of discretion ruins the best dinner parties, and besides, I always changed the names and salient details. And Bogdan's responses to my longer interview would be important data for the study of the mind of a man accused of heinous crimes.

He had initially refused my request for a second interview, but I was persistent in my hunt for Bogdan. If his was the face of evil, then evil's was an attractive face: clean-shaven, bespectacled, and with sensuous lips. His odd smile remained disconcerting, a furtive grimace, creepy like Mona Lisa's hint of wry amusement, not that I am suggesting she was a mass murderer - but you never know. Who would ever have suspected such a sweet, shy, mysterious girl as her? Perhaps Bogdan in his smile was merely expressing bemusement at this arrest and sudden torrent of attention, just as she had been bemused by da Vinci's artistic toil. Bogdan looked more podgy than you would expect, and his hands too were delicate, like Mona's.

Trapped in traffic on my way to prison, among the other commuting nonentities, I felt special, because I was not just listening to the news, I would be close to its subject - the allegedly murderous Bogdan. An audience with him made me a somebody. Bogdan's solicitor was being interviewed on the radio:

"My client is innocent until proven guilty. This is trial by media. I demand justice."

I looked around at my fellow travellers, ordinary people, men and women in the street, going from safe suburban homes to ordinary jobs. Some thought Bogdan did it: "Guilty as sin. Solicitors lie - look how many become politicians." Others saw him as a scapegoat, a bogus arrest, flung into jail to glorify the police effort.

After each day in court, Bogdan was briefly held in the pen near the clinic, where I approached him several times to arrange another interview. I tried to act casual, like he was just another subject in my research, one of the six hundred who happened to be selected for a longer interview, completely at random. He was loafing in the cell, hardly distracted by the afternoon TV. But each time I sauntered up to him, he would nod and say,

"No worries, doctor. I sleep fine," or "Appetite good. No problem," and wave me away with a whisk of his hairless forearm. He was always friendly, in an inscrutable sort of way. Once he said, "Sure, any time." But no time had yet arrived. Today he had been formally charged. This was a perfect opportunity. I simply had to see him, and waited all day in eager anticipation, hovering around the holding cell and badgering the remand reception officers.

"Truck in yet, Larry?" I asked.

"Nope."

"On the way?"

"Dunno."

"Should be in soon, shouldn't it?"

"Maybe."

This was all the information I needed. I devised my tactics. This time, I would use my wits. The honest approach had failed, so I would wheedle my way into Bogdan's trust by offering him a game of chess. Like all European émigrés, I felt certain he was a chess boffin, and if chess with the Devil was good enough for Ingmar Bergman, chess with the prince of prisoners was good enough for me. Then, at the end of the game, as I basked in the glow of the dying embers of battle - and Bogdan was still shell-shocked from the devastation of his army - I would surreptitiously begin my longer interview, slipping the questions under his guard. I was sure he would accept the offer of a game.

"I prefer to play yahtzee," he said.

"We lost our dice," I said

"Ah. OK. Chess. Bags be white."

I was even more confident now, given that chess had not been his first choice, and his chess etiquette was so appalling, but the game did not go according to plan. I was au fait with the fianchetto, the giuoco piano, the tooti frutti, the pistachio and the Sicilian, but none of these chess ploys, pizza toppings, and gelato flavours prepared me for Bogdan's opening gambit. Like the gelato genius who invented cassata, and the pizza patriot who first flung egg and ham on cheese and called it the "Australian", Bogdan had created something original: a new chess opening, the "Warsaw Special". When he unleashed the special on me, I walked straight into the trap: I took the King's pawn.

"My opponents almost always do," he later told me. "They can't resist." Things went well, at first, and by move ten, I felt I had the upper hand. My pieces were developed, I controlled the centre, and had a phalanx of pawns on the fourth rank, bearing down on Bogdan's queen side. But it was an illusory advantage. I was attacking like the Romans against Hannibal at Cannae, 216BC - with half my army. The Roman's lost. Bogdan regrouped swiftly, swinging his knight around to attack my exposed king side in a tactic known as the Mad Hanam. A move later, his bishop swooped to pin my knight. Bogdan had suddenly grasped the initiative. My position was weakened by what I now realised had been a hasty attack. He dictated the tempo, and I panicked. My pieces floundered on those sixty-four squares, a universe upon which Bogdan had cast a merry spell. Tentatively, I pushed out a pawn to challenge his bishop. But his move had been a feint, and now my king side was in disarray. He gripped his plastic queen, tapping the piece on the wooden board with a staccato sound like a rattlesnake's tail, before plunging her into my territory.

"Check!" he said. "And my tanks are in your capital."

I had never seen such a vicious onslaught. I tried the manic defence, in which the doomed player feigns a bout of uncontrollable hilarity and inadvertently knocks the pieces off the board. Unfortunately, Bogdan was too fast for me, and swept the board from my reach. There was nothing more I could do, given the paranoid-schizoid position of my pieces, and I resigned four moves later.

"Next time, we play yahtzee?" he asked at the end of the game. I returned, shattered, to the clinic.

"Do you think he did it?" Shauna asked me.

"Did what?" I snapped.

"The bloody crime."

"Oh, that. Dunno. Didn't ask him."

"I wouldn't expect HE'D tell you if he did it. I asked did YOU think he did it?!" Shauna sounded exasperated.

"Perhaps a dingo did it," I said.

"Dingos don't rape people."

"Well, I guess in YOUR case it wouldn't have to be rape."

Things were getting out of hand between us. I seemed to be arguing with everyone lately, but I was cranky about losing to Bogdan, and I also knew Shauna thought I was a tosser, a toff, a wanker. To her, I was "full of it", with my psychiatric training, and always putting on airs about my important research. I'd seen her look disdainfully at me when I was discussing scientific notions with Chia or Nick. She would glance up from her fag, curl her upper lip into a sneer, make the barest moan, and look away. She resented me, I could tell. It had taken a few months to crystallise, but it was there. She especially resented signing as witness to the consent procedure, a chore which I had foisted fully onto her since Sam's departure.

It was an unwritten law that you never asked a prisoner if he did it, but of course we all wondered, and offered opinions, particularly if it was as famous a case as Bogdan's. But Nick had been unable to resist asking the last major news figure, a notorious masked rapist/ murderer, perhaps because one of his daughter's friends had been a witness in the trial. When the bloke came in for some Panadol for a headache, Nick insisted he be thoroughly examined.

"You never know - it could be a brain tumour," he told the rapist, who had in fact worn the mask not for disguise but because he suffered from photophobia, an early symptom. Then, half-way through examining the rapist's cranial nerves, Nick had nonchalantly asked:

"So, ahh, did you do it?"

And his patient had replied: "I dunno what you're talking about."

"Well, why were you so violent with them - some of them were just kids?" Nick pressed on.

"Oh, that. To make sure they were dead. Didn't want no witnesses."

I did not ask Bogdan directly. Who knows if he did it? Did he himself even know? His denial in court was fact, fact enough for the vast legal mechanism to grind into action, beginning at innocence, and moving across a terrain without tracks - the geography of the past. These are the ideas and ideals of the law: today, whoever committed those crimes, it was not Bogdan. It happened, an act perpetrated by someone, not him, against someone, a victim, and another and another. The actions were final, frozen in time and stopped there, detached, split off and unregistered in another self. They were not here, not now - not in the man with whom I had just played chess, the inventor of the Warsaw Special. How could they be? The negation of life had no life of its own. Like the victims themselves, the past was dead and buried, in the processes of denial, but not in the eyes of the law. A disinterred corpse is as inanimate as those chess pieces we moved in acquiescence to the discontinuity of every existence. Self is a myth, just as plot is illusory. There is no one thread to unravel. Stories and life stories unfold organically, ending in death, itself an organic regrowth. But we cannot see around corners - that is the problem. It all looks straight, too straight. We miss the curves and parabolas and barely touched tangents which skew the fragile boxes we construct. Our pain-staking work - erecting and renovating certainty - might as well be a house of cards, built on a rickety raft of ideas and hopes and dreams (of justice, of love, of peace) cast out on an ocean, whose awesome expanse we cannot fathom. The best we can do is stay afloat, maybe do a bit of fishing, wear a hat. One wave will smash our fragile vessel, and toss us to the sharks - one indifferent wave.

We are no wiser than the sniffer dogs blindly and wordlessly following a scent, no more able to explain, still less understand. Call the expert witness, a scientist.

"What is a scent?" we ask him.

"An aromatic compound," Science tells us, and maybe draws a picture: "It looks like this."

"Oh, I see. Perfectly clear now, I'm sure. Yes, well, mmm. Don't just stand there, man, show it to the jury."

They nod knowingly, knowing nothing. It is an existential travesty to resolve some past action with a reaction, a conviction, to culminate in a calumny, a finding of guilty, a sentence.

What then must be done? If no plot is real, and nothing was done, how do we move on? There is no end to what never happened. It was sincere, Bogdan's plea of 'not guilty'. Listen to him:

"Don't you understand? I am still smiling. I am talking now. If I am guilty, where is the blood, where is the stain? Look at these hands. They moved the chess pieces. I won. You lost - and I taught you my Warsaw Special. What does that make me - a murderer?"

A murderer in the throes of denial will deny death throes allegedly inflicted. Was Bogdan a murderer, now asking himself to carry on, by telling himself the Big Lie? Truth has a way of intruding, because everything is related in life, although we try to keep things apart, split off and atomised. Turning different faces, it is always the same face. And yet there is no precision to our past, no latitude and longitude of memory's map, no ubiety of mind.

"Show me, show me up here in my cerebral cortex, the seat of my conscious being, where and when such a thing could be. It is not there - not in me. You are all wrong!"

Bogden was raving now, but he would settle down, and, true to the cliché, he would 'show no emotion' as he was led away from court for the last time. He wore no mask, for he was as innocent in his own eyes as he was guilty in the prosecutor's. Do not mistake the truth for justice. Courts do not seek truth, only that justice be seen to be done.

This is a charade, but it's easy to be critical. What are the solutions? The rough justice of the prison yard had a certain appeal in its due process - the law of the jungle, among noble savages. Bogdan was safe with them. The other prisoners respected him. A man accused of murder had a certain standing, as long as no minors were involved, so Bogdan did not need protection.

DIRTY

A night of mayhem in the wings slowed everything down the following day.

"One death, two suicide attempts," Larry told me as he opened the back gate. "A junkie. Probable OD."

"Another one down. How many this year?" I asked.

"Too many. It's... degrading," Larry said, searching his limited vocabulary for the 'bon mot'.

"For them and for us," I replied.

Let-go would be delayed, but I headed for the clinic, to catch up on the gossip, and maybe have another brush with Bogdan, although my enthusiasm for the pursuit of notoriety had dulled. Everything felt dull that morning.

"Oh, the quiet life for me," I said to Shauna.

"Well don't come in here then," she replied, friendly as a Rottweiler.

Another death meant another bunch of theories: was it a 'hot-shot', or accidental? Did he have someone out to get him? Was he a regular user? In that clinic tea-room, we produced dozens of coroner's reports without needing an autopsy. We might as well have been discussing last night's football: instant experts gathered in earnest, espousing their own guesses as fact, denigrating others' guesses as fiction. Knowing what happened and why and saying it loudly to other people who know why it didn't happen that way and why not.

There was an official response to this death: a memo telling the nurses to dispense more methadone. But a junkie explained that this was no solution:

"See, more 'done will only increase yer tolerance, doc, so you need to shoot up with more smack to get the same rush. It mucks up yer calculations, that's all."

At last the new prisoners arrived. Among them was old Stan, an alkie who lived in a bed-sitter, and was as well-known to the local Casualty as to the prison nurses. He was followed home twice in the last month from the pub along inner city lanes and bashed for a pittance. There would never be much change from his pension after he'd had a skinful. But the blue-black stain I saw over his bald pate was not from a mugging.

"Took a rum fit, doc. Bloody grog. Don't remember a thing," he said. His dentures clip-clopped as he spoke. His craggy hands trembled, but it was too early for a full-blown delirium.

"I get the horrors like a beauty," he said proudly.

I finished the interview with my usual question:

"Have you ever felt like you were useless, or sinful, or guilty?"

"All three in spades," he said. "Specially the guilts. I'm a lapsed Catholic, see, but don't get no comfort from mother Church no more. The priest says I outta be a lapsed alkie. But I'm a silly old coot. Don't even know why I'm here. This is prison, isn't it?"

Where else could he be - with the high walls, sturdy gates, barred windows - except maybe a zoo. It's an education, to see the animals close-up, although not in their natural habitat. They don't bite, and seldom snarl. If old Stan snarled, his dentures would drop out, clattering onto concrete.

"We don't let ourselves show it, doc, but a bloke who's been nicked is dirty - dirty mainly on himself. So dirty he could cry."

Listen to Stan, the lexicographer:
What's irritable mean, Stan?
Dirty.
What's frustrated mean?
Dirty.
What's depressed mean?
Dirty.

It's a useful word, if not pretty - 'dirty'.

The next prisoner was an alkie, too. There must have been a clean-up of alkie haunts, to get two in a day. Ces was as dirty as Stan, and no prettier, but where Stan would not have said 'boo' to a goose, Ces hit the holding cell like a dervish. He threatened anyone in sight with a "floggin'", unless they happened to be in a skirt, in which case he promised them something they'd never forget.

"It's ten on the slack and fourteen on the brute!" he yelled down the corridor at a female officer. He puckered his thick ruby lips between ginger stubble and pawed at Shauna's breasts.

"Siddown, Ces."

"Will if yer gimme a kiss."

Ces rested his elbows on his walking frame. A moist yellow globule appeared between the tips of his forefingers, pressed into the side of his ruddy schnoz.

"Blackheads," he growled.

Shauna groaned.

"I'll give yer somethin' to really groan about, cutie," Ces leered, running a beefy tongue over his blackened pegs.

The doctor to see Ces was old George, back after his run-in with Charlene. Nick must have had another overnight shift in Casualty, I assumed. George introduced himself in his usual jovial fashion.

"Why don't you fuck off," Ces replied. "Can'tcha see I'm talkin' to me girlfriend?"

George feigned indignation, but there was a bond between doctor and patient that such insults could not break.

"Bet you're a boozer, too, with a face like that, doc. You didn't get it from sunburn, I'll give yer the drum," Ces said.

"Well, Ces, you've found me out. Now how's about I get you up on the bed here," George said. "Have a feel of your liver, if it's still there."

"Corse it's there. How do yer think I do me metabolism? But if anyone lays a hand on me I'll flog 'em orright. And if anyone lays a hand on you, darlin', I'll flog 'em even harder," he said to Shauna. "I kin look after meself. I'm a southpaw."

Ces put up his dukes, wobbling without the support of his frame. Shauna tried to placate him, to allow George to get on with the examination.

"You've just had a birthday, Ces," Shauna said.

"Bullshit."

"Yeah - 30th June. It's on your ID card."

"Wot's today?"

"First of July."

"Oh yeah? Must've lost track. How old am I?"

"Sixty-two."

"Old enough to know better, eh darlin'?"

"You're right there, Ces."

But Ces was feisty as ever, and George had to abandon his laying on of hands. Bill, the helpful officer, knelt at Ces's feet to put his sandshoes back on. Ces got some valium for the night, and a cell on the bottom landing where he would await his trial in four days. His charges were 'assault police officer' and 'offensive language'.

"Swung me frame at 'em, the pigs. I'd do it again, too. I fight like a mongrel. I'd kick 'em in the head, orright, I'll give yer the drum. No-one messes with old Ces. I'm a southpaw."

The magistrate had refused bail, perhaps to ensure Ces a feed and a wash.

Back in the holding cell, an officer was yelling at him to "Shut the fuck up!" Of course, this incited Ces to ever louder obscenities, threats and demands. He steadied himself on his frame to harangue a frail and cowering prisoner awaiting transfer to the psychiatric ward. It was a pathetic contest. The other prisoner turned away, quivering in a corner of the bench. Ces could not believe his luck to have such a weak - albeit temporary - cell-mate.

"Come on - I'll fight yer, yer yellow dog!" Ces yelled at the other prisoner.

"Cut it out, Ces," an officer said wearily.

But Ces ignored him. He was edging closer to his victim.

"Ah, yer a nancy boy. Got them little Napoleons to stick up for you."

Ces was having a ball. Wherever he went, he attracted attention. Perhaps it was his charisma, or that people were curious to discover the source of all the commotion. This was a stage, with a captive audience. And Ces performed non-stop, a merry mayhem of curses and laughs and dismay he kicked up around himself. See the bill-board:

"Roll up, roll up! Ces on Show. Three nights only, exclusive to the Remand Prison. Tickets at the gate for the legendary, all-singing, all-dancing, all-night revue by the outrageous southpaw and raconteur, on his last ever tour!"

This would be one hell of a circus:

See Ces swig a flagon of brown muscat in one gulp while toppling from a moving bus and not spill a drop of grog, "but lose plenty of claret from me schnoz!"

See Ces take on all-comers in no-holds-barred fistic fury.

See Ces smoke the fattest and grubbiest ever roll-yer-own.

See Ces squeeze 18 gallons of pus from a single black-head.

See the fossil with the colossal tossil, a staggering fourteen inches on the brute. (Some nights the brute is slack, but still an impressive ten inches to ogle.)

Hear Ces produce the longest continuous stream of invective, and phlegm.

... Yes sirree, you're damned if you go, and damned if you don't. Remember to wear a rain-coat at the show. Bye now.

The prison circus carried on, after Ces, as it had before. Each morning an obese three-striper began his day with a Mantra: "Fuck I hate this place. Fuck I hate it." He would say it over and over, muttering as he opened the gate to let me in. I knew better than to take it personally. The officer was suffering from 'burn-out'. Perhaps he had some concerns about his prospects for promotion, and was serving his time until release, like everyone else there.

Even armed robbers got burnt out, and eventually contemplated retirement, like this 48 year-old recidivist.

"At my age, most blokes take it easy, throttle back a little. Not me. I'm a bloody mug. Spent everythin' I stole. Pissed it up against a wall in hotels up north. Funny thing when you haven't earnt it yerself. You spend it on any old thing. Like it's not even your own, which it isn't. Shit eh."

I remembered Sam.

TREE OF LIFE

"I just love trees, doctor,"

"Yes, me too. I think they're very nice."

"No, you don't understand. I LOVE trees. I can't live without them."

"No, none of us can. We need oxygen, see, which trees produce by photosynthesis. So we all need trees."

"Doc, look out at the yard. What don't you see?"

"Trees."

"Exactly. No trees, no life. I'll kill myself if I have to stay here, in a place with no trees."

But if there were trees in the prison yard they would be taken as scaffolds, prisoners dangling as strange blue fruit to meet the dawn.

I kept dealing myself a hand, convinced that this would be the biggie, this would make my name, set me up. As long as I could make a bid, exert myself at something - it didn't matter what - then I felt my life and its fantasies were sustainable. The hot air of narcissism would keep things buoyant, out of reach of the sharp jags of reality, or melancholia. I needed a buffer zone of desires and plans. As each sunk or disintegrated, I found another to take its place. So instead of achievement or purpose, I was devoted to a ceaseless scurrying from one distraction to another, all the while avoiding an inkling of the futility of my small ambitions, of my small life. I resolved to do my own thing, but until that came along, I did other things. Like this prison project, and this therapy with Gramsci which I had latched onto with typical zealotry. My hopes and aims were extravagant. "With this patient, my reputation will soar!" I had said to my professor, more as a plea for approval than as a boast. "With this case, I will rewrite the analytical oeuvre."

"That's not how you say oeuvre," she demurred. "And who are you trying to impress with your sesquipedalia?"

"My father."

How could I make a bid for greatness in the face of such nit-picking? I could concede, however, that even for me I was getting carried away. There had been an emotional investment in Gramsci that was, let's face it, unhealthy. But I couldn't see it at the time. We all have psychological blind-spots, regions of the mind and memory which are too painful to acknowledge, perhaps damaged by past trauma, or an innate tendency resulting from characterological factors. Gramsci was smack bang in the middle of my blind-spot. And all he left me was regrets.

ANSWERS

Even as my research interviews accumulated, Gramsci continued to dominate my thoughts like a riddle whose meaning I could not fathom, or lyrics muffled by a tune. I had not seen him since our rendezvous in the prison clinic, weeks ago, and had heard nothing further about him. He had disappeared into the prison ether. I had no answers.

This uncertainty reminded me of the effects of schizophrenia. The initial or prodromal descent into psychosis has been likened to stage-fright. The world becomes unnerving: things have changed, people are different, in a way that one cannot quite fathom. Dread begins imperceptibly. Asking the patient to recount just when things seemed to alter, or when he last felt OK, is like trying to hold onto a cloud. The patient, losing his mind, often casts about desperately for sign-posts, some mental hold on himself and his world. This is known as *'effort after meaning'*, and we all engage in it, with variable success, but in the case of schizophrenia, meaning is crystallised in delusional ways. The very fabric of mental life is ripped, and through the gaps, new vistas of experience appear, or erupt. The quality of being can no longer be trusted, as it too is a function of mind, and the mind has suffered a compound fracture. Bits stick out here and there, jagged edges where the boundary between inner and outer has burst. Just imagining this for a moment is enough terror for most of us. Try living like that.

After these morbid struggles with encroaching madness have run their course, a burned-out state may ensue. The so-called positive symptoms of hallucination and delusion are replaced by a negative state – a kind of shutting down. Engagement with the world grinds to a halt. The fires of natural enthusiasm are extinguished. This resembles melancholia, but may be distinguished by a more profound flattening of affective life, devoid even of suffering. The typical facial expression of a patient with long-standing schizophrenia has been likened to ground glass: it is opaque, an inscrutable blankness. I feel a more accurate hallmark of the condition is the sinking feeling, as into quicksand, engendered by schizophrenic circumlocution.

I recognised in therapy with Gramsci the same frustration, the frustration of striving for a deeper meaning, for some meaning. I had wanted to burst through his defences, to dive into the essence of the man's psychopathology. But Gramsci had allowed me only to dip my toes in the water, restricting my immersion into his psychic soup, even as he had dived into mine. His diagnosis was not schizophrenia: Gramsci was in control.

The morbid process, then, was in me. This is not the worst problem to have, not the gravest predicament. I was floundering, but squandered potential is what prisons are all about - for prisoners and officers and scientists. I obsessed over the details of my time with Gramsci, seeking markers along the therapeutic process. There were few firm holds in my own effort after meaning. Returning to facts, the knowledge of beginning, would surely resolve this uncertainty of ending. Detail gives some refuge, as words are a welcome flight from silent feeling.

I considered how our final engagement began at the remand holding cell had heralded my psychotic break, and a dog had died, and the fever of paranoia had arisen in my soul. Again, only more questions arose. Who could I turn to?

THE FALL

This is about me. I'm doing it for myself, and it's my right to find happiness: you only live once. This is my decision, my journey. I suppose I could be called selfish.

To hell with prison, with the research project, which after all had only been a template for the erection of a personal edifice, another unshared experience. Psychoanalysis, too, had failed to sustain me – either as Blind Freddy's patient or in my last fling as therapist with Gramsci. That crazy pinball of self was again flung between awareness and experience, before crashing into pieces. I attempted some simulacrum of intimacy in recorded observation, as if the act of representation could pass for love. This prison journal was my last bid for honesty, but I squandered its promise, as I had squandered this resurrection of my professional career. Onto the metaphors of crime and punishment, onto all the sorry tales of all the sorry men I saw, I had projected my own tawdry neuroses, knowing those prisoners were like me, and scorning them for it. If the pre-requisite for love is giving, the first gift to bestow upon love's object is attention. The essence of mature love – as opposed to infatuation - is awareness, to see things as they are. I had not seen or learnt a thing. I was as burned out as anyone with schizophrenia.

What, then, if there was no prison, no walled refuge, no asylum? Madness and badness flood the streets: huddled humanity, side-stepped by the scurrying purposes of society. Nothing could be further from the fact than fiction, from truth than falsity, but each needs the other as defining point. The hammer strikes the anvil, light hits the retina, and we see the spark. Action arises between an impulse dimly perceived, and an illusory outcome. Thought can be replaced by many things, subsumed in many guises. Thoughts appear as a convenient and seemingly necessary reflex, flowing over the felt spaces of emptiness. Actions follow. The moment is seized, not contemplated.

I must remove my hand from these eyes, to reveal something deeper than cynicism which itself is a shield from the suffering of the spirit, the purest ache for a beauty of love which deserves better than life's trituration, but who alive escapes that prison?

I reached perfect stillness - hovering attention - when in Gramsci's cell, under his malign influence. This was an addiction. I had listened too avidly, mesmerised beyond awareness, by a voice whose words meant nothing I can recall. But his meaning was immediate. Comprehension and memory are merely the residue of meetings between lesser beings. I did not need them then. I could not recall the slightest details of our last sessions, nor could I even see myself carrying out his commands during my psychotic break; I was enthralled. These actions were my downfall. From dream to the harshness of this: I now write in his place.

Few shames strike the psychiatrist as heavily as that of falling in love with his patient. Did I fall in love with Gramsci? There is no other explanation for what

I did. He polluted my character, by artful and abstract seduction he inveigled himself into my life. Gramsci applied his theory of political hegemony to the personal: the imposition of a system of beliefs on a people persuaded they are still free. So I was turned, from doctor to patient, and from master to slave.

CHANGING PLACES

One morning, an almighty explosion blew out the prison wall adjacent to Gramsci's cell. In the chaos of noise and dust and rubble, Gramsci fled to a waiting get-away vehicle, and was never found again. That day, the professor, too, disappeared without a trace.

The full apparatus of state counter-terrorism was mobilised to investigate the political prisoner's escape. Agents interviewed me in my clinic office. I did not think that I could help them in their enquiries, and was surprised at their aggressive tone. One of the agents produced a warrant to search my person. A signed credit card receipt for electrical wire, an explosive, a timer and a detonator were found in my wallet. I recognised my signature, but did not recall their purchase, which, by the date on the receipt, had occurred during my psychotic break. I was accused of smuggling these items to Gramsci one at a time via the prison clinic. And to think how fearful I had once been to even smuggle in a packet of cigarettes!

The court refused my defence that Gramsci's hypnosis rendered me not responsible for my actions, lacking *mens rea**. My barrister had argued, quite plausibly, I thought,

----

* mens rea is Latin for guilty mind. It is a legal term for criminal intent

that the murder of Gramsci's dog was a test to see if I had been put under his spell, and to see how far I would go in carrying out his mission. But the expert witness, Dr King, argued that hypnotherapy can only cause one to commit an act that accords with one's pre-existing volition.

I was found guilty, and sent to that same prison that I knew so well. But now I was to find out about it from the inside.

"We had our suspicions about you, doc. Your bogus research was a fine front for a while," Larry told me as I lined up behind the bars of the holding cell, being processed, numbered, and assigned to a wing.

I am placed in strict protection. Sanity's grip weakens, which opens new regions to explore, experience, observe, record.

I think about writing, about the transition from journal to story, from report to creation, from fact to fiction. I am my only reader and critic, which is reassuring, but makes progress difficult. These words reassure me, their blue scrawl relieves the whiteness of the page, as the self-inflicted laceration unites perpetrator and victim. Writing is mutilation's abstraction, an echo in ideas of the sound of the cutting up of the sweep of experience through time. I should write in red: at least blood flows like truth.

What is best for the writer - serenity or struggle? Perhaps writing itself is the struggle for serenity, which, of course, can never be attained. This returns us to a totality of process, means without ends, the unfinished, incomplete completion, which stops when it stops, commas spluttering and wheezing towards a gasped punctuation boldly signalling rest, cessation, annihilation. The End.

HOPES OF REPRIEVE

Chia came to see me. He bowed his head in respectful greeting as he entered my cell. "I am sorry to see you here like this, doc," he said. "You know the professor has not been seen since Gramsci escaped? It seems they have fled the country, together. I have evidence of their intimacy."

I interrupted his insinuations: "Listen Chia, don't try to tell me that there was some tryst between that vile creature and the professor. I am sure he was an incorrigible invert. And besides, sex with Gramsci would be like fucking a vulture."

"That is not what the professor seemed to think," Chia said. He frowned, and appeared for a moment disgusted. Then he continued: "I don't expect this will make things any easier, but the evidence indicates just what the professor was doing in setting you up as Gramsci's therapist. Don't you see? That allowed Gramsci to get you to help him escape. You already told the court how Gramsci hypnotised you before your break. It wasn't your fault, doc. There's no mens rea, so no guilt. We are planning to appeal your conviction. Meanwhile Gramsci gets away, and the professor goes with him. And you end up in his place – here. Even in the same cell that had once been Gramsci's. It breaks my heart."

My head was reeling with Chia's preposterous story. Then again, it sounded so bizarre, perhaps it was true.

"Chia, you said you have evidence. What is it?" I asked.

"This file was found on the professor's computer. No-one has linked her disappearance with Gramsci's escape… yet. You shouldn't have this, and I never gave it to you."

He handed me a document. It looked familiar: the title contained that same word – 'Desire' – as I had read on the pages which Gramsci had handed me during our therapy, and which I had so recklessly torn to shreds. But now I read the full title – 'Desire and Transgression' - and all that followed, and as I read, I became more and more nauseated by its contents.

Nothing could prepare me for this. My eyes widened, and my mind raced, as I learnt how the professor's clinical encounter with Gramsci had evidently taken on a more personal meaning to her. This explained why she had so hastily handed his care over to me. And that decision had coincided with the governor's edict that therapy no longer occur in the professor's office, but must take place in the prisoner's cell.

Each page of the professor's clinical record was dated, and headed with the name of the patient, but in the case of the Marxist Italian hunchback, her usually meticulous notes took a decidedly gushing and heated tone. Psychiatrists refer to the colleague who sleeps with his or her patient as committing a boundary transgression, but in this case, such euphemisms appeared lame, sanitised, almost irrelevant. For what I read took the erotic transference to new depths of depravity. There was no sense of a containing of mental experience, of a considered response to the patient's clinical material, or even of an awareness of one's own emotional responses. What her notes recorded was a shameless merging with the patient's infantile and sexualised neediness. This was not therapy; this was exploitation. But too many questions arose. To start with, who was exploiting whom? The professor as therapist obviously began with the balance of power tilted in her favour.

The deviousness of Gramsci, his predatory and destructive impulses, were precisely what she wanted, what she exacerbated. Beneath her veneer of self-control, her academic pretensions, lay a psychotic core which she opened up to Gramsci. She had succumbed to this rogue element in the social fabric of prison, this vandal, perhaps to revivify her own lost adolescent son. That was her desire fulfilled, and grief disavowed.

I now realised why Gramsci had dared to offer me the 'Desire and Transgression' piece all those months ago. His own desire was simply to transgress, to turn the world upside down, just as he had been strung upside down and encased in plaster as a child. So he turned his psychoanalysts into his patients, placed the slave above the master, and the id above the ego, and caused psychosis to spill out all around him. Whether he wrecked my research, my career, or hers, made no difference to him. As long as there was some sabotage going on, he was fulfilled. In the end, he had driven us both insane. I felt capable of recovery. Was she?

How could the professor have been so naïve as to put these inflammatory and incriminating events into written form, and what possessed her to give Gramsci a copy? In writing, it was likely that she was attempting to find some self-reflective space even as she was losing all therapeutic and rational focus. I also suspected her of hubris, that same pride which allowed her to ignore her need for supervision, and for a personal analysis. This is the requirement of all those who work closely with disturbed patients, let alone the most destructive psychopaths, like Gramsci. The professor had not only gone where others fear to tread, she had no map or compass, and endangered the lives of those who would attempt now to come to her rescue. I knew Gramsci would fight to the death. Live or die, she had certainly created a tomb for her career. I would never recommend a psychiatrist who has not had his or her personal therapy, and most haven't. The professor and I were both his victims. I had no doubt her relationship with him was doomed. Gramsci had manipulated our psychological blind-spots, those vast lacunae of narcissism, through which you could drive a truck and through which he had escaped. And which my own analysis had failed to seal over. What would Blind Freddy make of all this?

Here is what I read that sleepless night, over and over again:

DESIRE AND TRANSGRESSION

One gasp uttered towards a pleasure, in its grip, anointing tongue with tongue, thigh with moist and giving sex, one gasp takes away what cannot be taken in because it is longing incarnate, and risks so much.

She said, heart and mouth quivering hard against him - she said: "I am overwhelmed..."

All sense found its way into her breast, as his finger traced its outlines beneath the white blouse, and beneath her reluctance, against her flesh, whose lips pressed and moulded and gathered then the momentum to go on, going further, being taken and taking in the new delight of the lapping lash of their meeting tongues in whose dance she could immerse her being while still being enraged, affronted, aroused to spill in tiny shudders what his touch now brought. She doubted her own touch, she doubted the very presence beneath her finger tips of this chiselled, fine sculpture of a man. There was no deformity, no bruise, no blemish. Her grasp now reached for its decadent reward, and took in both hands the erection she had felt hard against her thigh as they had standing kissed, as now no longer upright, but beginning in a languorous motion to slide and fall along a slope, a trajectory of bliss, and ignorant of purpose or desire for it had them both in its swallowed breath. She took his cock in her two hands, slid their flesh along its delight, and he too knew that he was being taken as an object, as desire's demand surrendered. Her lips still pressed into his. He gave her naked form its intensity of worship beneath the lull and idle insistence of shared pleasure. She was in a fury, raising her sex to his, her sex made raw, her panting need outraged by the flick and stroke of that molten lava flow, that heat in its containing measure too much to not be taken in, for too long she hung suspended as a rocket fuse sparkled, spluttered, shortening its black line from flame to an inevitability of explosive rendering in sound and trembling, fecund joy: he had brought the dome of his desire again and again onto the softest need of hers, and brought her to a zenith. Still he held himself back from her fulfilment, from filling her as she needed now to utterly enfold that dome, its shaft, his buttock driven in beneath her grip, to hear that response of his larynx in spasm as she had been and again became around the lust in hers. She traced his torso with her tongue, she willed her hands into his muscles, into his thighs, onto his kyphosis, gyrating as her fingers worked and fed their way behind his balls, ending at the moist hole of his which by the tiniest invitation she entered her fond digit. That led up to the first of his orgasms, and the twitching mouthing apocalypse swooped her into her own response, as their pudenda had melted in a cauldron of unconscious rhythm, celebration of the danger of difference, and its miracle here beneath her body of his, this woman astride this man, again in movement, and again in bliss surrendered each to the other. He reached up, his neck brought mouth against her nipple, and her head flung back in the palm of his strong hand, stroking, never losing that sure feel for hers.

Some shudder of relief to be kept in such suspense, for he could still take her then, without pause, again taking her into the bed, and falling upon the fear to make of it a thrill. She had felt against her bare thigh the hard fascination of his lust. His eyes now took her utterance, faltering in their drive to know, because she had made a separate sound, made of herself a separate lust from his, from theirs which he had usurped, and he could not then demand her submission, much as they both longed for it. He was a desperate criminal, a political animal, an excitement in him to churn within her darkness, within the arousal now uttered and now declared as him. Could he not see her invitation? Could he not sense the moment with his hard knowing throb?

That brutal sexuality in the mouthing swirl, a falling return into the black abyss, no longer the girl whose lust had shamed herself with its power - this was the plunge beyond dreams to experience, and beyond self, spending with her body, with her carnal desire, all her accumulated and accustomed ways of pleasure. A choice now made to discard the moment, and the past, and yet rise with its potential into broken pieces of herself, as a pulverising ocean beats against the giving sand, rends its grains, gripping her back, now arching, longing, rising as a tidal moan from a forbidden submerged city of erotic totems, the beating now insistent, surging from the loins whose sinews pulsed and subsided.

That his caress had drawn her longing to its tautness, its wild extent aroused, she knew was a necessity for the girth which then would prise her still further, beyond the zenith, beyond the bed, the room, the embrace their bodies traced beyond the space where she had felt her pleasure melting into this vast time. It was now beyond any reckoning of control that even as she was spreading wider than she had ever been, and pierced deeper than the womb - that even then she drew him further, daring, madly longing, never losing that presence filling hers at her own ringing gasp and shudder. The pulse of ecstasy shook her to the bone; the climbing ever further into the meeting of his sex, his demand that she succumb, that she force her own demons now to kneel as he had been forced by his desire to kneel at her raucous cry, "Oh, God, Oh God, Fuck me, Gramsci, please FUCK ME!" And as she yelled his name, a reflex took her whole mind, its darkest continent now flowing into his, she gripped him in a full celebration of this sex, this carnality, and brought him ever deeper, further now that her infinity had been broached, and slipped its spasms in rings encircling this massive cock that she had to know, to which she had sold her misgivings and her doubts and the ruin of her soul, attaining in the victory a man, the great gift his now to make: "Will you take my seed? Take me?! Have this man?!"

She yelped, a guttural pursuit of his lust, as though in the back of her throat lay all the waves of all the oceans fit to toss his massive elongated craft upon them, and break it into pieces, as then the rolling crashing passion launched him yet further against the shores of her coast, the outlines now of their fused continents glistening as though a storm had burst and was riven then with beams of light, and still the waves crashed, and still the roar broke over them, a torrent, and a paradise. She had never, she could never, she was taken, given, tossed, and never retrieved: this was the man in her, around her own being, and she around his firm and beautiful purpose. Their gaze directed the slower pulse - the iris hue which dimmed with its perceptible contraction as he came and came and came to her shuddering welcome, the womb, the bodies flung.

There would be no regrets, no chance to doubt that this had to occur, as destiny is stuff of future fused with legend. She had waited, prepared, and then anointed an afternoon of her life with the possibility of the greatness of desire. This had been achieved at no cost, even as the tears of hers spoke dripping upon his now dormant torso, her moistness laid upon its quiescent mass, and the lapping of their tongues confirming pleasure, confirming more to come.

There is no spell cast as hard as theirs that can ever break, nor any joining now beyond them. That assurance made her proud to be with him, his idiosyncratic beauty as her bed, and her audacity and gorgeous form as his delight.

Others faded, others never existed - there was not even other time than this eternal now with him. A universal clock has struck, as sure as the daily wash of tides, the meeting of their desire forever more and more than ever. She could only apologise for taking so long to allow this belief in herself, and her sex its gift as its expression.

That sex expressed in the shadow of their imprisonment what must be set free. They could no longer remain in this place. Their plan was underway, and each knew who would take the fall.

THE SIX HUNDREDTH SUBJECT

For all the so-called progress of civilisation, sex and paranoia remain the base metals of motivation. I spent a restless night, filled with lewd images of Gramsci and the professor entwined. Chia was right: I had been set up. Each disgusting thrust and counter-thrust of the professor's pornography seemed to press me deeper into their trap. Now, like Gramsci, I had nothing to lose and resolved to take the evidence to the authorities the next morning. No doubt Chia's appeal would succeed. I could not be left to languish in prison. Every dog has its day, and mine would be the day of my release. I felt certain I would be vindicated. But then the real task would begin.

The professor must be exposed. Her self-confessed transgression would require a disciplinary procedure before the medical tribunal, and with her expulsion, the faculty would end, and so too would my dreams of research. Once again, I would have to rebuild my career, and my professional identity. I felt lonely, like a little boy who had stumbled upon his parents in the act of intercourse, the so-called primal scene. I was shocked. Besides anything else, I wondered at Gramsci's prodigious sexual performance, all the more so considering that disfiguring hunch-back.

And now I could recognise the core of my self-doubt in that aching knowledge that the professor cared less than a little for what I could produce. I was discarded, another shabby little Oedipus. I knew then that I would seek my vengeance upon her. But not in a sneaky way. I resolved to find her and confront her with the evidence: I would present those filthy pages and watch her squirm with shame. And after that, the consequences would follow as destiny determined. That seemed the path of self-righteous indignation, and duty. The dignity and good standing of the profession of psychiatry must be upheld. If my research was to crash as a result of my own noble actions, so be it.

I was interrupted while writing the next morning by another visitor to my cell. It was Dr King, my former colleague. He looked bright and keen and oblivious, which really pissed me off.

"Frightfully sorry to interrupt. Thought you might like some company, old chap," he said.

I was too lonely and bored to wave him away – which was probably how my research subjects had felt as I approached them in their holding pen - and nodded him to a seat on my concrete bed.

"I know how much your project meant to you - your life's work, I suppose. So as a tribute to your devotion to the mental health of prisoners, I resolved to complete it, and it just so happens that you are interview number six hundred. Congratulations."

"Thanks," I muttered. "But how did you get to six hundred so fast? I wasn't even half-way there."

"That was your problem, old boy – you were trying to do it all yourself. I am the professor now, so I really don't do any field-work at all. I have a whole team of research psychologists to do that. Being devoid of inner workings, they are marvellously suited to mindlessly repetitive tasks. In this respect, they resemble ants: a glossy cognitive-behavioural exoskeleton, industrious, efficient, and working like drones to some higher plan, of which they are content to remain oblivious. But I saved you up for myself," he beamed inanely at me.

"Well, Dr King, in exchange for the privilege of interviewing me, let me ask you one thing. You argued in court that I must have wanted to do what I did, despite being hypnotised. Helping Gramsci escape is one thing, but it makes no sense at all to suggest that I would want to murder a dog. I have no such desire."

"Tricky thing, motivation. No hard feelings old boy, I was merely a disinterested expert before the court. Who knows what that dog represented to you? Perhaps some universal archetype of the vast canine unconscious. Don't take it so personally. It was only a court report."

"You bloody Jungian fraud!" I yelled. "Your court report put me behind bars. Of course I take it personally."

Dr King's disarming prattle was too much to bear, but I was able even in my impotent rage to recall an episode with Blind Freddy. When I was once late with a fee payment, he had said: "You must stop biting mother's breast."

Yes, perhaps some canine complex persisted within me. Dr King, too, persisted. He had taken over my project, and was determined to see it through, and get the glory.

"Yes, well, here we go then. If I can just get your autograph right here. Yes, good."

He proffered a consent form. I signed hurriedly, and he sat at my desk - as once I had sat with Gramsci - and began asking the questions. About appetite. About sleep. About guilt. About sex. About hearing voices, and paranoia, and drug use.

When he had finished the interview, I asked him for help. One good turn deserved another, or so I thought.

"Look, King, can you take this and get it to the police. Chia gave it to me last night. It's from the professor's file, and it's about Gramsci and her having some lewd sort of relationship. I think she must have followed him after his break-out."

I handed him the incriminating pages.

"Oh, dear fellow. You haven't been taken in by all that, have you? Raunchy stuff, I'm sure, but Chia really has been trying to take the mickey out of you. These are the polymorphous perversities of a sad old woman. And that's putting it charitably. Mere fantasy stuff. But I think we are well rid of both of them. Rasputin and the Russian queen, ha ha. Look, I would like to stay and chat, but I had best be going. Articles for various prestigious journals to produce, now I have completed my research project. And lots of administration to do, as the new professor of forensic psychiatry. The last one really had left the place in a frightful mess. Someone had to take the fall. Pity it had to be you. No hard feelings, old chap. Cheerio."

I watched him disappear, with the evidence. I realised too late that Dr King wasn't interested in helping me. He was in it for himself. I later heard that Chia had been arrested on charges of smuggling material in to a prisoner - me. Dear Chia, that one good man, a *mensch*. I was left to languish in my prison cell, an object of my own study. As doctor turned prisoner, the research proceeded, and the serpent of Asclepius swallowed its tale, for these were my findings:

'I began my prison year as a visitor observing another world...'

www.ingramcontent.com/pod-product-compliance
Lightning Source LLC
Chambersburg PA
CBHW030655120726
47905CB00001B/220